A TRIUMPH OF SOULS

ALAN DEAN FOSTER

JOURNEYS OF THE CATECHIST ❉ BOOK 3

A TRIUMPH OF SOULS

ASPECT®

WARNER BOOKS

A Time Warner Company

Aspect® name and logo are registered trademarks of Warner Books, Inc.

Warner Books, Inc., 1271 Avenue of the Americas, New York, NY 10020
Visit our Web site at www.twbookmark.com

 A Time Warner Company

Printed in the United States of America
First Printing: March 2000
10 9 8 7 6 5 4 3 2 1

Library of Congress Cataloging-in-Publication Data

Foster, Alan Dean.
    A triumph of souls / Alan Dean Foster.
        p.   cm. — (Journeys of the catechist ; bk. 3)
    ISBN 0-446-52218-X
    I. Title. II. Series: Foster, Alan Dean, 1946–   Journeys of the catechist ; bk. 3.
PS3556.0756T75   2000
813'.54—dc21
                                                                                    99-41376
                                                                                      CIP

For my nephew, Joshua Francis Carroll

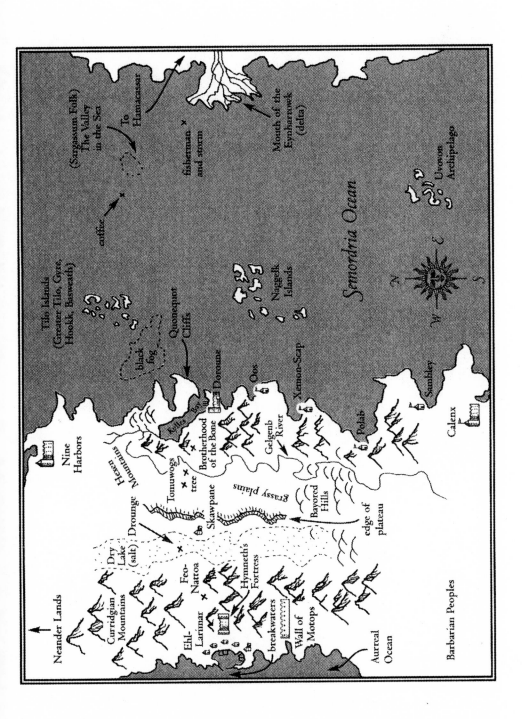

I

"He is coming. And he is not alone."

So spake the Worm.

It had started out to be a better day. Waking after a passable night's rest in a less discontented mood than usual, Hymneth the Possessed had chosen to dress in armor and accoutrements that were celebratory instead of intimidating. Gold-trimmed leggings tucked tightly into high boots of dark-crimson embossed leather. Scarlet armor covered him from head to thigh, and rubies so red they were almost black studded the gloves that encased his bare hands. Instead of horns, the high-ridged crimson helmet with its rearward-sweeping feathered crest gave him the appearance of some great and noble raptor diving to Earth.

Eyeing the result in the narrow floor-to-ceiling mirror at the far end of his dressing chamber, he found that he was well pleased with the effect. Today he would inspire only awe among his servitors and subjects, and leave terror in the closet.

At his high-pitched, intricate call, the twin eromakadi ceased their hunting of small bright things beneath the massive bed and came to heel. Intricately filigreed satin cape swirling behind him, he exited the sleeping chamber in a flurry of gold and crimson and made his way downstairs.

As usual, he ate alone, attended only by silent servants desperate to be free of his company but unable to show their true feelings. Their frozen smiles and polite inquiries after his health fooled him for not a minute. Their fear was as plain to hear in their voices as if they had been bound and bleeding in his presence. The slight tremolo at the end of every sentence, the swift darting of eyes whenever they thought he was not looking, the infinitesimal quiver of lower lips: Their emotions were as blatantly obvious to him as bulging eyes and hacking sobs.

He ignored it all, pretending to be taken in by the pitiful subterfuges as they served him. These were the best of the best, the few who could survive in his service without going mad or begging for dismissal. It made no sense. Was he not a kind and even generous master? Other nobles of wealth and power regularly beat their staff. Still others paid only a pittance for services rendered. In contrast to this, he was tolerant of oversights and paid well. And, in addition, there was the prestige that went with working in the house of the master of Ehl-Larimar. He could not understand why his people were not content.

Yes, it was necessary occasionally to discipline a menial for a job overlooked or poorly done. Yes, his methods for doing so were undeniably—well, different. As in everything, he prized efficiency above all. Why it should matter to people if a miscreant was crippled or given the face of a bat or frog instead of simply being broken on the rack or blinded in the traditional manner he could not understand.

Was it not better to have the teeth of a rat than none at all? Sometimes he felt he would never understand the reasoning of the common man.

Of the gustatory delights that burdened the dining table he normally would consume only a small amount. The remainder of the pancakes, eggs, meats, breads, jams, butters, fruits, cereals, juices, and cold drinks would be divided among his kitchen staff. He grunted to himself as he ate, passing food and liquid through the lower opening in the crimson helmet. They might tremble too badly to eat in his presence, but he knew that once he was done the food would vanish rapidly into hungry mouths. Which was well enough. Let them serve him. Love he would find elsewhere.

Love he sought, actually, in only one place.

Lifting his gaze to the stairway that entered the dining chamber from the left, he tried to imagine her descending to join him. Did his best to envision the fluid succession of perfect curves and contours concealed by clinging ripples of satin and silk, the hair like ribbons of night draped across bare shoulders that put the finest ivory to shame, and the eyes that were like sapphires. Eyes that he would have given half a world to have focused on him.

He imagined her approaching, not walking but flowing like mercury across the floor, weight shifting sensuously with each step, lips of blood-red brighter than his armor parting slightly as she raised one delicate hand to place it on his shoulder and whisper in the voice that turned men's legs to jelly and set their groins ablaze, "Good morning, My Lord."

Little enough, he agonized inside, to want. Little enough. Yet even now, after all this time, the best he could hope for was that she would not curse him aloud in his presence. She would eat later, he knew. In her room, or after members of the entourage he had assigned to her had assured her he had left to attend to matters of state. He possessed no more of her presence than he did of her passion.

Suddenly the morning no longer seemed so propitious. The food curdled in his mouth. Angrily, he pushed his plate away, and the two servitors attending him twitched visibly. Neither man ran, however. They knew all too well the fate of those who had fled the presence of the Possessed without first being properly dismissed.

Leaning back in the high, sculpted chair of carmine cobal, he rested his armored chin against one massive fist and brooded. After several minutes, the two servants exchanged a glance. The one who had lost the wordless debate took a step forward. His voice was deferential and suffered from only a slight quavering.

"Lord, if you are finished, should we clear away the dishes?"

He waved an indifferent hand. "Yes, yes, take it away. Take it all away!"

Bowing obsequiously and repeatedly, the man and his companion began to remove the masses of food and flatware. Hymneth sulked in his chair, contemplating aspects of life and death to which most living creatures were not privy, until a loud crash penetrated his pondering and brought his head around.

The second servant, a well-built and comely youth of some twenty and four years, was kneeling over the fragments of a shattered enameled tray. Muffins and sweet rolls, breads and breakfast cakes were still rolling away in several directions. From his crouch, he looked up to see the helmeted head staring down at him. The look on his face was one of sheer paralyzed terror.

"L-lord, I'm sorry. I'm so sorry. I—I will pay for it." Hastily, he began sweeping the larger fragments into a pile, not caring if he cut himself on the fractured ceramic.

"Pay for it? It would take six months of your wages, lackey. I wouldn't think of taking that from you. It would be cruel. In the absence of your salary I am sure you have loved ones who would go hungry. Besides, it's only a plate. In this castle there are hundreds of plates."

"Yes—yes, Lord." Some of the terror drained from the man's face. He swept faster, trying to gather up every last shard and white splinter.

"However," Hymneth continued, "while I could care less about a plate, you broke something else. Something much more valuable."

"Something else, Lord?" The attendant looked around helplessly, seeing nothing but broken crockery and spilled baked goods. Next to him, the other servant was already backing away, straining desperately to make himself invisible, discorporeal, nonexistent.

"Yes." The Possessed sat up straighter in his grand chair. "My train of thought. And that I cannot abide." One huge, powerful arm rose slowly.

"No, Lord, please!"

The other attendant turned away and wrapped his arms around his head so he would not be able to see what was coming. A twitch of sickly green leaped from Hymneth's armored hand, writhing and coiling like a giant heartworm. It struck the kneeling servant on the back of his neck. Instantly his entire body arched rearward as if struck by a

5

heavy hammer. With a muffled scream he snapped forward to lie prone on the floor, arms outstretched to both sides, unconscious.

Wearied by this constant need to discipline his staff, Hymneth slumped back into his chair and waved diffidently. "Take him out of here. Then come back and clean up the rest of this mess."

Shaking violently, the other servant slowly removed his hands from around his head and straightened. When he saw the figure of his friend lying on the floor, he screamed. It caught halfway in his throat, broken by the realization that the noise might offend the looming figure seated at the head of the table.

"Well?" the Possessed admonished him tersely. "Get on with it."

"Yes—yes, my Lord." Fighting to control his trembling, the other man reached down and grasped the unconscious servant by his wrists. Slowly, he began to drag the limp body from the room.

"Throw some water on him," Hymneth ordered. "He'll be all right. And maybe from now on he won't drop dishes when I'm thinking."

The other attendant did not reply. The Possessed's meaning was clear. Indeed, it would be much harder for the young servant to drop dishes or anything else. Because he now had four limbs to carry them with: his two arms, and the pair of slick, green, sucker-laden tentacles that had sprouted noisomely from his shoulders.

"And when he comes around, tell him that he's still on full pay!" Hymneth remembered to shout to the rapidly retreating menial.

Am I not the soul of tolerance and understanding? he thought.

As always, it was a puzzlement to him why his people did not love him openly, instead of from within the pit of fear.

Dispensing such magnanimity always made him feel better. He had started to rise when Tergamet entered. One of his many advisers, he was subordinate to Peregriff, who was no doubt even now reviewing his Lord's schedule for the day. Tergamet was wise, and the master of a magnificent long beard, but he had a regrettable tendency to tell Hymneth what he thought the Possessed wanted to hear, instead of the truth. Perhaps this was understandable, in light of the warlock's occasional tendency to set ablaze specific portions of the anatomy of the attendants in his vicinity whenever a piece of particularly disagreeable news was conveyed to him. In that respect, he supposed Tergamet was braver than most.

"Yes, what is it?"

"And how is my Lord this morning?" The elderly adviser bowed as low as his aging back would allow.

"Impatient, as always. So don't bother inquiring after my condition. I know that you, as much as everyone else in this benighted pile of stone, would rejoice at the sight of me dead."

Tergamet fluttered a protesting hand. "Oh no, Lord! How can you think to say such a thing to me, one of your most trusted and loyal retainers!"

"I don't trust anyone, old man, and loyalty is a commodity to be bought, like expensive wine and cheap women." His irritation was growing. "What news? Not the harbor pilots again, with this nonsense about Krakens interfering with their work. I've told them how to fight back, and what poisons to use."

"No, Lord. It is not the harbor pilots." Eyes that still saw

7

sharply rose to nearly meet his. "It is the Worm, Lord. It wishes to speak with you."

Hymneth considered, then nodded slowly. At this news, the two small eromakadi that attended his ankles danced excitedly around his legs. Termaget was careful to keep them in view. Simple contact with either one could suck the life out of a man. The Possessed they merely bounced off like agitated spaniels.

"The Worm, you say. What about?"

The senior adviser bowed again and spread his arms wide. "I do not know, my Lord. It will speak only to you."

"And quite properly so. Very good, Termaget. You may go."

"Thank you, Lord." Bowing and scraping, the old man retreated toward the main doorway. As he turned to depart, Hymneth considered whether to let the eromakadi take a playful nip at his heels. Nothing serious; just a week or so out of his remaining years. Days someone like Termaget would probably waste anyway. Hymneth decided against it, knowing that the old fellow probably would not see the humor in the situation.

His cape flowing behind him like blood running down the outside of a chalice, he exited the dining room. Instead of striding toward the audience chamber as he normally did this time of morning, he turned instead to his right in the middle of the main hall. The door there was bolted with a hex and locked with a spell, both of which yielded to the keys of his voice. He did not bother to seal it behind him. It would take a braver man or woman than dwelled in the castle to try the steps that began to descend immediately behind the door. Hex and spell were designed not to keep them out, but to seal something securely within.

Torches flared to life at his approach, the flames bowing briefly in his direction. As Hymneth descended the corkscrewing stairway, one of the eromakadi darted swiftly upward behind him to suck the life out of one torch. The flame screamed, a high-pitched conflagratory shriek, as it died. When Hymneth turned to reproach the black gust of horror, it hid behind its twin like a censured child.

Down the Lord of Ehl-Larimar went, below the sewers that carried water and waste away from the castle, below the dungeons where men and women and children wailed and whimpered in forgotten misery, below even the un-shakable foundations of the massive fortress itself. Down until there was nothing left but the raw Earth—and the Pit that had been gouged from its heart.

At this depth nothing could live that basked in the light of the sun. In the perpetual darkness, things that rarely saw the surface burrowed and crept, mewling and cheep-ing softly to others of their own kind, hoping to avoid the mephitic, malodorous monstrosities armed with teeth and claw that would prey readily on anything that moved. An eerie glow came from the phosphorescent fungi that thrust bulbous, deformed stalks and heads above the surface of the Pit, giving it the appearance of some ghastly, unwhole-some garden. In this place even the air seemed dead. All movement took place below the surface, out of sight, out of light.

Until Hymneth arrived, with eromakadi in tow.

Pausing on the last step, the final piece of clean, hewn stone that bordered the Pit, he gazed speculatively down into its depths. His boots, he knew, would require days of scrubbing to make them clean again. As he slowly lifted both arms up and out, his steady, sturdy voice shattered the diseased stillness.

"Alegemakh! Borun val malcuso. Show thyself, and speak!"

For a long moment there was nothing. No sound, no movement except the breathy stirring of the eromakadi. Then soil began to tremble, and shift, disturbed by some movement from below. Clumps of moist loam shuddered and individual particles of dirt bounced and quivered until at last they were thrust aside by something monstrous.

The Worm arose.

It burst forth from the earth, shedding dirt and uprooted fungi from its flanks. Pellucid mucus glistened along the length of its body. A length that no man, not even Hymneth the Possessed, had ever measured. The Worm might be ten feet long, or twenty, or a hundred. Or it might curl and coil all the way through to the other side of the Earth. No one knew. No one would ever know, because attempting the knowing meant death. Of all men, only Hymneth had power enough to meet the Worm in this place, chiseled out of the solid rock halfway between air and earth, and survive.

It lifted above him, shimmering and immense, its great tubular body arching forward like that of a questing serpent. Its upper girth, if not its length, was measurable. From where it emerged from the ground to its head it was as thick around as a good-sized tree. The last eight feet of it tapered to an almost comically small mouth, no bigger around than a barrel. From this darted and fluttered, like the tongue of a snake, a long, wet, flexible organ tipped with four tapering, sharp fangs that pointed forward. It was not a tongue, but a device for piercing the body of prey and sucking out their soft insides. The Worm's diet was varied—it would eat dirt as readily as blood.

Darting away from their master's side, the twin eromakadi began to feast on the light emitted by the bioluminescent fungi. Completely enveloping a helpless mushroom or toadstool, they would hover thus until its light had been consumed before moving on to another, leaving behind a shriveled and dying lump where before there had been life, however humble.

The Worm too pulsed with its own pale, necrotic glow, but they kept clear of that massive, hovering body. Not because they were afraid of it, but because they knew it was there to meet their master. And of all the things in the world, the eromakadi feared only Hymneth the Possessed.

Vestigial eyes no larger than small coins focused on the tall, armored figure waiting on the lowermost of the stone steps. Black as the eternal night in which they dwelled, they had neither pupils nor eyelids. But they recognized the tall figure. Long ago, Worm and man had struck an accord. Hymneth provided the Worm with—food. The Worm, in turn, kept a kind of watch over the realm of the Possessed. It had the ability to sense disturbances in That Which Had Not Yet Happened. The great majority of these it ignored.

But out on the fringes of the future it had detected something. Something active, and advancing, and imbued with might. In keeping with the covenant it had made with the man, it duly remarked upon this commotion.

"He comes. And he is not alone."

Hymneth had lowered his arms. As the eromakadi spread small deaths throughout the chamber, he concentrated on the tapering head of the Worm swaying high above his own. "Who comes, eater of dirt?"

The Worm's voice was a high hollowness. "A master of the necromantic arts. A questioner of all that is unanswered. One who seeks justice wherever he treads. He comes this way from across the Semordria."

"That is not possible. The eastern ocean is not a lake, to be crossed at will by casual travelers. They would have to travel far to the south, pass through the Straits of Duenclask, and then sail north against the current through the waters of the Aurreal."

"A strong boat guided by a bold Captain brings him, and the three who journey by his side."

"Only three?" Hymneth relaxed. This descent to the depths had been unnecessary after all. "That is a small army indeed."

"I render no judgment. I speak only of what I sense."

The Possessed chuckled softly, the crimson helmet reverberating with his laughter. "I will alert the navy to keep watch for any odd vessels entering the harbor. As always, I thank you for your attention, Worm. But in this matter your insight seems to be sorely lacking."

"Sense," the Worm whispered. "Not judgment." It was silent for several moments, its upper length weaving slowly back and forth above the churned surface of the Pit. "They come for the woman."

That piqued Hymneth's interest. "So the young Beckwith was not the last. I thought with putting paid to him and his crew I had seen the last of these misguided aristocrats. They worry me like fleas." He sighed. "Well, in the unlikely event that any of them should reach Ehl-Larimar I will tell Peregriff to alert the castle guards. But I have more confidence in the ocean. Even if they reach these shores my gunboats will stop them before they can cross the outer reefs." He shook his head sadly.

"You would think they would recognize who they were dealing with, and stop shipping their sons off to be slaughtered. The error of false pride. As if running this kingdom didn't make demands enough upon my time."

"Feed me." The immense, looming mass of the Worm swayed hypnotically back and forth, the flickering light of the stairway torches gleaming off its terrible piercing teeth. "I tire of soil. I have done my share. Feed me."

"Yes, yes," Hymneth replied irritably. He had already virtually forgotten all that the Worm had told him. As if a mere four possible invaders were anything to worry about, even if one happened to be a so-called master of the necromantic arts. There was only one dominating master of matters sorcerous and alchemical, and that was Hymneth the Possessed.

As he started back up the stairs he almost hoped these predicted intruders did manage to survive the impossible journey across the ocean. It had been a long time since he had fought a duel, and it would be good to have someone worthy to exercise his powers against. Though he doubted any of these potential assailants would qualify. To the best of his knowledge, there were no worthy masters living on the other side of the Semordria in the Thinking Kingdoms. For all the threat it posed to him, the Worm might as well have kept the information to itself and not disturbed him. He departed disappointed.

"Feed me!" The reverberant moan rose insistently behind him.

Where the stairs began to disappear upward, Hymneth

paused to lean over and peer downward. The head of the Worm vacillated below him now. "For information like that you deserve nothing. But I am mindful of the covenant between us. I'm sure Peregriff can find a few condemned, or condemnable, to bring to you. The axman will gain a rest."

"I await." With a wet, sucking sound the Worm began to withdraw into the damp earth. It would lie there, Hymneth knew, with only its head above the surface, until the promised unfortunates were brought. Cast into the Pit, they would be pierced by the creature's mouth parts, their internal organs and muscles and flesh liquefied, and the consequent putrid, gelatinous mush sucked out. No one could complain, Hymneth mused virtuously, that his dungeons suffered from overcrowding.

As he climbed upward, the two eromakadi reluctantly left the last of the surviving fungi to accompany him, impenetrable black clouds that hovered at his heels. Occasionally they would show very small, slanted red eyes, but most of the time they kept themselves as black as pitch. Visitors who knew what they represented were as terrified by their silence as by their shapes.

Hymneth had mounted nearly to the top of the corkscrewing stairwell when a voice, pure and melodious as the golden bells of a benign spirit, called down to him accusingly.

"So this is where you spend your time. In the depths of the Earth, consorting with demons!"

Taken aback by the unexpected intrusion, he tilted his head to peer upward. High above him, a portrait of beauty unsurpassed gazed down. Not even the look of utter disgust on her face could mar the perfection of her countenance.

"My beloved Themaryl, this is business of state! Nothing more. I converse in the depths. I do not consort."

Her face furrowed with loathing. "You smell of things diseased and rotting. I thought—I thought we might talk, so I sought you out. I'm glad that I did, for it gave me the chance to see yet again your true self!" With that she whirled and fled upward, back to her rooms, back to the tower that she had made a prison for herself.

Bad timing, Hymneth thought in an agony of frustration. Of all the mornings and moments to parley with the Worm, of all the hours available to all the days, he had chosen the one time she had relented enough to descend from her steeple. Falling to his knees, he let out a cry of utter despair, knowing even as he did so that it would have no effect on her. Delighting in his anguish, the eromakadi clustered closer, inhaling of the darkness that had suddenly suffused his soul.

Slowly, his clenched fists fell away from the eye slits of his helmet. Someone had told her where he was. Someone had shown her where he was. Admittedly, he had decreed that she be given the run of the castle. But whatever fool had believed that included access to the Pit had, while displaying adherence to the letter of his command, shown excruciatingly bad judgment.

He rose to his feet. With all of Ehl-Larimar to administer and govern, he could not afford to tolerate those who exhibited bad judgment. Especially not those who did so in his own home, his sanctuary. When she had inquired as to his whereabouts, someone had taken her by the hand and guided her to the door that led to the Pit. It was a given. Mere directions would not have allowed her to find the unprepossessing door by herself, much less to enter.

Talk. She had thought they might talk. It had been months since she had said a word to him other than to demand that he return her to her home and people, and today, this morning, she had been ready to talk. A major breakthrough in their relationship shattered like cheap glass. Another setback when he might have hoped, just a little, for progress. And all because of someone's bad judgment.

That night the villagers who lived below the castle, on the slopes of the mountains, put cotton in the ears of their children and laid extra blankets across their beds. They slept in the same rooms with them, sharing their beds or lying on linens spread out on the floor. They made sure all animals were secured tightly in their barns and corrals, paddocks and pens. They did this because of the screaming that drifted down from the castle like black snow.

Up above, the unfortunate were being punished for a lack of good judgment. It went on all through the night. As dawn neared it grew so bad that even the bats fled the vicinity. The children slept, but their parents were not so lucky. One family lost two horses, dead from heart attacks, and another a brace of goats that, maddened by the sounds, broke free of their pens and fled into the forest, never to be seen again.

All told, the slope-dwelling citizens of Ehl-Larimar counted themselves lucky when the sun finally appeared over the mountaintops and the last of the shrieking died in a sudden, violent choking. They proceeded to go about their morning chores and business as if nothing had happened, as if the previous night had been only a bad dream, to be quickly forgotten like any bad dream. The women of the villages, however, found themselves with extra wash-

16

ing. Having spent the night oozing fearful sweat in great profusion, they and their husbands had stained many a nightdress beyond immediate reuse.

High above, government officials and administrators came and went, unaware of the frightfulness that had subsumed the fortress the night before. If they noticed anything out of the ordinary, it was that the castle's retainers moved a little faster than usual, and that they were less inclined to meet the eyes of visitors.

Far below, in the depths of the mountain, where earth met rock and where normal folk did not go, the Worm slept, its midsection swollen and bloated.

II

So still was the morning that the gull feather Simna let fall fell straight down. When it landed on the deck it just lay there, a puff of discarded dirty white that could easily be shifted by a waking woman's sigh. But it did not move.

It was more than an absence of wind. It was as if the air itself had become paralyzed, petrified in place. Though they had seen and experienced many things in their travels, the crew of the *Grömsketter* murmured superstitiously among themselves while anxiously watching the skies for any sign of movement. But the clouds themselves remained exactly where they had appeared at sunup. It was one thing for a ship to be becalmed, quite another for the upper reaches of the sky itself to grow still as death.

The only way they knew for certain that they still lived in the realm of air was because they continued to breathe. It was possible to make a breeze by blowing, as Simna demonstrated when he dropped to all fours and blew hard against the abandoned feather. It scudded a little ways across the deck, twisting and flipping, before it settled once more into a motionless, trancelike state.

Just above the helm deck Stanager Rose stood in the rigging, shading her eyes with one hand as she surveyed the surrounding sea. It was smooth as a mirror, undisturbed by wave or, more importantly, wind. They were two days' sail out from the delta of the Eynharrowk on a due westerly heading, and no longer moving. Nothing was moving. Even the seabirds had deserted them in search of wind to help support their wings. It was uncanny, it was worrisome, and it was hot.

"Never been becalmed like this before," she murmured.

On the deck below, Hunkapa Aub was chatting with Priget, the helmswoman, and trying to learn something about the basics of open-ocean navigation. She had plenty of time to talk to him since the ship's wheel, left unattended, was not moving. Ahlitah lay on the main deck, sleeping in the shade. The utter absence of a breeze was making the morning too hot even for him. Simna ibn Sind had tied a strip of colorful cloth around his forehead to soak up some of the perspiration. Though as unhappy with the unnatural stillness as anyone else aboard, the sight of Stanager Rose clinging to rigging helped to mitigate his unease.

Etjole Ehomba stood just below and to one side of the troubled Captain. Though no mariner, he knew well the moods of the sea, and right now the Semordria was not behaving in a proper maritime fashion. He had experienced still air before, while standing on different beaches in the vicinity of his village, but never anything like this. Heavy, hot, and stagnant, it tempted a man to take a whip to it, as if the very components of the atmosphere themselves had gone to sleep.

Stanager climbed down from the rigging. "The longer

19

we sit here, the more of our supplies we waste. Too much of this and we'll be forced to return to the delta to reprovision."

"We could eat less," Ehomba proposed, "and catch rainwater to supplement the ship's stores."

"If it rains," she replied. "I don't gamble with the lives of my crew. Or my passengers."

"Do you ever gamble?" Simna's forced cheerfulness fooled no one.

"Only when it's a sure thing." Ignoring him as usual, she strained to see past the bow. "May have to try kedging, but in which direction I haven't decided. It would pain me to have to tuck tail and go back to the delta." She squinted upward. All sails were set, and hung loose as dead ghosts from both masts.

"What's this 'kedging'?" Simna wanted to know.

She sighed. "Landsmen. We lower all the small boats and put the anchors in them. They row out as far as the lines will go, then drop anchor. This pulls the ship forward. Raise anchors and repeat, as many times as necessary until a breeze fills the sails. It's hot, hard work. A last resort for desperate sailors."

"I cannot go backward," Ehomba told her. "I have spent too much time already just in going forward."

"Then find me some wind," she declared curtly, "so we can escape these cursed doldrums!"

"The sky-metal sword!" Simna blurted. "Surely even a moment's work with that would bring down enough wind to move the ship."

Stanager frowned. "What is the mad elf blabbering about?"

"Something possible, but dangerous." Reaching back,

Ehomba wrapped his fingers around the haft of the sword. Simna looked on expectantly. Among those aboard the *Grömsketter*, only he knew what that enchanted blade of otherworldly metal was capable of in the hands of his tall friend.

Reluctantly, Ehomba released his grip. Simna looked pained.

"Why the hesitation, bruther?"

"It is a chancy thing to consider, Simna, and not something to be attempted in haste. I have to think first how best to go about it. Too little wind is not a problem. But too much wind could shred the sails or even capsize the ship. And what if I thrust it wrongly to the heavens and call down another piece of sky? Here there are no holes in the ground for us to hide in, and nowhere to run."

"That's fine, Etjole." The swordsman made placating motions. "Take your time. Decide how to hold the weapon, which way to point it, what angle to incline the blade against the Earth. Only when you're satisfied that you know what you're doing should you go ahead."

Ehomba eyed his friend speculatively. "And if I'm not satisfied?"

Simna shrugged. "Then we sit. And sweat. And try to think of something else."

A thin smile curled the Captain's delectable upper lip. "I've heard you boasting endlessly to the crew, swordsman. Perhaps we should put you in a small boat behind the *Grömsketter* and let you jabber there all you wish. Maybe that would generate hot air enough to fill the mains'l just enough to get us moving."

He smiled back. "You don't like me very much, do you, Captain?"

21

"Not very much, no. If you were under my command, I'd have you swabbing decks and bailing bilges all the way to Doroune."

"I wouldn't mind being under your command, Stanager—depending on the commands, of course." He grinned irrepressibly.

She turned away, disgusted. "You are incorrigible!"

"Actually, I'm from a little village near Rakosy. Incorrigible is a bigger town that lies to the northwest."

"Boat ho!"

At the cry, everyone tilted their heads back to look up at the mainmast. The lookout was gesturing slightly to port.

It took the better part of an hour for the small, single-masted craft to drift into view. Stolid and unimpressive, a wholly utilitarian little boat, its aft half was piled high with pilchard and sardine, so much so that it rode lower in the water than otherwise would have been expected. Nets fashioned of strong cord and spotted with cork floats hung from the boom and over the sides. Its lone sail hung as limp from the mast as did those of the *Grömsketter*.

The single occupant was busy hauling in one of the nets, but not too busy to wave at the much larger vessel.

"Ayesh!" the fisherman sang out. "What ship?"

From near the bow, the first mate responded. "Good fishing?" Terious added by way of making conversation.

Grinning through his white-flecked beard, the lone sailor gestured at his catch. "As you see."

"You're not afraid to be out of sight of land, all by yourself?" the mate inquired. Several of the other members of the crew had moved to the railing to watch the discourse. In the detestable stillness, any diversion was a welcome one.

"Not I. Crice is the name, sir, and I am known throughout the delta for my bravery." He indicated his mast and
sail. "I know the winds hereabouts better than any man,
you see, and am always confident of finding one to carry
me home."

Cupping her hands to her mouth, Stanager shouted
across to the solitary harvester of the sea. "Ayesh, can you
find one for us, good sir? We have been stalled here this
past day and a half."

"Sorry." He waved again. "I have the last of my catch to
bring in and then I must return home. You know that every
ship must find its own wind. Not all have my skill."

Stanager flushed, her cheeks reddening. It was an
oblique insult and probably unintended, but it still set the
Captain's blood to racing. When it came to seamanship,
she took a back seat to no man or woman. This solitary
sailor who stank of fish guts and oil was taunting her, albeit
gently.

Persistent he might be, even irritating, but Simna knew
when to keep his mouth shut. Observing the look on the
Captain's beauteous face, he sidled away from her and
closer to Ehomba.

"What do you think, long bruther?" He nodded in the
direction of the little fishing boat. "Is his an empty boast?"

"I was admiring his catch." Ehomba gestured at the glistening mound that weighed down the boat. "All small fish,
all silver of side. Very difficult to see under normal conditions. When looking down into the water from the deck of
a boat, it is hard to separate such a school from sunlight.
But in these conditions, with the surface absolutely calm
and undisturbed by wind, they would stand out much
more clearly to a man with a net."

23

Simna's brows furrowed. "So the man is a good fisherman and brave to boot. What of that?"

"While he has been working and talking I have been studying everything on his boat. Though more than a little windy himself, I think he is no natural master of wind. He does not have the look. But there is no mistaking the confidence he has in his seamanship." Raising his voice, he called out to their visitor.

"Gatherer of fish, that is a most unusual bottle I see resting by your tiller. Though large and well blown it does not appear to hold drink, or anything else. Yet I espy something moving within. What does it contain?"

So startled by this unexpected inquiry was the fisherman that he dropped the net he was hauling in, letting it splash back over the gunwale. Once back in the water its contents, writhing and convulsing, wildly finned their way to freedom.

"It's only a bottle, sir. You have—remarkable eyes."

"From watching over my herd, looking out for predators. What is in the bottle?" Everyone on board the *Grömsketter* was watching Ehomba now. Men and women who had been resting in the shade rose from their places to crowd the railing.

"Nothing, good sir." Ignoring the fact that he had just lost the majority of his most recent catch, the fisherman resumed hauling in the one net that remained hanging over the side. He looked and sounded slightly agitated. "It's just an empty bottle that I carry about with me. For storing caught rainwater."

Simna was staring at his tall friend. Etjole was on to something, had seen something, he knew. But what? Now that the herdsman had singled it out, he too located the large bottle that rested near the tiller of the small boat. It was big enough to hold several gallons, with a bulbous body and a narrow, tapering neck that terminated in an elaborate metallic stopper the color of pewter. Hard as he stared, he could not discern any contents.

Ehomba, however, felt differently. Strongly enough to argue about it.

"I can see movement within the glass. To catch rainwater anyone would use a bottle with a much wider mouth. I know: I have had to do so in dry country on more than one occasion. So what is it, fisherman? Why are you lying to us?"

When the last of the net had been hauled in and piled on the deck of the little craft, its owner took a seat in the stern, resting one arm on the tiller. "You have no weapons that can reach me or you would have shown them by now. So I will tell you, landlord of sharp eyes. The knowledge will do you no good."

Baffled, Stanager had moved to stand close to Simna. "What nonsense is he prattling?" she whispered. "I can make sense neither of what he is saying nor of your friend."

Inclining his head close to hers, the swordsman murmured a reply. "I'm not sure, but Ehomba is a strange man. A good friend, to be sure. Straightforward and dependable. But different from such as you and I. He knows many things. I believe him to be a great sorcerer."

"What, him?" Almost, she laughed aloud. Almost.

"Say then that he is a sometime student of that which would mystify the rest of us. If he says there's something in that bottle, then I believe him, though I can't see it myself." He pointed. "It lies there, by the stern."

25

"I see it," she admitted, leaning closer. After a moment she shook her head dubiously. "It looks empty to me."

"Hoy, but then why is our trawling friend looking so uneasy, and speaking of weapons? Could it be that the bottle contains something of great value, whose nature he is wary of revealing?" In the course of their intense whispering his arm had slipped around her waist. Intent upon the byplay between herdsman and fisher, she took no notice of it, and thus allowed it to remain in place.

Lifting the bottle by its narrow neck, Crice held it up for all to see. Half the crew saw only a thick-walled container, perfectly blown and devoid of bubbles in the glass, sealed with a peculiarly sculpted pewter stopper. Among the rest there were many who thought they saw movement within the translucent vessel. Given the distance between the two craft, it was difficult to say what, if anything, occupied the bottle's interior. But it was now clear to the most sharp-eyed among the crew that something did.

Whatever it was, Ehomba had been first to espy it. Among them all, he was the only one to have an idea what it might be. Convinced of his invincibility, the fisherman proceeded to confirm the herdsman's suspicions.

"Here's your wind, sailors! You think yourselves masters of the sea and all that's above and below it—but I, Crice, command the air!" He held the glass container a little higher. "Here in this bottle I have all the wind that covers this portion of the sea. Found it at the bottom of a chest in a ruined ship. Must have been a thousand years old, she was, and reeking of magic fantastic and decayed. But the stopper on this bottle was intact, and I, yes I, discovered by myself how to open and close it. I let a little out when I need it and keep the rest shut up when I don't." He gestured at the perfectly flat, motionless water on which both craft floated. "That way I can see the fish I seek as clearly as if looking through a window. When I have enough, I let out just the right amount of wind in precisely the appropriate direction to carry me home."

"No wonder he's not afraid to travel out of sight of land," Simna whispered. His hand tightened a little on the Captain's waist.

"Not if he can control all the wind in this part of the ocean, no." Pressing forward against the railing, Stanager raised her voice. "Ayesh, fisherman, can you not let us have back a little of that wind?"

"Every ship must find its own," he reiterated implacably. "And if I give some to you, that will mean less for my sail. How much do you think a bottle like this can hold, anyway? I found the bottle, I captured the wind, and now it's mine! Seek out your own breezes."

Sitting back down in the stern, he pointed the neck of the bottle toward his mast. Slowly and very carefully, he unscrewed the pewter stopper just a little.

Emerging from the glass alembic, a gust of wind immediately filled his small sail, sending its thrusting curve billowing outward. Seeing this, several sailors on board the *Grömsketter* looked to their own masts, only to see their own sails luffing uselessly against spar and line. Yet to look at the little boat was to see it beginning to accelerate with a freshening breeze astern. Except no breeze advanced from the vicinity of the stern. It had emerged straight from the bottle that the fisherman was now firmly restoppering.

"Etjole, do something!" Simna blurted anxiously. At the same time, Stanager became aware of the arm coiled around her waist and stepped away. Her expression was a mixture of anger and—something else. "If he gets away with all the wind from this part of the sea we could be stuck here for weeks!"

"I know." Ehomba had not taken his eyes from the little boat heavily laden with fish and its contrary master. "I need a stone."

"A stone?" Simna knew better than to question his companion. If Ehomba had declared that he needed a purple pig, the swordsman would have done his best to find one.

Actually, on board a ship the size of the *Grömsketter*, finding the pig might have been the easier task. Of all the lands they had journeyed through together, of all the astounding places they had visited and countries they had traversed, here was the first that was devoid of stones, and here the first time Ehomba had required one.

"Ballast!" the swordsman yelped. "There must be ballast in the hold!"

Stanager was quick to disappoint him. "We carry base metals. Ingots of iron and copper that we can trade with the inhabitants of the towns on the other side of the Semordria. You'll find no rock in the belly of the *Grömsketter*."

"Well then, there must be at least one stone somewhere on this ship! Firestone in the galley, to protect her wooden walls."

The Captain shook her head sadly. "Firebrick."

"In someone's sea chest, then. A memento of home, a worry stone, anything! If Ehomba says that he needs a stone, that means he needs—" Simna broke off, gaping at his tall friend.

Reaching into a pocket of his kilt, the herdsman had removed the small cotton sack of "beach pebbles" he had carried with him all the way from his home village. As

Simna looked on, Ehomba selected the largest remaining, a flawless five-carat diamond of deeper blue hue than the surrounding sea, and shoved the remaining stones back in his pocket.

"No, long bruther." The swordsman gestured frantically. "Not that. We'll find you a rock. There's got to be a rock somewhere on this barge; an ordinary, everyday, commonplace, worthless rock. Whatever it is you're thinking of doing—don't."

The herdsman smiled apologetically at his friend. In his hand he held a stone worth more than the swordsman could hope to earn in a lifetime. In two lifetimes. And somehow, Simna knew his friend was not planning to convert it into ready currency.

"Sorry, my friend. There is no time." Pivoting, he returned his gaze to the little boat, now starting to pick up speed beneath the press of the freed breeze its sail had captured. "Soon he will be out of range."

"I don't care what—" the swordsman halted in midcomplaint. "Out of range? Out of range of what?"

"Rocks," Ehomba explained simply—so simply that it was not an explanation at all, but only another puzzlement. Raising his voice, he directed his words to the retreating fisherman. "Truly you are the master of winds! But you must control them through spells and magicks. No mere bottle that fits in a man's lap can contain more than the air that Nature has already placed inside."

"You think not, do you?" The fisherman turned in his seat, one arm resting easily on the tiller. "You'd be surprised, traveler, what a bottle can hold."

"Not a bottle that small," Ehomba yelled back. "I wager

it is not even made of glass, but some marvel of the alchemist's art instead!"

"Oh, it's glass, all right. Alchemist's glass perhaps, but glass incontestably. See?" Holding the bottle aloft and grinning, he tapped the side with a small marlinspike. The smooth, slightly greenish material clinked sharply.

As soon as the fisherman had begun to lift the bottle, Ehomba had placed the blue diamond in his mouth. At first a startled Simna suspected that the herdsman intended to swallow it, though for what purpose or reason he could not imagine. Not knowing what to think, Stanager had simply looked on in silence.

That was when Ehomba began to inhale. Simna ibn Sind had seen his friend inhale like that only once before, when on the Sea of Aboqua he had consumed an entire eromakadi. But there was no darkness here, no ominous roiling haze with luminous red eyes, not even a stray storm cloud. The sky, like the air, was transparent.

The herdsman's chest expanded—and expanded, and swelled, until it seemed certain he would burst. Those members of the crew close enough to see what was happening gawked open-mouthed at the phenomenon of the distending herdsman while Stanager, brave as she was, began to back away from that which she could not explain and did not understand. Hunkapa Aub looked up in dumb fascination while Ahlitah, as usual, slept on, oblivious to what was happening around him.

Just when it seemed that the skin of the herdsman's chest must surely rupture, exploding his internal organs all over the deck and railing, he exhaled. To say explosively would be to do injustice to the sound that emerged from his chest and mouth. It reverberated like gunpowder, echoing across not only the deck but the sea as well. The force of it blew its perpetrator backwards, lifting Ehomba's feet off the deck and sending him crashing into the smaller railing that delimited the fore edge of the helm deck. Hunkapa ran over to make sure the herdsman was all right.

As for Simna, he remained at the railing, realizing that Ehomba had expelled more than just air. There had been one other thing in his mouth, and it was not his tongue that had been violently discharged across the water.

In the little boat, the disdainful fisherman was preparing to tap his bottle a second time with the metal marlinspike to demonstrate the qualities of its composition when the ejected diamond struck it squarely in the middle, shattering the glass and sending green-tinted shards flying in all directions. The fisherman had barely an instant to gape at the ruined container, its neck and stopper still clutched tightly in one hand, before the winds it had held burst to freedom.

All the winds that had swept a section of sea greater than a man could see in any direction, and all of it released at once.

"Etjole, you right still?" The shaggy countenance of Hunkapa Aub was leaning low over his lanky friend. Ehomba sat, dazed but conscious, against the railing.

"I am . . ." he started to reply. Then a sound reached his ears—a rising sound—and he yelled out even as he wrapped his arms tightly around the nearest post. "Grab something and hang on! Everybody grab someth—"

The liberated winds struck the *Grömsketter* amidships, howling like a thousand crazed goblins suddenly released from an asylum for insane spirits as they tore through the masts and rigging. Struck hard enough to cause the sturdy vessel to heel sharply to starboard. For a terrifying moment, in the midst of that awesome roar, Stanager was afraid the ship was going to turn turtle. Her list reached seventy degrees. But as the initial blast began to subside, the ballast in her hold asserted itself. With maddening slowness, she began to roll back onto an even keel.

Clinging to the rigging, her skin and clothing soaked with gale-driven spray, the Captain screamed orders to the crew. Stays were drawn taut, the mainsail boom secured, the wheel steadied. Somehow, the sails held. Working his way aft, Terious Kermarkh silently blessed a succession of unnamed sailmakers. Tough fabric caught the wind and contained it.

But with demented gusts blowing from every direction, the sails kept wrapping themselves around the masts, making it impossible for the ship to maintain a heading, any heading. In the teeth of the disordered, chaotic gale there was no choosing a course.

Terious fought his way to within shouting distance of the helm deck. Standing below, he yelled up to the wheel. "Captain, we've got to get out of this! We're starting to take on water!"

"Keep the fores'l reefed, Mr. Kermarkh! All hands hold to stations!" Maintaining a firm grip on a storm line, her experienced sea legs absorbing the impact of every pitch and roll, she staggered over to where Hunkapa Aub and Simna ibn Sind hovered solicitously over their tall friend. Awakened from his sleep by the sudden, unexpected storm, the black litah stood nearby. The heaving, pitching deck did not concern him, not with four sets of powerful claws at his disposal to dig into the wood.

"Mr. Ehomba, you've taken us from the doldrums to the

roaring forties, from not a ghost of a breeze to all the winds of the four corners of the compass. But they've been let loose all together and all at once, and as a consequence blow from all directions unaligned. You got us into this, now you have to get us out, or we'll sit here and spin like a top until we sink!"

Still dazed from the blow to the back of his head, Ehomba accepted the help of his friends to rise. Simna helped him up. Once erect, Hunkapa embraced him in an immovable grasp that held him steady.

Observing the anarchic weather that had enveloped the *Grömsketter*, Ehomba thanked his friends and told Hunkapa to release him. The broad-shouldered man-beast complied reluctantly. All kept a wary watch on the herdsman as he half climbed, half slid down the steps that led to the main deck and disappeared below. Moments later he emerged with the sky-metal sword gripped tightly in one hand.

Simna eyed him uncertainly. Along with everyone else, he had to shout to make himself heard above the howl of clashing winds. "Hoy, long bruther, what do you want with that? We need less wind, not more of it!"

"Not less, Simna." Ehomba wiped perspiration from his eyes and forehead. "What we have is what we need. It only wants some guidance."

Climbing back onto the helm deck, he made his way to the stern railing. There he tried to assume a solid stance, but the pitching and rolling of the ship made it impossible. Without using at least one hand to grip a stay or line, he kept stumbling from side to side, forward or back. Leaning against the railing helped a little, but when the bow of the

Grömsketter rose sharply, the motion threatened to pitch him over the side.

"This is not working," he declared aloud.

"I can see that, bruther!" Spitting seawater, Simna clung to the railing next to him. "What do you need? What do you want?" Spume-flecked wind shrieked in their ears.

"My feet nailed to the deck, but that could cause problems later." Grimly searching the ship, the herdsman espied the big cat standing foursquare and four-footed to the left of the helm, as stable as the mainmast. "Ahlitah! I need your help!"

"What now?" Grumbling, the cat released its grip on the battered teak and turned. His extended claws held the decking as firmly as crampons on a glacier.

"I need someone to brace me," Ehomba told him. "Can you do it?"

The big cat considered, yellow eyes glowing like lamps in the darkness of the rising storm. When lightning flashed, it was the same color as the master of the veldt's pupils. "It'll be awkward. My forelegs are not arms."

Ehomba pondered, then shouted again. "Hunkapa! Brace yourself against Ahlitah and hold me! Hold me as high up as you can!"

"Yes, Etjole! Hunkapa do!"

The litah set itself immovably against the back railing, the claws of each paw nailing themselves to the deck. Then Hunkapa Aub stepped across the cat's back and straddled him, locking his shaggy ankles beneath the feline belly. With Hunkapa thus anchored to the litah, and Ahlitah fastened firmly to the deck, Hunkapa put huge, hirsute hands around the herdsman's waist and lifted him skyward. The *Grömsketter* rocked in the wind and waves, she rolled and pitched, but on her helm deck the unlikely pyramid of cat, man-beast, and herdsman rode rigid and straight.

Holding the haft of the sky-metal sword in both hands, Ehomba raised the otherworldly blade skyward, lifting it into the storm. When the flat, etched blade began to glow an impossibly deep, spectral blue, Simna immediately sought cover from something that he knew was more powerful than the conflicted storm itself.

A gust struck the pulsating glow—and bounced off, shearing away to the west. A complete concentrated squall bore down on Ehomba, only to find itself shattered into a thousand timid zephyrs. Swinging the great blade, secure in Hunkapa Aub's powerful grasp, Ehomba battled the winds.

No stranger to danger, Stanager crouched close by Simna and looked on in astonishment. "Ayesh, I was wrong to doubt you about your friend: It's a sorcerer he is!"

"Hoy, ask and he'll tell you it's not him but the sword that wreaks the magic. A sword he did not make himself, but that was given to him. No wizard he, he'll tell you again and again. Just a herder of cattle and sheep lucky enough to have learned friends."

She looked at him through the wind and rain. "Then which is he, Simna? What is the truth?"

"The truth?" He considered a moment, then broke out in the irrepressible grin that, when words failed, defined him. "The truth is a riddle wrapped in an enigma—or sometimes in a nice piece of hot flat bread fresh from the oven. That's my friend Etjole."

Stanager Rose was a woman of exceptional beauty and competence—but not a great deal of humor. "In other words, you don't know whether he's actually an eminent alchemist, or just a vector for the sorcery of others."

Simna nodded, rain dripping from his hair and chin. "Just so. But this I do know: I've seen renowned swordsmen battle a dozen skilled opponents at a time, I've seen them fight off beasts armed with fang and claw, I've watched others deflect the attacks of mosquitoes the size of your arm and thorn trees with minds of their own—but this is the first time I've seen anyone use a blade to fence with wind!"

Indeed, Ehomba was not merely parrying the gusts that swirled around him, but doing so in a manner that saw one after another line up aft of the ship. Deflected by the weaving, arcing sword and its attendant indigo aurora, gale after gale was forcefully merged to blow steadily from astern. Gradually the *Grömsketter* stopped sailing in ragged circles and resumed a westerly heading. The storm continued to rage, but now the bulk of it, aligned by blows from Ehomba's blade, raged from directly behind the ship, driving it across the wild Semordria in the direction it had originally been traveling.

Steer the winds as he might, Ehomba could not subdue them, not even with the wondrous sword. Priget once more gained control of the helm, and managed to keep the ship on course, but before the herdsman had been able to get the winds organized and under control the *Grömsketter* had taken a terrible beating.

"We need a respite." Stanager had taken one half of the wheel, opposite her helmswoman. "A blow from the blow." She flung her head to one side and slightly back, flipping sodden red hair out of her face. "An island in whose protected lee we could shelter would be best, but none lie close on our chosen heading." Tilting back her head, she examined the storm-swept sky. "Of course, we are no longer sailing on our original heading. I think we have been blown many leagues northward."

"Put me down, Hunkapa." As the hulking biped obediently complied, Ehomba smiled up at him. "You did well, my hairy friend. Are you all right?"

Through the rain and darkness the bulky figure beamed at him. "Hunkapa like to help. Hunkapa strong!" Long, powerful arms reached up and out, as if to encompass all ocean and sky.

"Strong enough." The herdsman blinked away rain, staring forward. Simna was at his side, trying to follow his friend's line of sight.

"What is it, bruther? What do you see? An island?" His tone was hopeful. Not that he cared overmuch for the condition of the *Grömsketter*, so long as she continued to float, but as a landsman raised on open plains and prairies, he felt himself overdue to stand on something that did not precipitously and unpredictably drop away from beneath his feet.

"No, not an island," Ehomba replied as softly as he could, given the need to be heard above the wind. "Something else." Turning, he addressed the stalwart redhead. "Captain, I think if you head your ship fifteen degrees to port you may find the respite you are looking for!"

Squinting into the squall, she tried to descry what her singular passenger was pointing out. "I don't see anything, Mr. Ehomba."

"Please, call me Etjole. If you do not see anything, then you *are* seeing it."

Her expression contorted and she barked at the tall

southerner's companion. "Simna! What nonsense is he talking?"

The swordsman could only shrug. "Sorcerers speak a language unto themselves, but I've learned these past many weeks to heed his advice. If he says to sail toward nothing, I'd be the first man to set my helm for it."

Stanager mulled over this second suggested absurdity in succession. "I see no harm in sailing toward nothing." Her gaze drifted upward. "The storm holds steady behind us. A little to port or starboard will not strain the stays any more than they already are. Helm to port!" she ordered Priget. Working in concert, the two women forced the wheel over.

It was late afternoon before they arrived at the place Ehomba had espied through the depths of the tempest. It was not, as he had told Simna, an island. Nor was it land of any kind. But it was a place of calm, and rest, in the midst of raging windblown chaos. That did not mean it was a haven for the exhausted crew of the *Grömsketter* and their battered ship. What the herdsman had seen and what they were about to enter into proffered an entirely unnatural and potentially perilous tranquillity. It was a valley.

A valley in the sea.

III

The bowl-shaped depression in the ocean's otherwise unbroken expanse was large enough to hold most of Hamacassar. Through the fulminating winds they could see that the ocean sloped gently down into the glassy green basin on all four sides. Attempting to analyze the impossibility, Stanager would have ordered the *Grömsketter* hard to starboard to avoid it, but there was no time. One moment the ship was thundering westward, driven by gales whipped into line by Ehomba's parrying blade. Then its bow was tilting downward into a trough the likes of which no sailor aboard had ever seen.

The concavity lay not between the crests of two waves, but between four uniquely stable oceanic slopes. Several women and not a few of the men held their breath as the ship's keel began to slide downward at a perilously sharp angle. As she descended she picked up speed, though not a great deal. It was not so very different from sailing upon level waters, save for the fact that a mariner had to guard against sliding along the deck until he fetched up against the bow.

The unrelenting gusts that had been flailing the ship from astern immediately began to moderate in intensity. Pounding squalls became gentle breezes. Ehomba estimated that the floor of the valley lay little more than a hundred feet below the surrounding surface of the ocean proper. Not a great difference, but one sufficient to provide them with a safe haven while the winds liberated from the mysterious bottle blew themselves out overhead.

They could hear those freed siroccos and emancipated mistrals blustering and raging overhead, but they did not blow down into the olivine depression to roil the serene waters. There was no perceptible current; only a gentle lapping of wavelets against the tired sides of the ship.

Climbing down out of the rigging, Stanager confronted her tall, laconic passenger. "For someone who's never been to sea, you seem to know much of its secrets."

Ehomba smiled gently. "I have lived by the shore all my life. The Naumkib learn to swim before they can walk. And there are many in the village who have been farther out on the waters than I. A wise man is a sponge who soaks up the experiences of others."

With an acknowledging grunt, she studied the walls of water that formed the basin. "I would've preferred the lee of an island."

"This was the only refuge I saw," he replied apologetically.

"I'm not complaining, mind." As the *Grömsketter* rocked contentedly in the mild swells, she turned and shouted commands. "Terious! Tell Uppin the carpenter to pick a crew to help him and have him get started on the necessary repairs. Once they've begun, see to the sails and rigging. Choose two men to settle the mess belowdecks!"

"Ayesh, Captain!" Turning, the first mate commenced to issue orders of his own.

Scrutinizing the enclosing green slopes, Stanager remained uneasy. "This valley we've slipped into; will it stay stable? If these walls decide to collapse in upon us, we'll become instant chum."

"When the old people of my village who have the most experience with the sea mention such a place, they speak of it as something that lingers long. I think we will be all right here. How long will it take your people to make the ship right again?"

She deliberated. "The damage is not crippling, but if left unattended to, it would surely have become so. We've a full day's work ahead of us, more likely two."

"Good!" Simna, for one, was not disappointed. Leaning on the rail, he surveyed their implausible surroundings. "I could do with a couple days of knowing where my legs are going to be at all times. Not to mention my belly." He glanced hopefully at the herdsman. "If this phenomenon is as steadfast as you say, bruther, maybe we could lower one of the small boats and do some fishing."

"I do not see why you could not," Ehomba replied encouragingly.

"Why not fish from the *Grömsketter*?" Stanager frowned at him.

"My tackle won't reach the water."

"Tackle?" Her puzzlement deepened in tandem with her frown. "I didn't notice any fishing gear among your baggage."

He winked at her. "You were looking at the wrong baggage." Turning, he yelled down in the direction of the mainmast, where a large black, furry mass lay half asleep, purring sonorously. "Hoy, kitty! Feel like some fresh fish?"

The litah yawned majestically. "I told you not to call me that. But I always feel like fresh fish."

"Then I'll be right down." Passing the Captain, the swordsman arched his eyebrows at her. "That's my tackle."

The sounds of hammering and sawing rose from the main deck where Uppin the carpenter and his commandeered assistants were already hard at work making preparations to carry out the necessary repairs to the ship. Something rose up behind Ehomba and the Captain, shading them from the intermittent sun.

"Hunkapa go fish too?"

"Not this time, my friend." Ehomba smiled sympathetically. "A little enthusiasm on your part goes a long way. I can see you catching a fish and in the excitement of the moment, drenching Simna and Ahlitah all over again." He indicated the bustle of fresh activity that filled the main deck. "Why not see if you can help the crew with their work? I am sure they could use an extra pair of strong hands."

More than human teeth flashed amidst the gray hair. "Good idea, friend Etjole. Hunkapa strong! Hunkapa go and help."

Stanager watched him descend to the main deck in a single, booming hop that disdained use of the stairs. "Sometime you must tell me how you came to gain the allegiance of two such remarkable creatures."

Ehomba grinned. "Simna would be upset that you left him out."

She snorted derisively. "In my time I've had to deal

with all too many puffed-up, self-important vagabonds and mercenaries like him. He aspires to far more than he can ever hope to attain."

"Do not underestimate him. He swaggers like a farm-yard cock, but he is brave, courageous, and, to a certain degree I have yet to measure accurately, true."

"I know what he is," she retorted sharply. "The question is, what are you, Etjole Ehomba?" One toughened yet surprisingly soft shoulder pushed, perhaps accidentally, perhaps not, against his side.

"What I am, Captain, is a humble herder of cattle and sheep. One with a loving wife and two fine children, whom I do not fail to miss every day of this seemingly eternal journey."

Eyes green as the sea and nearly as deep peered up at him. "Every day?" she inquired meaningfully. When he nodded slowly, she sighed and turned her gaze back to the panorama of sweeping liquid slopes and calm surface. "Ordinarily I have no time for landsmen, not even one who knows as much of the sea as yourself. Terious now; ayesh, there's a man!"

"A fine fellow," Ehomba agreed, perhaps a shade too quickly.

She noticed, and cut her eyes at him. "Do I make you nervous, herdsman?"

He composed his reply carefully, but sincerely. "Captain, until recently I would not have thought it possible for a flower to survive with only seawater to nurture it. Yet it not only survives, but blooms as brightly as any land-based blossom."

She smiled. "That's the difference between you and your friend." She indicated the longboat from which a chortling Simna ibn Sind and lightning-fast Ahlitah were hauling in all manner of edible fish. "I've always preferred the artful to the impertinent." Pushing back from the railing, she faced him squarely. "I have to go and supervise the repair work. I've known many men who, at the drop of a sailmaker's needle, will extol the surpassing virtues of their home port until a listener's ears grow numb. When those same men find themselves far from home in strange and stormy waters, they are grateful when a calm and inviting harbor makes itself known."

He smiled. "Though no mariner, I consider myself an experienced navigator in such matters."

"Then you should know that when in uncharted seas and hoping for a good night's rest it's the smart sailor who seeks a tight berth instead of a loose mooring." With that she brushed past him and descended to the main deck.

Simna's excited whooping and hollering as Ahlitah pulled in one fish after another with great, swift sweeps of his paws drew Ehomba's attention back to the water off the port side. Overhead, the liberated winds were finally starting to dissipate, borne aloft on their own wild energy as they dispersed to the four corners of the world. With its calm green slopes, mild temperature, and gentle breezes, the valley was a wonderfully tranquil space. A man could make a life in such a place, he mused, save for the fact that he would immediately begin to sink and drown. It belonged to the fishes, and to the seaweed that rode its small waves in broad, thick mats, and to the seabirds that from time to time descended raucously to hunt for fry and fingerlings among the lazily drifting greenery.

It reminded him of the beaches below the village, of a home that was distant in space and becoming increasingly distant in time. Glancing to his left as he leaned on the rail, he saw the shape of Stanager Rose stalking back and forth among her crew, barking orders and encouragement. Dangerously distant, he thought as he resolutely returned his attention to his two mismatched companions and their exuberant efforts to mine the piscine realm of its subsurface riches.

True to her estimate, the last repairs to the *Grömsketter* were completed by late afternoon of the following day. Fatigued but elated, Stanager emerged from her cabin and the luxury of a Captain's private sun-heated shower to join her passengers on the helm deck. Below as well as aloft, the reinvigorated crew was making final preparations for departure, as much rejuvenated by the respite from sailing and rough weather as was their ship.

Stanager refused to let the concern that had nagged at her ever since their arrival in the sanctuary dilute her high spirits. "All is in readiness," she told her guests. "We can leave now or on the morrow and resume our course westward. I have ciphered our position. Though we were blown far north into waters I do not know, the necessary adjustments are straightforward enough. We will sail a little more to the south, and still arrive at the trading port of Doroune less than a week later than originally planned. We carry more than enough stores to sustain us through the delay." She contemplated the placid waters.

"There is only one element I cannot account for, and that my experience is not equal to." Raising a hand, she gestured over the railing. It did not matter in which direction she pointed, because their surroundings were identical on all sides. And therefore, so was the problem.

"I have sailed through straits so narrow they would

pinch a coal lugger's gut, navigated my way past shelves of coral and rocks so black they could hardly be seen by the lookout. I have taken the *Grömsketter* safely past whirlpools strong enough to suck a lesser vessel down to its doom, and seen to a fire in the galley in the middle of the night. But I have never, ever, had occasion to try to sail uphill." She was watching Ehomba closely.

"This astonishing liquid vale has been a welcome refuge. Now, how do we escape it?"

Ehomba returned her gaze. Nearby, Simna ibn Sind leaned back against the rail and grinned. It always amused him when his tall friend startled the skeptical with one of his unexpected magical revelations. He looked forward with great anticipation to the look of amazement and realization that was soon to come over the Captain's beautiful face.

"I do not know," the herdsman replied frankly.

"What?" Stanager's expression hardly shifted.

Simna's grin widened. "Hoy, he's just toying and teasing with you." He smiled at his companion. "The stiffer they are, the harder it is for them to loosen up and have a laugh. Right, long bruther?"

Ehomba turned to him. "I am telling the truth, Simna. I do not know how we are going to get free of this place and back out onto the upper ocean proper."

"Right, sure!" The swordsman smiled at their hostess. "Would you believe that there was a time when I thought he had no sense of humor? Tell her, Etjole. Tell her now."

"I just did," the herdsman responded quietly. He considered the watery late-afternoon panorama. "I have no idea how one is supposed to sail uphill."

His expression falling, Simna straightened away from the railing. "This isn't funny, bruther."

Ehomba glanced over at him. "Why should it be? As you have said yourself, I have no sense of humor."

Stanager moved nearer. "If you had no notion of how to leave a place like this, why did you guide us into it?"

"Because you insisted you needed a place to rest and repair, and this was the only such shelter I could detect. Attend to the ship first, I thought, and deal with the leaving later."

"Well, the later has arrived, bruther." Simna was no longer smiling. "Time to deal with it."

"I am trying, my friend." He looked hopefully at their Captain. "Have you any ideas?"

Placing her hands on the rail, she regarded the valley in the sea. Soon it would start to grow dark again. "Terious and his people are stout of arm and strong of back, but I don't think even they could kedge uphill." She spared a quick glance for the sails. "We have some wind, but not enough to gain sufficient momentum to push us up one of these enclosing slopes. We might sail partway before sliding back. This is a magical place. Your friend claims you are a magician." Her gaze was steely. "Make some magic, Etjole, or we will surely all grow old together in this place."

"My friend is constantly overrating my abilities. It is a conceit of his."

"There must be a way out!" Simna was, however mildly and gracefully, feeling the gnawing edge of panic. "You speak to dolphins; I've seen you do it. Call them up and make a bargain with them! Have them pull and push us back to the surface above."

"I can speak to the sleek people of the sea, yes," Ehomba admitted, "but I cannot call them up, Simna. And believe me, I have been looking for them. But from where we are now I see neither spout nor fin."

"Then talk to the fishes! I know there are many here, and of diverse kinds. Strike a compact with them."

The herdsman flashed a look of regretful sadness. "Would that I could, my friend. But fish are of a lower order than dolphins, and can speak but few words." Peering out across the sea, he tried to see hope where there was only seaweed and water.

"The sky-metal sword! Call forth a wind strong enough to fill every sail and blow us out of here."

"Now Simna, remember what I have told you. Care must be taken in the use of that blade. If it is used too often and too many times in the same period, the consequences of its employment become dangerously unpredictable. Perhaps in a few weeks it might be safe to try again."

"A few weeks!" Whirling, the swordsman stalked off in search of a sympathetic ear to bend with his complaints. Knowing that the cat would not tolerate his ranting, he settled instead on poor Hunkapa Aub, who would sit and smile patiently through any tirade, no matter how lengthy or pointless.

"What are we going to do?" Stanager had moved to stand close to the herdsman—though not so close as before.

"As I said, I do not know." Ehomba brooded on the matter. "The answer is here. There is always an answer, or there could not be a problem. But I confess I do not see it. Not yet."

48

She put a hand on his shoulder. A reassuring hand, devoid of secondary meaning. "Look hard then, herdsman. I will look elsewhere, and between us it can be hoped that a solution will be discovered." Turning, she headed toward the main deck.

Left to himself, Ehomba contemplated fish and weed, sea and sky. Somehow the *Grömsketter* had to be pushed or pulled out of the valley and back onto the surface of the ocean proper. If it could not be done by wind or muscle power, then some other way must be found. His eyes fell to where the water lapped gently against the sturdy side of the ship.

If only Simna was right and I could talk to fish, he thought. But those fish he could speak with had little to say, fish not being noted even at their most amenable as being among the most voluble of conversationalists. Yet again it struck him forcefully what a wonderful place the valley would be to live, if only there was a little bit of land.

Of course, in the absence of land there were other things with which the appropriately equipped might endeavor to make a living. There was an abundance of fish, and calm conditions, and seaweeds in abundance.

A fragment of an old tale of Meruba's popped into his head. He struggled to remember the details, to envision all of it, but it hovered frustratingly just out of reach, skipping and skittering away from his most strenuous efforts at recall.

He went to bed with it nagging at him, and the ship still trapped within the haven that had become a prison.

"Put a boat over the side."

The morning had dawned a duplicate of the previous

mornings in the valley: calm, sunny, the water stirred by only the gentlest of breezes. Anxiety was now scribed plain on the faces of the crew, for, having completed even unnecessary repairs, they had begun to wonder why they continued to remain in the watery depression, and at the lack of explanation from their Captain and mates.

"Going fishing?" Hovering near the stern rail, Simna ibn Sind eyed his friend glumly.

"In a manner of speaking." The herdsman turned back to Stanager. "What I intend will demand my full attention."

"I'll send Terious to row you. Unless you plan to go far."

"I hope not. You are not coming?"

She gestured behind her. "The *Grömsketter* is my charge. A Captain does not leave her ship in the middle of the ocean unless it is at the invitation of another vessel to visit. But I will watch."

He nodded. "Let us not waste time, then. When the sun rises to the midpoint of the sky, it will be too hot."

"I know. What are you looking for, Etjole?"

"I am not sure. A part of an old wives' tale."

"That's not very encouraging."

He smiled hopefully. "The old wives of the Naumkib are not like any others."

As soon as the boat had been safely lowered, Ehomba followed the first mate aboard. Settling himself in the bow, he instructed the complaisant Terious to row for the thickest, densest mat of seaweed he could find.

"We won't make much progress through that," the mate warned his passenger as he pulled hard and steady on the oars. The boat moved away from the *Grömsketter*, out into the open water of the valley. "And not for very long, either. As soon as we're in among the weed it will be like trying to row through mud."

"Then we will back out and try another place." Ehomba stood in the bow, one foot on the small foreseat, his right arm hanging at his side and the left resting on his knee.

True to the first mate's word, they soon found themselves surrounded by thick green water plants, the little boat struggling to make any additional headway despite Terious's most strenuous efforts.

"This is the best I can do," the mate declared.

"Row us back out, then." Ehomba's sharp, experienced eyes scanned the mass of weed and saw nothing. It stank of salt and the open ocean. "We will try another patch."

They did not have to. A dark, slick shape was rising before them. Decorated with leafy structures that perfectly mimicked the surrounding seaweed, trailing streamers of glossy green the exact same size and shape as kelp roots, it regarded them out of black, pupil-less eyes that were gently bulging ovals lustrous as black star sapphires. The small slit of a mouth was a tiny oval set over where one would expect to find a chin, except there was none; the rest of the face was smooth and shiny as the seaweed it counterfeited. Gills on both sides of the neck revealed themselves only when they rippled to expose momentarily the pink beneath.

"*Kalinda uelle Mak!*" Terious exclaimed as he briefly lost his grip on the oars. "What in the name of all the ten seas is that!"

"A missing piece of memory," Ehomba told him, not flinching away from the aqueous apparition. "Part of a tale told since childhood to the young people of my village by

51

those of the Naumkib who have been to sea." Manipulating his expression in what he hoped was the appropriate manner, he made a round circle of his mouth and blew softly. "It is a sargassum man."

IV

The initial reaction on board the *Grömsketter* to the sudden eruption of the gilled, beleafed, brown-and-green homunculus directly in front of Ehomba was one of confusion and alarm. His sleep disturbed, Ahlitah stirred reluctantly to wakefulness. Simna and Hunkapa Aub rushed to the railing, and it was the swordsman who broke out into a broad grin and hastened to reassure the crew.

"It's all right! I told you my friend was a wizard. See what he has summoned up out of the sea."

"It didn't look like he called anything up," declared one of the crew from his position in the rigging just above the helm deck. "It looked like they were starting to back clear of the weed and the malformed thing just arose in front of them."

Simna threw the sailor a look of transient anger, then smiled anew at the uncertain Stanager. "No, Etjole called it forth. You'll see. Everyone will see." He returned his attention to the patch of drifting weed where the confrontation was taking place.

I hope, he thought uneasily.

Out on the open water, observing that his lanky passenger had not lost his, Terious regained his composure. "A *what* man?"

Not taking his eyes from the inquisitive dark green humanoid shape that now bobbed effortlessly in front of them, Ehomba endeavored to explain. "Sargassum man. They dwell in the mats of seaweed that float on the surface of all the oceans of the world. I have never seen one before, but they were described to me in stories told by the old people of my village." Glancing back over a shoulder, he regarded the astonished mate curiously.

"Did you not know, Terious, that the world is home to many kinds of men? There are hu-mans, like you and I, and sargassum men, like this fellow here. There are cavemen, and neander men, treemen and sandmen, and many other kinds of men not often encountered but as comfortable in this world as you or I."

The mate shook his head slowly. "I have never heard of or seen any of the kinds of men you speak of, sir."

"Ah well. It may be that living in such a poor, dry land as the Naumkib do, we learn to see things a little more clearly than other peoples. Perhaps it is because there is so little around for us to look at." Turning back to the leafy humanoid shape that waited patiently in the midst of the mass of weed, Ehomba pursed his lips in an odd way and made sputtering noises. To Terious they sounded like the gurgling a child makes when it blows bubbles underwater. After all that he had witnessed during the last several days, the mate was not at all surprised when the outlandish sea creature responded in kind.

"Good day to you, sargassum man." Ehomba hoped he

54

was remembering to make the sounds exactly the way his grandfather had instructed him.

In this he must have been successful, because the green-skinned being replied in kind. "Hello, landsman. You are an interesting color."

"I am not green, if that is what you mean." When Ehomba smiled, the sargassum man made a perfect round O with his lipless mouth. Tongue and gullet were entirely black. "I did not expect to find one of your kind here—but I had hope."

"'One'?" Lifting a supple, tubular arm that was fringed with kelp-like protrusions, the humanoid made a sweeping gesture. "My entire family is here; my wife and three children, and my uncle and his wife and two children, and an elderly cousin."

Strain his eyes as he might while surveying the surrounding floating weed, Ehomba could see nothing. "They must be far away."

A burbling noise rose from the depths of the sargassum man's throat. It reminded the herdsman of the sound a badly clogged drain might make. "They are right here." Turning slightly to his left, he pointed. Not off into the distance, but down.

Two sargassum children popped their heads out of the water not an arm's length from the boat, giggling like gargling eight-year-olds. They so startled Terious that for the second time he momentarily lost his grip on the oars. Watery laughter trailing behind, the effervescent pair ducked back beneath the weed mat. Though they were blowing bubbles less than a foot below the surface, their natural camouflage made them impossible to see even when Ehomba looked directly at them.

"We like this place," the adult was saying. "It is always calm here. The winds are mild and no landsmen ships with hooks and nets visit the valley." His expression, insofar as it was possible to do so, darkened. "No sharks, either. And this weed patch is thick and healthy and full of good things to eat."

"What do you find to eat in the weed?" The sun was still high, the languorous afternoon warm, and Ehomba was not above making casual conversation. Who knew when the chance to do so with another of these people might arise? Stuffed full of questions as always, he was reluctant to bring up the reason for his coming lest it cut the conversation short.

"The same sort of things a landsman would find in his garden. The weed itself is very tasty, and despite how uniform it appears to most landsmen, there are actually many different kinds of weed. Each has its own spice and flavor. Living in the weed are millions of little creatures; shrimp and small fish, and the larger fish that prey upon the smaller. There are comb jellies and moon jellies in many flavors, seahorses that crunch when you bite into them, and shellfish that have to be sucked out of their homes and down your throat. Oh, there is plenty to eat." Pushing a leafy hand down through the dense mat of green stuff and into the water, he drew forth a juvenile octopus.

"No thank you," Ehomba told him politely.

"What's he doing?" The first mate tried to see around Ehomba. "What are you two talking about?"

The herdsman glanced back. "Food."

"Oh." Terious was not displeased. He quite liked octopus himself. "What does he say about getting us out of here?"

"I am coming to that." With a reluctant sigh, Ehomba remembered that he was not here to discuss the delights of sargassum living, and that on the larger boat behind him waited anxious others silently watching who were depending on him to extricate them from what had become an inopportune situation.

"We think your valley is beautiful," he told the humanoid, "and we would like to stay and visit, but we have business to attend to on the other side of the ocean."

"Landsmen spend too much time attending to business and not enough time living. If you spent more time in the sea you would be happier."

"I could not agree with you more," Ehomba replied. "However, I am a herder of cattle and sheep, and they do not do as well in the ocean as jellyfish and clams."

"I fathom." The sargassum man popped something small and blue into his mouth.

"There is a problem with our leaving. Our ship cannot sail up the walls of your valley. There is not enough wind to make her go fast enough. Not even if we sailed in circles until we got going as fast as we can and then tried. We need help."

The humanoid nodded gravely. What strange thoughts must lie behind those impenetrable black eyes? the herdsman wondered. What sights must they have seen? To someone like himself who so loved the sea, the temptation to wish oneself a similar life was almost irresistible. Not all wishes in life, he reminded himself, could be fulfilled. He knew that despite his yearning, his desire to spend time at sea would have to restrict itself to long swims from shore and endless walks on the beach below the village. Perhaps, he mused, the sargassum man longs to walk on dry lands.

"We can do nothing." The sympathetic humanoid spread leafy arms wide. "We *could* pull your ship out of the valley, but it would take a thousand sargassum men, and there are not that many dwelling within many weeks' journey of this place. Most live farther to the south, where the water is warmer and the seaweed beds more extensive."

"Then there is nothing you can do for us?" Though disappointed, Ehomba was not surprised.

"Nothing. Nothing by ourselves." The humanoid pressed four kelp-like, nailless fingers to his forehead. "Others might well do better."

"Dolphins?" The herdsman's hopes rose. "There are dolphins in the area? I can tell them myself what it is that we need."

"No. No dolphins here. They like clear, open water where they can swim fast and breathe easy. None of their greater cousins are around, either. It is too bad. A few of them could easily pull your boat to safety. But I think I know someone who might be able to help you. This is not a certain thing, landsman. But I like you. You come to learn and not to lecture, without hook or net or line, and, unlike most of your kind, you have learned how to look into the water and see something besides food. I will do what I can." He started to sink back beneath the weed-choked surface.

"Wait!" Ehomba burbled. "When will we know if you can help?"

With only his head remaining above water, the sargassum man gurgled a reply. "When the king comes to you. If he is willing."

Then he was gone.

Leaning over the prow of the longboat, the herdsman

peered down into the water. There was a lot of life to see less than a few feet from his nose: tiny crustaceans crawling through the gently bobbing mat, the flash of falling sunlight off the silver sides of small fish, the fine patterns of jellyfish drifting near the surface like abandoned, sodden doilies of fine lace. But no sargassum man. He was gone. Or at least it appeared that he was gone. Like his offspring, he might well be lingering only a few feet away, laughing silently at the blind landsman who had eyes but could not see.

"Take us back to the ship." Ehomba turned away from the water and sat himself down. His back ached from leaning so long over the prow.

Reversing his position on the center seat, the first mate took a firmer grip on the oars and pulled hard to extricate them from the clinging weed. "Well, sir? What did the weed fella say? Will they help us?"

"They cannot. But he promised to speak to one who might, and entreat with him on our behalf."

"One what?" Looking back at his passenger as they pulled free of the weed and into open water, he hauled on one oar and pushed on the other, turning them toward the *Grömsketter.*

"I am not sure. One king, I think."

The first mate's heavy brows drew together. "There are no kings out here."

"There are watery kingdoms just as there are kingdoms of the land, friend Terious. Who are we to say whether these folk have kings of their own, and if so, what their nature might be? We must have help to escape this valley, and if that means treating some creature of the sea as a king, why, I will be the first to bow down before him and beg assistance." His gaze left the mate to travel out across the water, toward the surrounding walls of sloping sea that prevented them from continuing on their way.

"It will not be a king of dolphins, though. Or one of their larger cousins, nor sargassum people. It will be something else."

"How will we know it, then?" Impatient to be back aboard ship, Terious drew hard on the oars, putting his back and full weight into each stroke. "Will it come to us trailing a royal retinue, dressed in rich garment and jewels with a high crown perched upon its head?"

Ehomba shrugged. "I suppose you will know as well as I, my friend. We do not know what it is, but I suspect it will not be wearing clothes or crown. No creature of the sea that I have ever seen or heard tell of does so."

"Nor any that are known to me," the first mate replied as he strained at the oars.

They were right about the clothing, but wrong about the crown.

The sun slipped below the western rim of the valley, its shafting light turning the upper reaches of the slope into a sheet of emerald. Darkness descended on the valley in the sea, on the noble ship bobbing gently in the ripples that were not strong enough to qualify as swells, and on her apprehensive yet expectant crew.

Etjole Ehomba was no less anxious than any of them. With the ship's lamps alight and several secured high up in the rigging to mark the vessel's location to any passing craft—or king—he stood on the main deck and stared out to sea, wondering at the sargassum man's parting words. What dwelled out there that was not porpoise or whale yet was potentially strong enough to free the *Grömsketter* from her obstinate sanctuary? What mysterious acquaintances did the green humanoid intend to converse with on their behalf?

A familiar voice nudged up alongside him. "Hoy, long bruther: We're pondering the same thing, I think." The swordsman's gaze was similarly drawn to the black waters on which the ship rode, and to the unknown depths beneath her keel. What monstrous life-forms swam and fought and died there, down in the unfathomable abyss? Which of them could free the ship and her crew and send both on their way? Sea serpents? Simna had heard many tales of such. The horrid great Kraken, with its clacking beak and tentacles like a pack of pythons? A king, Ehomba said the weed man had told him. But king of what?

"Did you ever stop to consider what lies out there, Simna?" The herdsman spoke without taking his gaze from the water, even though in the hush of night nothing save a few fleeting phosphorescences were visible, minuscule ghosts scuttling across the surface of the sea.

"I'm not you, Etjole. I'm more inclined to ponder on what lies on the far shore, how expensive it is, how attractive, and how much longer I have to spend rattling around inside a wooden hull before I'll be able to investigate it."

Ehomba murmured something inaudible before replying with conviction. "You are right, my friend. You are not me."

"The treasure's to be found in distant Ehl-Larimar, isn't it?" As forthright as henna on a courtesan's cheeks, avariciousness rouged the swordsman's words. "Watched over by Hymneth the Possessed. He's obsessed by this Visioness he's abducted, and so are you, a little bit, but his real concern and yours is the treasure he guards in his castle."

"Simna, I really don't—" Ehomba's reply was cut short by a shout from the third mate. She was standing in the rigging on the starboard side, the opposite side of the ship from the two travelers.

"Ware the gunwales! Something's coming up!"

Everyone not on duty, passengers included, rushed to that side of the ship. With many of the crew already belowdecks either in their hammocks or preparing to retire, it was not immediately swarmed. There was room for each individual to peer over the side without crowding out a neighbor.

At first Ehomba saw nothing, only dark water and the barely perceptible reflection of a slivered moon. Then one of the sailors standing by the boarding ladder that always hung over the side as a precaution, should anyone fall in, shouted and gestured straight downward. What had moments before been apparent only to the mate from her elevated vantage point could now be seen by all as it rose from the depths.

Several members of the usually steadfast crew broke and ran as soon as they caught a glimpse of the apparition, hurling themselves belowdecks in hopes of hiding themselves away from the monstrosity. Others thought to find safety higher up in the rigging. That left the main deck clear save for Stanager and the bravest of her company. Terious was not surprised to see that the tall southerner held his ground, but the continued presence of the great black cat, the simple-minded brute, and the husky swordsman led him to comment admiringly on their unity of purpose.

"After what we've seen and been through together these

past weeks, my ponytailed friend, there's nothing above or below the waters that can frighten us." Even as he delivered himself of this characteristic burst of bravado, Simna was contemplating making a dash below for his sword, but he held back. For one thing, a smart man could judge the imminence of danger by monitoring the herdsman's posture and expression. Ehomba showed no sign of concern, much less panic. He had not stiffened or drawn back from the apparition that was ascending majestically from the depths. If he felt safe, then it was most likely that all who remained in his vicinity could likewise count themselves reasonably secure.

Also, bolting the scene in search of weaponry would not make much of an impression on Stanager, who stood tense but agreeably disposed to greet whatever was making its way up toward her ship.

The legs emerged first. Long and skeletal white they were, with touches of pink and carmine, as if a ghost had spent an evening making itself up to attend a masked ball. Fearsome barbs and spines protruded from each limb. They were tipped in ebony, legs armed with quill pens that had been dipped in the blackest of inks. Then the body appeared, equipped with an even more conspicuous array of anomalous weaponry. Bulging eyes stared up at the humans that lined the railing. They goggled from the terminus of stalks that weaved slowly from side to side.

Those terrible spines helped first one leg, then another, to secure a grip on the boarding ladder. Turning itself sideways, the visitant from the frigid ocean deep began to make its way upward. Muttering softly and swiftly to their respective chosen deities, two more of the crew fled for the safety and anonymity of their quarters.

From claw-tip to claw-tip, the creature hauling itself up out of the water was no less than twenty feet across. Seaweed clung to extruded spurs and hung from legs and eyestalks. Water dripped from its body while tiny bubbles oozed around the edges of the multipart mouth.

Simna was at once fascinated by and disappointed in the nocturnal caller. "Your weed man was right, bruther. He sent to us a king." The swordsman made a disgusted sound. "A king crab."

"A king crab, yes," Ehomba readily agreed, "but is that all it is?"

His companion frowned. "I don't follow you, Etjole. Not that it's the first time your reasoning has left me blind, deaf, and dumb."

The herdsman continued his line of thinking. "It is a king crab, but is it also a king among crabs? Look at its head."

"Must I?" Even as he objected, the swordsman complied. The longer he stared, the more his frustration gave way to dawning realization. There in the dim glow supplied by the *Grömsketter*'s oil lamps he saw those spines and projections in a new and implausible light. Squint a little, squeeze the eyes tight, and one could almost see those chitonous barbs and protuberances coming together to form, if not an actual crown, at least an approximation of a comparable configuration.

"What now?" he muttered. "Don't tell me, bruther, that you can talk to even so lowly a creature as this? Big as it is, it is still only a crab, a creature that spends all its life grubbing in the muck and ooze at the bottom of the sea."

"You have many good qualities, friend Simna, but you also have an unfortunate tendency to underestimate all manner of living things based upon their lifestyle. I know of men who abide at rarefied heights yet who cannot be trusted to tend to their own children, while others who live in the depths of poverty and homeliness I would charge with the safekeeping of my own wife."

Simna was not so easily rebuked. "Then if I underestimate, you overtrust, my friend."

Ehomba smiled. "Perhaps between us, then, we may make one sensible human being." He turned away as long, clawed legs came clambering over the side of the ship. "You are right to say that I cannot 'talk' to a crab. But there are numerous manners of speaking, Simna, of which the Naumkib know more than many other peoples. It is what comes of living in a lonely country. You learn to make yourself known to whatever inhabits the same land as yourself, however many legs it happens to walk upon."

The prodigious crustacean finally clambered over the railing to settle on the deck with a waterlogged *thunk*. Stalks swiveled bulbous eyes to right and then to left. Behind it, a captivated Stanager Rose spoke to Ehomba without taking her eyes off the visitor.

"If this is what your weedy man meant when he told you he would try to implore a king to come calling on us, then he must have believed you could communicate with it. I certainly can't. I would know how to boil it, but not talk to it. I certainly don't see what other use it can be of to us."

"Nor do I," Ehomba confessed. "But you are right, Captain. The sargassum man must have had a thought in mind or he would not have asked this creature to seek us out. I will try my best to find out what is afoot." As soon as he stepped forward, the huge crab scrabbled sideways to confront him. It was wary, but not afraid. Nor had it reason to be; not with those enormous sharp-spined arms with which to defend itself.

"What is afoot not indeed, but aplenty," Simna murmured to the hulking Hunkapa, who stood open-mouthed behind him. Unsurprisingly, the shaggy mountain did not react to what the swordsman felt was his best sally in some time.

Behind both of them, the black litah stood and stared in silence. From time to time its long tongue would emerge to lick heavy lips. The humans aboard were not alone in their fondness for the taste of crabmeat. The cat restrained the impulses that were surging through it. Ehomba had scolded him before for trying to eat an envoy. It was, the herdsman had pontificated at the time in no uncertain terms, not only bad manners but very poor diplomacy.

But oh, Ahlitah mused, what a meal this visitor would make!

Standing alone before the visitant, aware that those watching viewed it from perspectives as wildly different from one another as from his, Ehomba considered how best to proceed. The type of talking itself was no stranger to him. He had known it since childhood, albeit with a considerably lesser degree of eloquence. He simply did not want to get off on the wrong foot. Offend this noble creature and it would doubtless plunge itself right back into the depths it had risen from. It was not for nothing that its kind were called crabs.

Raising both hands, he began to wiggle several of his fingers in a certain manner. Though when it came to sheer number of limbs his counterpart had him outgunned, not all could be used simultaneously for conversation. Out of the water, at least, several had to be used at all times to support the weighty body.

"Well would you look at that!" Not for the first time Simna was all but struck dumb by an unexpected talent of his lanky companion. This time there was no question that sorcery was not involved. It was, as Ehomba had tried to explain, simply a different kind of speaking. One that made use of hand signs, or in the case of the crab king, foot signs, to express notions, emotions, and ideas.

After several minutes the giant crustacean and the tall human were practically shouting, so rapid and intense had the movements of their respective limbs become. It was certain that much was being said, but what, not a man jack among the crew had a clue. Neither did Simna ibn Sind, or the black litah, and certainly not the utterly engrossed Hunkapa Aub, who had to pause to ponder the meaning of any sentence longer than ten words.

Eventually the frenetic exchange of signs slowed. Bending low, Ehomba extended a hand. It was met by a thorny claw. They did not shake, exactly. The crustacean's armature would not properly allow it. But there was a definite physical meeting, following which those remarkable legs proceeded to carry their owner once more up over the railing and down the side of the ship. Rushing to the rail, those members of the crew who had remained on deck watched as the spiny, starlike shape sank once more beneath the wavelets, swallowed up entire by water the color of blue-black ink.

Direct as always, Stanager was first to question Ehomba. "Are we to make anything of that? Or was it no more than an unlikely dialogue?"

Turning to her, the herdsman smiled. "They are going to

try to help us. Not because it is in their nature to do so, or because it would ever happen under ordinary circumstances—but because the sargassum man asked it of them. As fellow creatures of the sea, it seems they have a compact of sorts that is very old, and inviolate. The king was reluctant, but as soon as he saw that I was able to speak with him, his last uncertainties disappeared."

"I'm glad they're going to try to help us," Simna put in. "If not, I'd hate to think we let such a superb meal just walk away."

Ehomba glanced over at his friend. "Odd you should say that, Simna. The king was thinking the same about you. About all of us. His people are quite fond of the taste of man, having dined on numerous occasions on the bodies of sailors drowned at sea. At the bottom of the ocean, it seems, nothing goes to waste."

The swordsman envisioned himself sinking, slowly sinking to the soft sands below, his face turned blue, his eyes bulging in a manner not unlike the crab's. Saw himself settling to the bottom, to be visited not long thereafter by first one small crab, and then another, and another, until dozens of tiny but sharply efficient claws were ripping at his saturated flesh, tearing off bits of meat to be stuffed into alien, insectlike jaws, there to be ground into . . .

"Like I said." Simna swallowed uncomfortably. "I'm glad they're going to try to help us." He blinked. "Hoy, wait a moment. Who are 'they'?"

"The king and his minions, of course. Apparently he commands a substantial empire, even if all of it is hidden well beneath the waves."

"I don't understand." Stanager's expression showed

clearly how much she disliked not understanding. "How can they help us to leave this valley?"

"The king did not say." Ehomba looked past her, to the east. "He told me that we should wait here until morning, and then we would all see if the thing was possible."

Her tone was sarcastic. "That we can certainly do! It's not as if we had plans to be anywhere else." Nodding past Terious, she indicated the hopeful, attentive crew. "Set the watch, Mr. Kamarkh. All crew to be sounded to quarters if anything, um, unusual should start to happen." Raising her voice, she addressed the others herself. "All of you, hear me! Get some sleep. With luck"—and she glanced at the studiously noncommittal Ehomba—"tomorrow will find us freed of this place.

"Though how," she murmured as she turned and strode past the herdsman, "I cannot begin to imagine."

V

It was not a perfect morning, but it would do. As was his wont, Ehomba rose with the sun. Normally one to sleep in, even aboard ship, Simna ibn Sind bestirred himself as soon as he sensed his rangy companion was awake. Whatever was going to happen, he was not about to miss it. And if nothing happened, as he half suspected it might, why then he would have a fine excuse for returning early to bed.

Hunkapa Aub was already awake, it being hard for him to sleep long in the cramped space he had been provided in the hold. There was no sign of Ahlitah, there being little that could rouse the big cat from its rest. Hands working against one another behind her back, Stanager Rose nervously paced the helm deck as she stared out to sea. She manifested more anxiety than she intended when Ehomba finally showed himself.

"Anything?" Shading his eyes against the sharpness of the early morning sun, the herdsman scanned the surrounding waters.

"Nothing. Nothing at all, unless you call the presence of a hundred or so flying fish significant. I hope your crab was

70

not keeping you hand-talking so long merely because he valued the opportunity for conversation."

"I do not think so. And he is not my crab, nor the sargassum man's. Whatever happens, he was most definitely his own crab."

A cry came from the lookout. It was indistinct, perhaps because the man was choked with surprise. But his extended arm, if not his foreshortened words, pointed the way.

Rising from the calm surface of the sea beneath the bowsprit was a line of crabs. All manner of crabs. Every type and kind and variety of crab the sailors of the *Grömsketter* had ever seen, as well as a goodly number that were new to them. Ehomba recognized some they did not, and there were many that he had never seen before. There were blue crabs and stone crabs, snow crabs and lady crabs, rock crabs and green crabs. There were tiny sand crabs and fiddler crabs, each sporting a single grotesquely oversized dueling claw. Pea crabs vied for space in the line with hermit crabs, while pelagic crabs shared the water with benthic crabs that were utterly devoid of color and nearly so of eyesight. There were king crabs, too, but of them all were subjects and none visibly a king.

The line they formed was a good two feet wide and stretched across the surface as far as one could see. Stretched all the way across the valley and up the nearest aqueous slope, in fact. Claws linked tightly to claws while spiny legs entwined, the chitonous queue continuing to thicken and grow even as those aboard the trapped vessel gathered to gaze at the astonishing sight.

"Millions." Much as he liked the taste of crab, Simna found he was not hungry. He remembered all too clearly what Ehomba had told him the night before about the crustaceans' traditional taste for the flesh of drowned men. "There must be millions of them!"

"Tens of millions," the herdsman agreed. Beneath the bowsprit the clacking of claws and scrape of shell on shell was almost deafening.

"How does this help us?" In her years at sea Stanager Rose had seen many strange things, but nothing to quite match the crustaceal armada presently assembling beneath the bow of her ship. "What do we do?"

"I know!" Never one to hesitate at venturing expertise in matters where he had none, Simna spoke up enthusiastically. "Etjole's going to magick them so that they carry us on their backs. As soon as enough have congregated, hoy?"

Ehomba eyed his friend dolefully. "There is no magic in this, Simna." Looking past him, he smiled encouragingly at Stanager. "When a hundred million crabs present themselves at the ready, Captain, I think it might be advisable to throw them a line."

"Throw them a . . . ?" For the barest of instants she gazed back uncomprehendingly. Then she turned and barked orders to Terious and the rest of the waiting crew.

The strongest cord on board was made fast around a fore capstan. When the mate was convinced it could be knotted no better, the unsecured end was heaved over the bow. It landed with a convincing splash just to the right of the line of floating crabs.

Immediately, those forming the end of the line nearest the ship swarmed over the rope. At any other time and in any other place they might well have tried to eat it, but not this morning. Sharp claws dug deep into the thick hemp, legs burying themselves into the folds of the triple weave.

"Line going out!" one of the crew monitoring the capstan shouted.

Stanager glanced briefly at Ehomba. He did not react to the warning and continued to lean over the bow watching the frenzied crustaceans. "Let it go," she directed the crew tersely.

The capstan whirred as more and more of the valuable cordage was taken up by the crabs, until at last only the terminal coils securing it to the capstan itself remained. Stretched out beneath the bowsprit, the rest of the line was completely obscured by swarming crabs. As those who managed to crowd into the bow observed, the thick cable was being drawn taut, and tauter still, until the visible portion that was suspended in the air between water and bowsprit twanged from the tension that was being applied to it.

Very slowly but perceptibly, the *Grömsketter* began to move.

"All hands to stations!" Stanager bellowed. Behind her, men and women swarmed into the rigging or to posts on deck. Priget stood like a barrel behind the helm, her eyes aloft as she searched for the first hint of a good stiff breeze.

When the ship reached the base of the oceanic slope there was a collective intake of breath among her crew. Exhaling in concert and producing a noise like a billion tiny bubbles all bursting at once, the line of crabs continued to pull the ship forward. That and the scrape of millions of carapaces rubbing against one another were the only sounds they made.

The elegant sailing vessel's prow rose slowly, slowly. Sailors reached for something to keep themselves from falling backward as the ship began to slide *up* the slope toward the smooth ridge above. At the halfway point someone erupted in an involuntary cheer, only to be quickly hushed by his superstitious fellow seamen. Who knew what might disturb the crabs at their arduous work? If the line broke, if a few hundred thousand claws and legs lost their grasp, then the ship would surely slide right back down into the peaceful but terminal watery valley—perhaps forever.

The rim drew near, nearer—and then it was beneath the *Grömsketter*'s bowsprit. Very gradually the ship ceased ascending and she leveled out. When the stern was once more on an even keel with the bow, several of the most senior mariners could no longer restrain themselves. They began to dance and twirl around one another out of sheer joy. Priget turned the great wheel, adjusting the ship's heading slightly. Wind began to billow her sails. Not strongly, but it was enough. And it was behind them. Picking up speed, the ship began to move away from the valley under her own power.

In front of it, the crabs were scattering, abandoning the line and sinking back down into the depths from which they had been commanded. Seeing this, Stanager ordered the heavy line winched in swiftly lest it back up and wrap around the bow, fouling their advance. She would have thanked the hardworking crustaceans who had joined together to drag them clear of the valley, but how did one thank a crab? She put the question to the most unfathomable of her unique quartet of passengers.

"Do not thank them yet." While, with the exception of the dozing cat, his companions celebrated along with the crew, the herdsman did not. He remained where he had been standing, hard by the bowsprit and staring at the water forward of the ship. "The crabs helped us because their king commanded them to do so. But I do not think they were alone. I do not see how they could have done such a thing by themselves."

"Why not?" Free of the valley and with a fair wind astern, Stanager was in too good a mood to let the solemn-faced traveler mute her high spirits.

"Certainly they were by themselves in their millions strong enough to drag the ship clear, but any line, however mighty, needs an anchor against which to pull." He waved diffidently at the gentle swells through which they were cutting. "What was theirs?"

"Who knows?" She shrugged, much too relieved to be really interested. "The top of an undersea mountain, perhaps, or a shelf of corals."

"Corals would not hold up under the strain. They would break off."

"Well, the submerged mountaintop, then." He really was a man to discourage good cheer, she decided. Not naturally grave, but given to an inherent reluctance to let himself go and have a good time. Simna ibn Sind was incorrigible, but at least he knew how to celebrate a success. Deciding to put the proposition to a small test, she reached down and pinched the stoic herdsman on his stolid behind. Startled, he finally took his eyes off the sea.

"So you are alive after all." She grinned cheerfully. "I was beginning to wonder."

His expression was one of utter confusion, which pleased her perversely. "I—I did not mean to dampen any-one's spirits. I am as gladdened as everyone else that we are safely out of the valley. You have to excuse me. It is simply that as long as I am afflicted with an unanswered question, it is impossible for me to completely relax. I can manage it a little, yes, but not completely."

"I'm surprised that you are able to sleep," she retorted.

Now it was his turn to grin. "Sometimes, so am I."

"Come and have a grog with me." She gestured over the bow. "Doroune lies that way, to the southwest. We'll have you and your friends there soon enough, and from then forward I'll be denied the pleasure of your company. Prove to me that there is some truth in that statement."

His uncertainty returned. "What, that we'll reach the coast soon?"

"No, you great elongated booby." She punched him hard in the thick part of his right arm. "That there's pleasure to be had in your company."

For an instant, inherent hesitation held him back. Then he relaxed into a wide smile. To her surprise, not to mention his own, he put his arm around her. "I do not especially like the taste of seamen's grog, but under the circumstances, it is the taste I think I should seek."

Even those members of the crew assigned to duty high up in the rigging joined in the festivities. Internal lubrication caused a number to sway dangerously at their positions, but by some miracle the deck remained unsplattered. The *Grömsketter* continued to make headway, albeit more slowly than the efficient Stanager Rose would have liked.

The celebration continued unchecked until one lookout, his vision blurred but his mind still vigilant, sang out with an utterly unexpected and shocking declamation.

"*Kraken!* Kraken off the port bow!"

On the main deck, conversing intimately with one of the female members of the crew, Simna ibn Sind heard the cry and sat up like a man stabbed. He had never seen such a thing as the lookout proclaimed, but he knew full well what it was *supposed* to look like. Stumbling only slightly, he abandoned his nascent paramour and staggered forward. Ehomba was already there, staring like a second figurehead out to sea.

"What . . . ?" The swordsman steadied himself as he slammed up against the railing. "What's happening, bruther? I heard the lookout. . . ."

"Hoy," the herdsman murmured, mimicking a favorite exclamation of his friend. "We had our rescue." Turning back to the water, he nodded to the southwest. "Now comes the reckoning."

It arrived with ten immense arms each weighing a ton or more. Pale pink in color, the benthic colossus had surfaced less than a mile from the ship. Now it moved effortlessly closer, making a mockery of the desperate Priget's attempt to steer clear of its cylindrical bulk. A few crabs and barnacles clung to its smooth flanks, while scars revealed the history of titanic battles with sperm whales that had taken place in the depths of the ocean.

In an instant Stanager was beside Ehomba, even as she was beside herself. She could only stare in alarm and astonishment at the abyssal apparition that was making a leisurely approach to her ship. What else could one do when confronted by the sight and reality of the Kraken?

"That is what was at the other end of the hundred million crabs," the herdsman informed her quietly. "That is the only creature strong enough to both grip and anchor them."

"But—what does it want? The crabs have gone, scattered back to their homes."

"They were commanded. This is no crab, and would have to have been asked. I do not know what it wants, but whatever that may be, we had better hope we can supply it. The elders of my village have spoken many times of the Kraken, and I do not recall them commending it for its placid nature." He tried to inject an optimistic note into the litany. "They are a diverse family. Hopefully this one will be amenable to reason."

"Reason? *That?*" She gaped at him.

"The Kraken and their smaller cousins are among the most intelligent creatures in the sea. I thought an experienced mariner like yourself would know that."

"I am a Captain of people," she protested. "I do not converse with squid!"

He turned from her, back to the many-armed monster that was approaching the ship. "Perhaps you should learn."

It swam right up to the bow. There was a sharp bump as the *Grömsketter*, jarred by the contact, shuddered slightly. The Kraken did not try to halt the ship's progress, though it was clearly more than massive enough to do so if it wished. Instead, it swam lazily alongside, paralleling the vessel's advance. One of the two major tentacles rose high out of the water, reaching up to probe curiously at the lookout nest that topped the mainmast. The sailor stationed there crouched down, painfully aware of the inadequacy of his pitiful shelter.

Sidling to the side, Ehomba leaned as far over the railing as he dared and found himself gazing into a luminous, very alert eye. It was quite similar to his own, except that the Kraken's was nearly three feet in diameter. If he was not careful, a man could lose his mind in that eye, he warned himself.

The glistening orb twitched slightly and stared right back at him. Its pupil alone was far larger than Ehomba's eyeball. Behind Ehomba, Stanager and Simna waited breathlessly, knowing that the monster could pluck the herdsman from the deck as effortlessly as they would pinch a bud from a long-stemmed flower.

Ehomba smiled, for all the good that might do, and as he had done with the king of all the crabs, commenced to twist and wriggle his fingers.

The Kraken floated alongside, its tentacles weaving lazy patterns through the air and water, and studied the herdsman's limber gyrations. If so inclined, it was easily large enough to drag the entire ship down into the depths, locked in an unbreakable cephalopodian embrace. Iridescent waves of color, of electric blue and intense yellow, rippled through its skin as it flashed chromatophores at the apprehensive and uncomprehending crew.

Lowering his hands, Ehomba made a single final, sharp gesture with one pair of fingers—and waited. Eyes that were full of unfathomable intelligence regarded him silently. Then the Kraken lifted half a dozen enormous tentacles from the water. Responding, men and women bolted for cover or tried to make certain of their hold on lines and posts. But the monster was not attacking; it was replying.

When those six gigantic limbs had risen from beneath the surface, a powerful urge to flee had surged through Simna ibn Sind. Mindful of Stanager's presence, he had held his position. Besides, there was nowhere to run to. Watching his lanky companion converse with the apparition by means of simple finger movements was akin to observing an infant engaging in casual chat with a mastodon via a confabulation of giggles. Only the possibility that the exchange might turn unpleasant, resulting in the sinking of the ship and the loss of all on board, kept him from smiling at the sight.

When he could stand it no longer, he let loose with the question that was on the verge of driving him and everyone else on board mad. "For Gojokku's sake, bruther—what's it saying? What are you two *talking* about?" He hesitated only briefly. "You *are* talking, aren't you?"

"What?" As if suddenly remembering that he was not alone aboard the *Grömsketter*, Ehomba turned to gaze reassuringly at his companions. "Yes, we are talking. In fact, we are having a most pleasant conversation." Even as he replied to Simna, the herdsman continued to twitch and contort his fingers into patterns that meant nothing to his fellow humans.

"Hoy, then how about letting us in on a bit of it?"

"Yes," agreed an anxious Stanager. "What does it want?"

"Want? Why, it wants what I told Simna any creature in its position would probably want. Payment. For anchoring the hard-shelled multitude that pulled us out of the valley."

Stanager was uneasy. "By all the sea gods and their siblings, what form of 'payment' could such a creature require?" Peering over the side, she observed the powerful, parrot-like beak protruding from the center of the mantle—a beak large and sharp enough to bite through the hull of a ship. "If it's hungry, I'm not sacrificing any of my crew. We have preserved meat aboard, and fresh as well as dry fish. Might it be satisfied with that?"

Turning back to the eye of the Kraken, Ehomba worked his fingers. Once again, immense tentacles semaphored a

80

reply. Wishing to make certain that there was no miscommunication, the herdsman repeated the query and for a second time made scrupulous note of the response.

"Coffee."

"What?" Simna and Stanager blurted simultaneously.

"It says it wants coffee. Not too hot, if you please. Tepid will do fine. With sugar. Lots of sugar."

It was the Captain who replied. "You're joking, landsman. I know it must be you because nothing that looks like that is capable of making jokes."

"On the contrary, though this is the first Kraken to come to my personal acquaintance, I know from experience in the shallow waters below my village that squid have a very highly developed sense of humor. But it is not joking. It wants coffee. I admit that it is a request that puzzles me as well."

"Well, that's something, anyway, if you're as bemused as I am."

"Yes," he admitted. "What exactly is 'coffee'? I gather from the description that it is some kind of food."

While Simna slowly and carefully elucidated to his tall friend the nature of coffee, explaining that it was a warm beverage not unlike tea, Stanager conferred with the ship's cook. They had tea and coffee both. Not being an addict, the Captain had no difficulty with agreeing to sacrifice their store of the darker beverage. Parting with an entire sack of sugar, more than half the ship's supply, was another matter. The alternative, however, was surely more dispiriting still.

"Have you a cauldron?" Ehomba asked her. "Perhaps for rendering out seal blubber?"

"This is not a fishing boat. Cook will use her largest kettle to prepare the brew." Stanager peered past him, to where the Kraken continued to hover like a mariner's worst nightmare hard by the port bow of the *Grömsketter.* "It will have to be big enough."

As matters developed, the iron kettle was more than sufficient to hold the multiple gallons of dark, aromatic liquid. After the sugar was added and stirred in and when it had cooled to a temperature Ehomba thought appropriate, it was presented with some ceremony to the waiting cephalopod.

A tentacle powerful enough to rip a ship's mainmast right out of its footing reached over the railing. The prehensile tip hooked beneath the kettle's sturdy handle. Without spilling a drop, the Kraken lifted the heavy iron over the side. Ehomba's companions rushed to the railing, expecting to see the contents of the kettle vanish down that clacking beak in a single prodigious swallow. Instead, the monster tipped the kettle ever so slightly forward, and sipped. A vast, invertebrate sigh rose from within, and the Kraken seemed to slip a little lower into the sea. As it drank, other tentacles dipped and waved.

"What's it saying, bruther?" An enchanted Simna looked on as his friend strove to communicate with the many-armed visitant.

"It is wondering why it is drinking alone, and why we do not join it."

Stanager replied absently. "It was our entire supply of coffee that went into that kettle."

"Tea will do," Ehomba assured her. "I could do with a cup myself. This has been thirsty work."

"Hoy, and I'll have a cup as well, Captain!" Simna grinned broadly.

"Just remember that I am the master here," she growled back at him, "and not some serving wench put aboard for your amusement." Muttering to herself, she went once again to confer with the cook.

So it was that Etjole Ehomba and Simna ibn Sind came to sit on the railing near the bow of the graceful sailing vessel, their sandaled feet braced against the rigging, delicately sipping tea while the herdsman conversed on matters of wind and weather, tide and current, the nature and flavor of various seafoods, and the vagaries of men who set forth to travel upon the surface of the sea, with as intimidating and alien a beast as ever plied the deep green waters.

In the course of their conversation the Kraken's skin would undergo dramatic shifts not only in color but of pattern. Merely by willing it so, it could generate the most captivating designs and schematics utilizing its own body as a canvas. By the time it was reproducing intensely colorful herringbones and checkerboards, the crew had abandoned its initial fear in favor of spontaneous bursts of applause.

"Just how," Stanager asked Ehomba as she stood nearby sipping her own tea, "does the Kraken develop a taste for something as foreign to the ocean as coffee?"

Putting the reasonable question to the multiple-limbed sea beast, the herdsman received an immediate and unequivocal answer. "It was once dozing on the surface at night when it collided with a merchant ship cruising down the eastern coast that now lies far behind us. Furious and alarmed, it reacted instinctively, and attacked. The merchantman was slow but well laid up, and fully loaded from a trading expedition to the eastern reaches of the Aboqua.

Included among its cargo were several tons of coffee. The smell, I am told, was quite powerful.

"Aboard the merchantman was another like myself who speaks the tentacle-claw-finger language of the sea. Attempting to convince their enormous assailant to grant them their lives and allow them to continue on their way, they plied it with every manner of goods on board. Some the Kraken accepted, like a pair of live bullocks. Others it rejected. None carried the weight of persuasion until it tasted the coffee one crewman brought on deck for the agitated Captain. It also ate the crewman, but apparently humans go well with coffee, and so the overall effect was not significantly diminished." Ehomba drained the last of his tea.

"It held the merchantman in its grasp and its galley busily brewing until there was no more coffee to be had from its stores and cargo. Only then, with both its taste and anger assuaged, did it allow the ship to depart. Ever since, whenever a vessel has sailed near, it has risen from the depths in hopes of encountering that dark brown liquid again. Until now, it was always disappointed."

Stanager nodded understandingly. "In every country that I know of, tea and wine are far more common libations than coffee. It is a luxury." She made a face. "One that will now be denied to us for the duration of our journey across the Semordria."

"Better to complete that journey with thirst unslaked than perish with full cup in hand," the herdsman admonished her sagely.

"I agree, but I know of drinkers of this beverage who would not. To them it is not a refreshment, but an obsession." Looking past him, she watched the monster gingerly drain the last drops from the iron kettle. "Who would have thought to count the Kraken among their number. I hope," she added at a sudden afterthought, "that having quenched its fancy it will not now request someone to munch upon. I am fond of every member of my crew, and would not willingly give the least of them over to such a fate."

"The Kraken was angry with the ship that ran into it." Ehomba did his best to reassure her. "It is not angry at us." Long, supple fingers moved rapidly. "On the contrary, it is delighted to have received the best coffee it has ever tasted."

As if to underscore the herdsman's observations, a massive tentacle reached back over the railing to place the empty kettle conscientiously on the deck. Sending a surge against the side of the ship, the Kraken slowly moved away as its tentacles wove a complex pattern in the air. A pattern only one man aboard the *Grömsketter* could unravel.

"We are free to go, with thanks and in friendship."

Nodding tersely, Stanager turned and shouted orders. Shorn of their many-armed source of wonder and entertainment, sailors snapped out of their phantasmagoric reverie and back to work. Sails were made ready, lines drawn taut.

"Several days we lost because of the winds you freed from the old fisherman's bottle, and several more from making repairs and waiting down in the valley in the sea." Achieving only partial success, she tried to keep the irritation and impatience out of her voice as she spoke to her tall passenger. "If the winds are favorable we might make some of it up. If not, the lost time will see certain of our stores sorely thinned."

"Maybe there is a way to regain a little of the time we

have lost." Turning back to the rail, Ehomba wagged his fingers energetically at the drifting Kraken. Simna paid little heed, certain that his friend was bidding their exotic erstwhile drinking companion good-bye. In point of fact, the herdsman had something different in mind.

Strikingly different.

Returning to the ship, the immense cephalopod promptly wrapped all ten of its tentacles one after the other around the vessel's sturdy sides. Startled seamen were shaken loose from the lower rigging or knocked off their feet by the repeated impacts. With its arrow-like tail pointing westward and its beak hard up against the prow of the ship, the Kraken held her in an unbreakable titan's grasp.

A gasping Stanager had instantly stopped handing out orders and directives to stumble back to Ehomba's side.

"What's going on? What went wrong?"

"Wrong?" Utterly unperturbed, Ehomba was as calm as the heavens. "Nothing has gone wrong, Captain." He gestured at the mammoth-eyed beast that even as they spoke continued to tighten its grip on the ship. "You expressed a desire to recover some of our lost travel time. I have coaxed our new friend into assisting us in this enterprise. See?" He gestured forward.

Seeing that he was trying to point out something beyond the bow, Stanager moved warily forward and looked down. At the base of the Kraken's mantle, a pale yellow tube had emerged. The translucent organ was pulsing slightly, as if readying itself to perform some unknown function. Having eaten many a squid, Stanager Rose was more than familiar with the organ, but not with its function. This was about to be made clear to her and to the rest of the *Grömsketter*'s crew.

"I suggest you grab something and hold on to it." Looking past her, Ehomba repeated the warning even as he took a firm grip on a nearby stay. "Everyone hold on tight!" Noticing the stocky helmswoman still standing at her post far back on the helm deck, he added as loudly as he could, "You too, Priget!"

"Just a minute." Stanager put a restraining hand on his arm. "If Priget steps down, who's to steer the ship?"

The herdsman nodded once more at the bulbous bulk that now blocked much of the view forward. "I have already given our friend a heading. You see, Captain, I have been watching you these past many days, and have learned much. It is my nature to be curious about everything, including the operation and navigation of a vessel like this." Looking down, he saw the cylindrical yellow organ contract slightly. "Hang on. I am going to." So saying, he turned away from her and made sure his fingers were wrapped tightly around the stays.

"Why?" she snapped. "What's going to hap—"

Impelled forward by the stream of water ejected by the Kraken from its rearward-facing siphon, the great sea beast shot westward across the surface of the sea. Held firm in its tentacular grasp, the *Grömsketter* went with it. Several sailors who had failed to fully heed Ehomba's warning were nearly left behind as the deck was all but yanked out from under them. The term "jet propulsion" was one that was as yet unknown to Stanager Rose and her crew, even as it applied to squid of all sizes and species, but the practical effects of the process were abundantly evident in their astoundingly swift progress across the water.

Her bow lifted largely clear of the surface, ship and squid shot across the sea at a velocity no sailing craft, however well crewed and captained, could ever hope to match. Once she was convinced of the stability of the arrangement, Stanager Rose ordered all sails reefed and pennants and flags broken out and hauled aloft, determined to show the Kraken that it was not the only one that could alter the color and design of its appearance.

How much lost time this astonishing tandem journey recovered Stanager was not prepared to say, though it was evident from her expression when the Kraken, tiring of the game, finally let them go, that it was significant. Flashing a kaleidoscope of colors and patterns at them as it sank beneath the swells, the sea's most intimidating monster disappeared back into the depths from which the king of crabs had originally called it forth.

The lesson of the extraordinary encounter was not lost on the members of the *Grömsketter*'s crew. To wit: Never wag an unknowing finger at a squid, and when crossing those stretches of ocean that are endlessly wide and eternally deep, always carry a sufficiency of coffee.

VI

The Land of the Faceless People

People invariably fight with their neighbors. How often and how seriously is just a matter of degree. It did not start out that way in the Tilo Islands. Originally, it is said, in the days when settlers first arrived, necessity compelled everyone to cooperate. Survival took precedence over the usual petty human squabbles and disputes. Imposing predators lived on several of the islands, notably Greater Tilo and Hookk. Dealing with them was a matter of concern for the entire community.

Eventually, farms spread across all the islands, of which there were six that boasted cultivatable land. Towns were raised, and fishermen set forth in small boats to net the silversides that gathered in substantial numbers in the shallows. A few hearty folk even settled the rock-strewn smaller islets. They could not farm there, but individual gardens were made possible by soil patiently carried boatload by boatload from Greater Tilo, Hookk, and Gyre. And there were always the eggs of nesting seabirds to collect and sell in season.

The settlers of the Tilos prospered. So isolated were the

islands that they were never threatened by seafaring
raiders. The climate was congenial, with only occasional
severe winters and drenching summers. No one much
minded, as long as the fields continued to yield significant
crops. With the use of guano hauled from the seabird rook-
eries, the fertility of the land was not only maintained but
enhanced. There was even a modest deposit of dragonet
guano, which as any farmer knows makes by far the best
fertilizer due to the eclectic nature of dragon diet.

How and when the disputes began no one can say. History being a succession of individual memories clouded by
lies and personal agendas, it was impossible to ascribe
blame. Some insist it all started when a rogue from Greater
Tilo stole away the love of a Gyre man's wife. Others believe it had something to do with cheating involving a load
of potatoes from Basweath, potatoes being the staple food
crop and therefore a matter of some gravity among the
Tiloeans. Still others insisted the arguments began when a
group of villagers on Middle Tilo took to calling an old
woman by the name of Granni Scork a witch.

Disagreements soon gave way to fighting. Shifting al-
liances between islands and even between individual villages were made and broken. Fights occasionally escalated
into full-blown battles. Crops were carried off or de-
stroyed, fishing nets stolen or shredded, young women
treated with less than the respect that had formerly been
accorded to them. Given the vagaries of weather that sea-
sonally assaulted the islands, these clashes drew much-
needed muscle and energy away from the business of
growing and gathering food, repairing and building homes
and shops, and generally maintaining the seemly level of
civilization that the Tiloeans had hitherto enjoyed.

It was at this point (though no one can put a precise date to it) that a fed-up Granni Scork revealed to one and all that she was actually truly indeed a witch, as had been claimed all along but had since been forgotten by neighbors more interested in slaughtering one another than in following up on such hazy accusations. Observing the chaos that was consuming her beloved islands and threatening the very fabric of civilized society there, she resolved to deal with it in her own particular peculiar manner.

Seeing the faces all around her distorted with hate, and suspicion, and fear of one's neighbors, she dealt with the problem in a manner most admirably straightforward. From that point on, she declared, faces would be banned from the islands. Unable to narrow their eyes and draw up their noses and twist their mouths in expressions of animosity and dislike, the people of the Tilos would not be able to provoke reactions among their fellows. It would no longer be possible to flash looks of envy, of loathing, of disgust or dismay.

Of course, the absence of faces also eliminated any expressions of love, or caring, or just casual interest, but that was the price of peace among people too embittered to deal with the situation that had arisen and gotten out of hand in any other way.

At first there was panic, general and profound. But as soon as the initial pandemonium died down and people discovered that they could go on with their lives much as before, it was generally agreed that life was far better without the incessant fighting and conflict. Despite the absence of faces, people found that they were somehow able to perceive their surroundings sufficiently to carry out every activity that was necessary to life. To a certain extent they could still somehow see, hear, and smell. These senses were much muted, but not entirely absent. This impossible contradiction was generally ascribed to the magic of Granni Scork.

As for that redoubtable old lady, she saw to it that her own countenance traveled the same path as those of her neighbors. The loss didn't bother her. She had never particularly liked her face, and had in fact ceased caring for it very much some forty years earlier. When queried about its absence, she readily admitted that she was glad to be rid of the damned thing.

Much to the Tiloeans' surprise, they discovered that many of them agreed with her. One unexpected consequence of the loss of face (so to speak) was that within the society of islanders, all jealousy was eliminated. Without a face, no one could be accounted beautiful on sight or, more importantly, ugly. With everyone possessed of the same flat, blank visage, other qualities came to define a person's worth. Kindness, intelligence, good humor, skill at work replaced the superficialities of beauty when it came to judging another individual. With nothing to covet, covetousness too vanished among the Tiloeans.

Gradually they came not only to resign themselves to their loss of face but to give thanks for it. Fighting not only vanished as a social component of island society, but life among the Tiloeans was better than ever. They returned to the tending of their farms, to their harvests and gathering, and to the cordial neighborly relations that had prevailed when the islands were first settled.

So convinced did they become on the subject that a special corps was designated to make the rounds of all Tiloean buildings. It was their job to remove faces from every piece of art, sculpture, and craftwork in the islands, so that these artifices would appropriately reflect the new look of the inhabitants and the restored peace it had brought them. Only one problem remained.

What to do with all those expunged human facades.

For while Granni Scork had been able to remove them, her skills did not extend to obliterating them entirely. For many months, dislodged eyes, noses, ears and mouths drifted like clouds of fleshy butterflies over the islands, fitfully seeking places to rest. After Granni Scork's death, the now faceless people debated what to do with these persisting flocks of aimless facial components. While they did not want them to threaten the wonderful peace that had settled over the islands, neither could they quite bring themselves to extirpate something that had, after all, until recently comprised an intimate part of their individual selves.

There was much debate on the matter. Friendly debate, since it could not be disrupted by angry expressions among the participants. Eventually it was decided to make a celebration of the business at hand. Fishermen busied themselves weaving more of those ultrafine nets that were used to catch the very smallest fish. An islands-wide party was held, following which there was a great roundup of face parts in which every citizen participated.

With much shouting and yelling and waving of hands and reed screens, the emancipated noses and mouths, eyes and ears were herded together to be caught in the mesh nets. These were then taken to a small but secure central repository that had been built into the mountainside of

Greater Tilo, where they were stored in a large locked chamber with no exit. And everyone was satisfied.

People passed on, and when they died their respective facial components perished with them. As part of the ritual attendant on the birth of a new child, that infant's face was ceremonially expunged and evacuated to the repository, there to join hundreds of similar floating bits. Each year a festival was held to commemorate the original gathering of the emancipated faces, with the celebration terminating at the repository in the presence of much good food and drink. For the islanders were still able to eat, passing sustenance through narrow, inexpressive slits in the lower portions of their faces where lips and teeth had once reposed.

Similarly, they could hear through tiny dots in the sides of their heads, and smell through dots in the center, and see, after a fashion, through dots situated higher up. The arrangement was too minimal to be called a face, and each was utterly identical to that of its neighbor. These openings only manifested themselves when they were required. When a person did not need to smell, for example, no dots were present in the center of his or her head.

Occasionally, visitors arrived in boats that pulled up on the shores of the Tilos. They were immediately taken in hand lest they disturb the delicate faceless balance that made life in the islands so agreeable. Their faces were removed and placed in the repository with all the others. After an initial period of anguish and despair (but no screaming, in the absence of mouths), these unwilling immigrants slowly adapted to their new lives, blending in successfully with the original islanders and adding vigor and energy to what otherwise might have become a decadent and inbred stock. Because of this, the Tiloeans actually looked forward to the rare visitations from representatives of the outside world.

There came a day when a much larger vessel than usual arrived in the archipelago, sailing on a westerly heading between Greater Tilo and Hookk. It did not run up onto a beach but instead anchored offshore. This was understandable, the local fisherfolk knew, due to the visitor's size and the water she drew. As was standard procedure in such cases, a formal greeting committee was chosen from among the most respected islanders and given the task of visiting the ship preparatory to welcoming its occupants into Tiloean society.

There was no reason for those on board the visiting vessel to suspect treachery. From experience, the Tiloeans knew that craft that called at the islands were usually in search of replenishments for their stores. So the fishing boats that sailed out to greet the newcomers were loaded down with the best the islands had to offer: marvelously fresh vegetables and fruits, baskets of shelled nuts, racks of filleted fish, and cooked carcasses of the eocardia and isocromys and other strange rodents and rabbitoids that roamed the islands' rocky reaches.

Observing this approaching bounty, those on board the vessel overcame their initial revulsion at the sight of the people without faces. Their queasiness quickly gave way to camaraderie as the Tiloeans boarded the craft and announced their intention to supply the visitors with whatever they might require in the way of food and water. This was not a lie. The islanders thoroughly enjoyed sharing the munificence of their harvest with callers from the outside world. It was a way of introducing them to the good life that Tiloean society had to offer.

Through their subdued senses the islanders wandered about the ship, finding much to admire in its construction and design. As experienced sailors, the crew of such a vessel would find plenty of work on the islands. It was a bit of surprise to find that they came not from the west, as was commonly the case for those who found themselves in the Tilos, but from much farther away, from the distant eastern lands that lay far across the open reaches of the Semordria.

No matter. They would make good citizens one and all, as soon as their initiation was complete. A feast was decreed to celebrate their arrival. It would take place on the deck of the ship that very evening. The Captain proved agreeable to this offer, and her crew positively enthusiastic. In the calm, safe anchorage formed by the two islands, it would be possible to enjoy the promised festivities on a steady deck.

Everything was supplied by the islanders: food, drink, and entertainment. Their excitement was infectious, and they quickly had the crew relaxing and enjoying themselves. And why not? The enthusiasm of the Tiloeans was genuine, reflecting their delight at the imminent prospect of so many new bloodlines from outside joining with their own. Indifferent to all the noise and human activity, Ahlitah promptly abandoned the main deck in search of a quiet place below where he could sleep undisturbed.

Engulfed by such a sea of open and honest conviviality, the sailors let themselves go with an abandon they had not felt since their last days on the mainland. The upper deck of the ship became a scene of riotous exuberance, lit by the lamps hung in the rigging and marred only by the inability of the islanders to laugh in concert with their new friends. For that, real lips and mouths were required.

96

But the Tiloeans managed to convey their pleasure in other ways that readily communicated themselves to the exhilarated sailors. Among other things, the islanders had become masters of dance. When several of the extremely comely men and women who had come aboard for the celebration proceeded to divest themselves of their attire, a corresponding number of mariners happily joined them in mutual dishabille.

The party went on well into the early hours of morning, by which time nearly all the celebrants had fallen unconscious either through the effects of strong drink or simple contented exhaustion. Nothing was suspected by the crew since the visiting islanders had eaten and drunk of the same victuals as they. Unbeknownst to them, subtle seasonings that affected a person's consciousness had been cooked into all the food. As a consequence, they slept harder than would normally have been the case.

A small flotilla of fishing boats soon surrounded the visitor. From within, islanders ready with ropes and nets boarded the silent ship. The carousing citizens who had partaken of the night's celebration would be returned to their homes to recover from the effects of the soporific seasonings in their own beds. As for the somniferous members of the crew, they were carried one by one into the fishing boats and taken ashore.

Zealous, willing hands affectionately unloaded them onto waiting wagons for the brief journey to the repository. There they were lovingly placed on clean cots, one for each man or woman. When the last had been transferred from the wagons, the priests entered. These were the heirs of Granni Scork, insofar as she had any. They were there to bless the transformation of the sailors from irritable, anxious folk capable of such primitive emotions as rage and envy and mistrust into serene, gracious residents of the Tilos.

When the priests had finished their work, bestowing their benedictions on the new citizens-to-be, they relinquished the repository to a solemn line of villagers carrying ropes and soft leather cuffs. Among them were many fishermen, these being the best and most knowledgeable people when it came to the securing of bindings and knots.

One by one they tied the visitors to their beds. Not to make prisoners of these nascent friends and neighbors, but for their own good. Tradition held that travelers newly deprived of their faces were not always immediately receptive to the painless transformation, and tended to go on wild, mad rampages of despair and self-destruction, injuring themselves and sometimes other unwary Tiloeans. So they would be kept secured until they came, each in his or her own fashion, to accept the inevitability of their new lives.

Earnest attendants maintained a watch until the faces of the visitors began to reflect their new surroundings and the work of the priests. Ears were usually the first to go, followed by nostrils and then the rest. As these rose like newborn moths from the faces of their sleeping owners, they were shooed and herded into the back of the repository and into the great domed chamber where hundreds of other facial elements waited to greet them. One by one, the sleeping countenances of the newcomers were reduced to smooth, featureless blanks.

Commotion filled the room when they began to wake and discover themselves faceless. Instantly, gentling attendants were at the newcomers' sides, soothing them with soft, wordless sounds and reassuring touches. These would be needed in quantity over the next few days, until the panicked sailors began to exhaust themselves or otherwise calm down.

All of the frenzy and hysteria was physical. The newly faceless tried to scream, but in the absence of lips and mouths could utter only terse, noncommittal sounds. They tried to cry; an impossibility in the absence of eyes. Communication with one another and with their new benefactors would have to wait until they were taught the language of soft utterances and signs.

The largest among them, a great hairy creature who was as much beast as man, had required the largest chains on the islands to restrain him. His oversized cot rocked and bounced with his struggles, but strive as he might, he was unable to free himself. The Tiloeans took no chances, and had overbound the shaggy mountain just to be sure. In his frantic, undisciplined exertions he was nearly matched by several of his much smaller shipmates. None succeeded in breaking free, though a number continued to exert themselves well into the later part of the day.

With nightfall came a certain calm as the newly defaced company realized the hopelessness of continuing to struggle. The watch within the outer repository was changed and new islanders (if not new faces) arrived to replace the first attendants. These murmured soothingly to the bound guests, striving to assuage their understandable distress. After all, one does not lose one's face every day. But they would all be the better for it; they would see. Or rather, perceive, seeing in the old sense being one more unnecessary aptitude that had been painlessly excised from their personages.

No lights were lit in the chamber. None were needed, since those within perceived rather than saw, and for perceiving, light was not necessary.

The Tiloeans were much taken with their new residents. Nearly every one was of sound, hearty physical stock. They would constitute a wonderful addition to the general population. Already, eligible young men and women from all the islands were choosing favorites in hopes of striking an acceptable match. There were many to pick from, since every member of the ship's crew had been brought onto Greater Tilo from the fine ship now bobbing unattended at anchor in the little harbor.

But in taking her crew, the islanders had overlooked one who was not.

Something that was not even faintly human stirred in the bowels of the otherwise abandoned vessel. It had retired there in search of some peace and quiet during the raucous festivities of the night before. Perceived as entirely inhuman by the Tiloeans who had scoured the ship from stem to stern in search of slumbering crew, it had been relegated to the category of livestock or ship's pet and subsequently ignored.

Now it stretched, yawned, and slowly made its way upward until it was standing on the main deck. Confusion confounded it. A whole day had obviously passed, yet the detritus of the wanton celebration supplied by the faceless islanders still lay scattered everywhere about the ship. The big cat's heavy brows drew together. This was most unlike the human Captain, who experience had shown not merely favored but demanded a taut, spotless vessel.

Wandering through the quarters of officers, crew, and passengers, the black litah's unease increased as every successive cabin turned out to be as empty as the one before. Padding to the railing, it observed numerous lights onshore, indicating that while life had abandoned the ship, it was present in plenty on the nearby island. Clearly, something was seriously amiss. Not that the cat particularly cared about the individual fates of an assortment of ill-smelling, ill-bred humans, but it was painfully conscious of a still unpaid debt to one of them. Also, despite its exceptional physical abilities, it could not sail the ship by itself. For lack of an opposable thumb, it thought, many things were lost.

It was the possessor, however, of certain compensations, not the least of which was exceptional physical strength and senses that would put those of the most sensitive human to shame. Putting both massive forepaws on the railing, it pushed off the deck and plunged over the side, landing with a surprisingly modest splash in the calm black water. Powerful legs churning beneath its sleek body, it paddled steadily toward shore.

Arriving safely on a deserted beach south of the main cluster of lights, it shook itself several times. Ignoring an inherent impulse to pause and dry itself further, it contented itself with fluffing out its magnificent black mane before heading north. Trotting along the beach with eyes and ears alert and nose held close to the ground, it inhaled an excess of odors both familiar and exotic. No stranger by now to salt water, it was able to discard quickly hundreds of natural scents as immaterial to its search. When it encountered human spoor it slowed slightly, continuing onward only when it identified the odor as unfamiliar.

When at last it intersected a shallow beach that reeked not only of one but of a number of familiar body odors, it knew it had come to the place where its friends had been brought ashore. There was neither smell nor sight of a struggle, which the cat found most peculiar. Knowing that the human Captain would not have left her ship wholly untended and therefore suspecting foul play, the litah had expected to find evidence of a fight. In the absence of such evidence, it grew, if possible, more wary than ever.

Voices approached and the litah hunkered down behind one of the small boats that had been drawn up onshore. Two figures passed, faceless like those who had come aboard the ship to participate in the human festivities. The litah could have killed them silently and easily, with a single bite to the neck of each. But ignorance made it cautious. Not knowing what it was up against, the big cat held off doing anything that might alert the locals to its presence on their island.

Instead, it waited motionless for the two blank-visaged humans to pass. Dark as the night, it was virtually invisible in the absence of a bright moon, and the strollers did not even look in its direction. When their silhouettes and voices had faded into the distance, the litah left the beach and moved inland.

So recent and strong were the multiple smells of his friends and the crew that he was able to diverge from the actual path whenever it seemed he might pass into the open. Always picking up the scent trail after such momentary digressions, the litah soon found itself concealed within a patch of brush, eyeing the entrance to a single impressive stone structure. A quick circumnavigation of the edifice turned up no traces of his companions. Therefore it was reasonable to assume that they had been taken inside, where the spoor vanished.

Two islanders stood guard at the entrance. At the moment they were chatting with one another, relaxing beneath cloudy but otherwise clement skies. As guards their presence was more ceremonial than necessary. More than anything, they were there to attend to the needs of those fettered within should any of them become hysterical beyond the bounds of expectation or tradition.

This pair the litah slew. Not because it was unavoidable or because it felt a sudden surge of bloodlust, but because it was the quickest way to ensure their silence for as long as should be necessary. Padding through the unbarred doorway, it entered a corridor awash in darkness. Any human wandering about in such circumstances would have quickly stumbled into walls or tripped and fallen to the floor. The litah's eyesight, however, was infinitely sharper than that of any man.

Those same feline senses enabled it to locate its companions quickly. Faceless they might be, but nothing could disguise their individual odors, especially after a day and a night of struggling frantically against their bonds. Delicately employing bloodied teeth and claw and always keeping an ear alert for the sounds of approaching islanders, the litah freed them one at a time from their restraints.

Freedom brought only minimal joy to men and women who had lost their faces. It was one tall, easily recognizable individual who, exhibiting profounder perception than any of the others, caught hold of the litah's mane and led it not outside but deeper into the structure.

Turning a final corner, they confronted an elderly wise man with an impressive white beard that covered most of his otherwise vacant face. Sensing their presence, he rose from the cross-legged position in which he had been resting to brandish the ceremonial spear he held. Before he could throw it or utter a warning, he fell beneath the litah's huge paw, his neck broken and his upper spine shattered.

Behind him was a heavy wooden door. From the other side of that door arose a constant, relentless hum. It was the kind of noise a hundred subdued beehives might generate. Striding forward, the tall faceless human began to pound on the door. It was braced with double bolts and the bolts themselves secured with large padlocks.

Backing up as far as it could in a straight line, the black litah let out a reverberant roar that shook dust from the walls of the enclosed space and exploded forward. Beneath its onrushing mass, bolts, locks, and door went down together.

Beyond lay a single expansive, domed chamber. Buzzing like a million wasps, hundreds of eyes, ears, noses, and mouths rushed the sudden gap. The intruders, human and cat alike, ducked away from that torrent of fleeing lineaments.

Separating themselves from the choleric mass, six specific features slowed before the tall man. Pausing to ponder the vacant countenance-as-canvas to make certain it was the appropriate blank, they slowly drifted forward to reattach themselves to the smooth skin. The eyes went first, signaling to their fellow facial traits the correctness of the decision. Mouth followed, and then nostrils and ears, until the face of the tall man had been fully restored.

In the outer chamber other bits and pieces of individual countenance were searching out and relocating themselves on the faces from which they had been detached. It seemed impossible that every feature should find its proper owner, and there was some contentious bumping and fussing when, for example, two noses tried to fit on the same face or two ears to occupy the same side of a head. But eventually everything straightened itself out, much as individual seal pups somehow manage to find their mothers amidst tens of thousands of identical-appearing females.

Faces reinstated, the members of the ship's crew vowed to die fighting rather than surrender them again to the pernicious machinations of the islanders. The faceless bodies of the two guards lying athwart the entrance were favorably remarked upon by the escaping sailors. Arming themselves with branches of wood or pieces of stone, they made their way down toward the waterfront where the fishing boats were beached.

As it developed, there was no need to take up arms. The islanders were far too busy trying to fight off their liberated facial traits. Virtually attacking their former owners, the organs that had matured in isolation now instinctively sought to reattach themselves to visages that had never known them.

Tiloeans were seen fleeing their homes in the middle of the evening, swatting and flailing at aggressive noses and ears, their arms swinging wildly to keep persistent eyes from taking up residence in the location of former sockets. Never having known the senses that had been banished since birth, they had no idea how to cope with them. Those islanders whose ears found the right heads were stunned by the loudness a couple of convoluted slabs of flesh could convey. Others kept newly restored eyes shut tight lest they be mentally blinded by the shock of sharply outlined images delivered direct to the brain. Noses brought not satisfaction but nausea, and mouths a mind-less, disconsolate wailing that began to spread all across the island—and to other islands, as freed features flocked to owners living there.

With the aid of nets and clubs, the aroused populace te-diously began to bring the situation under control. Eyes and ears were rounded up and bagged for return to the domed chamber. Stunned noses fluttered and hopped on the ground, to be recovered and placed in bags by busy, faceless children. A carnival of the grotesque was on view as Tiloeans with one eye and a mouth, or two ears and nothing else, struggled to clean up the mess engendered by the mass release of features.

Nor were the impatient, agitated organs always precise in their deployment. Stumbling along the paths and past the village, the departing crew saw men and women with ears where their eyes ought to have been, noses taking the places reserved for mouths, and individual eyes occupying the high points of faces where nostrils ought to reside. All of which contributed to the general chaos and allowed the sailors to escape unchallenged.

Commandeering several fishing boats, they rowed their way back to the waiting *Grömsketter.* Ignoring the danger inherent in attempting to pass through close-set islands at night, the Captain ordered all sail put on. Not one of the grateful crew challenged her decision. Had she so ordered it, they would have jumped into the water in a body and pushed and kicked the heavy craft with their own hands, so frantic were they to flee that gentle, kindhearted, ac-cursed land.

It was only when they were safely clear of the Tilo Isles and their bizarre inhabitants that the mariners took the time to note that not everything had been put back the way it had formerly been. There was some question as to which eye belonged to whom, and what lips ought rightly to reside above certain chins. This posttraumatic confusion was understandable and was soon sorted out. Personal disappointments aside, it was understood that everyone had recovered his or her rightful features, and that if anyone held any second thoughts on the matter, they were best kept to oneself, since nothing could be done in any event to further alter the current state of affairs.

What lingering discontent existed was quickly swallowed in the wave of euphoria that followed the last peak of the Tilos falling behind the horizon astern. Everyone realized they should be grateful for having had the proper complement of features returned to them. After all, everyone knows it is better to have the wrong nose than no nose at all.

There was one attempt made to honor and praise the black litah for effecting their freedom and the restoration of their countenances, but the big cat forcefully demurred. Such frivolities were time-wasting activities fit for humans, it avowed curtly, and not for nobler species like himself. Besides, it went on to explain, it was by nature already lionized, and had no need of gyrating, genuflecting humans to remind it of that fact.

But despite the cat's insistence, a few brave sailors did manage to slip in a stroke or two when it was not looking, before dashing quickly back to their posts. After a while the litah gave up trying to frighten them off, even going so far as to tolerate their accolades and attention. Once when it was being the recipient of such attention, the lankier of its human companions caught it purring thunderously to itself. Confronted with this embarrassing contradiction, the litah promptly retired below, and thereafter showed itself as little as possible except at mealtimes and when taking the occasional feline constitutional around the deck.

VII

After the remarkable occurrences of the past week it was a relief to passengers and mariners alike to find themselves navigating a calm sea devoid of preternatural spectacles. Except for the flock of web-footed pink and white sea dragonets that glided gracefully past one morning, nothing out of the ordinary presented itself for their perusal. Life aboard ship resumed a normalcy it had not known since the *Grömsketter* had first cleared the mouth of the now distant Eynharrowk delta.

They were still in waters foreign to Stanager Rose and her crew, but sailing on the right course to make landfall somewhere north of the trading town of Doroune. The sometimes gruff Captain seemed pleased with their progress, and voiced aloud the hope that they would encounter no more unaccountable interruptions.

It was a false hope.

Contrary to what landsmen think, there are many kinds of fog. These are as familiar to mariners as the many varieties of wind and rain are to a farmer. There is the fog that sneaks up on a ship, scudding along the surface of the sea until it begins to cling in bits and pieces to its hull, gradually building up until it is heavy enough to creep over the bow and obscure a skipper's vision. There is fog that arrives in thick clumps like gray cotton pulled from some giant's mattress. Some fog drifts down from the sky, settling over ship and crew like a moist towel, while another fog rolls over the ocean in the proverbial bank that is more like a dark gray wall than a line of mist. There are almost as many species of fog as dog and, like dogs, each has its own peculiarities and unique identifying characteristics and habits.

There was nothing striking about the fog that began to assemble itself around the *Grömsketter.* At first. It announced itself as a single patch drifting out of the west, neither especially dense nor dark. Gray and damp, it floated toward the bowsprit and sailed past on the starboard side. Few of the crew paid it any heed. All of them had seen fog before, sailed through it, and come out safely on the other side.

When additional patches showed themselves later in the morning, it occasioned some comment among those on duty. The lookout in particular was concerned, and announced that they appeared to be entering a region of fairly contiguous mist. Stanager Rose directed Terious to make the usual preparations for running through cloud. These consisted of placing additional lookouts in the rigging and reefing some of the canvas. Better to go a little more slowly and be sure of what lay ahead than to charge blindly onward at full speed.

Sensing the ship slowing, her passengers came out on deck, to find themselves greeted by the congealing grayness.

Ehomba commented on the unhurried activity aloft. "You are taking in sail."

"Ayesh." They were standing on the helm deck. Stanager's attention was focused on her crew, not on curious passengers. "When general visibility's cut, a wise seaman doesn't take chances with what can't be seen. Don't want to run into anything." She smiled tersely. "Don't worry. Either this will lift or we'll plow right through it. That's the nature of sea fog."

"Run into what?" Standing at the railing, Simna was peering into the thickening gloom, struggling to penetrate the damp haze. "Another ship?"

"Possible, but most unlikely," she told him. "A floating log could do real damage, but I am more concerned with drifting ice." She squinted skyward, sighting along the mast. "As far north as the liberated winds blew us, we run the risk of encountering one of the great floating mountains of ice that sailors sometimes pass. Run hard into one and we could easily be hulled. I've no wish to be cast adrift, marooned on an island that's steadily melting beneath me."

"I'd melt beneath you."

"What's that?" Her gaze swung sharply from sky to passenger.

Turning and leaning back against the railing, Simna smiled virtuously. "I said that I felt you entreating your crew."

"Oh." Eyes narrowing, she looked away from him and back toward the main deck. "Certainly is thick. I'd hate to wander into another group of islands like the Tilos. No way to navigate unknown straits in this. We'd have to drop anchor and wait for it to lift."

No islands presented themselves, but neither did the fog slide away. Instead, it continued to thicken, to the point where sailors could only see but a little ways in front of them, and had to do a certain amount of work by feel. It was not the density but the darkness that began to concern Stanager.

Standing by the wheel, she surveyed the brooding layer that had engulfed her ship. "Never seen fog this dark. This thick, ayesh, but never so black. And it seems to be growing worse. But that's not possible. Fog, even the heaviest fog, is gray and not black."

Simna's eyes widened as he remembered another boat crossing. "Eromakadi!"

"What's that?" She blinked at him.

Ehomba interrupted before his companion had a chance to explain. The silent herdsman had been studying the fog for some time now. "No, Simna. It is not what you fear. Bad enough, but not what you fear." Reaching out, he swirled one long-fingered hand through the dank atmosphere. "Not thick enough to cut, but not eromakadi, either. See how I stir it?" He waved his hand back and forth. "Being a live thing, eromakadi would react. This is truly an ocean fog, and of a kind I have seen before, that rolls in off the ocean as easily as it clings to it." He looked over at Stanager, partially obscured by the black fog even though she stood only a few feet away.

"But on land, it does not linger. And a man carrying a lamp through his village does not have to worry about running into floating logs or drifting mountains of ice." He smiled encouragingly. "Only into sleeping dogs and laughing children."

"This is no game." Her expression was grim. "If it gets

any thicker or darker, my people won't be able to see well enough to perform their duties." Without being able to see him, she shouted to her first mate, knowing that he was somewhere below on the main deck. "Mr. Kamarkh! Light and set all lamps! And be careful! A burning ship will cut through this fog, but that's not the kind of light I want to see!"

"Ayesh, Captain!" came the mate's stalwart reply.

Moments later, pinpoints of light began to appear throughout the ship: in the rigging, at the ends of spars, atop both masts and along her sides. But so dense and dark had the mist become that they barely shone bright enough to illuminate their immediate surroundings, much less the water through which the *Grömsketter* was cutting.

"This won't do," Stanager muttered. "Lookouts can't see a thing. Even if they did, it'd be too close to avoid. We're going to have to furl all sail and put out the sea anchor until this thins or lifts."

"That will cost us time." Ehomba did not phrase it as a question.

"Ayesh. But I've no choice." She stared at him through the gloom. "I won't risk my ship."

"How long do you think before it clears enough to continue?" Simna asked.

Her response was not encouraging. "Impossible to say. Something this intense, it might be days. Or weeks."

"We do not have weeks," Ehomba observed quietly.

"I know. I hope you gentlemen like fish, because if we're forced to remain here for very long, we're going to be eating a lot of it." She turned away from them to give the necessary orders.

"Wait."

Her gaze swung back to the tall passenger. "Wait for what, herdsman? I respect you for what you've done, but don't try to tell me my business."

"I would not think of it. It is only that I would like to try something." He glanced in his friend's direction. "Simna, would you bring me the sky-metal sword?"

"Would I like to be locked in the Pasha of Har-Houseen's harem for a week?" Elated, the swordsman dashed to the nearest hatch and vanished within as swiftly as a meerkat diving into its burrow.

Stanager eyed her enigmatic passenger warily. "More wind? Should I alert the crew to be ready for some sorceral gale?"

Ehomba sighed heavily. "As I have had to tell my friends repeatedly, there is no sorcery involved. I am only making use of what the wise people of my village have been kind enough to provide me."

"I'm only interested in the consequences, Etjole. Not the source."

"There will be no wind." He smiled to himself. "Simna is a good man and a fine fellow, but sometimes his enthusiasm gets the better of his thinking. The sword of sky metal is not for calling up a casual breeze when one is too hot, or a gust of wind to fill a sail. When loosed to do all that it can, it is an extremely difficult blade to control." He nodded skyward. "It might as easily sink this ship as blow it free. But there are all kinds of winds. Eminent sailor that you are, you know that there are winds within the sea as well as above."

"Winds within the sea?" She frowned. "Are you speaking of controlling the currents?"

"I am not mariner enough to chance such a thing, and

the effects of the sword are not so precisely controlled. But I think there is one path I might explore." His smile widened even as his tone grew increasingly speculative. "It is a good thing that I have lived all my life close to the water. One does not have to spend time on a boat to know what wonders lie beneath the waves. Simply walking a beach can also be highly instructive."

He was interrupted by Simna's return. The swordsman held the sky-metal sword carefully in a double-handed grip. Having seen what it could do, he had no wish to find out what might happen if it was accidentally dropped.

"Here you are, bruther!" He passed the sword to its owner. "Now, by Geulrashk, call us up some wind and disperse this muck! Clear the air, Etjole!" Eyes shining, he stepped back.

"I cannot," Ehomba told him. "Too dangerous. A ship is a fragile thing. We already have enough wind. What we need is a way to see clear to making use of it."

"Gojom help me, I don't understand, bruther." It was a sentence Simna ibn Sind had come to use frequently in the presence of his enigmatic friend.

Grasping the hilt of the sword firmly in both hands, Ehomba slowly raised it skyward in front of him, the blade held vertically and as straight as one of the *Grömsketter's* masts. An intense blue glow began to emerge from the metal, pale at first but intensifying rapidly to azure and then indigo. It pushed back the fog instantly—but only for a few yards on either side of the radiant sword.

Expecting something grander, Simna was openly disappointed. As for Stanager, she was quietly grateful for the modest improvement in the clarity of her immediate surroundings. At least the men and women on deck and up in the rigging would be able to see her without straining. Down by the mainmast, a seated Hunkapa Aub saw the blue luminescence and delightedly clapped two massive hands together.

"Pretty light!" he exclaimed in the tone of a delighted child. "Pretty, pretty blueness!"

"It's pleasing to look upon, all right." Simna grunted. "But it's no beacon sufficient to guide this ship."

"No, it is not. Nor is it intended to be. But perhaps like will follow like." Holding the resplendent sword as carefully as if it were a cauldron of boiling oil, Ehomba turned and slowly made his way to the side of the ship, trailing the gently pulsating blue aurora around him.

One of the several emergency boarding ladders that always hung over the side scraped wetly against the stern. Still holding the blade vertically, Ehomba transferred his grip to one hand. With the other, he grasped the uppermost rung of the rope-and-slat ladder and started over the side. It was a delicate balancing act that did not allow the herdsman to relax for a second.

"Hoy, Etjole, what do you think you're doing?" Seeing his friend disappear over the side, Simna rushed to the railing. Leaning over, he watched as Ehomba, carefully balancing the length of refulgent metal in a single-handed grip, made his way down the ladder toward the dark sea below. Only the circle of blue light from the blade made it possible for the swordsman to follow his friend's progress. Without it, the frightful thickness of the mist would have quickly swallowed him up.

"What's going on?" Though intensely curious as to what the tall passenger was about, Stanager would not abandon her position by the helm.

"I don't know." Tensely, the swordsman watched his friend continue his descent. "But I can tell you this much—he's not out for an afternoon's swim."

The bottom of the ladder trailed backward in the dark water. Ehomba reached a rung where his feet were occasionally submerged and stopped there. Still firmly grasping the tough, sea-cured rope with one hand, he abruptly let gravity take hold of the mass of the weapon and swing the point downward. Keeping the fine edge facing forward, he was able to maintain his grip as the blade cut through the water. The deep blue radiance was clearly visible beneath the surface.

Even though the edge sliced easily through the gentle swells, the ocean still tugged and pulled on the sword. Gritting his teeth, Ehomba held on, the hilt locked in his long-fingered grip, the blue glow penetrating deeply into the waters that tried to steal it away from him. Above, Simna and Hunkapa Aub watched from the rail. The swordsman could see that the strain of holding on to the ladder with one hand and the submerged blade with the other was tiring his friend.

"Want me to spell you awhile, bruther?" he called out.

The herdsman's face turned upward. Somehow, he managed to grin. *He'll grin when he's on his deathbed,* Simna mused. *It'll be the last expression he wears.*

"Thank you, friend Simna, but all is well."

"Well as what?" the swordsman retorted. "What is it you hope to do?"

"Light a way through this confusion." With the effort of looking upward putting additional stress on his body, Ehomba lowered his head.

117

Hunkapa dropped a massive, shaggy arm over the side. "Look, look! More prettinesses!"

Simna squinted. Something was rising from the depths of the ocean. It was not large—no longer than one of the *Grömsketter*'s small boats—but it was lined with lights that flashed bright yellow and pale red. As it loomed nearer the surface he saw that it was a fish—but a fish unlike any finned denizen of the deep he had ever seen before, either in kitchen or in art.

Its body was more than nine feet long and silvery black, but it was no thicker around than a ribbon. A single long fin ran the length of the spine, and two tiny pectoral fins fluttered just beneath and back of glaring eyes the size of dinner plates. Above the head three long spines bobbed and weaved, and each was tipped with a bright yellow light. Prominent in the narrow, gaping mouth were fangs like shards of broken glass.

It was soon apparent that it was not alone.

Drawn by the light of the sword, all manner of wondrous deepwater creatures were rising to the surface. They swam and drifted and hovered about the cerulean halo of the sky-metal sword like moths romancing a candle on a summer's eve. As the abyssal ascension gave rise to this luminescent benthic epiphany, more and more of the crew crowded to the port side to gape. Though somewhat muted by the persistent fog, their reactions were a mixture of awe, wonder, and sheer childlike delight in an exotic and beautiful phenomenon the likes of which none of them had ever encountered before.

Up came a pair of fish like bloated black bladders, one thirty times larger than its companion. Each had a single long, curving appendage like a thin filament fishing line attached to its forehead, from whose tip twitched a lure of irresistible intensity. Their eyes were so small as to be almost invisible, and they burned with the fire of a hundred natural lights. Nearby swarmed a school of a thousand small silvery fish, each flashing a thumb-sized soft blue light from just aft of its eye.

There were jellyfish larger than any the sailors had ever seen, their pulsing bells decorated with blue and green and yellow lights that trailed fifty-foot-long tentacles of unbroken luminescence. Deep-sea sharks swept tails full of sapphire light in steady arcs, like glowing oars in the water, and all manner of toothy fish darted to and fro in balls of intense yellow or green.

But it was when the tiny lanterns of natural luminescence finally arose that the sea around the *Grömsketter* turned from dark to light. There were billions of them, seemingly in as many shapes and sizes, many so small that even sharp-eyed seamen wearing spectacles could barely make them out. Ehomba could. The herdsman's vision was particularly acute.

Then the mid-ocean merfolk arrived, showing oval, slightly protuberant eyes and gills that flashed gold around the edges. They displayed elegant patterns of light along their sides and fins and carried short staffs tipped with transparent crustacean bodies scavenged from the hidden places of the sea. These were filled with glowing krill individually selected for their color and brightness. A number of merfolk rode in shell chariots drawn by man-sized seahorses that glowed brown and were harnessed with kelp and sea-grass strips radiating an intense crimson.

The lightwhals came too. Looking like crosses between oversized dolphins and blind seals, they radiated a ghostly, pellucid purple. There were night penguins that emitted green light only when hunting in dark seas, and merlions whose manes were fringed with pallid lavender. The mournful, watery moans they exchanged with their land-bound cousin Ahlitah resounded regretful and forlorn across the mist-shrouded swells.

There were deep-ocean crabs whose shells boasted imbedded iridescences in lines of intense green spotted with azure, and strange turtles whose carapaces wore diadems of lights like pulsating jewels. Eels slithered and writhed like living lightning, while squid and cuttlefish ranging in size from palm-sized to giants that might have been family of the Kraken itself sent waves of opalescence rippling through their skin. Sea butterflies more colorful than any of their terrestrial counterparts flew beneath the surface on wings tinted emerald and topaz and tourmaline, occasionally emerging from the water in jubilant bursts of dazzling effulgence.

Drawn by the incomparable blue glow emitted by the sky-metal sword, all this great upwelling of light and life swirled around the *Grömsketter*, disturbing neither water nor sky but overwhelming and beating back the darkness imposed by the clinging fog. Whereas before Stanager and her crew could barely see one another clearly enough to avoid running into each other on the deck, now the excess of spectacular natural light illuminated the sea around the ship for nearly half a mile, making not only onboard activity but also navigation possible.

"Terious!" the Captain shouted. "Set the mains'l and the lower fores'ls! Let's punch through this murk before our herdsman's flock grows bored and decides to sink back from whence they came." Her classic profile was aglow with light from the thousands of luminescent deep-sea dwellers that had gathered around the ship.

Simna had not left his position by the rail. "Better to worry not about losing their interest, but about my friend losing the strength in his arm."

It was a procession never to be forgotten by all who saw it: the graceful *Grömsketter,* sails set and making her way southwest, englobed by millions of colored lights worn by as fantastic a profusion of undersea life as could be assembled in one place. Even experienced seamen would have been paralyzed by all that beauty, had they not been so busy. Stanager Rose kept her crew occupied lest they lose themselves in the embarrassment of natural magnificence.

Thrust back by the luminescence, the fog began to shrivel and disperse, until a single light brighter if not more beautiful than all those assembled began to illuminate the scene from above. Then even the blue intensity of the sword could not sustain the interest of the visitors from the deep. In their tiny millions and larger pairs and trios they began to sink back into the abyss from which they had risen, untold numbers of lights descending and dissipating, until, with a last silent wave of a phosphorescent scepter, one of the deep-sea mermen saluted the ship and turned his glowing chariot ultimately downward.

The sun burned away the last of the fog, enabling the crew to put on still more sail and to flee from that darkling, benighted patch of ocean. Then it was time to bring forth a small quantity of the ship's precious supply of ice, kept sealed in the darkest, coldest depths of her hull. Not to cool her crew, who were certainly sweating heavily enough to deserve it, but to ice down the muscles of one of her passengers. Held in one position for so long, Ehomba's left arm and fingers had become badly cramped. The application of ice wrapped in towels might not equal the recent display of magic, but it was blessedly effective.

While the herdsman sat on the helm deck trying to restore the flow of blood to his aching muscles and tendons, Simna gingerly held the sky-metal sword. As always, the crosshatched lines on the blade fascinated his eye.

"How do you make it work, Etjole, if you are not the sorcerer you keep insisting you're not?"

The herdsman would have shrugged, but his cramped shoulders would not allow it. "Practice, friend Simna. Otjihanja showed me some things, and other elders had suggestions. It is not something to be described. You must *feel* the proper motion, the way the weight of the metal travels through the air and fights the pull of the Earth."

Simna nodded. "You know, it's funny. When I was younger I would have taken that as a challenge, and as a result probably tried something stupid."

"I do not see much that has changed with age." Curled up against the railing that separated the helm deck from the main deck below, the black litah murmured sleepily.

"And I do not take criticism of my profession from a yowling devourer of carrion." When the big cat chose not to respond, Simna turned back to his lanky friend. "Having seen what this remarkable blade can do, I would no more try to make use of it than I would a sculptor's chisel or a musician's lute."

Ehomba smiled softly. "You did, once."

A startled Simna looked sharply at the seated herdsman. "I thought you were asleep!"

Ehomba looked away. "I was."

The swordsman started to reply, discovered that he did

not have an adequate response at hand, and decided against it. Instead, he laid the wondrous weapon carefully down alongside his seated friend and pulled the thin blanket a little higher on Ehomba's narrow shoulders. The herdsman had spent far too much time with his hand and part of one arm immersed in the cold water. Sorcerer or not, he was starting to shiver.

"I will be all right." He smiled reassuringly up at his concerned companion. "The ocean below my village is much colder than this, and I have spent many an hour wading and swimming in its waters."

"I don't care," Simna told him. "Any man can catch a chill and die from the complications." He looked out to sea. "Attract like to like, you said. More like light to light. It was a grand sight. I never dreamed quite so many splendid phantasms dwelled in the sea, and all of them lit from within by sorceral glow."

"Not sorceral," Ehomba corrected him. One hand held the edges of the blanket tight against his throat. "The lights you saw were all natural, manufactured from within their own bodies by the creatures themselves. There was nothing of sorcery about it."

The swordsman's forehead furrowed. "How do you know that?"

"Because many such creatures wash up dead on the beaches near my home. Their bodies are flaccid and their lights dimmed, but they still glow for a little while after dying." He nodded toward the clearing sky. "The waters offshore from my village go down very deep. It must be exceedingly dark in the depths, like a perpetual night, for the creatures that live there to need to make their own light."

"A handy property," Simna agreed. "There have been

times when I would have liked to have been able to shine a little light from my own body."

The herdsman looked at him strangely. "Everyone does so, Simna. It is just that it is difficult to see. It takes practice to separate it out from the natural light that surrounds us every day."

The shorter man laughed easily. "So you're saying that I glow like those fishy things? Like a jellyfish, maybe?"

"No, not like a jellyfish. The light that people, or at least most people, emit, is something very different. But you do glow, my friend. Less intensely in ways than you would like to believe, and more brightly in other kinds. There are many, many different kinds of light."

"Well, at least I'm not dark." Simna enjoyed the notion, even though he was not sure he understood at all what his cryptic companion was talking about. "How about everyone else?" Turning, he gestured at those nearby, not really expecting the herdsman to respond.

Instead, Ehomba rested his chin on his knees and squinted, pausing once to wipe away a lingering droplet of salt water. "The Captain, she glows only a very few colors, but those colors are as pure and strong as I have ever seen in a person. The helmswoman Priget emits light in fits and bits, like the sparks from a fire. That man working the ropes over there, his lights are few and dim, but far from being absent." The herdsman's gaze roved the open decks.

"The lights of the first mate are also strong and unadulterated, but not nearly of an intensity approaching that of the Captain. Certain shades and tints are completely absent in Ahlitah, but those colors he does manifest are almost overpowering." He sniffed and, lifting a hand from beneath the blanket, rubbed his nose.

Simna's natural reaction to all this was to laugh heartily. But seeing the seriousness with which Ehomba was rendering his appraisals, the swordsman could not quite bring himself to do so. The herdsman was jesting, of course. Having one of his silent, slightly taciturn chuckles at the expense of a friend. People, much less cats like Ahlitah, did not glow. If they did, someone as sharp-eyed as himself would surely have noticed it by now. But he was happy to run with the joke, enjoying the fertility of his laconic companion's imagination. His friend might or might not be the mighty sorcerer Simna supposed him to be, but he was certainly a fine storyteller. The sincerity with which he spun his tall tales only added to their seeming veracity.

"You overlooked someone." He indicated a large, unkempt gray mass resting on the deck like a pile of discarded rugs. "What about Hunkapa Aub?"

Ehomba gazed thoughtfully in the direction of their humble companion. "He is a strange one. I can descry occasional bursts of light from him, but they are very subdued and difficult to catch." He grinned gently. "Maybe it is all that fur. Certain things can block out a person's light. Although I have never before known hair to do it, neither have I ever known anyone covered with quite so much hair." His attention drifted. "I think the rest of the day will be fine. I wonder how far we are from Doroune?"

Simna straightened. "I'll go and ask Stanager."

"Yes," Ehomba commented, "I have noticed that you and the Captain have begun to get along better these past several days."

The swordsman winked conspiratorially. "You've been around me long enough by now to know that I'm a very persistent fellow, long bruther. And not just in the matter

125

of lost treasures to be found." Grinning, he turned and marched off in the direction of the helm, where Stanager Rose was conversing with Priget.

"Be careful," the herdsman called after him.

"Why?" Simna smiled back over his shoulder. "Afraid I might figure out how to see her 'light'?"

"No," Ehomba responded. "Afraid that you might see it. You're all too easily blinded by such things, Simna ibn Sind."

VIII

After so long out of sight of land (the Tilo Islands being a horrific recollection that every man and woman aboard firmly desired to expunge from their memories), the majestic spectacle of the Quonequot Cliffs looming on the western horizon roused a throaty cheer from passengers and crew alike when they finally hove into view. Rising vertically a thousand feet from the waves that broke against their base and plunging to untold depths below the surface, the white-chalk precipices terminated in a massive headland that marked the entrance to Kylles Bay. Beyond and within lay the fabled western trading city of Doroune.

Stealing a moment from her navigational duties, Stanager Rose left the helm in the capable hands of Priget, who had guided the *Grömsketter* into the bay several times before, and walked over to stand alongside the most puzzling passenger she had ever carried. At present, he was gazing thoughtfully over the starboard side, studying the lofty white escarpment as the ship neared land. Dragonets of many sizes and colors glided regally along the cliff faces, where they found safe nesting sites among the sheer walls.

In this they were not alone. Ceaseless screeching and cawing and hissing testified to the competition for prime sites
among dragonets and puffins, gulls and terns. As Captain
and passenger stood side by side at the rail, a formation of
great osteodontornids glided by overhead, their twenty-
foot wings momentarily blocking out the sun, their tooth-
filled beaks intent on tracking a school of small fish
shoaling by just beneath the breaking spume.

"What will you do now?" she inquired of the silent
herdsman.

He did not turn to look at her, but instead kept this gaze
on the immense chalky headland. "As I told you before we
set out on this crossing, I am bound by personal covenant
to journey to a land called Ehl-Larimar, there to seek out a
woman called the Visioness Themaryl, and return her to
her family in Laconda. Ehl-Larimar lies to the west of
here, so it seems I must keep traveling west." Shifting his
attention from the imposing headland, he smiled down at
her. "I have already been too long away from home. I hope
I do not have to travel so far west that I meet myself coming."

She laughed, caught herself, and choked slightly on the
unusual reaction. "That's silly, Etjole. Nobody can meet
themselves coming."

With a sigh, he returned his attention to the place where
the incoming swells shattered themselves against the
white ramparts. "It depends how far west one has to go,
and what one means by 'west.' This Doroune, is it as big
as Hamacassar?"

She shook her head. "Haven't been that far inland—the
crew and I keep pretty much to the harbor because that's
where both our business and recreational interests lie. But

from all that I've seen and heard on previous trips, it's a much smaller place. Most of the coastal towns we visit and trade with are like that. Transit points for goods from farther inland. They don't get many visitors from across the Semordria." She grinned confidently. "Everyone knows only fools and imbeciles dare attempt the ocean crossing."

Solemnly, he put a hand on her shoulder. "As one fool to another, let me say that it has been an honor to travel on your ship, Captain Rose."

She nodded once, as eloquent an acceptance of the compliment as she could manage. Straightforward praise made her uncomfortable. Easier for her to deal with a storm or a mutinous crew than an unabashed encomium.

"Thanks." They were silent for a while, standing side by side, watching the sea and the birds and the dragonets as Priget and Terious deftly maneuvered the *Grömsketter* around the southern tip of the headland and into Kylles Bay. Heading north once again but this time in calm, sheltered waters, Ehomba soon found he could make out the steeples and peaked roofs of Doroune in the distance.

"Look," she said finally, "I'll be a goodly while sailing down the coast and then back up again, selling off not only our own trade goods but those we pick up along the way. Can't give you exact times and dates because this sort of unscheduled trading isn't done to a timetable. But we'll for sure be calling at Oos, Xemon-scap, Polab, Sambley, and Calenx. Can't say if we'll go farther than that. The weather south of Calenx can turn at the drop of a line." It was her turn to put a hand on his arm.

"If your travels take you to any of those cities, don't depart without asking about us. If—when you've accomplished your quest, you'll be wanting passage home. Can't

take you to Ehl-Larimar—don't even know where it is—
but we *can* carry you back across the Semordria." This time
her grin did not surprise her. "Try and hang on to a few of
your pebbles. I like you, Etjole Ehomba. I find much to
admire in you. And much that bewilders me. But while I
like to think there's much goodness in my heart, that doesn't
include free passage."

He nodded understandingly. "A few pebbles. Thoughts
of them will keep your supercargo feeling younger than his
years."

"Broch's a good fellow. Sharp mind, sound seaman. He's
devoted to me, and to the ship, and has made it his mission
to see to it that both of us stay afloat. Enjoy your last moments on the *Grömsketter*, Etjole Ehomba. She'll miss you,
and so will I." She stepped back from the railing. "There's
much of interest to see on the final leg of our approach into
Doroune. Now if you'll excuse me, I have some small matters of navigation to attend to below."

He watched her until she disappeared down one of the
ladders that led to the main deck. Straight of back and purpose, she was a fine woman. The sea had burnished her
like bronze, had knocked off all the rough edges and replaced them with the sharpness of salt and the fire of red
coral. Mirhanja would like her, he decided.

High on the white cliffs above, dragonets and seabirds
screamed as the ship came around. It would be strange, he
thought, to have again beneath his feet a floor that did not
roll. Were he not so devoted a herdsman, he had often
thought he might have become a sailor.

But such a thing was not possible for a Naumkib. They
were a people of their land. If men such as he went off to
sea, who would watch over the village and the herds? He

inhaled deeply of the fresh, pungent salt air, knowing that it might be some time before he could fill his lungs with it again.

Activity busied the docks of Doroune, but the crowds and freneticism he had encountered in Hamacassar were absent. There was about the people here a sense of purpose, but not desperation. They wanted to make money, but none were dying of the need to do so. It was a simpler place, an easier place, especially for four strangers.

What, he found himself wondering, would Ehl-Larimar be like?

After spending the night on the boat, the following morning Ehomba was more than a little shocked to see Hunkapa Aub carrying Simna ibn Sind down the unloading ramp, with a dour Ahlitah padding behind. From above, Terious and Priget waved good-bye. Of Captain Stanager Rose there was no sign. He was not surprised. She had made her farewell to him the previous day.

"Simna, what happened? What is wrong with you?"

"Wrong?" Tired eyelids fluttered and a wan smile flashed across the swordsman's countenance. "Hoy, nothing's wrong, bruther." With a shaky hand he gestured toward his feet. "Me legs aren't working right just now, that's all. A little rest and they'll be fine." Looking away from his tall friend, he let his eyes roll skyward. "Me, I'm already fine. Very fine indeed. Except for me lower appendages, thank you." With that he closed his eyes, and was almost instantly asleep.

Hunkapa bore Simna's limp body effortlessly as they made their way inland from the docks. Puzzled, Ehomba sought enlightenment from Aub, even though he felt he

131

was attempting to mine a strata devoid of that particular ore.

"What happened to him?"

"Don't know." Brows like shredded rags drew together as the big biped struggled to cogitate. "Friend Simna not much speak today." The bestial visage brightened. "Simna say he talk navigation with Captain Rose. Last night."

"Naviga—?" Finding understanding where he had expected to unearth none, the herdsman concluded the excavation silently. Clearly, for his friend Simna, whatever else they might stumble into, Doroune had for him already proven a propitious port of call.

Halting in the middle of a small plaza with a public drinking fountain before them, Ehomba considered the shopfronts that ringed the circular square. "We need a guide, some information, and instruction."

Still carrying the swordsman, who was by now awake, moaning, and holding himself, Hunkapa gestured with his great shaggy head. "Ehomba want go west. Hunkapa guide! That way, west." Next to him, Ahlitah commented by farting.

Leaning on his spear, the herdsman smiled tolerantly at his oversized companion. "That is very good, Hunkapa. I am glad you know which way is west. But before we start we should try to learn something about the country we must pass through."

Eventually a resident brave enough to stop at Ehomba's request directed them to a large dispatch house where wagons of many sizes and descriptions were being fitted out with sails. The travelers had already encountered several of these sturdy, wind-powered vehicles steering their way around the city. According to the helpful citizen, the dispatch center was a good place to find not only transportation inland, but also a guide to convey them there.

Their inquiries met with the same kind of amused skepticism Ehomba had encountered before. It was a reaction that, on repetition, was beginning to grow tiresome. Was he the only man who believed that to travel from one place to another, no matter how reputedly dangerous or difficult, all that was required was for one to start walking in the requisite direction?

"Lissen, you," stammered the ancient pathfinder who was too bored not to talk to them, "we all every one of us knows where Ehl-Larimar lies." Raising a shaky finger that resembled a strip of rolled saddle leather, he pointed westward. Behind Ehomba, huge hands clapped delightedly together.

"See, Etjole, see! Hunkapa know, Hunkapa guide!"

"Be quiet, Hunkapa," the mildly annoyed herdsman admonished his hulking friend. The matted one fell silent.

"If you all know how to get to Ehl-Larimar, why cannot one of you guide us there?"

"Because the difficulty's not in the knowin', it's in the goin'." Peering behind his questioner, the elderly guide considered the herdsman's blond hair. "Why you braid up your locks like that, man? Seen wimmens do it, but never 'til now a buck."

"It is the style among the men of my village." Uncharacteristically, Ehomba was becoming impatient with this short, skinny sage, who reminded him of chattering macaws. "What is so difficult about the going to Ehl-Larimar that you and all your colleagues refuse to take us?"

Aged eyes that had seen much rolled in their sockets as

if loose. "Why, out west there's dangerous wild critters everywhere, some of 'em monstrous big, others with long fangs that drip poison." To emphasize the latter, he protruded his upper jaw far beyond the lower and flapped it to simulate biting motions. "First you have to get through the Hexen Mountains. Then there's the demons what live in the interior, and hostile tribes of things thet ain't always human." He was waving his birdlike arms wildly now, using them to magnify the drama of his own declamations.

"Get past them, and then there's the Tortured Lands, and beyond thet, the Curridgian Mountains with their ice fields and rock slides." Lack of wind finally forced him to call a halt to the hymn of horrors.

"And after that?" Ehomba asked quietly.

"After thet? After thet!" Calming himself with an effort, the senior pathfinder took a deep breath. "Why, after thet is Ehl-Larimar its very self, and beyond there, the Ocean Aurreal."

"Another ocean?" Raising himself up, Simna had his hirsute nurse place him on the ground. On shaky legs, he confronted his lanky friend. "By Guisel's gearing, Etjole, no more long sea voyages! I beg you!"

Ehomba's brows rose slightly. "I thought you enjoyed our sojourn on the sea."

Anxious eyes gazed up at him. "Hoy, long bruther, it wasn't the voyage that leaves me looking like this. It were the arrival."

The herdsman nodded noncommittally. "Somehow I do not think we would face a similar situation on another ocean entirely, but I will certainly keep your concerns in mind. I do not see why it would be necessary for us to take passage on this western ocean anyway, since if it lies to the west of Ehl-Larimar, we should reach our destination before we encounter it." Turning back to the guide, who was by now feeling sorely left out of the verbal byplay, he offered his thanks for the information.

While not one of the available pathfinders could be induced to travel with them, the master of the dispatch center was persuaded to sell them a windwagon and supplies. Ehomba was once more astonished to see in what exalted regard other peoples held the humble colored beach pebbles he had brought with him from the shore just north of the village. While the supply in the little cotton sack was diminished, it was by no means exhausted, suggesting that if the same responses were to be encountered elsewhere, they might be able to pay for their needs the rest of the way to distant Ehl-Larimar without misgiving.

Though with Hunkapa Aub and the black litah aboard, the windwagon was a bit crowded, it held them all, together with their newly purchased supplies. Steering was by means of a straightforward tiller-and-axle arrangement, and manipulation of the single simple square of canvas that provided the wagon's motive power posed no problem for travelers who had just spent weeks aboard a large sailing vessel. To the cheers and jeers of the personnel at the dispatch station (their respective individual reactions being directly related to how much of the visitors' story they had happened to overhear), the four adventurers once more set sail, this time in a craft both smaller and noisier than the graceful and recently departed *Grömsketter.*

A plentitude of roads and wagon tracks led off in all directions from Doroune. By far the greatest number led north or south to the other trading towns and farming

communities of the fertile coastal plain. A lesser selection
offered access to the western horizon. Choosing the most
direct, the travelers soon found themselves clear of the
city and its suburbs and among tillage of grain and vegetable. People working in the fields would look up and
wave, at least until they caught sight of Hunkapa Aub or
the black litah. Unlike the worldly citizens of sophisti-
cated metropolises such as Hamacassar or Lybondai, the
peoples living on this side of the Semordria were of a far
more insular nature.

So while they were cordial, they tended to keep their
distance whenever the wagon pulled up outside an inn or
tavern. Though less openly friendly than the inhabitants
of distant Netherbrae, they were at the same time more
accepting of the ways of others. Soon enough Ehomba and
his companions began to receive warnings similar to those
that had been voiced by the aged guide in Doroune.

"You might as well turn back now." The blacksmith
who had agreed to perform a final check on their wagon
spoke meaningfully as he rose and knelt, rose and knelt
while moving from one wheel to another.

"Why?" Ehomba shielded his eyes as he gazed westward, to where the track they were following vanished
into looming hills densely forested with ancient beech
and oak, sycamore and elm. "My companions and I have
crossed many high ranges, and this that lies before us does
not look either very high or very difficult to scale."

"The Hexens?" The affable blacksmith moved to another wheel. "They're not. Takes a while to get through
them, but the road goes all the way across. At least it did
last I heard tell of it. Even a child could make the walk."

The herdsman was openly puzzled. "Then what is the danger from these mountains?"

Taking a hammer and chisellike tool from his heavy work apron, their host began to bend back and tighten a bolt that was threatening to work its way loose.

"From the mountains, none." Looking up, he stared hard at the lean and curious visitor. "It's what lives in the Hexens that you have to watch out for. Deep in the inner valleys, where the fog lingers most all the day long and people never go." He shrugged and turned away. "Leastwise, those people that go in and come out again. What happens to the ones who go in and don't come out, well, a man can only guess."

"Hoy, we're not easily frightened," Simna informed him. Nearby, Ahlitah was playing with the blacksmith's brace of brown-and-white kittens, having promised Ehomba not to eat any of them. They assaulted the big cat's mane and tail while he batted gently at them with paws that could bring down a full-grown buffalo with a single blow. "Go ahead and guess."

The blacksmith paused in his work. "You really mean to do this, don't you?"

Simna made a perfunctory gesture in the herdsman's direction. "My friend has a fetish for the west. So that's the way we go. Would it be safer to head north or south and then turn inland toward our destination?"

The blacksmith considered. "I'm no voyager like you." He indicated the sturdy house and shop set just back off the road. "Family man. But settled here, at the foot of the Hexens, I meet many travelers. Go north and you're liable to run into bad weather. But south—head south and then turn west, and you'll skirt the base of the mountains." He turned back to his work. "Of course, there are other dangers to be encountered when traveling in the south."

"How long must we move south before we could turn west again and miss these mountains?" Ehomba was willing to consider reasonable alternatives.

"A month, maybe two, depending on the condition of the roads and the weather. This time of year, traveling weather's best between Oos and Nine Harbors. That's where you are right now, more or less."

The herdsman nodded tersely. "Then we go west from here."

"Why am I not surprised?" Simna's sigh was muted. He knew his tall friend well enough by now to have put money on his response. "You were going to tell us about the dangers we might run into in these Hexens."

"It's not a certain thing," the pensive blacksmith replied. "Many people make the crossing and return safely to the coast. For traders who do so, the rewards are considerable."

"I can imagine, if so many folks are too scared to even attempt it. What happens to those who don't make it back? Bandits?" The swordsman was extrapolating from similar situations that existed on the borders of his own homeland.

The blacksmith was shaking his head. "Bandits people can deal with. Tolls can be met, bribes paid, ransoms raised. Highwaymen would not discourage more people from traveling to the west. It is the Brotherhood of the Bone that terrifies would-be travelers and keeps them at home." Hitherto ringing, his voice had dropped to an edgy whisper.

"Do we have to ask what that might be?"

"Doesn't matter." The blacksmith's tone remained subdued. "I can't talk about it. Not openly, in front of others. You're determined to push on, so I'll just wish you good luck." He indicated the front of his shop, where Ahlitah was toying with the delighted kittens and Hunkapa Aub lay half asleep, sitting up against one side of the entrance, his mouth open wide enough to reveal a gap sufficiently commodious to accommodate both nest- and abode-hunting birds. "You are obviously knowledgeable wayfarers, and you have powerful nonhuman friends of your own. With luck, you'll make it. You might not have any trouble at all." He spread his hands wide and smiled regretfully. "Iron and steel I can forge for you, but not luck."

"You said 'nonhuman,'" Ehomba remarked. "Are the members of this Brotherhood of the Bone not human?"

"Some are, some ain't. I hope you don't have occasion to find out." Rising, he replaced his tools in his apron and wiped his hands. "Come inside for a cold drink and we'll settle your bill." His expression darkened ever so slightly. "You have money?"

Simna smirked knowingly. "Money enough. Before we left Doroune we took the time to cash a pebble."

In the depths of the mountains it was difficult to remember the admonitions of blacksmith and guide, so congenial were the surroundings. Though the splendid forest crowded the wagon track on both sides, it was not oppressive. Heavy broad-leaf litter covered the ground, making a carpet for deer and elk, broad-shouldered sivatherium, and droopy-horned pelorovis. Squirrels of many species foraged among the ground cover, methodically conveying found foods from the surface to their homes high up in the

139

accommodating trees. Ehomba was particularly taken with one short-tailed gray-and-brown variety that built endless tiny ladders to assist them in reaching the highest branches. Communities of these enterprising rodents traveled safely back and forth between boles by means of tiny carts suspended from thin but strong ropes.

Rabbits scurried about in profusion, providing effortless hunting for Ahlitah and a welcome supplement to their purchased provisions. Since no one had been able to tell them exactly how far it was to Ehl-Larimar, they availed themselves of every opportunity to feast off the land. Stowed food was to be conserved, since it might prove vital to their well-being should they encounter less-productive country.

Acorns and chestnuts could be easily gathered from beneath heavily laden boughs, and small rushing streams were everywhere. Morning and evening mist kept the temperature on the chilly side, but to travelers who had successfully crossed the great Hrugar Range hard by the base of Mount Scathe itself, the occasional discomfort was minor at most.

Birds in their colorful profusion nested in the forks of branches. Their darting songs echoed through the woods. One persistent archeopteryx in particular kept attacking their provisions in hopes of stealing one of the smaller brightly wrapped packages of food. When their attention was diverted it would dive-bomb the wagon, attacking with teeth and claws, until one of the travelers shooed it away. Cawing huffily, it paralleled them for quite a ways, flapping awkwardly from tree to tree until the next opportunity for avian larceny presented itself. Eventually it

140

gave up and fell behind. As poor a flyer as a hoatzin, it could not trail them forever.

After a number of days of easy, relatively comfortable travel interrupted only by the occasional need to get out and pull or push the wagon where there was an absence of wind, Simna had begun to relax. It was a state of being that Hunkapa Aub never exited and Ahlitah pursued with feline determination. Of the four travelers, only Ehomba remained on perpetual alert. This situation the swordsman was content to live with.

Lying against the back of the wagon, hands behind his head, he looked up contentedly as his lanky friend adjusted the single sail. Today's breeze was not strong, but it blew steadily from the east, driving them through the narrow canyon they were currently traversing.

"The people of this coast are really missing something by restricting their settlements to the flatlands east of these mountains." He waved a casual hand at the enclosing forested slopes. "This is wonderful country. Clean, bracing air, lots of small game, no dangerous predators that we've encountered, fertile soil, and some of the best timber I've ever seen. There are trees in here old and strong and big enough to supply lumber for a hundred thousand homes and ten thousand ships the size of the *Grömsketter*."

Intent as ever, Ehomba was watching the forest slide past on either side of the track. Tugging on a line, he trimmed the wagon's single sail slightly. "It may be that this Brotherhood would object. Certainly if they harry individual travelers they would rise up against any organized settlement. Perhaps that is why none exists."

Simna waved diffidently. "Gwouroud knows that's not it, bruther. They're just fearful folk hereabouts. They feed off the tall tales and spook stories of their neighbors. I've been through provinces like that, where everyone is so credulous they're scared to set foot beyond their own village." Closing his eyes, he inhaled deeply of the brisk, unpolluted air, its innate refreshingness enhanced by the extra oxygen being pumped out by the forest.

The wagon hit a rut and bounced, jarring Ahlitah momentarily awake. "Pick your trail with care, man," he rumbled.

"There is only one." Ehomba's response was curt. "And while we have the wind with us, this is no flying machine to soar smoothly over what water has cut." Moments after Ehomba composed his terse rejoinder, the wagon began to slow.

Opening his eyes again, Simna ibn Sind saw that the wind still blew in gusts sufficient to drive the vehicle. It was Ehomba who was bringing them to a gradual halt as he turned the sail sideways to the breeze. Frowning, the swordsman sat up.

"Hoy, bruther, why are we stopping?" A glance at the sky showed that it was too early for the midday meal. It was time for them to be covering as much ground as possible, not pausing to rest or engage in casual contemplation of their surroundings. "This wind is meant to be used."

"So are your eyes." Standing near the rear of the wagon, the herdsman held his long, slim arm out straight, parallel to the ground and pointing to his right, off into the woods.

Blinking, Simna glanced in the indicated direction. So did an insouciant Hunkapa Aub. Curled up near the back of the wagon, the black litah ignored the delay in favor of sleep.

"I don't see anything, bruther." The swordsman's confusion showed itself in his face. "What are you pointing at? What am I supposed to be looking for?"

"In that big elm. A bird." Ehomba sighted along his arm. "I understand your difficulty. It is not very big. About the size of a sparrow."

Simna made a face. "You stopped so we could look at a sparrow?"

"There!" Ehomba's identifying finger shifted slightly to the right. "It just flew into the tree next to it. It is a little closer now. See?" He gestured impatiently with his arm. "Near the outer end of the lowermost large branch, among the leaves."

Realizing that to resume headway meant humoring the herdsman, Simna muttered under his breath. As he adjusted his position slightly in the wagon, he was nearly knocked over by the abrupt shifting of the hairy mass next to him.

"Hunkapa see, Hunkapa see!" Their oversized companion was pointing excitedly, bouncing up and down in the wagon. The stalwart wooden bed creaked dangerously. "Bird without!"

"Without?" Time to put an end to whatever nonsense had afflicted his friends, Simna decided. "Without what?" Straining, he followed the pair of pointing arms and used them to fix his gaze on a particular branch in a certain tree.

He located the bird, and as he did so the small hairs on the back of his neck erected. That was more than the bird could do. It had no hair to stiffen, or feathers either. Nor skin, nor muscle or insides.

Sitting on the branch and preening itself with its naked white beak, the small flying creature ignored all the attention its presence had prompted. Satisfied, it spread proportionate, compact wings and rose from its perch, flying off into the forest, a small white specter comprised of nothing but naked, fleshless bones.

Ehomba had watched many birds in flight, and dragonets, and even certain specialized lizards and frogs, but this was the first time he had ever seen a skeleton fly.

IX

The skeletal sparrow was but the first of many they encountered as they drove deeper into the heart of the Hexens. There were more birds: crows and robins, jays and grosbeaks, neocaths and nuthatches. But they were not alone. It was not long before they found themselves traveling through a dense and dismal section of forest where flesh was scarce and scoured bone dominant.

Skeletal hares hopped among the roots of sheltering trees. Four-footed white skeletons scampered through the branches trailing furless vertebrae like the whiptails of scorpions. Once, a cluster of capybara peered up at the travelers from the shelter of their stream, staring at the wagon from the mindless depths of dark, voided eye sockets. For the travelers, it was unsettling enough to encounter such sights. To see them staring vacantly back was more unnerving still.

Devoid of skin and muscle they might be, but the inhabitants of these woods ran and flew and hopped and jumped with as much energy as their more fully rounded, naturally fleshed-out counterparts. The only other observable difference between them and their tissue-heavy relations was the degree to which they stared at the passing visitors: stared with a degree and intensity that grimly belied their dearth of eyes. If not for the presence of healthy trees and bushes, Simna could well have believed that they had rolled on into the land of the dead.

Studying the forest as they rattled along the increasingly ill-maintained dirt track, bumping over rocks and clumps of uncropped weeds, they watched a misshapen panoply of normal life play itself out among the vegetation. Ehomba pointed out a skeletal badger busily excavating a new burrow with more than adequate claws—but no pads on its feet. A great bull elk trotted past, displaying horns that in its entirely emaciated state seemed certain to make it too top-heavy to stand up, much less run. But it managed to stay erect nonetheless.

Once, a bobcat of bones leaped from concealment to take down a large rabbit. Normally, there is no more piercing and heart-rending sound in the wilderness than the cry of a dying rabbit, but this one could only emit the noise of bare bones rubbing together. Settling down to its meal, the ghostly feline began to gnaw on its victim, pinning it to the ground with limber white paws. Biting and ripping with sharp teeth, it methodically dismembered its prey, cracking open the smaller bones to get at the marrow within.

Tiny skeletal fledglings croaked in nests carefully built by osseous parents. A trio of cassowaries loped across a clearing, their exposed ribs clacking against one another like castanets as they ran. Cumbersome grizzly skeletons grazed in a dense path of wild blackberries. Occasionally one would become entangled as the thorny vines wrapped tightly around ribs or arms. One bear-shape pushed its snout deep into the copse, emerging with it stained blue-black by berry juice. A vine thrust upward through the underside of the jaw to emerge from one eye socket. This vegetal invasion appeared to have no effect on the lumbering ursinoid.

Why a skeleton would need to eat was but one of many questions contemplated by the travelers. As was his nature, Ehomba very much wanted some answers, whereas his companions simply wished to be clear of the blighted chasm as rapidly as possible. Even Ahlitah, who had a particular taste for marrow, sensed the unwholesomeness of the place and expressed his desire to leave it behind.

Abruptly, the wagon made a sharp swerve. "Hoy!" Simna called out as he was thrown off his feet. "Who's steering?" Looking around as soon as he managed to recover his equilibrium, he caught sight of Ehomba taking in the sail. "Etjole, what are you up to, man? Surely you don't mean for us to camp here?"

"Not camp." The herdsman spoke while continuing his work. "But we have to stop for a moment." By way of explanation he nodded forward.

A large tree had fallen across the wagon track, blocking it completely. Thick underbrush on either side prevented them from going around. The toppled trunk would have to be moved, or cut through, or else the wagon would have to be unloaded and hauled across, with their supplies following from hand to hand, one package at a time.

"By Givouvum, what a place for a rest stop!" Grumbling loudly at the inconvenience, the swordsman vaulted over the side of the wagon to inspect the impediment.

"A stop, yes, but from the look of it, no rest." Ehomba was soon standing alongside his friend. Together they pondered how best to proceed, whether to try to remove the log or move themselves across it.

Not one given to much pondering, Hunkapa Aub lumbered over to the top of the tree where it lay among a host of smaller saplings it had smashed in the course of its fall. For a long moment he stood in silence, considering the supine column. Then he bent his knees, gripped the upper stretch of the tree in both huge hands, and with a rolling grunt lifted it off the ground and began to pull it deeper into the woods and off the road. Joining reluctantly in the effort, the black litah put its forehead against the shattered base of the tree. Digging in with all four sets of claws, it pushed while Hunkapa pulled.

It took them less than ten minutes to move the trunk far enough off the track for the wagon to squeeze past. Starting back to their vehicle, Ehomba found himself wondering how much more of the blighted forest they had yet to traverse, and whether they would be out of it by nightfall. Hopefully, they would be far away before darkness fell, provided nothing else materialized to impede their progress.

That feared something else took the form of several dozen figures who emerged from behind the wagon and the brush off to one side. Each skeletal warrior carried a heavy wooden club or spear, save for several who brandished weapons confiscated from unlucky predecessors. A few wore scavenged armor. Ill-fitting helmets of bronze and steel bounced loosely on naked, bony skulls. Feathers and iridescent insect parts protruded from the metal crests, supplying a macabre touch of color to warriors whose appearance was otherwise almost entirely the bleached, chalky white of naked bone. Many of the animate advancing cadavers were missing teeth or limbs.

Worse, they stood between the travelers and their vehicle, in which all their weapons were stored.

However, they were not entirely defenseless. As sepulchral shouts rose from the gaunt, ghastly regiment and weapons were upraised, Hunkapa Aub and Ahlitah took matters into their own hands and charged.

The shaggy man-beast's unearthly howling combined with the big cat's thunderous roars were enough to give even the dead pause. As the skeletal raiders hesitated, the improbable duo tore into them. It was a revelation to Simna to see the ferocity with which the gentle, soft-voiced Hunkapa scattered their attackers. Sword cuts failed to penetrate his thick, hairy coat, and spears he knocked aside with sweeping sideways blows of his massive arms. Grabbing up one clattering, cackling cluster of bones, he dismembered it as easily as the swordsman would a chicken. Ripping another assailant into pieces, Hunkapa threw chunks of bone at its companions, bowling them over with the force of his throws. Skeletons were knocked askew or trampled underfoot.

Eyes blazing, Ahlitah was not relying on his stentorian bellows to scatter the enemy. Powerful, curving claws severed skulls from shoulders while heavy paws shattered vacant rib cages and limbs. The crackle of bones being crunched echoed through the woods every time the litah's powerful jaws locked onto another gaunt figure.

While their two nonhuman companions wreaked havoc among the surprised attackers, Ehomba and Simna made a dash for the windwagon. Ducking beneath a spear thrust, Simna rolled into the legs of his assailant, bringing the startled skeleton down on top of him. Reaching up and around, he locked both hands and forearms around the skull. Much to his surprise, it was warm. Gritting his teeth, he twisted his hands and arms in opposite directions. With a snap, the neck broke and the head came away in his fingers. As the decapitated skull tried to sink its exposed, gleaming teeth into his arm, the sickened swordsman flung it as far as he could.

Ehomba leaped sideways to avoid a sword stroke and brought his right leg around the way Asab had shown him and the other young men of the village when they were of an age to learn about fighting. Its legs taken out from under it, the skeleton went down on its back. As it rolled toward him, flailing energetically but wildly with its sword, the herdsman was able to reach the wagon. Simna joined him seconds later. While Hunkapa Aub defended one side of the vehicle and Ahlitah the other, the two men scrambled for their weapons.

"Send the sharks after them!" Simna shouted as he picked up his own sword. Long knife gripped between its teeth, a skeletal soldier was attempting to scramble over the side of the wagon and into the bed. The swordsman dispatched it with a single blow that cleaved the raider from collarbone to sternum. Cut vertically nearly in half, it fell back, clutching at itself.

"I cannot!" Ehomba fumbled among the supplies. "The magic of the sea-bone sword works only on attackers made of flesh and blood. Sharks will not attack bones. Neither will the spirit of my walking spear."

"Hoy, then take up the sky-metal sword and call down the wind from between the stars to blow them apart!" With a grunt, Simna stabbed a climbing warrior between the ribs. Since his weapon met only air, it did no damage. With a curse, the swordsman drew the weapon back and hacked sideways, beheading his adversary. That stroke had the desired effect.

"Remember, Simna, the sky-metal sword is not a shaman's instrument, to be so casually wielded." The herdsman indicated the surrounding forest. "This place is too confining. If I were to succeed in bringing down the wind it would uproot trees and send them flying in all directions, as likely to do away with us as our attackers." He continued to busy himself in the center of the wagon.

With barely enough time to glance in his friend's direction, Simna finally shouted in exasperation, "By Gokhoul, bruther, what are you doing?"

"Setting sail. Hold them off, my friends, hold them off!"

With the battle-tested Simna shouting orders, he and Hunkapa and the black litah did just that, giving Ehomba time to ready their vehicle. As soon as the sail was up and fully set, he called out to his companions to join him within. Simna was first back aboard, followed by Hunkapa Aub. As the wagon, under full sail, began to pick up speed, Ahlitah ran alongside, dispatching those skeletons that tried to keep pace. Any that drew near found themselves crushed between powerful jaws or knocked asunder by claw-tipped paws.

Only when the last of their jabbering, gesticulating, spear-waving pursuit had fallen too far behind to pose any threat did the big cat rejoin his companions, clearing the space from ground to wagon in a single long, easy leap. Once on board he sat back and began to lick his wounds. They were minor, nothing worse than a few scrapes and the occasional shallow cut.

151

"It's nothing," he insisted in response to Ehomba's so-licitous inquiry. "I've taken worse from wildebeest." As the cat spoke, it groomed its face and mane with moist-ened paw. "One time I took a blow to the stomach from the spiked tail of a full-grown female glyptodont protect-ing its young. Now, *that* hurt." Twisting its head around, it began to lick a bloody gash on its right flank. "Made the kill anyway."

"Hoy?" Sword laid out across his knees, Simna was sit-ting down, his back resting against the interior wall of the wagon. The was no blood on the blade: only the accumu-lated white stain of powdered bone. "I always wondered what glypto tasted like."

"Like pork." The black litah lifted its head suddenly, ears pricked, listening intently. Seeing this, Simna imme-diately scrambled to his knees and turned to scan the dense woods through which they were racing.

"What is it? More of them in the trees? They can't hope to run us down. As long as we have wind at our backs and clear road ahead they'll never catch us."

"Footsteps." The litah sat still as a sculpture in obsidian, listening. On the other side of the wagon, an intent Hunkapa Aub was likewise scrutinizing the forest. "Not human. Not human skeletons, that is. Something else."

"Something else, how?" Standing tall in the rear of the wagon, Ehomba steered them expertly down the track and past the most egregious ruts and potholes.

"Heavier," the litah explained bluntly.

They came tearing out of the trees off to the left, the cavalry riding not to the rescue but intent on total destruc-tion. There were too many to count as the windwagon, with full canvas up and traveling at top speed, negotiated one dip and curve after another in the increasingly uneven track.

Baying like a hundred xylophones all playing in concert, skeletal warriors came pounding out of the forest on skeleton mounts, waving their weapons over their bleached skulls as they sought to ride down the fleeing wagon. Naked pelvises sat astride the ivory-colored spines of horses and mules, zebras and okapis, kudu and pronghorn. It was a charge the likes of which even an experienced horseman like Simna ibn Sind had never hoped to see, a charge from Hell.

But even as their mounted assailants bore down on the fleeing travelers, the forest was thinning out around them, giving way to more open country. A grateful Ehomba had more room in which to maneuver. No longer restricted exclusively to the narrow wagon track, he was able to utilize the windwagon not only as a vehicle to effect their escape, but as a weapon.

When a pair of high-riding, mace-swinging skeletal warriors turned their mounts toward the rattling, bouncing wagon, Ehomba adjusted the sail to angle the heavy vehicle not away from but directly toward them. The front end of the wagon slammed into the startled attackers, sending a shower of broken, splintered bone flying over the passengers as their assailants were smashed to bits. Meanwhile, any raider that rode too close risked a blow from Hunkapa Aub's fist, Ahlitah's paws, or Simna ibn Sind's sword. Grimacing ferociously, the swordsman stood up in the unstable wagon bed to taunt their attackers. He still had his sea legs from their weeks on the *Grömsketter,* and this especially allowed him to keep his balance.

"Come on, you offspring of bastard boneheads!" Gleefully, he waved his sword in expert circles. "Here's a tooth longer than any of yours. Come close and see how it bites! What's the matter—afraid of dying?"

"Simna, it is not good to taunt the dead."

The swordsman threw his long-faced friend a wild-eyed glance. "Tend to your tillering, bruther, and leave me to deal with the departed. They should have stayed dead."

Emitting hollow, sinister cries, the remainder of the skeleton cavalry whipped their mounts with whips of slivered bone and closed on the windwagon. Try as they might, they could not surround it in sufficient numbers to overpower its passengers. Every time it looked as if more than two of the attackers might have a chance to leap or climb aboard, Ehomba would steer the vehicle away from their skeletal chargers. Cut down by Simna's flashing sword or pulverized by the strength of Ahlitah or Hunkapa Aub, their numbers were steadily reduced even as their determination was redoubled.

Compared to the horde that had participated in the initial assault, few were left when the windwagon struck the brush-covered gully. It bounced once, flew into the air, struck the hard ground on the far side, and overturned. Ehomba barely had time enough to warn his companions to grab something to hang on to before he was slammed to the ground and thrown from the wagon.

Everyone but Ahlitah lay dazed and unsteady. All cat, the black litah had reacted to the imminent crash by leaping clear of the wagon, twisting his body in midair, and skidding to a stop on all fours. Snarling warningly, it took up a position in front of the overturned wagon bed as the mounted skeletons stumbled down one side of the narrow chasm and up the other.

By the time they reached the site of the crash, the wagon's occupants had recovered their equilibrium and their weapons. With nothing left to steer, Ehomba had picked up the sky-metal sword. While it might not be time to make use of it to call down pieces of the sky or the wind from between the stars, its blade was still sharp and functional. The overturned wagon lay on its side, one wheel still spinning futilely in the air like the kicking hind leg of a dying lizard. With its solid wooden bed against their backs, they readied themselves to deal with the remaining skeletal warriors arrayed against them.

Instead, the mounted skeletons drew up in a line opposite the toppled vehicle. Weapons at the ready, they sat staring with empty eye sockets at the contentious living. Their mounts pawed with skeletal hooves at the ground, snorting through ragged-edged nostrils of varying length.

"What's this, bruther?" Not taking his eyes from their hesitating attackers, Simna whispered to his tall companion. "What are they waiting for?"

"I do not know." Holding the sky-metal sword out in front of him, Ehomba considered the surrounding forest. Though much reduced in density, there were still too many large trees scattered nearby to chance drawing down the wind from the heavens. But if the attackers persisted, he realized that he might have to chance it. Certainly if their assailants were reinforced by others from within the deep woods, he would be left with no choice. Warmed by his hands, the sword quivered expectantly.

The skeleton that dismounted was neither the tallest nor the most stout of those pale white specters that were arrayed against the travelers, but it strode forward with a stiff-jointed dignity none of its demised confederates could match. With plucked feathers streaming from the gilded helmet that rocked atop its bleached skull, it approached the living. Simna's fingers whitened on the haft of his sword and Hunkapa Aub growled deep in his throat. Ahlitah stood almost motionless, his massive chest heaving slowly in and out with his steady breathing, ready to pounce the instant Ehomba gave the word.

Halting barely a spear length away, the skeleton placed one bony arm across its splayed rib cage—and bowed. Then it straightened, steadying the flamboyant helmet on its naked skull, and began to speak in a voice that was deeper than a whisper but not much stronger.

"You fight well." The wind carried away the last syllable of every word and the straining travelers had to listen closely to make out the meaning of each. "You put a great many of the dead to sleep, for which they are eternally grateful."

"Hoy?" Simna smiled tautly. "Come a little closer, Mr. Bones, and I'll gladly assist you in joining them."

The white skull swiveled. Empty sockets peered into the swordsman's living eyes. "That is not to be the way of things, master of a steel tooth."

"Then what is the way of things? Tell us." Without lowering his guard for an instant, Ehomba queried the expired but animate mediator.

Simna muttered knowingly. "Always the questioner, Etjole, even when the one replying is Death itself."

"We are not Death," the skeletal envoy explained softly. "Only dead. The difference is of significance." With a sweep of one white-boned arm, it indicated those mounted warriors waiting patiently behind it. "We are the Brotherhood of the Bone. This forest we claim as ours, a place of quietude and darkness in which to linger after life has given us up but before death claims us forever. Here we dwell but do not exist, occasionally taking out the frustration of being neither or either on those mortals foolish or courageous enough to dare the byways that we haunt." A chalky arm pointed in their direction.

"You are sufficiently brave to pass, but there is a problem."

"A problem?" Simna laughed humorlessly. "You send dozens of your own to try and slay us where we stand and now you say there is a 'problem'?" He tossed his sword easily back and forth, swapping it from hand to hand. "Come forward, the lot of you, and we'll show you how Simna ibn Sind and the great sorcerer Etjole Ehomba deal with their problems!"

"You might yet escape." The envoy made the confession even as it looked to their overturned wagon. "Yet your vehicle will need time to be put right, something you cannot do while fighting us. Even as we speak, hundreds more of the Brotherhood are riding to our aid, called hither by the sounds of battle and breaking bones. If you flee right now and the wind holds, you might well outdistance them all. But if you are delayed by fighting—" This time it was the envoy's meaning and not his speech that trailed off.

"It's a damned bluff!" Simna wanted very badly to rush forward and separate the taunting skeleton's skull from its shoulders. "Let's finish them!"

Ehomba ignored him, straining to listen, to pierce the distant woods with hearing that was more acute than that of most men. Strive as he might, he knew that there were among his companions ears far more sensitive than his own.

"Ahlitah?"

The big cat sniffed the air even as it listened intently. After a moment, yellow eyes looked in the herdsman's direction. "I think I hear something. It might be the wind— or it might be fleshless feet. Hundreds of them."

"Might be, might not be—what need for speculation?" Simna took a step forward. "By Geewenwan, I say we put an end to this!"

"They are mounted and we are afoot," Ehomba sensibly pointed out. "It is a doable thing, friend Simna, but as the envoy points out, killing even the dead takes time. All of you have come this far because of me. I will not give up your lives for a cause become yours only by accident." Lowering his sword, he approached the envoy.

An alarmed Simna looked on uneasily. "Etjole, I don't know what you're thinking, but don't think it!"

Halting several feet from the skeleton, Ehomba met vacant eyes with his own speculative gaze. "You said something about us being brave enough to let pass, except there was a problem."

The bleached skull nodded slightly. "You have dispatched many from the Brotherhood and sent them on their final path to rest. Those who do so must take the place of at least one who has departed our company. If this is done willingly, then the others may live, and will be allowed to quit our presence still citizens of the world of the living."

Ehomba nodded understandingly. Behind him, Simna was growing rapidly more agitated. The herdsman continued to ignore him. "I have your word on this?"

"Here is my hand on it." Skeletal fingers reached toward him. "What remains of it."

158

Wrapping his own long, weathered fingers around the bare white bone, Ehomba embraced the warm, smooth grip.

"Which of you will come willingly to the Brotherhood?" The envoy was looking past him. He need not have done so.

"I will."

"What?" Behind him, Simna took a confrontational step forward. "What's all this ungodly mumbling about? Etjole, what have you promised this—this fugitive from an unhallowed grave?"

Rejoining his companions, Ehomba put both hands on the swordsman's shoulders. Inclining his head slightly, he stared hard and evenly into the smaller man's eyes.

"Simna, do you still believe I am a mighty sorcerer?"

"Yes—but you've always denied it. I know your way with words. What trick of sophistry are you playing now?" The swordsman eyed his friend warily.

Dropping his hands from the other man's arms, Ehomba looked up at the hulking, hirsute form of Hunkapa Aub. "What about you? Do you believe in me, my hairy friend?"

"Hunkapa—believe in Etjole." The broad figure replied slowly and solemnly, his response tinged with uncertainty over what was to come.

"And you, Ahlitah? What about you?" The herdsman gazed affectionately at the big cat.

It yawned. "Do what you will. If you die, I go home. If you live, I continue with you. Only one thing I know for sure: I'm sick of the taste of marrow. So do something."

"I will." Turning back to the swordsman, the tall southerner smiled reassuringly. "No matter what happens, no matter what you see here, you must promise to continue

159

the journey westward away from this place. Watch, friend Simna. Watch, and trust me."

"Trust you? Trust you to do what? Etjole . . ."

The swordsman reached for his friend but was unable to restrain him. After placing the sky-metal sword in Hunkapa's hand, a resigned Ehomba walked back to confront the expectant envoy. Halting before the skeletal warrior, the herdsman nodded once. "I am ready."

The envoy made a gesture and started to raise his sword. Ehomba lifted a hand to forestall the first cut. "Hold! I will save you the trouble."

Standing between the living and the dead, the herdsman parted his jaws to form a wide oval—an oval that grew large, and then larger still. It was impossible for any human mouth to open so wide. Even among the mounted skeletons there was a stirring at the sight. Among all the onlookers only Simna ibn Sind and the black litah were not shocked by the gape of the herdsman's expanding maw, for they had seen Ehomba do something similar before.

No human could part its jaws so wide—but Etjole Ehomba was more than human. He was also eromakasi. There was no darkness to eat here, no threatening eromakadi to consume. But that did not prevent him from making use of his remarkable oral abilities. Wider still stretched his jaws and lips.

Then, with a delicacy of step and perfect aplomb, his skeleton emerged from the container of his body, stepping out from within through the accommodating aperture of the herdsman's unnaturally distended mouth.

X

Like a prosperous merchant discarding a favorite dressing gown, Etjole Ehomba's skeleton continued to slip free of his clothing and skin until it stood, white and glistening, before the silent, approving envoy. When the last lingering flesh had been sloughed off, the mounted warriors vented a cadaverous cheer, waving their weapons in the air and reining their assorted skeletal mounts up on their hind legs in celebration.

"No!" Sword upraised, a horrified Simna rushed forward—only to fall hard as something tripped him. Looking down, he saw, staring back at him from amid the pile of attire and skin and muscle that had moments before cloaked his companion in the garb of life, the face of his good friend. Though unnaturally flaccid and flattened in the absence of its usual sturdy frame, it was smiling reassuringly.

"Calm yourself, Simna. Did I not tell you to trust me?"

Shocked, the swordsman scrabbled back on hands and knees. "Etjole, is it you? Are you alive?"

"Alive but limp. As a wet rag, like the saying goes. Lift me up, my friend. I want to see what is happening."

Placing a hesitant arm beneath the flattened head, Simna fought down the queasiness in his gut as he raised the soft, slightly rubbery remnant of his friend and held it where it could face their former assailants. Having turned away from the living, Ehomba's expelled skeleton was following the envoy to the line of waiting skeletal mounts. There the envoy swung himself up onto the bare-boned back of a once noble but now wholly desiccated steed and reached down. Taking the proffered hand, the tall, slim skeleton that had just walked away from its owner leaped up onto the exposed spine.

With a final salute, the grisly members of the Brotherhood turned and, passing in review in double file, trotted away, leaving the living to their own devices. Slack as a sack of beans, Ehomba watched them and a part of him go.

"I hope it can hang on for a while. The Naumkib are not known for their horsemanship."

"It wouldn't matter anyway, bruther." Simna followed the line of mounted skeletons as they disappeared into the trees. "No amount of practice could prepare one for riding saddleless astride bare bone." He looked down at his friend. "Why have you done this?"

"To put them off." The eyes that stared back up at him sank deeply into the limp, unsupported flesh. "Ahlitah was right. I could hear the approaching hundreds also."

"But the sky-metal sword! You could have tried to use it."

"Not in a place like this. We would have died of it," the herdsman replied simply.

"So we would have died." Simna's frustration came pouring out. "Anything's better than living like this!" He ran an open palm down the length of his freshly pliant friend.

The fold of flesh that was Ehomba's mouth smiled. "Did I not ask you to trust me?"

"Hoy, so you did, but to what end? Do you expect us to cross the remaining unknown country that lies between here and Ehl-Larimar with you in this condition? And what if we were to do so, and succeed? How will you fight this Hymneth the Possessed? Am I supposed to stand behind you and work your legs and sword arm like some kind of mad puppeteer? I'll have none of it, I tell you! I consider myself a brave man, but not a fool." His tone turned bitter. "If there is good magic in this, I don't see it."

"You will, my good friend. Lay me down easy. Take up the tiller and lines and sail us out of here."

"Hunkapa!" Simna exclaimed. "Give me a hand and let's right this wagon." As soon as their transport was once again resting upright on all four wheels, the swordsman proceeded to check the axles and undercarriage. Despite the jolt it had received during the hard landing, everything appeared intact. "Here, hold him up so he can see. I have to steer."

"Steer where?" Gently, the shaggy hulk took the limp body of the herdsman in his massive arms, cradling the empty but animate human envelope as easily as he would a child.

"West. Where else?" Settling himself in position, the swordsman tore into ropes and lines, adjusting the sail to catch the wind that, fortuitously, continued to blow from the east. Almost immediately, the wagon began to move. It creaked and groaned in places that previously had been silent, but nothing fell off. Very soon, they were scooting along the increasingly bumpy track at a respectable rate of speed.

They made good progress with no more interruptions. Ahlitah hunted, bringing back rabbits and small antelope to feed not only himself but his companions. For Ehomba there were mashed-up berries and chopped fish. His mouth and teeth still worked, but the lack of any bony support left him unable to chew all but the softest foods. Much to Simna's continued surprise, the herdsman seemed content. He could not walk, but he could pull himself along the ground with his long, lean-muscled arms and kick out with his legs. So long as he did not try to raise up any higher than his arms could push him, he did not appear to be suffering greatly.

The swordsman marveled at his friend's stoicism. Anyone else he had ever known, upon sacrificing their skeleton, would have lapsed into melancholy. Not Ehomba. He was positively buoyant, commending Simna on his steering, Ahlitah on his hunting, and Hunkapa for his help and perpetual good spirits.

"By Gierbourne if I don't think you're a happier man without it," the swordsman finally commented on the fifth day after the fateful final encounter with the representatives of the Brotherhood.

"A skeleton has many uses." Lying in Hunkapa Aub's trunklike arms, Ehomba twisted himself slightly to meet his friend's gaze. "But traveling upright is not always the best way to live. It exposes one to the wind, and to the spears and arrows of enemies. There are advantages, too, to a low profile. Ask any snake."

"I agreed to help a man, not a snake." Grumbling, Simna

concentrated on his steering. "Looks like a river up ahead. Big one."

Ehomba had Hunkapa hold him high. "I think the wagon track stops before it reaches the bank. But there are not as many trees on the other side, and the land is more level than what we have just come through. We should be able to make use of this vehicle for a while longer yet."

"Good," the swordsman snapped. "I'm starting to wonder if maybe I haven't done too much walking for too little reward these past several months."

"Why Simna, are you starting to have second thoughts? What about the treasure?" From within sagging pleats of flesh the herdsman smiled at him.

"Hoy, what about the treasure?" The swordsman trimmed a line. "In all this time I've heard nothing about it from you, except when you chose to deny its existence. Now that things have turned troublesome, you tease me with it." He stared hard at the flaccid figure. "When I wax enthusiastic on the subject, you claim it doesn't exist. But if I express skepticism, you lose no opportunity to remind me of it." His expression tightened.

"Don't think to play me the fool, long bruther. If I decide that's what you're about, I'll drop you like a year-old egg and vanish into the bush."

Ehomba managed to shrug, a ripple that ran through his right shoulder like a small wave lapping repeatedly at a sand beach. "You are right, friend Simna. There is no treasure. It is only a trick to keep you with me, to buy your aid. I am ashamed before the elders of my village." A limber, boneless hand fluttered in the swordsman's direction. "Go now. Leave with your dignity still intact. I release you from your vows."

"Don't tempt me, bruther! Don't think that I won't. I'll stop this gut-churning box on wheels right here and get out, and leave you in the care of one too stupid to know better and another who'd as soon eat you for supper as help you!"

"Do it, then. Stop now, Simna, and take your leave while there's still time." Ehomba rarely grew angry, or raised his voice. "Forget about the treasure. It does not exist. It is only a phantom you have raised up in your own mind to justify your continued journeying in my company. Free yourself of it! Abandon the wagon and make your way back to the coast and its welcoming towns. I will not think ill of you for doing so. Only a fool risks his life for an illusion."

"That's right. By Gworjha, you're right!" Pulling in on the lines, the swordsman trimmed the sail. The wind-wagon slowed to a stop. Behind him, the black litah looked up sleepily.

"What now?" it growled softly.

Hunkapa supplied a ready explanation. "Big river." He looked uncertainly from Ehomba to Simna. "Big argument."

"That's right." Securing the lines, a determined look on his face, the swordsman was gathering up his kit and a limited share of their dwindling supplies. "I'm leaving!"

The big cat was only mildly interested. As always, it found sleep of more interest than the often unaccountable doings of humans. "What for?"

Ehomba elucidated. "Simna has realized that the treasure he sought in my company does not really exist, and he will no longer waste his time seeking it."

"That's right!" The swordsman fumbled with his gear. "Only a fool and an imbecile risks his life for no recom-

166

pense." Having arranged his kit and stuffed his backpack full, he put one hand on the side of the wagon. Looking back, he glared at the rubbery, limp length of the herdsman gazing back at him from within the cradle of Hunkapa's arms.

"Well?"

"Well what?" Ehomba's demeanor was as pleasant and placid as ever. "I wish you a safe journey back to the coast. One man traveling alone and making little noise should be able to avoid the attentions of the Brotherhood. Perhaps we will meet again someday."

"Hoy, not if the fates are kind to me." The swordsman started to lift himself over the side of the wagon. He had only gone partway when he paused. While he hovered between wagon and ground, the look on his face underwent a slow but profound change.

"*Hoyyyy*—you think you're very clever, don't you, wizard?"

"Clever?" Ehomba considered. "My mother and father thought that I was. Among the herders of my age I am considered tolerably adept."

Simna let himself down, back into the wagon. He was grinning ferociously. "Master of magic you may be, or you may not, but the day will be long indeed when your kind can outwit Simna ibn Sind!"

The flaccid shape looked puzzled. "I do not follow you, my friend."

Even as he spoke, the swordsman was disencumbering himself of pack and weapon. "You're a shrewd fellow, Etjole Ehomba. Far more subtle than most. You almost had me!" He wagged an admonishing finger at the slack outline. "Your language is simple, but you know how to

167

use logic to twist a man's thoughts. You actually had me convinced there was no treasure! Planted the notion anew in my mind until it seemed to be my own. Well, it won't work! I'm a little slow, long bruther, but I'm not like other people. When I get a grip on something, I don't let go until I've shaken all the nourishment out of it. You won't cheat me of my share so easily!" Settling himself at lines and tiller, he prepared to swing the sail around to catch the wind.

"Try all the thought-twisting you wish, but you'll not be rid of me. No one talks Simna ibn Sind out of his share of treasure."

Ehomba sighed, his ribless chest rising and falling less than it would have had it been properly supported from within. "You are certainly a most determined man, friend Simna. Once you get an idea in your head, nothing can take it from you."

"That's right, and don't you forget it, mentor of calves." The swordsman pulled hard on a line.

"Wait!" Ehomba rose up as far as he could in the cradle of Hunkapa's arms.

"What for?" Jawline set, Simna continued to ready the windwagon. "So you can try more of your sorceral tricks and word games to discourage me? I don't think so."

"It is not that. Someone is coming." A shaky, rubbery arm rose to point back in the direction they had come.

Frowning, a reluctant Simna turned to gaze back up the wagon track. "I don't see anything. If you're trying to stall so I'll leave before we cross the river, you're wasting your time, Etjole. Like it or not, I'm coming with you. All the way to Ehl-Larimar."

"From out of the trees, a little to the north. A lone rider. An old friend."

"What 'old friend'?" Exasperated, Simna turned fully on the bench seat. "We have no friends here, and no member of the *Grömsketter*'s crew would leave her to come this far inland. We don't—" He broke off in midsentence as a single figure hove into view. Ehomba was right; it *was* an old friend.

It was the herdsman's skeleton.

Pushing its mount hard, the long, lanky collection of bones kept low, head forward and arms locked around the neck bones of its osseous steed. Legs pounding, the skeletal stallion picked up speed as it struck the slight downslope leading to the edge of the river.

"But how . . . ?" Simna's query trailed away, and he could only turn a look of bafflement on his friend.

From within the folds of flesh that comprised his sunken face, the herdsman smiled back at his companion. "If deprived of the rest of him, a man's skeleton gets lonely."

"You knew it would come back to you," Simna declared accusingly.

"I knew it would try. I hoped it would succeed. I have always had confidence in all of me, my friend." A boneless hand fluttered in the swordsman's direction. "Keep sail up. It will be back among us soon."

"Not soon enough." Rising to his full height and lifting Ehomba effortlessly as he did so, Hunkapa Aub nodded in the direction of the densest part of the forest. "Bones come also."

Instantly, Simna was on his feet and staring along the line of Hunkapa's sight. Sure enough, from among the trees there now poured an entire battalion of the Brotherhood. They came streaming toward the windwagon, some on foot, others riding an even greater assortment of skeletal grotesqueries than the travelers had seen previously, yelling and screaming in their hoarse, ossified whispers while waving all manner of weapons above their bleached skulls.

"Gipebwhen," Simna murmured nervously. "There must be hundreds of 'em!" He looked sharply at his soft friend. "What do we do?"

"Cross the river," Ehomba told him. "Cross it quickly, I should say. Sail, Simna. Fill the sail."

"Hoy, right, sure!" Settling himself back on the seat, the swordsman hastily brought lines and tiller into play. As the single canvas filled with the steady breeze, the high-wheeled wagon once more began to move toward the water.

"Just one thing, bruther." As he spoke, Simna deftly controlled the lines that kept the vehicle's sail properly trimmed. "What do we do when we reach the river? Swim for it? This conveyance is no boat."

"No indeed," the pliant figure of his friend replied, "but save for a few braces and nails it is all wood, light and strong. I am hoping it will float."

The windwagon continued to pick up speed. "And if it doesn't?" an anxious swordsman inquired further.

"Then I will float better than any of you." The eyes that gazed back at the swordsman did not smile.

Howling and moaning, the Brotherhood of the Bone angrily pursued the turncoat skeleton and its fleshy friends. Repeatedly looking back over his shoulder, Simna ibn Sind tried to cajole more speed out of the solid but clunky windwagon. It had been built for durability, not speed.

The breeze held behind them, but he found himself wishing for one of the gales they had encountered at sea. Occasionally he inhaled deeply and blew into the sail, more as a gesture of encouragement to the wind than out of any expectation of increasing their velocity, however minutely.

"Come on, hurry!" Holding Ehomba easily in one arm, Hunkapa Aub was using the other to beckon repeatedly at the herdsman's fleeing skeleton. Spears began to fall around the fugitive. One struck its mount, but passed harmlessly through the rib cage without becoming entangled in the bleached white legs.

Then it was racing alongside, barely keeping pace with the steadily accelerating windwagon. With its bony mount exhausted and beginning to fail, Ehomba's insides had no choice but to risk the jump from vertebrae to vehicle. Letting go of the ossified stallion's neck bones, it leaped, arms outstretched—and fell short.

Only to be caught at the wrist by a massive, hairy hand. Thick fingers wrapped around the delicate bones and strained, pulling the skeletal structure bodily into the wagon.

"Set me down," Ehomba directed his massive friend. Obediently, Hunkapa complied.

Having no breath to catch, the skeleton did not hesitate. On hands and knees it crawled over to the limp form of its outer self. With an effort, Ehomba opened his mouth. It was the mouth of an eromakasi, trained to expand sufficiently to swallow darkness of any size. Inserting first a hand, then an entire arm, the wayward skeleton wriggled and wiggled itself back into its fleshy sheath.

Slowly, Ehomba's shape and silhouette filled out, returning to normal. When the last of the animate white

171

bone had disappeared down his gullet, he contracted his greatly distended mouth and sat up. Working his jaws up and down and from side to side to realign his skin with his skull, he twisted and turned as he sat in the bottom of the jouncing, rocking wagon. Finally satisfied, he stood up for the first time in days, and stretched. Simna had not heard so much creaking and groaning and cracking since he had been forced to spend a stomach-churning night alone in their cabin aboard the *Grömsketter.*

Looking over at him, the herdsman smiled contently. "That is better. Much better. Life is easier without a skeleton because there is less strain on the body, but being unable to stand up soon grows tiresome." His smile vanished as he grabbed quickly for the mast and shouted. "Watch out!"

"Hoy?" Simna sat up straight and gripped the tiller and control lines tightly in his fingers. So entranced had he been by his friend's structural renascence that his attention had wandered from their heading. In the interim, they had run out of road.

The windwagon hit the water hard, sending up a fan-shaped shower of water that sprayed higher than the mast. Instantly, the boxy vehicle slowed. Caught by the sluggish current but still powered by the wind out of the east, it began to drift with agonizing slowness across the broad, flat expanse of the unnamed river.

Lying in the rear of the vehicle, the black litah lifted its ebony head and yawned, trying to work up an interest in the proceedings. "They're still coming. Better get a move on."

"We're making as much speed as we can! This is no pinnace." Glancing down, Simna saw water beginning to filter

up between the slats, threatening to submerge his sandaled feet. The wagon was caulked against the weather,
but it was never the intention of its builders to make it wa-
tertight. How long the seals would hold against the pressure of the river its hopeful passengers could only guess.

The army of the Brotherhood reached the bank where
the wagon had driven into the languid flow. Many halted
there, pulling up and reining in their mounts. Dozens of the
more determined dead, driven by anger and fury at the de-
ceitful betrayal of the living and his promised contribution
to their ranks, did not. Urging their ashen mounts onward,
they plunged headfirst into the current.

"They're still coming!" Frantically, Simna tugged on
lines and tiller, trying everything he could think of to aug-
ment their sluggish pace.

Himself fully restored, Ehomba quietly contemplated
the skeletal spectacle aft. "Easy for the dead to be brave."

"Complimenting them is not likely to save us," the
swordsman snapped.

His tall companion smiled over at him. "Keep your hand
on the tiller and your mind on the sail, friend Simna. Bravery and intelligence do not always go hand in hand." He
turned his attention back to the onrushing skeletal horde.
"Oura says that after they have been dead for a while, people tend to lose their mental edge. They may remember
well the little things, but the greater picture starts to escape them."

Simna frowned, and despite the herdsman's admonition
turned to look at the waters behind them. What he saw
raised his spirits far more than any gust or gale.

Charging forward without pause, those members of the
Brotherhood of the Bone intent on punishing the retreat-

ing living who had dared to take back one of their own struggled out into the current of the wide, deep river. Struggled out—and began to sink. For while the living carry within their bodies the means with which to accomplish natural, unforced flotation, the long dead do not. Bone sinks. Confronted by this inescapable fact, mounts and riders closed no more than a few yards between themselves and the escaping windwagon before, despite their frenzied determination, they began to slip beneath the surface.

The blanched skeletons of once-powerful coursers kicked futilely at the water that dragged them down. Not to their deaths, for they were already dead, but to a river bottom gluey with accumulated mud and decomposing plant matter. Their furious riders sank with them. From a position of safety halfway across the river and slightly downstream, the wagon's passengers watched as a number of their would-be pursuers crawled laboriously out onto the bank they had so recently and precipitously left, there to dry themselves in the sun as they rejoined their more conservative deceased comrades. Not all of them made it back out, some having managed to mire themselves forever in the grip of the shifting, glutinous river bottom.

Simna would have given a cheer, but he was too tired. Besides, he knew he might need his remaining energy for a swim to the far bank. With every gust of wind they drew nearer to that gently sloping haven, but at the same time the wagon continued to take on water.

"Will we make it, do you think?" he asked Ehomba.

The tall herdsman contemplated the dirty backwash swirling around his feet. "I do not know, Simna. I am an expert neither on wagons nor boats. The sides are well made, and will hold. But that will not do us any good if we sink below the surface like our pursuers." He raised his gaze to the sail that continued to billow westward. "If the wind holds . . ." His contemplative murmur trailed off into the sustaining breeze.

Amazingly, when there was nearly a foot of water inside the windwagon, it stopped sinking. The natural buoyancy of the wood that had been used in its construction kept them afloat, though with so much water inboard their progress was greatly reduced. They were no longer sailing so much as drifting with the current.

Before long, the small army of the Brotherhood had vanished from sight as the river took a westward bend. They were very close to the opposite bank now, tantalizingly close, but if they jumped overboard and swam, it meant that their supplies, not to mention themselves, would be drenched. Ehomba elected to try to ride it out, hoping that the combination of current and wind would carry them safely to shore. Simna concurred.

"If it sinks under us, we'll have to swim for it anyway," the swordsman pointed out. "Might as well stay as dry as possible for as long as possible."

Even as he concluded the observation, something jarred the wagon sharply, bringing it to a shuddering halt. Simna grinned cockily. "Nothing like having a request filled on the spot. We just hit a sandbar." Leaving the tiller set, he sloshed to the left side of the wagon and peered over the side. The murky water obscured and distorted everything that lay more than a foot below the surface, but by leaning over, the swordsman was able to make out the broad, dun-colored, slightly curved shape that had brought their aimless odyssey to a halt.

"It's a sandbar, all right," he informed his companions confidently. "Looks like it stretches all the way to shore." Still grinning, he gathered up his sword and backpack. "We can walk from here."

Ehomba hesitated. "Simna, I am not sure. . . ."

"Not sure?" The stocky swordsman hefted his pack higher on his shoulders as he prepared to step over the side. "Not sure of what, Etjole? With those long legs most of you will stay drier than most. Hunkapa's the one to feel sorry for." He nodded in the shaggy hulk's direction. "With all that fur he'll soak up this brown muck like a sponge."

"Hunkapa be okay," their massive companion assured him.

"Hunkapa always okay." After mimicking his ponderous friend's childish tone, Simna pointed out a spar splint floating on the floor of the wagon. "Sandbars are usually firm enough for walking, but I don't want to step onto one made of silt and sink up to my neck. If I'm going to look like an idiot I want company. Hand me that length of good wood, Hunkapa."

Obediently, Aub passed it across. Gripping it firmly in one hand, the swordsman threw a leg over the side of the nearly motionless wagon and thrust the length of lumber downward, anxious to see how far it would slide into the upper reaches of the sandbar. To his surprise and gratification, it didn't sink at all. The gently convex surface was firm, yielding only very slightly to his exploratory prodding.

"There, you see?" He took some pleasure in being able to chide Ehomba. The soft-voiced, solemn-visaged herdsman was right so often it was beginning to grow irksome.

"Easy walking. Get your stuff and let's get out of here while we're still afloat."

Leaning around the mast, Hunkapa Aub tried to see into the murky water. "Is strong enough to hold me, Simna?"

"Sure! Here, see for yourself." The swordsman thrust the wooden pole hard into the water.

Taking offense at this latest and most flagrant outrage, the sandbar promptly erupted in Simna's face, drenching him with dun-colored water, decaying plant matter, and smatterings of the snails, freshwater crustaceans, and startled amphibians that had been living on its back. The swordsman was knocked down by the impact. Ehomba nearly went over backwards into the river, catching himself on the tiller only at the last moment, and Hunkapa Aub was knocked to his knees.

Wrenching its head from the mud in which it had been buried, the great eel whipped around to confront its assailant. Normally placid and somnolent during the heat of the day, it could no longer ignore the stabbing annoyance near the center of its spine. Rising from the shallows, it arched skyward for an instant to get its bearings. Tooth-lined jaws parted in the middle of the streamlined green-black head while tiny black eyes struggled to focus. Espying the intruder nearest to its back, it plunged downward, mouth agape. Simna was reciting his last will and testament as rapidly as he could, but he saw that he would not be able to finish it in time.

Something like a gout of black flame exploded past him, rising into the sky to meet the descending fanged skull before it could strike. Instinctively, Simna thrust his sword upward in a parrying gesture, but it never made contact. The enormous eel had been jolted sideways, back into the water. The concussion as it struck rocked the windwagon, once more knocking all three of its occupants off their feet. Three, because one had gone missing.

Clinging to the tiller for support, shaking water from his face and braids, Ehomba hung on as their waterlogged transport rocked in the waves stirred by the stupendous underwater encounter. "Can you see anything? Simna!"

Dazed and drenched, the swordsman fought to get a grip on the rim of the wagon. Clinging leechlike to the rocking sideboard, he struggled to peer over the side. "No!" A small geyser hit him square in the face, forcing him to turn away and spit river water. "Can't see a thing—nothing!"

Squinting through the dirty, flying liquid, the herdsman sputtered, "Ahlitah! Where's Ahlitah?"

Of them all, only Hunkapa Aub, utilizing his prodigious strength, managed to struggle to his feet in the midst of chaos and tempest. "Hunkapa see him!" Sodden hair hanging in triangular, downward-facing points like limp, gray pennants from the underside of his arm, he pointed.

"How . . ." Ehomba spat out another mouthful of water. "How is he looking?"

There followed a pause, which ended when Hunkapa Aub declared, "Hungry."

The highly localized squall subsided almost as abruptly as it had struck. Around the waterlogged windwagon the river once again grew calm. Within, everything that had not been tied down was afloat, bobbing in the water that had bubbled or sloshed in. Not even the inherent buoyancy of the sturdy planking would keep them afloat much longer, Ehomba saw.

In front of the wagon and paddling steadily for shore was the black litah. In its powerful jaws it gripped the broken neck of the great eel. The nightmare head hung severely to one side, the black eyes glazed with death.

"Hunkapa, we must go with Ahlitah," Ehomba told his husky companion. "You are the only one strong enough to pull the wagon."

The massive man-beast regarded the herdsman with limpid, mournful eyes. "Hunkapa would do, Etjole. Only one problem. Hunkapa cannot swim."

"Cannot . . . ?" It was rare indeed for Ehomba to be taken aback. When they had first plunged into the river to escape the pursuing minions of the Brotherhood, all the time they had been sailing and drifting across, even after they had become dangerously waterlogged and had begun to sink, the big brute had not said a word.

Simna was lying with his back against the inner wall of the wagon, his chest heaving, his sword hanging limp in the tepid water. He was still trying to recover from the experience of having been less than a few seconds away from being eaten by his "sandbar." Ehomba pushed past him to peer over the front of the saturated vehicle.

The eel had been lying half-buried in the ooze that stretched out from the nearby bank. Though no sandbar, the mud bank did incline gently shoreward. He and Simna would have to swim for a little bit, but Hunkapa's head should remain above water.

When informed of this, the shaggy biped hesitated. "Don't know, Etjole." He peered warily over the side of the wagon. "Hunkapa afraid."

"You have to try," the herdsman told him. "I think it is shallow enough so that you can walk, but if not, you will have to try to swim. I knew how to swim before I could walk. It is a more natural motion than walking." He started to gather up his kit and spear, securing the two swords to his back.

"If you find yourself in trouble, just watch me." He smiled encouragingly. "We cannot stay here, Hunkapa. This wagon is coming apart. If the current catches it, there is a good chance it will drift out into the deep part of the river. Then there will be no opportunity for you to walk."

He could see the fear on the creature's face. So powerful, and yet so afraid of an element in which Ehomba found himself very much at home. Reaching up, he took one massive paw in his hand.

"Come with me, Hunkapa. We will go in together. Do you understand? We have no choice."

Slowly, the shaggy head nodded. "Hunkapa—Hunkapa understand. Go together. Ehomba look out for his friend." Huge fingers squeezed painfully tight, but the herdsman did not complain. He glanced back over his shoulder.

"You coming, Simna? Or does your love for this vehicle extend to floating downriver with it?" He mustered an ironic smile. "Swim a little ways and your feet might strike a sandbar."

"They might strike something else, too," the swordsman growled ominously. Sheathing his sword and holding his backpack above his head, he slipped both legs over the side of the steadily sinking wagon. With a grimace, he dropped into the cloudy, silt-rich water.

"Together now." Ehomba allowed his hand to be half crushed as he stepped resolutely over the side. River buffeted him as Hunkapa Aub's much greater mass displaced water. The ungainly hulk disappeared—only to reappear seconds later with its head well above the surface. Astonishment and delight beamed from the guileless, hair-covered face.

"Hunkapa not have to swim! Hunkapa's feet on bottom!"

"I hoped it was so." Treading water while struggling to keep his pack dry, the herdsman started to kick for the shore. Against his back, the sea-bone sword quivered orgasmically at the sensation of being submerged. Anyone else would have found the unexpected vibration unnerving, but Ehomba had anticipated it. What more natural than that the wondrous weapon should react to being placed in the surroundings from whence it had originally evolved?

Suddenly he was out of the water, high and dry, heaved skyward by a robust thrust from below. No gigantic eel bursting from the depths this time, but the hand of Hunkapa Aub, lifting him from beneath. Effortlessly, the herdsman's huge companion placed his angular friend on broad, hirsute shoulders. In this manner Ehomba rode in comparative comfort the rest of the way to the shore. Only his ears suffered, bruised by an unending stream of blistering profanities from the struggling Simna, who, forced to swim, trailed well behind.

XI

As they drew themselves up on the reed-lined, accommodating bank, they scanned the now distant opposite shore
for signs of their pursuers. But the Brotherhood of the
Bone, unable to cross by swimming or riding, had given up
and gone back to the dark, sheltering forest that was their
refuge and abode. The weary travelers were safe, if once
more afoot.

Taking a seat on the gentle, grassy slope, Ehomba un-
packed his gear and spread it out beside him to dry in the
sun. Like a high-priced overstuffed rug liberated from a
sultan's palace, Hunkapa Aub sprawled nearby, basking
gloriously in the heat of midday. The herdsman watched
gravely as the windwagon that had carried them so far and
so well slowly drifted off downstream, sinking slowly into
the riverine depths.

Nearby, an exhausted Simna finally emerged, dripping,
from the water. Stumbling up the bank, he tossed his pack
to one side, not caring if it spilled its contents all over the
grass. Through no effort of his own, it did not. His sword
he slipped back into its scabbard, which he then removed

and dumped next to the pack. Swaying slightly, murky water and the occasional tadpole running off him in rivulets, he staggered over to where the black litah lay panting. Its forepaws lay on the crushed throat of the great eel. As the sodden swordsman approached, the magnificently maned cranium swiveled slowly to regard him.

Halting before the cat and its kill, Simna stiffly dipped his head and made a sweeping gesture with one arm. "Look before you leap, my master at arms always told me. I admit it: There are times when I'm forgetful."

The litah replied thoughtfully. "There are times when you're an idiot."

Gritting his teeth, Simna looked off to one side for a long moment. Still breathing hard, he rested one hand on a knee. "You're not making this any easier for me, cat. I came over to thank you for saving my life."

Massive eyebrows rose haughtily. "Saving your life? Did I save your life? Dear me, I suppose I did." Ahlitah turned back to his kill. "If it will make you feel any better, I assure you it was coincidental. It's just that I happen to be very fond of eel." With that, the great head dipped forward and puissant teeth tore into the slick, green-black flesh.

"Hoy, well, thank you anyway, thou maestro of piquant sprays. Simna ibn Sind embraces chance salvation over intentional abstention any day." Stumbling as he turned, he made his unsteady way back to the place on the bank where he had dropped his gear. Behind him, the clear warm air of afternoon was filled with contented crunching sounds.

Exhausted, and mentally as well as physically spent from their exertions of the morning, they made camp in a thick copse of impressive shade trees not far from the river. The woods on the western bank closely resembled those they had passed through on the opposite shore, except that on the western side larger trees were fewer and farther between.

"These woods seem to be thinning out." Seated next to the campfire, Ehomba reached down to give the wooden spit on which their evening meal of freshly caught fish was broiling another turn. "If that turns out to be so, it is a great shame. We could have made good use of the windwagon on open plains."

Lying on the other side of the fire with his head against the pillowing flank of Hunkapa Aub, Simna watched the meal cook. Hungry as he was, the tantalizing aroma that rose from the sizzling fish verged on the sensuous.

"Hoy, long bruther, we've traversed desert and veldt, mountain and marsh on foot before. By Gumitharap's calluses, we'll cross whatever lies before us as well."

Ehomba smiled fondly over the flames at his sometimes trying but ever willing friend. "Optimism becomes you, Simna."

The swordsman looked up and grinned. "Not being dead does wonders for a man's spirits." Lifting his head and glancing to one side, he indicated a slowly heaving dark mass lying off by itself a little ways away from the fire. Having ingested an unholy vast quantity of eel, the black litah was locked in a sleep that mimicked the deceased.

"Kitty there won't own up to it, but he saved my life. I don't buy all that pompous indifference about his just being after a meal. He could catch fish anytime. He knew what he was doing."

"I suspect that you are right, my friend." Rising, the herdsman wiped down the front of his kilt. "I was thinking how nice it would be to have something else to eat with the fish. I think we passed a fruit tree a little ways back, and I know I saw some mushrooms." Picking up his spear, he started away from the fire and into the forest.

"Don't go too far, bruther," Simna exclaimed warningly. "We don't know these woods. There may not be any possessive, ambulatory collections of bones click-clacking about, but unknown nights often hide all sorts of hungry beasties."

Ehomba replied without looking back. "I remember the tree as only being a little ways from camp, Simna. You rest here, and do not let our supper burn."

"No chance of that, famished as I am." Sitting up and away from Hunkapa Aub, who snorted and rubbed his nose briskly in his sleep, the swordsman gave the improvised spit another turn.

With half the moon and all the stars to guide him, the herdsman worked his way back through the woods until the campfire was only a distant flickering among the trees. Convinced that he had already wandered too far, he tried a little more to his left—and there was the tree he had remembered passing. It was a wild orange, its limbs bristling with long thorns. Their presence did not worry him because he had no intention of trying to climb into those protected branches.

Using the ancient but still sharp tooth that tipped his spear, he cut away the ripest of the brightly colored spheres within reach. Each time a severed stem fell, the faintest, most ethereal of roars could be heard. Sometimes the spirit of the tooth could be invoked for purposes other than engendering mass confusion and destruction: gathering oranges, for example.

With the aid of the spear it only took a few minutes to accumulate enough of the juice-heavy fruit to more than sate himself and his friends. He knew that Hunkapa Aub would probably eat Ahlitah's share. To the best of Ehomba's knowledge, large carnivorous cats were not fond of fruit.

Slinging his spear against his back, he made a basket out of the folds of his kilt and filled the resultant concavity with the best of the oranges. Nearby, he located the mushrooms he had passed earlier and added several handfuls of the tasty fungi to his growing accumulation. Satisfied, he started back toward camp.

He was within sight of the fire when something sprang silently from behind one of the trees he was passing to press an incredibly sharp knife tightly against his neck. His hands dropped, sending mushrooms and oranges spilling to the ground, rolling away from his feet. Despite his acute herdsman's senses, he had not seen or heard his assailant. Or smelled it, which was not surprising when its nature became apparent to him. It had no smell.

Old bones generally did not.

"Surprised to see me, swindler of promises?" The voice was breathy, unnatural, and familiar. It belonged to the envoy of the Brotherhood of the Bone.

"Very much so." The edge of the bone knife dimpling his throat was sharp enough to cleave a notion. "From what I saw, I did not think any of you or your brethren could swim the river, or walk across its bottom."

Whispering in his ear, the skeleton smiled. "Who said anything about swimming or walking?"

"Then how did you get across?" With the bony rib cage pressing hard against his back, Ehomba could not reach his spear. His swords lay back in camp, laid out neat and useless alongside his blanket.

"Flew, of course." A spectral chuckle rattled the vacant chest. "Dead dragonets carried me. It was hard for them, but there was no choice. I couldn't use dead birds. When they die, they lose their feathers along with their flesh. But bats and dragonets retain their wing membranes for quite a while. Took a dozen of them to bring me over, and they'll never make it back. Their wings are too frayed, too desiccated. It doesn't matter. They were dead before they took off from the other bank anyway. Dead here, dead there: Location means nothing, and doesn't change anything."

Ehomba stood perfectly still. "That means you are marooned here now as well, and will never be able to rejoin the Brotherhood."

Teeth chattered. "No, but I'll have something better. I'll have their revenge. You promised your bones to us in return for our letting your friends go. Then you called them back. Charlatan." The edge of the knife pressed a little deeper. The herdsman felt a tiny trickle of warmth start to flow down past his collarbone to his chest.

"I did no such thing," he protested softly. "I left you my insides, as was agreed. If they preferred my company to yours, that is no reason to blame me."

"Isn't it? As if you didn't know they would find a way to return to you."

"Actually, I was not sure. I hoped they would. I need my insides. They are of more use to me than to you."

"They won't be, in a moment."

"Bruther, what . . . ?" Holding his sword in a firm, two-handed grip, Simna stepped out of the shadows. The looming mass of Hunkapa Aub stood to one side of him, a softly growling Ahlitah on the other.

"Keep your distance!" the envoy shouted warningly.

"Etjole . . ." Seeing the knife that was gripped in the skeleton's hand, the swordsman measured the distance between them. Too far. "If you cut him . . ." he began.

"What?" The envoy cackled amusedly. "You'll kill me? You're more than a century too late to make that threat hold up, traveler. When I'm through with him, maybe I'll have your bones too. They look to be an interesting set, all squashed down and out as they are."

Simna looked as if he wanted to say something else, but he was interrupted by a loud *crack*, the dry cry of splitting wood. Automatically, everyone's gaze snapped upward into the night. Everyone's, that is, except Ehomba's. The instant the skeletal assassin's attention was diverted, he broke free of the bony grip and threw himself forward and down. Reacting, the envoy of the Brotherhood raised the knife, hewn from the shinbone of a comrade, and was about to strike lethally downward when the enormous broken bough landed on top of him with a reverberating crash.

Bones and splinters went flying in all directions. Rolling away from the impact, Ehomba stared at the branch that had crushed his would-be executioner. The bleached skull was no longer intact or visible, having been pulverized by the considerable weight of falling wood. Leg and arm and rib bones lay scattered everywhere.

His friends were at his side before the dust settled. Hunkapa Aub simply lifted the herdsman bodily and set him on his feet. Feeling of the cut that had been made to his throat, Ehomba knew he would have to wear a bandage there for a few days at least. Had it gone half an inch deeper his life would be gushing out between his fingers. The falling branch had startled the envoy for barely an instant, just long enough to allow his captive to break away.

Now the bones of the murderous, spectral visitant lay strewn across the ground, dispersed and harmless.

Satisfied that their friend and guide was not seriously injured, Hunkapa Aub and the black litah returned to camp. Simna remained to inspect the shattered bough. Having fallen from somewhere halfway up the side of a truly imposing trunk, the branch was greater in diameter than many of the mature trees nearby.

"That's what I call a lucky break," the swordsman commented. "It doesn't look rotten, and I see no evidence of termites or other insects having been at work, so something else must have caused it to fall." He gazed evenly at his tall companion. "Fall just then, and just there. I don't suppose a man who continually denies being a wizard but who can step out of his own skin would have had anything to do with that?"

Having brushed himself off, Ehomba had bent to recover as many of the spilled mushrooms and oranges as he could. Like the envoy, many had been squashed beneath the weight of the broken branch. Whatever he scavenged would have to do. He was not going back into the forest in search of replacements. One nearly fatal fruit-gathering expedition a night was enough.

"As a matter of fact, Simna, I did not. Grateful as I am, it was as much of a surprise to me as to the rest of you."

"Hoy, right, sure." The swordsman wore a peevish expression. "That's what you always say, bruther. You just happened to be standing under that branch, and it just happened to break and fall right on that homicidal stack of bones. No magic, no sorcery. Just coincidence, and nothing more."

Having picked up those oranges and mushrooms that were unbruised, Ehomba glanced over at his companion. "I cannot explain it, Simna. But I know that there are times in a man's life when it is best not to question things too closely." Tilting his head back slightly, he sniffed of the night air. "Something is burning."

"Our supper!" Whirling, Simna broke into a run, but not before looking back over his shoulder as he darted past his friend. "By Gnomost's gneels, if I didn't know better, I'd *swear* I'd seen that tree before. Funny thing, that."

"Yes." Ehomba too spared a last, lingering glance for the immense old oak as he followed his frantic companion back into camp at a more leisurely pace.

The incident was not discussed as they ate, but everyone watched the surrounding woods a little more closely, paid a bit more attention to the distant rustlings and rattlings of the nocturnal forest creatures. The fish was delicious, not badly burned as Simna had feared, but only thoroughly cooked. As Ehomba had surmised, the addition of broiled mushrooms to the meal and wild oranges for dessert was an excellent complement to the main course. Even Ahlitah tried a little of everything, much to the surprise of both his human companions.

"I'm always open to new experiences," he told them as he spit out orange peel. "That's one I won't have to open myself to again. Paugh!" Nothing wrinkles in disgust, Ehomba mused, quite so exhaustively as the face of a displeased cat.

With Hunkapa Aub agreeing to take the first watch, the others retired, the two men to their blankets and the black litah to the mat of leaves and grass he had assembled with his paws. Ehomba drifted off with one hand feeling gingerly of his throat and the strip of cloth that now separated it from the beaded necklaces he wore.

As he slid into sleep, his thoughts drifted into dream—but it was most unlike any normal dream, or even a normal nightmare.

He was running, running hard, but on all fours. Bushes and grass sped past at an astonishing rate of speed. Though he could feel the ground beneath his feet and therefore knew he was not flying, with each prodigious stride he left it below him for an impossibly long time.

Startled by his sudden appearance, something with wide eyes looked up to encounter his gaze. Utterly paralyzed by the unexpected eye contact, it stood frozen for an instant and then flashed by as he raced past. A rabbit, too small and scrawny to bother with. Little more than a mouthful or three, certainly not enough to satiate the voluminous hunger that burned in his belly. He needed, and was after, bigger prey.

When he exploded from the high grass the herd panicked. Though it meant he would have to exert himself a little more to make a kill, he was exhilarated by the fear his appearance had incited. Eland and elk bolted in every direction, eyes rolling with fright, tongues lolling from open mouths. Impala and syndyoceros crashed into one another and bounded away wildly as they sought the safety of the herd that had not yet re-formed.

In the confusion Ehomba had an entire minute to single out a victim: more than enough time. Settling on an old bull elk, he accelerated to maximum speed. The elk never had a chance. Ehomba hit it head-on, his open jaws slamming into the hairy throat and locking like a vise. The elk tried to lower its head in order to bring its massive horns to bear on its attacker, but, already caught and held in a death grip, it had no real chance to defend itself.

Blood flowed into and through Ehomba's jaws, exciting every nerve and sensation in his body. Unable to fight, the elk tried to run. His assailant's weight made sustained flight impossible. The prey sank to its knees, then its belly, and finally went limp, suffocated by the tightening of its attacker's jaws.

Ehomba held on for another several minutes until he was sure death had arrived. Then, crouching alongside the body, one paw placed possessively on the carcass, he began to eat. Blood and muscle, organs and bone, all vanished into massive, efficient jaws. Lingering over the kill, he ate intermittently for the rest of the afternoon and on into early evening. Only then did he rise and move away, belly dragging low, back into the high grass. There he found the stream, and drank for long minutes.

Locating a small clearing, he lay down heavily in the shade of a cluster of yellow-blooming hopak trees and began to groom himself. It was impossible to get all the blood off his muzzle no matter how many times he licked a paw and ran it across his face, but he made a start. The rest of the stain would come out later, following repeated washings. Glutted and content, he slumped down on his side and fell into a sleep any passing traveler might easily have mistaken for death. But despite his seeming somnolence, the sound of a snapping twig would be enough to rouse him instantly. In the depth of his deep sleep, one foot kicked out repeatedly.

Wrapped in his blanket beside the campfire, Ehomba's left leg twitched restively.

Ahlitah was dizzy. Not from chasing his tail, which when absolutely convinced no one and nothing else was watching he would occasionally do to relieve unrelenting boredom, but from trying to maintain an alien and utterly unaccustomed posture. With each step he took, no matter how short and cautious, he was convinced, absolutely certain, that he was going to fall over. Yet despite his fear and misgivings, he did not.

By all that ran and crawled and swam and flew, what had happened to his other pair of legs?

And his eyes. And his ears, and his nose! Though he could see adequately, the acuity of vision he usually enjoyed had been replaced by a pale, fuzzy imitation of normal sight. Objects located more than a short distance away were unidentifiable. Anything at a reasonable distance blended invisibly into the landscape or the horizon. Furthermore, it was as if he were gazing through a steady downpour. Colors were washed out or absent entirely. It was horrible: He felt half blinded.

Nothing was audible except that which was in his immediate vicinity. The familiar panoply of distant sounds, the constant susurration of animate life, was entirely absent. It was as if the world had suddenly gone silent. There were noises and the echoes of movement close by, but nothing else. No complaining insects, no scuttling lizards or slithering snakes, no chirping birds. The wing-beats of dragonets no longer whispered in his ears, and the delectable murmur of prey animals cropping grass was sorely wanting.

As for the wonderful universe of scents that normally filled his nostrils, its absence constituted a kind of olfactory blindness that made his severely impacted vision that much worse. It was a struggle, a strain, a surreal effort to smell anything at all. What odors he was able to identify were so homogenized it hardly seemed worth the effort to inhale.

Simply keeping his ridiculous body from falling down demanded a preposterous share of his considerably reduced energy. And yet he was conscious of the fact that, though shorter, it was a much better body than many of those that were in motion around him. Feeling greatly enfeebled and not knowing what else to do, he instinctively sought shelter.

A nearby enclosure seemed to promise privacy if not enlightenment. Given his severely diminished capacity for perceiving the world around him, it was hardly surprising that he should be wrong about this, too. The edifice was not empty.

Ordinarily he would have attacked and killed the pair of two-legged young females that came running toward him. For reasons unknown and inexplicable, he did not. Instead, he allowed them to carry out a mock attack on his person; striking him about the chest and arms, gamboling around his middle, and prattling inanities into his ears. They made muted howling noises. The younger, a lithesome female not long past the cusp of puberty, was only slightly more respectful of his person than her elder. The air of commingled anticipation and affection they projected was oddly unnerving, as if it were forced rather than natural. Their strongest efforts to pull him farther into the enclosure notwithstanding, they struck him as wretchedly weak.

So did the third female figure that appeared from another part of the enclosure to throw both fore and hind legs around him. To his astonishment and disgust, instead of extending her tongue to lick his face by way of greeting, she thrust her tongue deeply into his mouth. So startled was he by this unexpected, unnatural act that he forgot to bite it. She, however, was not averse to nibbling on his ear. At least something about the otherwise inane interaction between himself and the unknown female made sense!

Most unexpectedly, given the extreme distaste and inner turmoil his extraordinary situation had brought about, he felt the heat rising in his loins. Disturbed and bewildered, he did not bother to resist as the female led him to another, darker portion of the enclosure. At least, he thought with relief, she had dismissed her irritating, overly exuberant predecessors.

When he realized what she had in mind, he knew only one way to react. Evidently, this did not displease her. Quite to the contrary. The mechanics of the act as well as its immediate consequences were surprisingly conventional, a touch of familiarity in alien surroundings for which he was grateful. After they both rested awhile, he was prepared to repeat the process. Again, the female had no objection.

By the fourth time, she was regarding him with unabashed awe. By the fifth, with hesitancy. When he ventured to initiate a sixth reiteration with as much enthusiasm as the first, she retreated precipitously from the darkened portion of the enclosure. Her reaction only confused him further. As was typical of his kind, he was prepared to continue for the rest of the day and far on into the night. Clearly she was not.

His head hurt. Agitated and bemused, he stumbled back to the enclosure's entrance. A pair of very large two-legged males were waiting for him there. They bore weapons and grim expressions. Standing behind them, the female with whom he had recently consorted appeared in a state of extreme agitation, pointing and jabbering in his direction. The looks on the faces of the two armed males grew ominous.

If there was one thing he was in no mood to tolerate at that moment, it was the absurd verbalizations and oral circumlocutions of a brace of irritable bipeds. To let them know how he was feeling, he voiced a warning roar. The effect was salutary. The fur stood up on their heads, their eyes grew as big as emu eggs, and they turned and bolted in the opposite direction as fast as their hind legs would carry them, flinging their weapons aside while screaming at the top of their lungs. From other enclosures, startled faces peered out in search of the source of the sound. Feeling much better about things, he strode out of the bordello. Though he had neglected to pay, no one dared to confront him.

Lying well away from the campfire, Ahlitah smacked his lips as he rolled over onto his back.

Simna frowned as he entered the city. The golden towers, the marble archways, the teeming crowds of barkers and bazaaris, the fragrant smells of fine cooking—all were absent. In their place were simple houses of stone and wood and thatch. In lieu of richly garbed horses and moas, dogs and rodent-hunting cats roamed the streets. Where he normally would have expected to see paving stones of granite there was only packed earth.

A few women tracked his progress as he advanced. Some were ancient, others not yet old enough to understand. Those of young and middle age were tall, proud, and comely, with elegant necks and straight backs, full breasts and curving backsides. He grinned at them and a few smiled back, though there was a hesitancy in their expressions that bruised his ego.

Where was he? Was this not the entrance to Vharuphan the Radiant, renowned capital of the Dhashtari Emperors? Where were the great domes of polished green verdite and the fine gilded latticework famed near and far across half a continent? The nearest thing he saw to fine latticework was a sturdily constructed well. As for domes, there was one of brick for firing pottery, and it was not habitable.

As he wandered in a daze something struck him in the legs. Looking down, he saw a young girl clinging to him and beaming delightedly, her sweet innocent features blushing with love. As he struggled weakly to disengage himself from her pythonic embrace, a young man stepped down from the porch of a nearby house and approached. In one hand he carried a spear suitable in size and weight for someone no longer a child but not yet an adult. It was more than toy, less than weapon. Bowing low, he then put a hand on Simna's arm and smiled, revealing a blaze of perfect white teeth.

Stunned and not knowing what else to do or where to go, Simna allowed himself to be led by hand and arm up the steps of the porch and into the house. In a back room an astoundingly handsome woman stood before a stone counter, using knives of differing size and heft to slice and butcher what remained of a human hindquarter. When Simna made gagging sounds, she turned. A conflagration of a smile spread across her face, making her appear more beautiful than ever and somewhat minimizing the effect of the bloodstains that spotted her apron and overblouse. The ensuing kiss she bestowed upon him almost, but not quite, allowed him to overlook the import of the three harrowing words she spoke to him.

"Welcome home—husband."

Simna ibn Sind woke up screaming.

The sounds of his yelling and thrashing about startled his companions to wakefulness. This included Hunkapa Aub, who, having never been relieved of his watch, had fallen asleep where he sat. Around the dying embers of the campfire the forest was silent, and night still held sway over the world.

Ehomba rushed to his friend's side. "Simna, what is wrong? Is there anything I can do?" Nearby, Hunkapa Aub was still trying to shake the sleep webs from his brain while the black litah looked on unblinkingly.

"Anything you can . . . ?" The swordsman looked up at his rangy companion. "Yes, by Guquaquo. If you ever hear me making noises like that in my sleep ever again, wake me instantly." Putting both hands to his head, he stared blankly at the corpse of the campfire. "Hoy, what a nightmare! I—I was domesticated!"

His expression twisting, Ehomba stood up and stepped back. "Is that all?"

Simna fixed the herdsman with a look of utmost seriousness. "Bruther, every man has his own fears. I do not mock yours. Grant me the same courtesy."

Ehomba nodded soberly. "You are right, my friend. I

apologize." His expression tightened slightly. "I am curious, for I also had a most peculiar dream. I had four legs and the keenest imaginable senses, and was hunting."

"And I," Ahlitah put in with a reverberating growl, "walked on two legs like humans, and visited a place where intercourse was expected to be paid for with human money."

It was left, unsurprisingly, for Ehomba to sort out what must have taken place.

"I do not know what happened, or how, but it seems that some unknown mechanism has caused our dreams to slip from one individual to the next." He nodded at the swordsman. "You got my dream, Simna." His gaze shifted to the intent big cat. "I dreamed Ahlitah's dream. And he must have suffered through yours."

The swordsman nodded vigorously. "Hoy, that's crazy, but crazy logic is logic still. I certainly . . ." His expression twisted. "Wait a minute. What do you mean, 'suffered'?" He turned sharply to the watching litah. "Did my dream then cause you suffering?"

"Beyond doubt," the big cat replied. "I dare say you would have enjoyed it."

"Cursed unfair," the stocky warrior grumbled. "Every man—and cat—should keep to their own dreaming. Who asked you to snatch mine?"

"Believe me," Ahlitah replied, "if I had been allowed any choice in the matter, I would have opted instead for the dream of the nearest rodent. At least in such a dream I would have had the proper number of legs."

"Hoy, that's no given because—"

Ehomba cut him off. "Hunkapa Aub; you were asleep

when Simna's nightmare woke us all. What did you dream?"

Enormous shaggy shoulders heaved, framing a look of utter ingenuousness. "Hunkapa not dream, Etjole. Sleep soundly."

Simna uttered a rude noise. "The slumber of the dumber. In ignorance there is purity."

"We must take care in the future." A thoughtful Ehomba gazed into the last dying embers of the campfire. "It could be dangerous for one to dream too often the dreams of another, be it man or beast."

They sat awhile together, discussing the remarkable occurrence. Eventually, fatigue overcame concern and they retired once more, this time to sleep the sleep of vacuity that refreshes the mind. In the morning they were rejuvenated—and much relieved. In the future they resolved to monitor their own sleep as well as that of one another more closely, the better to prevent a recurrence of the unfortunate slippage of the night before.

They resolved also to eat no more mushrooms gathered from this particular forest, no matter how nourishing or tasty they looked.

XII

Very soon they no longer had to worry about the unknown properties of forest mushrooms of any variety, because those delightful but often mysterious edible fungi soon vanished, along with the last remnants of the forest itself.

They did not lose the trees entirely, but instead of dense woods or even isolated thickets, individual boles grew in isolated hollows or followed the course of the occasional stream. Otherwise, the ground was covered with a tall yellow-green grass that came up to Simna's hips. They had traveled through worse before, but it still would have made for slow going if not for Hunkapa Aub. With his thick coat of hair to protect him from cuts and scratches, he was virtually immune to stickers and sharp-edged grasses. Following him as he plowed a path westward, they made steady progress.

The presence of many small creeks and streams meant they did not have to burden themselves with full bags of water, and the shade their gullies supplied provided a welcome respite at mealtimes and at night. After sundown, tiny covert creatures ringed each campsite with querulous cheeping sounds. Whenever one of the travelers attempted to locate the source of these gentle fanfares, they quickly evaporated into the surrounding grass. Whether animal, insect, or wee folk of the prairie, their true nature remained shrouded in mystery. Whatever they were, Ehomba decided, they were curious but not hostile.

Monstrous bison ranged the grassland, browsers larger than any Simna or Ehomba had ever seen. The travelers gave these hulky dark brown herbivores a wide berth. Ahlitah had to be restrained from testing his skills against such tempting, oversized game.

"There is no need," Ehomba argued with the big cat as they traipsed along in Hunkapa Aub's wake. "There is plenty of smaller game. What would be the point of risking your well-being to bring one of the beasts down?"

"To prove that I could do it." Passionate cat eyes looked up at the herdsman. The litah was panting in the heat of the day, thick black tongue lolling out one side of its mouth. "I know you don't understand. It's a predator thing."

"I understand that if you were to spark a stampede with one of your attacks we could all be killed. There is no shelter around here. I understand that if you go down beneath those great hooves and break a leg or two we would not be able to carry you."

"Man, you waste almost as much time worrying about things as you do wondering about them." Idly, Ahlitah slapped a big paw down on a field mouse that was unwisely attempting to cross behind Hunkapa and ahead of them. As it was not even big enough to chew, the cat swallowed the snack whole. "When it comes to matters mystical, I defer to you. When it comes to the business of killing, you should trust in me."

"Very well then," Ehomba argued. "Suppose you catch one and bring it down. What if it falls on you? I know how strong you are, but these grazers are huge. A dying one would be difficult to handle."

The great maned head nodded slowly. "That is a valid point. Even the most skilled hunter can fall victim to an accident."

"Besides," the herdsman went on, "what would we do with all that meat?"

"Ordinarily, I would live nearby until it was consumed." The litah snorted. "But since we are traveling on a human timetable, something that sensible would be out of the question." He was silent for a while, pacing easily alongside the herdsman. "Perhaps you are right. I'll find something else to kill."

"Thank you," Ehomba told him.

They camped that night in a depression where a small natural dam of rocks and debris had formed a narrow but deep pool. Not only did it provide them with a source of fresh water, but it also offered a chance to bathe and even, to a very limited degree, to swim. In this Ehomba took the lead, demonstrating once again the natural affinity for water that he had demonstrated on more than one occasion. Simna was a fine swimmer, while the black litah contented himself with rolling about in the shallows and following his immersion with a dust wallow. Unable to swim, Hunkapa Aub splashed about near the shore like a happy child.

It was therefore surprising that Ehomba woke not to the

smell of damp vegetation or surroundings, but to an odor that was distinctly acrid.

Sitting up and pushing aside his blanket, he tilted his head slightly and sniffed. The sun was just considering the eastern horizon and none of his companions were yet awake. The smell was as familiar as it was distinctive, but from what direction was it coming? Of one thing and one thing only he was certain: Something in their vicinity was ablaze, and it wasn't the extinguished campfire.

Turning his head slowly to his right as he tried to locate the source of the odor, his gaze fell upon the black litah. As was its manner, it had awakened noiselessly. Now it was sitting back on its hindquarters, nose in the air, inhaling silently.

"You smell it also," Ehomba murmured.

The big cat nodded once. "Something burning. What I can't guess yet."

"Can you tell where? Which direction?" Knowing how much more sensitive the big cat was to odors of every kind, Ehomba ceased his own efforts in favor of the litah's.

There was a pause, then Ahlitah lifted a forepaw and pointed northward. "That way. And coming closer, fast."

"Better get everyone up."

While he roused Simna, the black litah prodded Hunkapa Aub to wakefulness. By the time the swordsman was sufficiently conscious to communicate, the sharp, acrid smell of burning vegetation was thick in Ehomba's nostrils.

"Etjole?" Raising himself up on his elbows, Simna blinked once, then wrinkled his features. "Somebody making breakfast?"

Satisfied that his friend was awake, the herdsman

straightened and gazed soberly to the north. "I think this grassland is on fire."

It came roaring toward them like a wall, advancing in a solid line from horizon to horizon. Orange flames framed in red fed hungrily on the dry grass. Their superhot crowns licked at the sky, rising fifty feet and more before transmuting themselves into gouts of dense black smoke that obscured the clouds. Fleeing before the blaze was a rampaging menagerie of terrified creatures large and small. Broad-winged raptors and agile dragonets swooped and darted in waves before the flames, feasting on the insects and small game that were being driven from their hiding places by the onrushing conflagration.

Wind drove the fire forward. Where it advanced too rapidly for those in its path to escape, charred corpses littered the smoking, blackened earth in its wake.

"By Gapreth!" Suddenly wide awake, Simna was scrambling to gather up his gear. "The pool! Into the pool!"

"It is not wide enough," Ehomba countered. "The fire is too big. The flames will consume the grass on both sides and merge above the surface. They will suck the air from above the water, burn the lungs and suffocate anyone who is not fish or frog." Even as he spoke, the towering flames had advanced another ten feet nearer to the campsite. "Downstream! If we can find a pool too broad for the flames to overreach we will be safe."

Carrying everything, they fled from the onrushing blaze. Ahlitah flew effortlessly over rocks and gullies that slowed less nimble companions. Burdened by packs, lesser individuals than Ehomba and Simna would have fallen fatally behind. Hunkapa Aub was not graceful, but his expansive stride compensated for his occasional un-gainliness.

As they fled, the stream continued to flow strongly alongside them, holding out the promise of a hoped-for refuge somewhere up ahead. When the ground showed signs of sloping slightly upward, Ehomba took heart. The slight alteration in terrain strongly suggested that the water that was now flowing downhill beside them would soon have to come to rest in a large, still body.

It was the tallest of the travelers who sang out moments later. "Hunkapa see water!"

"Another pond?" a gasping Simna inquired. He was panting hard not so much from running as from the rising temperature. In spite of their exertions, the wall of flame was gaining on them, and the fire gave no indication of tiring.

"No pond, Simna." The shaggy biped stumbled, caught himself, and loped on. "Hunkapa see lake!"

Unless their hirsute companion's definition of a lake was radically different from their own, Ehomba knew they would soon reach a place of safety. Seemingly intent on proving that good news came in bunches, like grapes, the wind chose that moment to drop to almost nothing. The grass fire continued to burn behind them, but it was no longer racing south at high speed.

"Watch yourselves." The composed warning came from Ahlitah. "We're not alone. There are animals up ahead. Big animals."

"Of course there are," Simna wheezed. "Probably seeking safety in the lake just like we are."

"No." The big cat sounded puzzled. "Actually, they're coming this way."

That made no sense, Ehomba reflected as he ran, covering the uneven ground with long, supple strides. His swords bounced against his back. Why would any creature deliberately be heading toward the fire, even if the wind had fallen?

As he topped a slight rise he saw them for himself, an irregular line of golden brown shapes arrayed between the fleeing travelers and the looming silvery sheen of the prairie lake. Its calm, expansive waters beckoned, promising relief from the heat and refuge from the raging blaze.

The beasts initially espied by the black litah boasted dark stripes along their lower flanks and each of their six legs. They had short, nobby tails and oddly flattened skulls like the heads of digging spades. The slightly protuberant eyes that gazed out at the world from the upper corners of the weirdly triangular skulls were covered with transparent membranes that glistened in the sun. Double rows of sharp incisors were visible in the long, flattened jaws. From the summit of the skull projected a single bizarre horn that curved forward and up.

They were built like grazers, Ehomba saw; heavy of body, thick of fur, and short of leg. But their teeth were designed for biting and chewing flesh, not grass or other plant matter. Yet among the dozens of incisors he could see not a single canine tooth or tusk. Such teeth were suitable for biting off and slicing up large chunks of meat, but not for killing. This singular orthodontic arrangement marked them as scavengers. So did their stumpy legs, with which they could never hope to run down even the smallest of healthy herbivores.

As for what they scavenged, that was abundantly clear. At least two of the sturdy, stockily built creatures could be seen chewing on the charred, blackened remains of less fortunate animals that had been mortally injured by the fire. Apparently these extraordinary beasts tracked the advancing flames much as the opportunistic raptors hunted in front of them. Since they plainly could not move very fast and would be unable to outrun any blaze, he decided, they must be exceptionally sensitive to the smallest shifts in the fire's or wind's direction.

Moments later, evidence was given to show that he was only partially correct. The bizarre hexapods did indeed feed upon those unfortunate creatures who had been caught and killed by the flames. But the striped carnivores were not scavengers: They were hunters. They did not follow behind the grass inferno or measure its progress from in front.

They caused it.

Even as he and his companions ceased running and slowed to a stop, the true function of the curious "horns" that projected from the center of each of the beasts' foreheads made itself known. They were not horns at all, but hollow structures formed of hardened keratin. From these organic nozzles the slow-moving carnivores expressed streams of liquid that caused the long, dry grass to ignite on contact. Flames erupted between the fleeing travelers and the lake as the line of beasts began to set fire to everything in their path.

And the wind was rising again.

Enclosed by raging wildfire, the only place in the vicinity that promised any safety was the stream. Barely a few feet wide and not as deep, it offered only temporary shelter at best to Ehomba and Simna. Hunkapa Aub and Ahlitah were far too bulky to be able to conceal themselves beneath the rushing waters.

Had they made an immediate charge, they might have succeeded in bursting through the oncoming flames with only minor burns. Already, that option was denied them. Like the grassland behind, the fresh growth ahead was now fully engulfed.

With the flames advancing and the heat rising from the merely uncomfortable to the unbearable, they clustered together. Trapped within his thick, shaggy coat, Hunkapa Aub was suffering terribly and on the verge of passing out. They had to do something quickly.

Head inclined forward, Ehomba was searching the tops of the grasses intently. An agitated Simna watched him, wondering what he was doing when they should be picking a direction in which to make a run for it.

"Bruther, there's nothing there but grass!" Above the roar of the approaching flames he gestured sharply to his left. "I say we try back to the west. The stream should delay the fire for a minute or two!" Instead of responding, the herdsman maintained his intent exploration of the wind-whipped yellow-green blades. "Etjole! We're out of time! What are you looking for?"

His lanky friend replied without looking up from his search. "Tomuwog burrows! They are our only chance."

"*What* burrows?" Sweat streaming down his face and neck to stain his shirt, the swordsman blinked as his companion continued what appeared to be an aimless examination of the grass. Why, he wasn't even directing his attention groundward, where one's gaze would be expected to be focused if he was hunting for some kind of den.

It made no sense. Never mind that Simna had never heard of a tomuwog and had no idea what such a creature might look like. Even if it dug a burrow large enough for a human to crawl into, anything large enough to accommodate Hunkapa Aub or the black litah would have to be a veritable cave, harder to avoid seeing than not. And they had passed no such opening in the earth in the course of their flight. With the constricting blaze crackling all around, he turned a slow circle. There were a few small holes in the ground, the largest of which would prove a tight squeeze for a corpulent mouse. Anyone trying to burrow away from the flames would need not only a physical refuge, but one large enough to sustain a sizable air pocket.

"Bruther, this is crazy!" Spreading his hands wide, he implored his companion. "We have to make a break for it! Otherwise we'll . . ."

Ehomba disappeared. Not instantly, as if he had evaporated in the rising heat or vanished into some sorceral otherwhere, but gradually. It happened right in front of the swordsman's disbelieving eyes. One moment the tall southerner had been standing before him, scanning the tops of the blowing grass. Then he started to go away. First his long spear, prodding and probing. Then the hand and arm holding it, followed by the rest of him, until all had been erased from view.

Simna was not the only one startled by the herdsman's unexpected and inexplicable disappearance. Hunkapa Aub walked all around the area where Ehomba had vanished, and Ahlitah paced the spot sniffing like a huge black dog.

The flames were closing in, narrowing the circle of unburned grass and breathable air. Simna started to cough, choking on the ashes from the carbonizing vegetation and the air that had begun to sear his lungs. Surely Ehomba hadn't abandoned them for some mystical refuge only he could access? The swordsman had to admit that such a development was not beyond the bounds of possibility. How often had Ehomba spoken of the need first and foremost to fulfill his perceived responsibility to the deceased scion of distant Laconda? How many times had he made it clear, to Simna as freely as to total strangers, that the resolution of that journey took precedence over everything else?

A sweating Simna ibn Sind scanned his surroundings. Encircled by leaping flames, with the earth itself seemingly beginning to incinerate around him, he saw nowhere to run, no place to hide. This was not a good place to die, out in open country witnessed only by insects and rodents, his body about to become food for indolent meat-eaters that under normal circumstances he could run circles around. From the time he had been old enough to understand the significance of life and the finality of death he had planned to depart this plane of existence in a blaze of glory that would be immortalized in ballad and song. Now it seemed he was to expire simply in a blaze, as something else's dinner. Where were the cheers, the shouts to admire him as mind and body shriveled and dissolved? The circumstances were ignominious to a fault.

On the verge of passing out from the encroaching heat, Hunkapa Aub had fallen to his knees. Panting like a runaway bellows, the black litah sat back on his haunches, waiting for the end.

Then a hand appeared out of nowhere, beckoning. It

was followed by a familiar face. "Hurry! There is little time."

"We don't need you to tell us that, bruther!" Without stopping to realize that Ehomba was beckoning to him from within a circle of nothingness, Simna stumbled toward the gesturing hand.

It grabbed hold of his own and pulled. Almost immediately, the unbearable heat disappeared. The swordsman found himself standing in a corridor of coolness. Mere feet away now, the fire continued to rage. But he could no longer feel it.

Mouth slightly agape in wonder, he extended tentative fingers toward the blaze. They halted inches from the nearest tongue of flame. Pushing experimentally, he found that there was a slight give to the invisible surface that kept him separated from instant incineration, as if he were pressing against transparent rubber. There was no noise. Whatever was protecting him from the flames also shut out all sound from beyond.

Turning, he reached out in the opposite direction. The corridor in which he was standing was no more than six feet wide, in places a little less. As he stared in amazement, the flames seemed to burn right through to continue their march of fiery destruction on the other side. Within the miraculous passageway everything was a calm, cool blue-green: the soaring but silent flames, the scorched earth they left in their wake, the bodies of small animals too slow to flee, even his own clothing and flesh.

Looking back the way he had come, he saw that Ehomba too had acquired a soft tinting of pastel blue-green. So had Hunkapa Aub, who had followed the swordsman to safety. Reflecting his own coloring, Ahlitah was a dark shade of green. Among them all, Simna was the lightest in color.

Walking back toward his friend, he found that he could begin to feel the heat from the fire again. Pivoting, he discovered that as soon as he took a few steps in the opposite direction, the threatening warmth dissipated. Hunkapa Aub joined him to make more room near Ehomba.

"Where are we?" the swordsman heard himself wondering aloud. He did not expect an explanation from the hulking Hunkapa, much less a reasonable one.

A hairy hand reached out to stroke the resilient, transparent wall. "Somewhere else." It was as sensible an answer as Simna could have hoped to receive.

As soon as the black litah had been brought to safety, Ehomba squeezed past them to take the lead again. Gesturing for them to follow, he led the way through the last of the fire, heading west once again. Behind, the line of pyro predators began to root among the charred rubble for well-done meals.

The blue-green corridor was not straight. It changed direction several times, winding through unburned brush and grass, down gullies, and up over small hills. After an hour of this, Simna was moved to comment.

"It's not for me to question how you saved us, bruther, but we're well away from that range fire and the creatures that keep it going. Why can't we just step back out into the real world?" Behind him, Hunkapa Aub was having to advance bent double. The ceiling of the passageway was not much higher than the corridor was wide.

"You can try," Ehomba informed him without looking back, "but I do not think you will have much luck."

Taking this as a challenge, the swordsman pushed

against the pellucid barrier. Beyond, unburned brush pressed right up against it, and a pair of small yellow and black birds were courting only inches from his questing fingers. Ordinarily, they would have fled in panic, chirping wildly. But they did not seem to see or smell him and did not react to his near presence at all.

He pushed harder, then leaned all his weight against the boundary.

"Here. Let me try." Stepping up beside him, the black litah lifted a paw to expose five-inch-long talons, pointed like knives and sharp as razors. Claw and dig as he might, they made absolutely no impact on the wall. The litah could not even leave scratches. It was the same with the dark blue-green floor underfoot.

Having stood patiently by while his friends satisfied their curiosity, Ehomba now turned and once again headed off westward. A thoughtful, somewhat chastened Simna followed. He was not upset or uneasy: only curious.

It was delightfully cool within the corridor, with even the sun having acquired a blue-green tinge. The surface underfoot was smoother than the ground outside but not slippery: ideal for running. Only the absence of water concerned him. Their water bags were more than half full, but despite the containers he toted on his back, Ahlitah needed to carry drink for Hunkapa Aub as well. That portable source would begin to run out in less than a couple of weeks.

In response to his query, Ehomba assured him that he had no intention of keeping to the corridor for anywhere near that length of time. His sole intention in disappearing into it was to find a means of escape and a temporary refuge from the fire.

"What is this place, bruther?" Within the passageway, voices acquired a deeper cast, reverberant and slightly echoing.

"I told you when I was looking for one." The herdsman angled to his right. "Careful, there is a bend here. We are in a tomuwog burrow."

"Hoy, this is a burrow?" Looking to right and left, Simna could see clearly in every direction. The only difference from what he would have accounted as normal was that everything he saw was tinted varying degrees of blue-green. "By Geletharpa, what is a tomuwog? I've never heard of such a creature, much less seen one."

"You will not see one," Ehomba told him. "Unless you know how to look for them. They are difficult to track, even for the Naumkib. I am considered one of the best trackers in my tribe. There is no reason to hunt them, since they make poor eating. But in times of difficulty, their burrows can provide a place to hide. We were lucky." He started to slow. "Ah, this is what I was looking for. We can rest here awhile."

A baffled Simna slowed his own pace to a walk. Try as he might, he could discern no difference in their surroundings, and said so.

As he took a seat and began to unburden himself of his weapons and pack, Ehomba smiled patiently. "Stretch out your hands. Walk around a little."

The swordsman proceeded to do so. To his surprise, he discovered that they had entered a blue-green chamber some twenty feet in diameter. The ceiling had also expanded, allowing poor Hunkapa Aub to straighten up at last. He stretched gratefully.

Simna found himself drawn to a seven-foot-wide zone

of glistening aquamarine-tinted light. It formed a translucent mound that reached perhaps a fourth of the way to the ceiling. Extending a hand, he found that his fingers passed completely through the phenomenon, as would be expected of something that was composed entirely of colored light.

"What's this? Some distortion in the corridor?"

"Not at all." Taking his ease, Ehomba was unpacking some dried fruit from his pack. "That is a tomuwog nest." When the swordsman drew his hand back sharply, his lanky friend laughed softly. "Do not worry. It is empty. It is the wrong time of the year."

While Hunkapa Aub sighed heavily and stretched out on the floor, trying to work the accumulated cricks and contractions out of his neck and back, the black litah explored the far side of the enclosure. Realizing that he was hungry too, Simna rejoined his friend. Outside, beyond the walls of the enchanted chamber, blue-green antelope were methodically cropping blue-green grass, entirely oblivious to the presence of the four travelers conversing and eating not more than a few feet away.

"These tomuwogs," the swordsman began, "what do they look like?"

"Not much." Ehomba gnawed contentedly on dried pears and apples. "The tomuwog live in the spaces between colors." Mouth half full, he gestured with his food. "That's where we are. In one of the spaces between blue and green."

"Excuse me, bruther? That doesn't make any sense. There is no space between colors." The swordsman's brow furrowed as he struggled with a concept for which he had no reference points. "There's blue, and then there's green. Where and when they meet, they melt together." He made clapping motions with his hands. "There's no 'space' between them."

"Ordinarily there is not," Ehomba readily agreed. "Except where the tomuwog dig their burrows. It is just a tiny space, so small you and I cannot see it. Cats can." He nodded to where the litah was still exploring the far reaches of the chamber, poking his head into bulges and side corridors. "Ask Ahlitah about it sometime."

"But this is not a tiny space we have been running through, and are sitting in now," Simna pointed out.

"Quite true. That is because it has been enlarged by one or more tomuwog to make a burrow." He gestured with his free hand. "As I have already told you, this is one of their nesting chambers. Tomuwog burrows are hard to see and harder to find, as you would expect of something that only occupies the space between colors. I was hunting for one while the fire was closing in around us. As I said, we were lucky to find it." Finishing the pear, he started on a dehydrated peach.

"The walls of their burrows are very tough. They would have to be, or people would stumble into and break through them all the time."

"And we've passed these things before?" Simna made stirring motions in the air with one downward-pointing finger.

"Of course. They are not common, but are widespread. I remember a particularly large burrow from the mountains near Netherbrae, and one in the desert where we encountered the mirage of the houris. And there were a number of others."

"By Guoit, why didn't you ever point one out to me, bruther?"

Ehomba shrugged. "There was no need to. You would not have enjoyed entering them anyway. Most were warm burrows."

The swordsman's expression twisted. "There are different kinds of burrows?"

"Certainly. It depends which colors the tomuwogs are burrowing between. If red and yellow, which are hot colors and seem to be more common, then the burrow will be warm, or even scalding. If the blue is separated by black instead of green, then conditions inside the burrow can be extremely cold." He smiled appreciatively. "Blue-green is best, though it is still a little warm for running. A darker blue, more indigo, would have made for an even more comfortable refuge."

Simna sat shaking his head in amazement and disbelief. "To think that such wonders exist all around us, in every time and place, and want only the knowing of them to be seen and utilized."

"Oh, there is much more, my friend. Much more." The herdsman bit into a large, crunchy piece of preserved apple. "The world is awash in marvels that most men never see. Usually it is because they are too busy, too hurried, to look. Looking takes time. One does not become a good tracker overnight."

Simna nodded slowly. "Or a good hand with a sword. In the learning of that, I bled a lot. It took me many years, many curses, and many cuts before I became proficient."

"As does the accumulation of any worthwhile knowledge," Ehomba agreed.

Tilting and turning his head, Simna took in more of the

remarkable chamber. "The corridor we came through was not large for a person, but pretty big for a burrowing animal. These tomuwogs must be of good size."

"See for yourself." Putting the remainder of his food down slowly and carefully, Ehomba nodded to his right. "Here comes one now."

XIII

Simna paused with food halfway to his mouth. Sensing the approach of the burrow's owner, the black litah growled a warning as it moved off to one side. Eyes shining, Hunkapa Aub put both hands together and murmured delightedly.

"Pretty, pretty."

The adult tomuwog was bigger than any of the travelers, but it was only partially there. A glittering, roughly cylindrical shape, it entered the nesting chamber on noiseless feet of aquamarine light. One moment it stood out in sharp relief, the next it was reduced to a drifting cloud composed of splintered sapphires. With each step, portions of its supple, streamlined body slipped in and out of sight. Half solid, half illusion, it inspected them warily out of eyes that were pale blue mother-of-pearl.

It had a short tail that struck blue-green sparks from the air as it flicked nervously from side to side, and a narrow snout of a face that glittered as if faceted. Huge sparkling pads front and rear resembled flippers more than feet. The edges of these appendages caught the ambient light and bounced it back in clipped, prismatic jolts to the retinas of onlookers. The shimmering claws had to be sharp, Simna reflected, to slice a path between two colors.

Filtered blue-green light danced off the creature's flanks, so bright that from time to time the entranced intruders were forced to turn their faces away from so much brilliance and blink away tears. Simna found himself wondering what a tomuwog that inhabited the space between red and orange might look like, or between purple and red. Certainly they would be no less colorful than the singular slow-moving one before them.

That the tomuwog was aware of their presence there could be no doubt. Twinkling eyes examined each of them in turn. Upset at their presence but apparently convinced they posed no immediate threat, it proceeded to haul itself over to the glittering, glimmering nest and settle itself atop the pile of carefully scavenged color.

Resuming eating, but slowly so as not to startle the placid creature, Simna leaned over to whisper to the herdsman. "Where do they come from, bruther? Eggs?"

"I am not sure." Observing the remarkable beast, Ehomba wore a satisfied smile. "I believe they lay light. This light then matures according to the predominating colors within which it is brought up, and becomes a full-grown tomuwog. As I have said, they are shy creatures and difficult to see. They almost never wander outside their burrows."

A sudden thought caused the swordsman to put down the remainder of his food. "Hoy, what do they eat? Doesn't look like it has any teeth."

"That is a real mystery, Simna." In contrast to his hesitant companion, Ehomba had no trouble finishing his food. "No one has ever seen a tomuwog eating. I would not think there was much to eat between blue and green, but if my elders had not explained it to me I would not have thought there was much space there, either. Perhaps they forage on little bits of wandering moonlight, or the motes we see dancing in a shaft of afternoon sunshine. Since no one knows what they eat *with*, it is understandable that nobody knows what they eat." Seeing the look on his friend's face, he added, "Whatever it is, I do not think that people are a part of its diet."

"Hoy, I certainly don't see any blue-green teeth." Cautiously, the swordsman resumed feeding.

They were soon finished with their meal. When Ehomba decided they had rested long enough, he led his companions out of the chamber. Choosing a corridor that led west, they left the tomuwog sitting serenely on its twinkling nest. It made no move to interfere with their departure. From the time it had arrived until the moment they departed, it had uttered not a sound.

The passageway provided a smooth-floored, controlled-climate means of making progress. As they jogged along, they passed other herds of grazing animals, and flocks of birds large and small. As far as these active inhabitants of the prairie were concerned, the travelers were invisible. And so long as they kept to the tomuwog tunnel, they effectively were.

The extent of the corridor did not surprise Ehomba. Tomuwogs, he explained to his friends, dug very elaborate, very complex systems of burrows that boasted but few entrances. After a number of days, however, he decided it was time to sacrifice concealment and convenience for the world that lay beyond the tunneled realm of blue and green. For one thing, the corridor was devoid of anything except cool air and blue-green light. They would soon need to find food and fresh water.

Simna fingered the transparent, unyielding wall that enclosed them. "So how do we get out, bruther? Cut ourselves a hole?"

"Only a tomuwog can do that, Simna." As they trotted down the corridor, the herdsman was scanning the ceiling. "We must find a natural entrance."

"You said there weren't many."

Ehomba nodded. "That is so. It is why I want to find one before our food or water begins to run any lower." With his spear, he gestured behind them. "I would hate to have to retrace our steps all the way back to the place where the firemakers nearly entrapped us."

Simna grunted his agreement and thought little more of it. But by the evening of the following day he was starting to grow concerned. The thought of starving to death in plain view of rolling fields of edible plants and herds of plentiful game, pinned like an ornamental butterfly between layers of blue and green, was singularly unappealing.

It was therefore with considerable relief, and not a little confusion, that he slowed to a halt behind Ehomba. The herdsman had raised a hand and was staring off to his left. Squinting in the same direction, Simna could see nothing. Or rather, nothing that differed from the rest of their surroundings.

"There is our exit." Though he did not manifest it outwardly, Ehomba was greatly relieved. Entrances and exits to tomuwog burrows were even more scattered than he had led Simna and the others to believe. Knowing that if he appeared worried it would have weighed heavily on them, he had maintained an air of quiet confidence ever since they had left the nesting chamber. He had also eschewed mentioning that tomuwog burrows were subject to a variety of external strains and pressures, and therefore prone to collapse. What would happen to anyone who found him- or herself caught in a tomuwog cave-in he could not imagine, except to be certain it would not be pleasant.

"I don't see anything," Simna murmured.

"There's nothing there." The black litah snorted.

"Exactly." Ehomba started forward, toward something only he could see. Or rather, toward nothing only he could see.

When Simna emerged from the burrow, the return of multihued light together with the sounds and smells of the world outside threatened to overwhelm his senses. Hunkapa Aub took to running about in little circles, grabbing at grasshoppers and beetles, while Ahlitah promptly lay down in the yellowed grass and rolled, immersing himself in the delicious convocation of aromas.

Looking back the way they had come, Simna could see only ground and growth, rock and soil. There was nothing to indicate to his eyes that they had just exited a corridor that tunneled between the color blue and the color green.

"It's really there?" he found himself asking his tall companion.

"Yes, Simna. It is really there."

The swordsman nodded somberly. "Wizardry. I've grown used to your denying it, Etjole, but that doesn't mean I accept it. We both know what you are."

"How can we both know what I am when I do not even know myself what I am?" Ehomba was not smiling. "I am a good tracker, friend Simna. Good at finding things."

"Things that no one else can find, or even suspect exist." Together, they resumed the trek westward. "If that's not sorcery, I don't know what is." Idly, the swordsman plucked a striking blue wildflower. He did not hold on to it for long, though, having had enough blue to last him for a while.

"Not true, Simna." Once again, Ehomba was using his spear as a walking stick. "Many of the Naumkib could have done what I just did." He grinned. "I am just a little better at such things than most of the villagers. I think it is because I am always questioning my surroundings that I have become good at seeing what others overlook." With his free hand he pointed slightly to their right. "For example, standing right there is a Gogloyyik, a fantastic animal with four eyes, purple wings, a tail three times the length of its body, and a head that is a mass of absurd-looking horns."

Following his friend's lead, Simna strained to locate this phantasmagoric creature. All he saw were insects whizzing back and forth above the tops of the grass, and something like a chartreuse bunny that scampered frantically out of sight on all fours.

"I don't see anything, Etjole. Is it only semi-invisible, like the tomuwog?"

"It's right there, right before your eyes, Simna! What's the matter with you?" The herdsman's irritation was palpable.

Simna's forehead was beginning to throb. Breaking away from the others, he jogged off in the direction Ehomba had indicated. Halting at what he thought was an excessive distance from his companions, the swordsman turned a slow circle.

"By Githwhent, bruther—there's nothing here! Where is this . . . ?" He stopped. Hunkapa Aub was chortling softly, his enormous chest heaving with muted laughter. Even the black litah was grinning, insofar as a cat is capable of such an expression. And the herdsman—Etjole Ehomba had a hand over his mouth and was shaking his head slowly as he strode along.

Simna's expression darkened. "Very funny, long bruther. Oh, vastly amusing, yes! Scare the insides out of a man one minute and make him the butt of jokes the next! How clever you are, how witty! How droll." Rejoining the group, he fell in step behind the herdsman, forswearing his company.

Padding up alongside him, Ahlitah was uncharacteristically sympathetic. "I understand, little man. Don't take it to heart. If it's any consolation, I don't agree with what your mentor just did."

Simna eyed the big cat warily. "You don't?"

"No. He can't make you the butt of jokes one minute, because to me you have been and will always be nothing more than a butt." With that the cat sauntered off, choosing to parallel rather than follow the herdsman's lead.

Will I ever figure him out? the swordsman mused as he gazed broodingly at the back of the tall southerner. "If you are a sorcerer, Etjole—and I still hold to that belief as strongly as ever—you will be the first one I ever met that had a sense of humor. Such as it is," he hastened to add.

Still grinning, the herdsman looked back at his friend. "I come from a simple village, friend Simna. You should expect my sense of humor to be simple as well."

"Hoy—that I won't argue." After a while he increased his pace to move back up alongside his companion. There followed an exchange of jokes that caused laughter to ring out across the plain. The guffawing was wholly human. It did not matter whether the jape was told by Ehomba or Simna. Strive as he might, Hunkapa Aub never got it, and the black litah did not want to.

As the resolute propounders of intermittent jocularity strode onward toward the beckoning sunset, accompanied by a hulking and perplexed mass of hair that lumbered after them on legs like hispid tree trunks, and one brooding black cat of striking size and grace, the Gogloyyik lifted its outlandish cranium and watched them go, not overlooking a chance to fenegrate the sookstrum that unexpectedly darted between its legs.

XIV

Peregriff wondered if he dared knock. The south castle aerie was but one of many that his master used for his regular rendezvous with the costly courtesans he imported from the city. Despite the many wild and scurrilous rumors that attended to his master, the chief of staff knew that Hymneth the Possessed was indeed a man, with all the needs and desires that implied. He was, however, glad that it was the job of others to select and escort the often reluctant women into his master's presence. What happened subsequently comprised scenarios he preferred not to speculate upon.

It had been some time since the last such visit to the castle, though. It might well be that the omnipotent ruler of fabled Ehl-Larimar had simply decided to spend the afternoon in solitary, alone with thoughts only he could appreciate and assimilate. That only he would want to, Peregriff mused. Taking a deep breath, he rapped several times on the carved wooden door. A lesser man might have fled. But lesser men did not rise to the position of most valued aide to the Possessed.

At first there was no reply. Having done his duty by knocking, Peregriff was tempted to retire. If he had guessed wrongly and his master was otherwise occupied, persisting could draw the kind of reprimand that would reduce anyone else to a quivering sack of human jelly. His fist hovered before the door, hesitating.

A voice from within bade him enter. Neither irate nor expectant, it offered no clue to its owner's state of mind. Making certain his uniform was straight and correct in every detail, Peregriff lifted the heavy iron latch and pushed the door inward.

No suit of armor could really be called "playful," but the ruler's attire of the day was designed more to impress than intimidate. Dark blue leather banded with chased steel, it consisted of vest and lower skirt beneath which Hymneth wore mail of very fine links. His helmet was likewise fashioned from the finest, smoothest steel, engraved with scenes that were less than usually horrific. The eye slits were long and narrow, while the front of the helmet descended in a straight line from forehead to chin, hiding nose and mouth alike. It gave to the skull the look of a ship preparing to cleave the open waters.

Helmet and point turned away from the window out which they had been staring to face him. "What is it, Peregriff?"

The reverberant, commanding voice was tinged with indifference: a good sign, as far as the general was concerned. Yet still he hesitated to step into the room. Leaning imperceptibly forward, he managed a look to his right. The rack and bench were empty and showed no sign of having been subject to recent employment. As he bowed, he cut his eyes in the other direction. Likewise, the bed was undisturbed.

A pair of small, seemingly innocent dark clouds lolled above the richly embroidered spread. They grew active when he entered, only to become still as they recognized him. They knew that within the castle certain life lights were not for eating, and his was among them. When he straightened, it was with less concern and more confidence. Not that he ever really relaxed. Only fools and the deathly ignorant relaxed in the presence of Hymneth the Possessed, and Peregriff was neither.

"Don't you remember, Lord? This is the morning you wished to review the household guard." Turning slightly, he gestured at the open doorway. "I have come to escort you."

"Ah, yes. My mind was elsewhere, good Peregriff. On other matters."

The general hazarded a guess. "The one whose coming the Worm predicted?"

"Actually, no." Straightening, Hymneth rose to his full, towering height. "I have begun to believe no such person exists. If he did, and had power enough to inconvenience me even remotely, surely he would be here by now. I thought at the time that the Worm's words made no sense, and I've seen or heard nothing since to make me change that opinion."

"Still, Lord, it pays to be cautious."

From behind the burnished steel, unblinking eyes narrowed ever so slightly; the timbre of voice from beneath the helmet's projecting lip grew infinitesimally softer.

"Are you presuming to advise me on this matter, Peregriff?"

The general did not miss a beat in his reply. If there was one fault Hymneth could not tolerate in his senior advisers, it was hesitancy. "No, Lord. It is only my abiding concern for your welfare that impels me to comment on the matter at all."

"Yes, well. Good intentions are always to be applauded." The voice returned to normal, and the slight tremor Peregriff had experienced was not repeated. He had lived and labored too long in the Possessed's service to frighten easily. It is hard to panic a man who has long since resigned himself to the possibility of perishing on the spur of the moment at the whim of another.

"It is not caution that eases my concern, Peregriff." Stepping away from window and wall, the autarchic ruler of Ehl-Larimar approached the doorway. "It is confidence." A mailed hand rose and gestured. The fingers were thicker and blunter than those of any normal individual. "Come, and let us review the troops before they grow bored."

Those servants who were not forewarned of the approach of the Possessed in time to scurry out of the way were compelled to stop whatever they happened to be doing at that moment and prostrate themselves before him. Hymneth considered himself a kind master, full of forbearance, a trait that he felt he displayed on numerous occasions. This morning was no exception.

When two serving maids engaged in animated conversation failed to notice his approach and continued to gab between themselves, the Possessed put a finger to the lower rim of his helmet and commanded Peregriff to silence. Advancing silently, he stole up behind the two before one of them noticed, or felt, a presence. Turning, she saw who it was and let out a heart-rending scream before fainting dead away. Instinctively, her friend caught her, or she too might have swooned with fear.

Hymneth found this vastly amusing. Reaching out and down, he tousled the hair of the unconscious servitor. "Get her some wine," he ordered the other woman. "When she awakes, tell her that I am not displeased. After all, fainting may be accounted a kind of bowing."

"Y-y-yes, Lord." Utterly terrified by her proximity to the looming, guttural figure, the other woman tried to curtsey and support her friend at the same time, with the result that both went down in a heap. This caused Hymneth to burst out laughing, a sound that many of his retainers found more dismaying than his explosive fits of anger.

"It's good when one's people can exalt and amuse you at the same time, eh, Peregriff?"

"Truly, Lord." Debating which expression would be suitable for the moment, the general settled on a slight smile.

There were no further interruptions, mirth-provoking or otherwise, as they descended the rest of the way to the main floor. Exiting the great hall, they emerged into another of the warm, spectacular days for which Ehl-Larimar was famed. Below the mountain to which the fortress clung, the city and harbor and ocean beyond spread out in three directions, a vision of consummate municipal harmony over which Hymneth the Possessed wielded unchallenged dominion.

Drawn up in three parallel lines before the castle entrance was his household guard, a small regiment of cavalry maintained by him and kept separate from the realm's regular army and police. As soon as his tall, overawing figure appeared in the arched portico of the castle's entrance, horns and drums struck up a welcoming tattoo.

With Peregriff hurrying to keep up, Hymneth strode forward to inspect the first line of fighters. Watching his master, the general could not help but feel that he was preoccupied.

Nevertheless, Hymneth moved down the first line of mounted soldiers with his eyes set left and not wandering. Peregriff noted that he scrutinized each and every individual fighter from boot to crested helmet. In any emergency or ultimate showdown, these were the men and women who had sworn to lay down their lives for him. There was no place in the household guard of the Possessed for slackers.

Leather boots pressed firmly into steel stirrups. Backs straight, armor shining, helmet visors up and locked, the men and women of Ehl-Larimar's most elite military force sat at attention in their saddles, eyes front and lances perfectly perpendicular to the ground. Even their mounts, a unique assortment of the finest steeds the country had to offer, remained motionless and poised in the presence of their commander in chief. A few heads bobbed and shook, an occasional leg lifted or twitched. These deviations Hymneth was willing to forgive—in a horse.

He could feel eyes flicking around to follow him as he and Peregriff came to the end of the first line, pivoted, and started down the second. Formal inspection of the ranks was a duty he could have delegated to the general, or even to one of lesser rank, but it had been some time since he had performed the task, and it was beneficial for the troops to see the individual to whom they had pledged their lives. Beneficial, and sometimes instructive.

Would Peregriff have noticed the way certain soldiers looked at him? Would he, sensitive and alert as he was, have remarked on the combination of fear and respect that dominated their expressions as he passed by? Despite their elevated equine seats, Hymneth the Possessed's great height allowed him to regard them almost eye-to-eye. None met his own. That was as it should be, he felt. Let them match stares with their officers, and not with him. A little terror was like soap: all-cleansing while leaving an almost imperceptible film in its wake. A remembrance of who stood above them.

Halfway through the third rank Hymneth stopped, his thoughts distracted. Behind the sloping helmet, penetrating eyes drew slightly together. Mailed hands clasped behind his back, he turned slightly in Peregriff's direction.

"Do you see that?"

The general, who had allowed himself to relax slightly, stiffened. "See what, Lord?"

High above him, the helmeted skull nodded slightly. "Sixth rider from the end."

Peregriff's gaze narrowed. He badly wanted to lie on behalf of the young man thus singled out, but did not for a moment seriously consider doing so. "Yes, Lord. I see it."

"What do you think we should do about it?" Behind Hymneth's back, steel-clad fingers tick-ticked against one another.

"I'm sure my Lord will think of something suitable."

Again the single, singular nod. "I dislike rendering precipitous judgments. Let's give him another minute or so to straighten himself out."

"Yes, Lord." As they resumed the inspection, the general betrayed no outward shift in expression or emotion.

Inside, he found himself praying for the soul of the unfortunate young warrior.

Instead of improving, the soldier's condition continued to worsen. Already trembling badly, his shaking grew worse as Hymneth and Peregriff drew nearer. Halting beside the man's mount, the lord of Ehl-Larimar looked up at him speculatively. Quaking, the man looked down.

And dropped his lance.

Not knowing whether to dismount and recover it, flee, or remain as motionless as he could manage, the terrified soldier stayed where he was. Glancing down, Hymneth contemplated the fallen weapon. The ever-present pair of juvenile eromakadi circled it excitedly, inhaling of the potential darkness it represented.

After a moment or so, Hymneth looked up. "I'm afraid there's not much use in my household guard for a man who is spineless. It's one thing to fear me, something else to completely lose control in my presence." Extending a long arm, he indicated the lance lying in the short grass. "If you drop your weapon during an inspection, what would you do with it during a battle? Fling it aside and run?"

"No, Lord," the man stammered desperately. "I-I was nervous today, that's all. This is only my third full-dress inspection, and the first you have graced with your august presence." Risking all, he looked down and met the gaze of the Possessed. "Please, Lord. I have a wife, and a babe of six months. Give me another chance and I'll serve you well! My life is yours. It was—"

"Yes, yes, it was promised to me when you agreed to become a member of the guard. I know." Hymneth made a sweeping gesture that took in the rest of the mounted troop. Not a head had turned in the direction of the confrontation. The man and woman mounted on either side of the unfortunate one sat rock-steady and unmoving in their saddles, eyes front, backs stiff.

"But how can I rely on someone who shakes so badly he can't even keep control of his primary weapon during an inspection? I could give you another chance, but what if one wasn't enough? What if you needed a third chance, or a fourth?"

"Please, Lord, I beg you to—"

"And what sort of example does that set for your fellows? I don't see any of them asking for second chances when they make mistakes. Could it be that's because they don't make mistakes? Because I can't afford to tolerate mistakes in my household guard." Turning away, he looked back toward the sea that lay downslope and far away.

"You know, there are those in Ehl-Larimar who would give a great deal to see me dead." When Peregriff started to offer the requisite ritual objection, Hymneth waved him off. "No, it's true. For whatever reason, I am not universally loved by my people. I tolerate this because I must. A certain amount of dissension is valuable because it allows the discontented to let off steam, and to preserve the illusion that they enjoy a greater degree of personal freedom than is the case." With a resigned sigh he turned back to his general and to the heavily perspiring soldier.

"But I must strive for perfection in those who serve me, even as I aspire to perfection in myself. Especially among my personal bodyguard there can be no room for hesitation, or incertitude. The irresolute must live with the consequences of their own spinelessness." Having abandoned the fallen lance, the two eromakadi were now darting and dancing about his ankles. Clenching his fingers tightly, he lifted them up to the sweating soldier—and opened them.

Uttering an inarticulate cry, the young man wrenched on the reins of his mount, whirled, and bolted from the ranks.

Rotating slowly perhaps half an inch above Hymneth's open palm was a fist-sized sphere of dark green vapor shot through with black streaks. It was lit from within by a dull, miasmatic light. Miniature clouds roiled across its surface, evolving and vanishing after a few seconds of life. Lips tight, Peregriff held his ground. At Hymneth's feet, the eromakadi bounced and spun in a paroxysm of deviant delight.

With a gesture that reeked of bored indifference, he flicked his wrist in the direction of the deserting soldier. The fleeing fighter was already through the outer gate and racing down the road that led to the city, driving his mount hard with repeated blows of his ceremonial whip of gold braid. Seeing this, Hymneth frowned darkly behind his helmet. One thing he could not abide was unreasoning cruelty to animals—especially those that served him better than his people.

Trailing a long tail of ichorous green mist, the ball of vapor lifted from Hymneth's hand. It soared over the outer wall and down the mountainside. Having no need for road or trail, it made its own.

"Come, Peregriff. Let's finish this."

Together, lord and servant resumed the inspection. None of the assembled soldiers had moved during or subsequent to the unpleasant confrontation, and none of them moved now as Hymneth the Possessed strode past them, hands still busy behind his back. Only two mounted fighters remained to be scrutinized when an agonized, distant shriek wafted over the outer wall from somewhere on the road not far below. It carried with it all the horror of death without dying, of some finely conceived yet transitory torture. It expressed eloquently the shock of sudden realization of an exquisite torment artfully delivered. Pausing before the last soldier in line, Hymneth smiled, his revealed teeth concealed behind the protective steel.

"Good job, soldier." Reaching out, he patted the white-and-black gelding firmly on the side of its neck. The horse reacted with a slight shake of its head, ruffling its mane. At a terse nod from Peregriff, the individual thus singled out felt free to respond.

"Thank you, Lord."

"Think nothing of it. Good work is to be rewarded. Failure is—well, why don't you and this fine young gentleman here next to you ride out and bring back your hapless former associate?" At a gesture from their master, the two riders turned their mounts and galloped off in the direction of the outer gate.

Peregriff was uncertain. "Lord, he is not dead?"

"Of course not. What do you think of me, Peregriff? He had to be punished, and of course he is dismissed from the troop, but I would not kill someone simply because they proved unable to live up to the standards set for the guard. Besides, the man has a wife and infant. Having only the standards of the lower classes to aspire to, they have done nothing wrong. Therefore I will not deprive them of this man's company, however graceless it may be."

Walking back to the front of the troop, he eyed them from beneath his helmet for a long moment. Hands on hips, he addressed them prior to departing.

"You are a credit to your countrymen and to all of Ehl-

Larimar! I am proud to call you members of my personal household, and am confident that should the time ever come that it is necessary to place my life in your hands, then it will be in the finest care available anywhere in the world. I salute you!" Raising one mailed hand, he held it, palm outward, toward them.

Lances rose, the small gold and blue pennants secured just below where blade met shaft dancing in the slight breeze that always blew from the mountain heights down toward the sea. Thus dismissed, they broke ranks and prepared to return to their barracks.

As Hymneth and his general were mounting the steps that led back into the inner castle, trailed by the snuffling, silent eromakadi, the two soldiers who had been dispatched to bring back the deserter returned, leading the man's mount between them. Across the saddle lay an oddly slack body. Its legs and arms were twitching, as was its neck, but it was as if they were no longer connected to one another. The man was beyond screaming now, reduced to a piteous sobbing that shook the spirits of all within and without the castle who happened to overhear it.

Dismounting, the pair of soldiers relieved the other horse of its burden. The man screamed anew when they pulled him off the saddle. He could no longer sit on his horse, or anywhere else. As he could not stand, he had to be carried off by his former comrades in arms. Since he had lost weight they were able to move him without much effort, though they had to be careful of his middle. It sagged flaccidly, chest and stomach sinking toward the ground as if that part of him were melting in the sun.

Hymneth paused long enough to watch the unfortunate being carried out of sight. "I suspected he was spineless when I first set eyes on him. Now he is for sure." Turning away, he led his second in command back into the castle. The inspection had made him hungry.

They ate together. Not in the formal dining room, but out on one of the second-floor terraces that overlooked the city and the sea. If there was anywhere else on earth that could boast of weather as serene and tranquil as that of Ehl-Larimar, Hymneth had not heard of it. Peregriff agreed; it was another fine day.

"You must be pleased, Lord, to know that you are so well protected. It must help you to sleep well at night." Before imbibing, the general considered the white wine in the superb fluted glass set before him, savoring the bouquet while admiring the color.

"The guard is a window dressing, Peregriff. Stalwart men and women in shiny uniforms to awe the people. I have never relied on them to protect me."

The general looked surprised. "But Lord, you said—"

"I said what I did for their benefit. It's hard to motivate those who serve if you tell them that ultimately even the potential sacrifice of their lives means nothing." Enjoying the sun that struck his face through the helmet, he gazed out across his realm, at ease if not content. "Oh, they are fine for making minor arrests and for dealing with undistinguished miscreants like that deserter or ordinary assassins. But anyone or anything powerful enough to seriously threaten me would toss them aside like straw." He sipped at his own drink. "Still, they look fine on parade."

The general considered carefully before commenting. "So you still feel that the Worm's warning was inaccurate, and that those whose coming he predicted will not reach

Ehl-Larimar? Or is it that you do not believe the necromantic powers it spoke of are strong enough to pose a threat?"

"Pose a threat? There is no threat, Peregriff. It doesn't matter if the Worm's prophecy proves to be correct or not." He gestured diffidently. "You may pass the order to the navy to relax their alert. The household guard may stand down, and the instructions that were given to the border patrols to be on the alert for any unusual group of travelers seeking to enter the country are to be withdrawn."

Despite his master's mellow, even exuberant mood, the general was not reassured. "Is that wise, Lord? Maintaining a heightened military status does not require a great deal in the way of additional effort or expenditure. If it will ensure your safety . . ."

Hymneth waved him off. "I'm telling you, Peregriff: It doesn't matter. If these individuals exist, and if they manage to reach and cross the border, and if one of them happens to be a sorcerer of some small skill, it does not matter. Even if they succeed in reaching the castle there is no need for concern." Setting his wine aside and leaning across the small feast that had been provided for the midday meal, he lowered his voice in what the shocked general could only interpret as an intimate manner.

"There is no longer any reason to worry about such matters, Peregriff. Everything is well in hand. More so than you can imagine. Things have changed. Let them come to the castle. I am curious to meet those who would suffer such hardships and travel so far on behalf of the stiff and self-important aristocracy of far Laconda." Sounding as satisfied as the general had ever heard him, the lord of Ehl-Larimar sat back in his chair and did a most remarkable thing: He put his long legs up on the banister and crossed them contentedly. Rising from the porch, the eromakadi hovered above his feet, shading them from the sun.

To Peregriff's way of thinking, only one explanation seemed possible. "You have made some unique preparation in expectation of their possible arrival, Lord. Groundwork that you feel sure will counter anything they can do, no matter how unexpected or powerful."

"Something like that." More than anything, the ruler of Ehl-Larimar sounded amused. Peregriff was at a loss to know how to proceed.

"You want no special measures carried out, no extra guards posted either in the city, here at the fortress, nor even in your private quarters?"

"Peregriff, calm yourself. Should anything untoward occur, and it will not, no blame will accrue to you. I know perfectly well what I am doing. If the augury of the Worm turns out to be true, no harm can befall me. If it turns out to be false, no harm can befall anyone else. I await with anticipation the resolution of this conundrum that has so bedeviled my thoughts for far too long. You will see." He sipped from his glass. "Life will continue not as before, but better than ever. You have my word on it." He extended the chalice.

Automatically, the general picked up his and touched it to that of his master. In the placid light of midday their glasses clinked musically. Even as he swallowed the wood-tinged blood of the grape, Peregriff wondered what it was that he was toasting.

He was overlooking something, he knew. Priding himself as he did on his thorough knowledge of everything that went on both in the castle and in government, the omission was maddening. It was good that Hymneth seemed content, but the general knew all too well how rapidly and radically his master's moods could change. That insight had kept him alive and prospering far beyond the time of uncounted colleagues in the service of the Possessed who had long since fallen by the wayside.

But what could it be? As regularly as Hymneth consorted with the powers of darkness, it might involve some malevolent spell of unimaginable power. Peregriff knew that the baleful green vapor that had crippled the errant soldier was as nothing compared to the malign energies his master could muster if the circumstances demanded it. He had seen him do things in the privacy of his chambers that would have left lesser men huddled mewling on the floor, their eyes fastened to carpet or cold stone, their bodies curled into tight fetal positions.

He dared not probe. If and when the time came, Hymneth would reveal all to him. Peregriff knew the master did not trust him. That was to be expected. One in a position of absolute power could not afford to trust anyone. It was one way in which absolute power was maintained. But the ruler of Ehl-Larimar *would* occasionally confide in him. Their relationship was based on mutual respect for each other's abilities. That, and Peregriff's blood oath to support his master in everything he did.

It had been a good life and, if Hymneth was to be believed, one that the general could look forward to for many years to come. Had not the Possessed, through means of sorcery most profound, given him back the arm he had lost at the battle of Cercropai? He sat a little straighter in his chair. All was well in the kingdom, the nuncupative oozings of the Worm notwithstanding. Hymneth's confidence was reassuring.

Though he had not met and knew nothing of them, Peregriff found himself beginning to feel sorry for the unknown, unenlightened interlopers whose advent the Worm had foretold.

XV

Ehomba halted before the stark yet beautiful panorama. They had been walking for many days without a change of terrain, and it was unreasonable to think that it would not eventually give way to a different landscape. It was just that he had not expected the shift to be so abrupt, or so harsh.

"By Gowancare's jennies." A somber-voiced Simna stood next to him, contemplating the identical vista. "Surely we're not going to have to cross *that?*"

"I am afraid we must." As usual, the herdsman's voice betrayed no tightness, no unusual emotion. Raising an arm, he used the point of his spear to indicate the far horizon. "See those distant peaks? If all we have been told is true, those should be the outermost ramparts of the Curridgian Range. Beyond lies Ehl-Larimar. Once we cross over, we are near the end of my journey."

"First we have to reach them," Simna observed, noting the sun-blasted desolation that lay between. His water bag was full, but already it felt perilously inadequate against his back.

Before them lay a land of weathered promontories devoid of vegetation. Predominantly beige and white, some of the hills were shot through with streaks of carmine and yellow. Where intermittent flash floods had carved more deeply into the eroded sandstone, layers of black and brown were visible. Stunted trees and battered brush huddled together in the deepest gullies, seeking protection from the unrelenting sun.

Beyond the hills and fronting the base of the mountains, the light gleamed brutally off a strip of perfectly flat whiteness. Ehomba recognized it from his deepest forays into the interior of Naumkib country.

"Salt pan," he informed his companions. "There was once a lake at the foot of those peaks, but the water all dried up long, long ago. Now there is nothing, and because of the salt not even a weed can grow there. They are terrible places." From his elevated vantage point on the edge of the grassy plateau he surveyed the land that had to be crossed. "So long as we have enough water, we should be able to cross the salt flat in two nights and a day." He indicated the beckoning, snow-capped peaks. "We should find springs at the base of the mountains."

"Should find." Simna's tone was flat. "And if we don't?"

The tall herdsman looked down at him. "Then we will get very thirsty. We will have to find water somewhere because we will not be able to carry enough to make a return crossing. I do not know what sources might lie between here and the pan. If we can find any it will be a great help."

Behind him, the black litah growled impatiently. "Naked veldt." Padding past the two humans, he started down the loose, scree-laden slope. "We waste water standing here."

As they descended from the ridge, the temperature rose

perceptibly. Beneath their feet, the unstable surface made for poor walking. Except for the sure-footed cat, each of them slipped on more than one occasion. Conscious of the danger, however, no one suffered any injury. Everyone realized it would be an especially bad place to incur a twisted ankle or broken bone.

"This must remind you of home, Etjole." Pebbles sliding and bouncing away from beneath his sandals, Simna picked his way carefully down the slope.

"Not really." Ehomba used his spear to steady himself on the steeper portions of the descent. "It is true that the land of the Naumkib is dry, but there are many rivers that flow through it to the sea, and springs even along the beach that bring fresh water from distant mountains. The hills behind the village receive rain in the winter and heavy sea fog in the summer, so that there is almost always grass to be found somewhere. There are trees in the ravines and washes, and plenty of game." Sweat coursing down his face from the exertion of the descent, he paused and nodded at the terrain that lay before them.

"The country of the Naumkib is dry, but much cooler than here until and unless one travels far to the east. This is land that has been tortured."

They drank their fill and topped off their water bags from springs that bubbled from the base of the ridge. From there until they reached the mountains there was a real chance they would find no more water. The deepest gullies separating the low, rounded, multicolored hills held out the promise of moisture in their depths: The vegetation that grew there was proof enough of that. But it might well lie far below the surface, within reach of ancient roots but not desperate hands. They could not count on supplementing their supplies for many days.

"We'll need to watch what we eat as well," Simna commented as they headed off into the rolling, uneven terrain that lay ahead.

"Dry country often yields a surprising amount of food." Ehomba maintained a steady pace, his face a picture of determination. "Plants that look dead sometimes provide unexpected nourishment, and where there are plants there is at least some game." He nodded to his left. "We are lucky to have with us a game-catcher supreme."

"I can only kill what's there." The litah acknowledged the compliment with a terse grunt.

"Hunkapa hunt too," the hirsute hulk bringing up the rear added plaintively.

"Hoy, I'm sure you're well skilled at sneaking up on small burrowing creatures," Simna commented sarcastically. "No matter. We all need to be sharp of eye and alert of ear 'til we're through this hell, lest we overlook even one opportune meal."

Ehomba's dry-land lore and Ahlitah's hunting prowess notwithstanding, they could not eat what they could not find. In the days that followed, no game of any size showed itself, and the nearest thing they found to a water hole was a damp depression in the sand between two hills. Digging exposed only more sand; moist, but not drinkable.

The herdsman did locate a colony of honey ants. Digging out the bulbous bodies of the storage workers, he showed his companions how to make use of them.

"Hold them up by their heads, like this," he explained as he demonstrated, "and bite off the sugar-water-filled abdomen." This he proceeded to do, flicking the useless head and thorax aside when he was through.

Simna swallowed uncomfortably. But after trying one of the bloated insects, he found the sensation in his mouth surprisingly agreeable. The taste of the taut, thumbnail-sized golden sphere was sweet and refreshing.

It would have taken a dozen such colonies to slake their thirst, but the supplement to their dwindling reserve was welcome, and the sugar gave a boost to their energy and spirits.

Both had waned considerably when Ehomba, following a gully that led slightly northwestward, stepped around a sandstone column and ran into the demon.

Though understandably startled, the unflappable herdsman quickly regained his composure. Bunching up behind him, his companions were less sanguine. For its part, the demon regarded them warily but without fear. After all, there was very little reason for a true demon to dread the living. Protected as they were by all manner of spells and enchantments, there was not much a mortal could inflict on their person in the way of bodily harm.

Realizing this full well, Simna pressed close to his tall friend. Knowing that his own weapons would be useless against such a profoundly base creature, the herdsman's hand did not stray in the direction of his weapon. Swords and knives were no match for the hexes of the underworld. Fortunately, he was traveling in the company of one of the few people he had ever met who possessed the knowledge to ward off evil enchantments. Assuming, of course, that Ehomba had been lying to him all along about not being a wizard.

On the other hand, he decided as he edged out slightly

from behind the herdsman's shadow, the appearance of this particular demon, though its ancestry and origins were never in doubt, was not of a kind to inspire immediate and unremitting terror. Above its slick bald forehead it wore a wide-brimmed hat, battered and notched, with two holes cut out to allow its horns room to protrude. The arrangement had the added benefit of helping to keep the hat on the apparition's head in a high wind. Needless to say, it was not perspiring.

In addition to the dusty hat, the creature wore long pants in the back of which a hole had been cut to allow the curling, pointed tail room to roam. Trouser legs were tucked into calf-high boots. Above the belt the hairy chest was partially covered by a checked vest of many pockets whose contents Simna decided he would prefer to remain in ignorance of. A red bandanna around its neck was decorated with an embroidered pattern of interlocked human figures writhing in torment. On its back it carried a huge pack secured with multiple straps of well-worn leather. Tied to the pack were a pick and two shovels, a shallow, broad-bottomed iron pan, and a tent and bedroll. The bloated, oversized load would have taxed the strength of Hunkapa Aub. Supernatural strength and stamina notwithstanding, it clearly taxed the endurance of the red-faced phantasm.

Herdsman and demon considered one another. Then the profane apparition clasped one clawed, long-fingered hand to its exposed scarlet chest and shivered.

"Sure is cold out today."

"We find it tolerable," Ehomba replied.

"You would." The demon began slapping its arms against its sides. It momentarily tripled their length so that it could also slap at its back and lower legs.

For once, Simna had nothing to say, preferring to let his lanky companion conduct the entire conversation. If he could at that moment have rendered himself wholly invisible, he would gladly have done so. While the physical appearance of the demon was no more abhorrent than that of certain bureaucrats the swordsman had known, its face was a mask of pure horror, a promise of all the torments and suffering the netherworld was heir to. One joked with such a hideous specter at the risk of one's life and limb.

Yet while his companions remained anxiously in the background, Ehomba took a step forward and calmly extended a hand. "We are strangers in this blasted country, and could do with some information."

"Information you want, is it?" Grinning to reveal a maw packed with jumbled, broken, sharp-pointed teeth, the bare-armed fiend accepted the proffered fingers, shaking but leaving them attached to Ehomba's hand. "I'll help if I can. I have to say, your ignorance does you proud. Like now, for instance." The clawed hand suddenly tightened around Ehomba's.

Instantly, steam began to rise from the virulent grip. Simna started to shout a warning that was already too late, then caught his breath. As the herdsman continued to sustain the handshake, the slitted yellow eyes of the demon began to widen. Eventually it released its hold.

To the amazement of fiend and friends alike, Ehomba's palm showed no evidence of damage from the searing handclasp. He smiled slightly. "It is also hot in my homeland. My skin is toughened from season after season of moving rocks that have lain in the sun for many years."

The demon nodded understandingly. Turning to one side, it spat out a soggy blob of brimstone. The impious spittle sizzled where it struck the sand. The chaw that bulged one of the creature's cheeks must have been composed of solid sulfur.

"I'd heard that some mortals could handle heat better than others. You must be one of them. What brings you to the Tortured Lands?"

Ehomba nodded in the direction of the demon's enormous pack. "I might ask you the same question."

"Fair enough." The back of a scaly red arm wiped thick, blubbery red lips. "I'm a prospector, plying my trade. It is by nature a solitary business, only rarely rewarding, but it suits me."

This was something Simna ibn Sind felt he could relate to. Stepping out from behind Ehomba, he essayed his most comradely smile. "What is it you're prospecting for out in this desolation? Gold, I would imagine. Or silver, or another of the precious metals? Gems, perhaps, or the rare ingredients for arcane powders and potions?"

The horned skull shook slowly from side to side. "I am digging for lost souls." Once again extending an elastic arm farther than was natural, the demon fumbled at its pack. "Exhumations have been meager these past few weeks, but there's a little color in the pouch. Care to have a look?" From a small, tightly fastened, intricately inscribed leather bag there arose a faltering chorus of moans.

"That's all right." Making motions of demurral, the momentarily confident swordsman once more hastily took refuge alongside his lean companion.

With a shrug, the demon retracted his arm. "I understand. There's really not much to look at. Fair size, decent opacity. Impure, of course, or they wouldn't be here."

Perking up, he smiled horribly. "I've been following traces for some time, hoping to hit a vein."

Not mine, Simna hoped feelingly. Despite the veneer of civility that overlay the ongoing exchange of pleasantries, he could not escape the feeling that if Etjole Ehomba were not standing between him and the eager phantasm, he and the others would already be staked out on the searing sand with their body cavities ripped open and their entrails exposed to the sun. Why this should be he could not have said. The herdsman had evinced no special protection, had thrown up no obvious defenses. But Simna was certain their continued salvation was due solely to the herdsman's presence among them. In this he believed as firmly as he believed in his own existence. Perhaps more so.

It was plain to see that even as they conversed amiably, the demon was sizing them up and paying particular attention to Ehomba. Either there was something about the herdsman's soul that rendered it unattractive, or else it was shielded by means and methods beyond the ken of a wandering swordsman. Whatever it was, Simna was exceedingly grateful for its existence, because it appeared to be protecting not only its owner, but his friends as well.

"I'm Hoarowb." The creature did not extend its hand again. "What do you want with the Blasted Lands? You don't look like soul miners to me."

"We are not," Ehomba admitted quietly as he leaned slightly on his spear for support.

"That's good. I don't much care for competition in my territory. Rich pockets of lost souls are few and far between, and it's the smart fiend who keeps their location a secret."

"Our business does not lie in this country." Raising his

spear, the herdsman pointed to the distant, glistening crags of the Curridgians. "We travel through to the mountains, and beyond."

Sniffing like a pig snuffling for offal, the demon extended its head forward in the direction of the spearpoint. "Interesting poker you've got there. Positively rank with dead millennia." Again the hideous grin. "I don't suppose you'd consider trading for it? I have a couple of really quality souls, prime stuff. Fetch a good price on the nethermarket."

"Thank you, no." Ehomba smiled to show that he was not offended by the offer. "I need all my weapons, and I already have a soul."

The demon spat a gooey glob of yellowish brimstone to one side. It struck an ankle-high clump of green weed bursting with tiny purple flowers and promptly set it ablaze. "Everyone can use a spare soul or two. Comes in handy at the moment of Determination. But never mind. I can sense that you're not the trading type." Peering around the herdsman, the demonic countenance focused on Simna.

"You, on the other hand, smell like someone I could do business with."

"Maybe another time." The swordsman ventured a wan smile. "My soul's all tied up just now." He pointed to his companion. "With him."

"Pity." Straightening, the demon smiled affably at Ehomba. "I could split your sternum, tear out your heart, and leave you to bleed to death here in the sand." He shuddered slightly. "But I can tell that you'd spoil it all by resisting, and anyway it's too cold out this morning for sport. I've a ways to go before I dig a hole and make camp."

"Since you are not going to kill us," the herdsman replied good-naturedly, "could you tell us how far it is to the nearest water hole?"

"Water hole?" The demon eyed him in disbelief, then burst out roaring. It was laughter wild and withering enough to scald bare skin. Indeed, unprotected by fur or learning, Ehomba had to turn away from it to keep himself from being scorched.

"There's no water holes in this country. Hot springs, yes, and boiling mud pots, and steaming alkali lakes a being can take a proper bath in—but water holes?" One crimson, clawed finger elongated enough to reach up and over the specter's skull, pointing to the northwest.

"Only one place you might find running water, and that's Skawpane. They got everything in Skawpane. Another month or so and I'll be due for a visit there myself, depending on how well the prospecting goes." From the vicinity of the occulted leather bag, small screams bereft of all hope seeped futilely. Simna ibn Sind shuddered. The chill he felt had nothing whatsoever to do with the temperature, perceived or otherwise.

"What is this Skawpane?" Ehomba asked.

The demon sniggered at some private joke. "Only decent place in the Blasted Lands. There's other flyspecks claim to be, but Skawpane's the only real town." Oculi that reflected righteously hellish origins stared into the herdsman's. "Go there if you dare. If you seek water that's unboiled and nonpoisonous, that's the only place you might find it. I guarantee you one thing." It nodded knowingly.

255

"You and your familiars will be a novelty. Don't get many mortals in Skawpane."

With that, the apparition tipped its hat politely, set it neatly back over the protruding horns, and ambled off down a side gully. In its wake the stink of masticated sulfur and burning brimstone corrupted the air, and bootprints fused the sand where they had trod into dungy glass.

Smiling pallidly, Simna was quick to offer a suggestion. "If we ration our remaining water carefully, we might well make it to the base of the mountains."

Ehomba considered. "That is what I wanted to believe. But I think now that I was allowing my common sense to be swept aside by optimism and hope. Hunkapa Aub in particular needs a lot of water." He sighed. "We must make our way to this Skawpane and refill our water bags there."

The swordsman was reluctant to concede the point. "How about we just let our common sense be swept, and hope that we find a spring as soon as we strike the foothills?"

Ehomba pursed his lips disapprovingly. "You are more afraid of what we may encounter in this town than you are of dying of thirst?"

Simna jerked a thumb toward the gully where the prospecting demon had disappeared. "If that thing was representative of the general citizenry of this particular metropolis, then my answer is yes."

It did not matter. He was outvoted. Having followed Etjole Ehomba this far, neither Hunkapa Aub nor the black litah was about to dispute his judgment. That was because both of them were dumb animals, Simna knew, though he was loath to point it out. Grumbling, he hoisted his pack and water bags and followed along.

Maybe he was worrying needlessly, he told himself. Maybe the demon had been having a little fun at their expense. Skawpane might prove to be a quaint, if isolated, little oasis of a community, its dusty streets shaded by palm trees, its inhabitants serene and content with their lot. Believing this, wanting to believe it, he marched along beside his tall companion with a renewed feeling of confidence. Even if he was wrong and his hopes were to prove unrealized, how bad could it be? A town was a town, with all the familiar urban baggage that implied.

When they finally reached the municipal outskirts, he saw that he was only partially correct. Skawpane was a community, all right.

But it was no oasis.

XVI

Do we have to go in there?" Simna stood atop the smooth-surfaced, rounded boulder of yellow-white sandstone look-ing across the flat, hardscrabble plain that separated the travelers from the first outlying structures.

Ehomba did not squint as he contemplated their immi-nent destination. He was used to the sun. "Unless you want to chance running out of water before we reach the mountains. I have seen men who tried to reach the coast of Naumkib from the interior but ran out of water before they found a stream or village. Even those who had not yet been located by scavengers were unpleasant to look upon."

"A fine choice," the swordsman grumbled. Resigned, he started down the gentle slope. "Hoy, maybe they'll have cold beer."

After a last, speculative glance, Ehomba followed and caught up to him. "Do you really believe that?"

"No," Simna confessed, "but here lately I find that I prefer refreshing delusions to the reality of our actual sur-roundings."

Skawpane turned out to be less appalling from a distance. From the disgusting state of the dirt streets that ran with dull green putrescence to the sewer grates designed to carry off flash floods of mucus, the act of merely walking quickly degenerated into a detestable activity. No edifice rose to a height of more than three stories, perhaps because of the lack of suitable building materials. Storefronts were fashioned of skin tanned to woody toughness by the repeated application of hot blood and salt water. The origin of these skins was a question the travelers by mutual unspoken consent decided not to ask.

Sidewalks rose a foot or more above the abominable streets. Instead of wooden slats, their planks were fashioned of split bones with the rounded side facing downward. Larger bones such as scapulae had been made into gleaming white shutters that flanked windows of thinly stretched corneas. Occasionally a poorly fashioned pane would blink desperately, reflecting its organic origin.

There were tall, narrow chimneys made of interlocking vertebrae, though what a home or shop would need with a chimney and fireplace in such a hellish climate Ehomba could not imagine. Troughs of liquid sulfur stood outside several of the establishments. Standing patiently at their hitching rails and nuzzling the noxious, toxic brew they contained were a diversity of infernal steeds. The herdsman saw desiccated horses whose pointed ribs protruded from their sides and whose lower incisors pierced their upper jaws like the tusks of bastard babirusas. All had prominent, protuberant eyes that shone with the madness that resided within.

Nor were they the only mounts secured or occasionally spiked to the railings. One storefront they passed had a pair of enormous, hirsute hogs roped to a trough at which they rooted ferociously. When these glanced up to espy the travelers, they strove hard to break their bonds. In so doing they exposed mouthfuls of long, sharp teeth that seemed to belong to some other animal. The saddles fastened to their backs were small and narrow, with disproportionately high pommels. What their riders looked like the visitors could only imagine.

Across the street three elephantine orange-green slugs lay melting in the sun. Their glutinous bodies renewed themselves as they liquefied and they emitted an odor so foul that it rose above all the other myriad stinks that afflicted the noisome concourse. In place of saddles they wore simple handgrips that were buried deep within the slimy flesh itself. Once more, their riders were thankfully conspicuous by their absence.

That did not mean that the streets were devoid of denizens. While Skawpane would never pass for a bustling metropolis, neither was it a ghost town—though ghosts shared the streets and fronting establishments with the rest of their fellow citizens. In addition to reddish demons who might have been related to the prospector they had encountered out in the layered hills, there were demonic folk of every stripe and color. Some were dressed in styles that would have been considered shocking in cities as far apart as Lybondai or Askaskos, but which in their current surroundings seemed perfectly appropriate. Others were content with plainer attire.

The population was a mélange of all that was disturbing and horrific, a veritable melting pot of the diabolical. Besides demons and ghosts there were less familiar phantasms, from towering, spindly brown creatures with bulging pop eyes to winged horrors boasting circular mouths that covered their entire black faces. The crows that haunted the tops of buildings and pecked at offal in the streets had membranous wings like bats, and sickly toothed beaks that looked fragile enough to crumble at a touch. A flower-crowned, tentacled horror lazing in a rocking chair made of human bones tracked their progress down this boulevard of horrors with organs that were not eyes. Next to where its feet would have been if it had had feet, a dog-sized lump of multilegged one-eyed phlegm lifted its rostrum and sniveled threateningly.

Wherever they went and whatever they passed, they attracted attention. Exactly as the prospector had predicted, the arrival of mortals in town was cause for comment. When a tubby yellow blob whose midsection was lined with gaping multiple mouths came bumbling off the sidewalk toward them with self-evident mayhem on whatever it possessed for a mind and both Ehomba and Simna drew swords and proceeded to cut it to pieces, none of the fiendish onlookers voiced a warning or raised an objection. In fact, several evinced what appeared to be evidence of macabre amusement. A few interested horrors that had been considering participating in the anticipated butchery changed their minds at this exhibition of formidable resistance on the part of the visiting quartet.

"I need to stop and clean myself." Repeatedly licking one forepaw, the black litah applied it to his eyes and snout. "I don't think I've ever felt so filthy."

"It is not the street here that makes one feel unclean." Striding along, the always curious Ehomba tried to identify the composition of the slimed, slaglike substance beneath his sandals. "It is the atmosphere."

"Hunkapa no like," declared the hairy mass that lumbered along in his wake.

"We agree on something." Holding his sword like a long gray flag of warning, Simna put all the confidence and cockiness he could muster into his stride. At the first sign of weakness here, he suspected, the four of them would go down beneath a horde of horrors, torn apart for a midday snack—and that was if they were lucky. It was vital to maintain an appearance of invincibility.

In this Ehomba was of no help. Ever since they had entered the town, the soft-voiced herdsman had altered nothing. His expression, his posture, the loose, casual manner in which he held his spear: all were unchanged. Whether this seeming indifference was perceived by the ghastly inhabitants of Skawpane as an invitation to feast or supreme confidence in powers they could not descry remained to be seen.

At least they were not immune to the effects of a well-honed blade, skillfully wielded, the swordsman reflected. He gripped his sword a little tighter.

"Hoy, bruther, where's the water you promised us?"

"Promised?" Ehomba glanced down at his friend. "If you would put food in my mouth with as much ease as you do words, I would never grow hungry again." Simna might think him detached, but his cool dark eyes missed nothing. "We need to ask someone."

"Don't you mean some*thing?*" The swordsman skipped agilely to one side as a crow soaring past overhead relieved itself. The dark red dropping sizzled where it struck the moist, mephitic street.

"I wonder why someone—or some*thing*—chose to put a town here, in the worst place imaginable?" Ehomba mused as they walked on. The buildings were moving slightly apart as the street widened. They were coming to some kind of central square or plaza.

Simna's retort was tense and edgy. "Maybe it's a summer resort, where the residents can come to escape the heat of their customary surroundings. Who knows what monstrosities like these consider attractive in the way of climate or countryside?"

"For one thing, we like it beautifully barren and destitute, visitor. To most of us this is splendid country."

Thus hailed, they halted. The figure that had spoken had paused in its stroll down the osseous promenade. It was a lizard, but while both Ehomba and Simna were familiar with the four-legged reptiles from their respective travels and homelands, neither man had ever encountered a lizard like the one they confronted now.

Standing on its severely bowed hind legs, the reptile was a good three feet tall. It wore a military-style cap, maroon vest with gold stripes, long, tattered brown pants, and no shoes. Stretching another three feet behind it, a brown-and-green tail whipped nervously back and forth as it spoke. Completing the unexpected costume were a pair of pince-nez glasses that rode comfortably halfway down its snout.

Inclining its head slightly downward so it could peer out over these at the visitors, the lizard tut-tutted softly. "I declare, you lot are the most peculiar collection I've seen in some time. If you don't like it here, I suggest you move on."

"That is exactly what we are planning to do," Ehomba responded politely. "Just as soon as we are able to top off our water supply."

"So it's water you want, is it? In Skawpane." The head bobbed rapidly up and down. "Interesting. We don't get many calls for water here. Sulfur now, or antimony, or cinnabar; those the general store stocks in bulk. But water—your options are mighty restricted." Slitted eyes blinked as they stared up the street. "So's your time."

"Why?" In the face of danger, it was typical for Simna's tone to turn belligerent. "Don't the locals like company? Who are you, anyway?"

"I'm the town monitor. As for my fellow citizens, they're an intemperate lot at best. Never know how the individual members of such a mixed bunch are likely to react in any given situation. There's folks here who'd like to talk to you, some who might invite you in for a game of cards or bowls, but most would probably prefer just to tear you limb from limb."

"Hungry?" Hunkapa Aub asked.

The lizard nodded. "Or just surly. Or wanting the exercise. Even established locals have to watch their step. The fiends among us are no respecters of residency. Skawpane's a popular place among the damned and doomed."

"Which are you?" Hunkapa inquired innocently.

"The downtrodden. In fact, things have been so bad hereabouts lately that I'm thinking of taking off for open country. You get tired of looking over your shoulder every minute. Trying to make a living in the midst of unrelenting demoniac anarchy takes a toll on one's health."

Holding firmly to his spear, Ehomba watched as a pair of blue demons with four legs and long, warty snouts crossed the street in front of them. They were trailed by three magnificently ugly but well-dressed miniature versions of themselves. Much to their parents' satisfaction, the young demons fought continuously among themselves. Darting in and among the impish offspring was a small, yapping bundle of thorns that had feet but no legs. Or head.

"You said that our options were restricted. That implies that options exist. What are ours?"

"For obtaining water?" The lizard turned, claws clattering on the bone sidewalk, and pointed. "The central plaza lies just ahead, on the other side of the memorial municipal ceremonial slaughterhouse. In the middle of the plaza is the town fountain. That's where you'll find your water."

"And no one will object to us filling our bags?"

The reptile shrugged. "Your very presence here is an insult to all that is profane and unredeemed. Mortals don't belong in Skawpane. Frankly, I'm surprised you're still alive. I would've thought by now that some enterprising perversion would have killed you, skinned you, and hung you out to cure in the sun. Or done so without killing you." Cold reptilian eyes regarded them speculatively. "As I said, you're an odd lot. You might get your water. Of course, after that you still have to make it safely out of town." A scaly thumb gestured.

"Remember: on past the slaughterhouse, middle of the central plaza. And good luck."

With that it resumed its stroll along the sidewalk and had not gone more than a couple of yards before something long, leprous, and scarlet shot out from within a shaded storefront to wrap snakelike several times around its middle. Hissing violently, the lizard was drawn back into the depths of the aperture. From within arose the sounds of violent and desperate conflict.

The travelers did not linger to witness the outcome. Ehomba led them onward, away from the noise of fighting.

Not only was it the safe thing to do, it was the accepted reaction. None of the other locals out walking the streets paid the slightest attention to the shrouded life-and-death struggle taking place nearby. They went about their business as if nothing untoward were taking place—which for Skawpane was perfectly true.

Simna placed his feet carefully, doing his best to avoid stepping on the pale white maggots that infested the street slime and snapped hungrily at his ankles. They could not catch him, but there were certain places on the public avenue where it would clearly be unwise to loiter. Though everywhere awash in corruption and decay, some spots were perceptibly worse than others.

"Hoy, I've seen too many tentacles since joining your company, Etjole." The swordsman nodded back the way they had come. "That one was particularly long and vicious. Reminded me of our encounter with the Kraken, but at least in this case there was only one of them."

Ehomba kept his gaze alert as he unblinkingly scrutinized shadows and side passages. "Yes, but that was no tentacle, Simna. It was a tongue. And the storefront from which it emerged was not a place of business at all, but a mouth most carefully disguised. Little here is what it seems, and visitors such as ourselves can be sure of one thing only: the omnipresence of death."

"Hoy—thanks for that explanation, bruther. I feel so much better now." Behind them, the black litah paused repeatedly to flick slime from its paws.

"I am only pointing out what is true," Ehomba countered.

"Sometimes it's better to keep what's true to yourself."

The swordsman nodded forward. "Looks like more of the friendly citizenry has come out to greet us."

From the ominous, looming double door that sealed the end of the slaughterhouse, more than a dozen of Skawpane's diverse inhabitants had emerged. They formed a line across the volcanic paving stones that marked the outskirts of the town plaza, blocking the only visible access to the center.

From their attire and accoutrements Ehomba decided that all or most of them must work in that dismal, odiferous structure. Several wore long aprons encrusted with revolting dark stains. Their expressions were frightful, their posture dire. It was clear that they had no intention of stepping aside to let the travelers pass.

Several stood more than ten feet tall and boasted multiple arms or boneless limbs. Others had three eyes, or no eyes at all. One of the creatures most nearly resembled the many-branched cacti that grew in isolated thickets back of the Naumkib's grazing lands. Toxic pus oozed from each quill, and the drool that ran in a steady trickle from a central orifice dissolved whatever it came in contact with.

All were armed. Not with weapons, but with the tools of their horrific, evil-smelling trade. Much in evidence were oversized skinning knives: long punctuation marks of metal, sharper than razors and blotchy with dried blood. The largest among the coterie of inhuman butchers fingered meat cleavers the size of small doors, weighty with malevolence. Standing in line, blocking progress, they watched the approach of the diverse quartet of advancing mortals. While most sported no expression at all (and indeed, some had nothing to express with), a few wore macabre grins that were crescent moons of pure evil.

Simna casually raised his sword. "Maybe we should go around; try entering the square from another part of town?"

"What makes you think these wicked corruptions of all that lives and breathes would not be waiting for us there as well?" Keeping his voice down, Ehomba slipped his spear into its sling on his back. "Besides, I have a strong feeling that if we were to turn our backs on any of the inhabitants of this place, they would take that as a sign of unqualified weakness and fall upon us in a body. From the moment we entered into the boundaries of Skawpane I sensed that sooner or later we would have to defend, and prove, ourselves." Reaching back over his shoulder, he drew forth the sword of etched sky metal. As always, it emitted an imperceptible hiss when drawn from its scabbard. "It seems it is to be sooner."

One of the biggest of the brutish butchers laughed hollowly at the sight of the two bright, slim weapons. Its impure tittering resonated through the soles of the travelers' feet.

"Puny mortal weapons will not serve here, little meat. We're going to carve you up, dress you down, and pick our teeth with your bones!"

Something that looked like it had been run over twenty times by a wagon laden with building stone weaved slowly back and forth on powerful, if unsteady, feet. It had one oversized, bloodshot eye and a second that seemed to float around the lower portion of its face like an iniquitous afterthought.

"Use your jugular for a straw and suck your blood. Nice 'n' salty."

"Eyes," declared something else that had no name, nor want of one. "I claim the eyes."

"Not all eight!" The cleaver-wielding hulk swaying next to it objected strenuously. "Half are mine." It raised the immense blade.

Holding his sword at the ready, with a tensed Hunkapa Aub guarding his left side, Simna ibn Sind brayed defiance. "Come on then, you piss-poor pack of putrescence! You motherless self-fornicators! We'll see who's skilled with a blade here, and who's ripe for butchering! I'm thirsty, and I mean to drink my fill at your town fountain. And if that means going through you instead of around, then by Gucoron, have at it!" He nodded to his right, where a tall figure stood silently holding a larger sword before him.

"This here is Etjole Ehomba, the most powerful wizard on either side of the Semordria Ocean! Press him, and he'll blow out your eyes and pickle your entrails!" He gestured with one hand. "Come on then, you long-winded flock of featherless foulness!"

"A wizard." One of the other butchers cackled. "Mortal magic doesn't work here, little meat. The atmosphere is all wrong. Too dry, or too hot, or too disrespectful. Skawpane is rife with impudence and contempt for anything that seeps in from the world outside. Your magic, if you command any, which by the looks of you I seriously doubt, will not save you here." Saclike, malignant eyes bored into those of the swordsman. "You're going to *die* here, little meat. But you won't be food for worms, because we leave no scraps for our pets."

"Had a pet once," mumbled the thing with one over-sized eyeball and one too small, "but it made too much

269

noise one day. So I ate it. It was greasy." Rubbery lips smacked. "I like grease."

With a roar that would have chilled the blood of less hardened pilgrims, two of the largest abominations lurched forward. Simna ducked a slice from a skinning knife that was easily big enough to decapitate a buffalo in a single swipe. Charging forward, Hunkapa Aub struck the creature beneath two of its four arms and knocked it off its feet. Ahlitah was an ebony blur, slashing and snapping anything that came near. Several of the rapacious monstrosities tried to surround the big cat, but it was much too quick for them.

Like a runaway guillotine, a gigantic meat cleaver descended in Ehomba's direction, aiming squarely for the herdsman's head. Bringing the sky-metal sword up and around, he parried the blow. Sparks flew as metal struck metal with a reverberant ring that echoed back and forth across the street. The attention of his own assailants momentarily diverted by Hunkapa Aub, Simna saw the two blades make contact—and his heart sank.

A chunk the size of a small plate had been taken out of the side of the sky-metal blade.

He wanted to shout at his friend, to hear an explanation for what had just happened. Sorcerer supreme Ehomba might be, or simple herder of cattle and sheep as he claimed, but there was no disputing the power of the singular sword. Simna had seen it in action too many times to doubt its alchemical provenance. Whatever happened to its owner, it was impossible for the weapon to fail. Impossible!

Yet, a second blow from the raging demon's cleaver took another piece out of the blade. Many more impacts like that and Ehomba would be left without anything to fight with. Somehow Simna knew that the herdsman's other weapon of choice would not save them here. The efficacy of the sea-bone sword this far from the ocean would be much in doubt. Butchers from the netherworld would probably greet the sharks the blade's teeth would bring forth as another welcome source of meat, be it solid or numinous.

As for the herdsman's spear, that was a last hope held in reserve, but the swordsman remembered his tall friend saying on more than one occasion that its startling effects were of brief duration, and therefore could not be counted upon for more than momentary salvation. As he looked on, the herdsman parried still another weighty swing. A third section of sword shattered violently.

The blighted butchers pressed their assault. Hunkapa was holding his own, and the black litah doing real damage. In a fair fight the visitors might well have prevailed. But they were outnumbered, and by creatures for whom Death itself was an old friend. Their assailants had relentless confidence and no fear.

Simna had to admire the way Ehomba fought on, stolid and expressionless, swinging his failing blade with steadfast determination as if nothing were wrong. By himself he was holding off the three biggest of their assailants, whose heavy cleavers were taking a terrible toll on the herdsman's weapon. The stocky mercenary was about to shout the suggestion that Ehomba throw away his deteriorating weapon and try the magic of the spear, when a glint out of the corner of his eye momentarily diverted his attention.

It was one of the many splinters the frenzied demons had struck from the surface of the sky-metal sword. The tiny bit of metal was glowing brightly, emitting a vaporous fragment of the deep azure light that Simna had seen the whole sword give off when justly held in both Ehomba's long-fingered hands. As he stared, still vigorously defending himself but keeping an eye on the splinter, it rose from the slimed street, shining more brightly than ever. Beneath his disbelieving gaze it expanded until it was more than a foot long and pulsing with an intense blue light. He had seen that same fierce, cold, cobalt effulgence before—at moments that had preceded deliverance.

Something else put a claim on his attention. Three more of the shattered splinters were rising from the ground, elongating and glowing. Off to his left rose still another half dozen, burning with an angry, internal, azure radiance. Ahlitah gave ground as a handful of metal shavings beneath his feet lifted to luminous attention, and Hunkapa Aub paused in his exertions to stare mesmerized at the shards that were rising from the ooze beneath his very feet.

Everywhere splinters and fragments from the sky-metal sword had landed it was the same. Every flake and chip, no matter how small, no matter how seemingly insignificant, was rapidly regenerating itself as a smaller version of the matriarchal sword. At the sight the diabolic butchers slowed but did not halt their attack.

Then Ehomba took a step back from the conflict. Holding the sword hilt tightly in both hands, he raised the remnants of the primary blade over his head. In concert, a thousand smaller versions of the original weapon rose skyward and hung, glowing, parallel to the ground. The field of battle before the demonic slaughterhouse was engulfed in lambent blue.

When next the herdsman swung the peerless weapon aggressively, a thousand lustrous offspring mimicked the blow to glistening metallic perfection.

XVII

A cerulean wind moaned as the thousand blades struck at the loathsome assailants. When the demon-butchers attempted to rally and strike back, Ehomba dipped his sword and their blows were met by a thousand unyielding parries. At that moment more than the tide of battle turned: The dark heart, the evil essence of the enemy, evaporated like a palmful of water on the scorched approach to Skawpane.

Not that they ran. Flight was not in their nature. They fought on, continuing their efforts to slaughter the handful of obstreperous mortals. All that had changed was that one of their human opponents now wielded a thousand blades where moments ago there had been only one.

Come to think of it, everything had changed.

So elated by this unexpected turn of events was Simna ibn Sind that he forgot to taunt his lanky companion about his supposed lack of sorceral skills. The swordsman was too busy thrusting and hacking as he threw himself at their adversaries. One on one, he was convinced that nothing lived, of this Earth or anywhere else, that could stand against him. Part of this was due to actual skill, part to confidence, and part to pure bluster. Stirred together in the anima of the stocky swordsman, they made him a dangerously unpredictable opponent.

Bellowing defiance, Hunkapa Aub was breaking limbs and heaving opponents into nearby walls with unbridled gusto, his great strength and boundless energy giving even the most formidable of the fiends pause. The black litah was a dark streak of feline dynamism; blurred destruction. Fang and claw left their multiple marks on many assailants, who searched in vain for a tormentor who had already moved off to attack someone else.

A monstrous cleaver descended, only to have its path blocked by a hundred blades. Many splintered under the impact, but many did not. Bringing his weapon up and around, Ehomba visited a hundred deep cuts on his assailant. The towering brute gasped and clutched at its flank, unable to stop the flow of green blood from its side. And each of the metallic splinters from the dozens of smaller swords it had shattered arose afresh to give birth to a hundred new sharp points and edges.

Amputated arms and tentacles lay twitching in the street, some still futilely clutching their weapons. Green blood ran in rivers into animate sewers that sucked greedily at the flow. Blinded and crippled, sliced into smaller and smaller pieces, confronting a hostile and terrible magic where traditionally there should have been none, the would-be butchers fell back. Those that were still capable of movement retreated into the depths of the slaughterhouse and the unmentionable horrors that hung curing within. Others limped or crawled or dragged themselves into side alleys and away from the theater of battle.

They found neither safety nor surcease there, and certainly no compassion, the latter being an emotion as alien to Skawpane as love or understanding. From their places of concealment in dark byways and dank vents, fanged orifices and greedy claws shivered forth to drag the wounded away. Drifting faintly back to the main street, the sounds of this muted slaughter were dreadful in the extreme.

Only two of the foul crew of expectant butchers that had originally confronted the travelers were still capable of rapid movement. Without a word, they gave up at the same time, throwing their weapons and butchering tools aside as they hobbled for the safety of the slaughterhouse, slamming the great doors shut behind them and sealing themselves tightly inside.

Face alight with blood-lust, Simna was all for pursuing and finishing them off. Ehomba first restrained, then calmed, his friend.

"It is enough. I do not think they will trouble us for the duration of our stay in Skawpane."

"Gierot well right they won't!" Breathing hard, the swordsman employed his weapon to make several obscene gestures in the direction of the shut-up slaughterhouse. "What say you, shit-spawn? Not bad work for a few scraps of 'little meat,' hoy?"

Nearby, Hunkapa Aub was picking curiously through a pile of severed limbs, holding each one up for closer inspection, then tossing it aside as he moved on to the next. Ahlitah was sitting on the highest chunk of volcanic paving stone he had been able to find, one that was moderately free of slime, and was cleaning himself, licking his forepaws and using them to glean green gore, varicolored guts, and bits of torn flesh from his jaws and feet.

As Simna relaxed and his levels of excitement, energy,

275

and adrenaline began to decline, he and his companions were treated to another piece of sorcery that, if asked, Etjole Ehomba would insist he had nothing to do with. Using a slightly different two-handed grip to hold the damaged sword out in front of him, the herdsman held himself steady and watched blue effulgence expand. Soon the chipped and scored blade was throbbing and vibrating like a live thing. The effort Ehomba was expending to hold it in place showed in the whitened knuckles of his fingers and the strained lines of his face.

Gradually, and then more swiftly, in ones and twos and small groups, the thousand-plus miniature swords that the conflict had given birth to returned to their metal of origin. Streaks of drifting, razor-edged silver-gray and blue bolted in the herdsman's direction, the combined rush of their mass returning generating a small blue typhoon that roared and howled above Ehomba's clenched hands. Steel swirled giddily about the parent blade. The etched span of sky metal drank them down, soaking up each and every sibling sword in an orgy of resplendent sapphire metalogenesis.

Then the last was gone; vanished, redigested and amalgamated by the original length of star steel. The cerulean glow faded, the complaining roar of displaced air fell to a whisper, and the sky-metal sword was once again whole.

Without a word of comment, its owner slid it back into its empty sheath. As was usually the case, Ehomba's expression could not be read, but it was clear that the effort had cost him. Perspiration poured in small vertical rivers down his face and body, staining his shirt and kilt and running off down his legs and between his toes. If he was not breathing as hard as Simna, he was certainly fatigued.

"I need something to eat," he informed his companions, "and a place to rest."

"Not rest here." As he delivered himself of the obvious, Hunkapa Aub kicked aside a mutilated, multimouthed length of tentacle as thick around as his thigh.

"No." Tired as he was, Ehomba was in complete agreement with his hirsute crony. "We will find a suitable place once we are well away from this blasphemous community." Straightening to his considerable, full height, he gestured ahead. "But first we will have the water that we have fought so hard to gain."

Eyes and photoreceptors that were not eyes and organs that did not even require the presence of light in order to see watched from the shadows as the four vanquishing mortals strode purposefully past the locked-down slaughterhouse and the remaining few buildings that barred them from the central square. Now and then, Simna ibn Sind would raise his sword and take a step sideways as if to confront one of the hidden watchers. In response, the concealed eyes always retreated—albeit some with greater reluctance than others.

When they finally reached the plaza that lay at Skawpane's heart, it was with a feeling of mutual relief. The unlucky lizard had not played them false: The fountain was there, exactly as it had told them it would be. Fenced off by blocks of volcanic scree, it bubbled and foamed to a height of more than fifteen feet. From all appearances, it was a natural spring. Fed from below, it could not be turned off. Hundreds of gallons of fresh water spouted into the sky, spilling down into cracks that carried it away, and all of it theirs for the taking. Except that it was perfectly useless to them.

Because Skawpane's fountain was a geyser.

It made sense, Ehomba mused. What more fitting as the centerpiece for a hellish town like this than a permanent font of boiling water? It was so hot that they could not get near it. Hunkapa Aub and the black litah had to keep well clear lest the sizzling droplets singe their bare feet and paws. Much of the water turned to steam before it could fall back to Earth. Even if they could figure out a way to approach close enough to catch the searing liquid, there was no way they could transport it: The heat would destroy their water bags.

As he considered the predicament, Ehomba felt a hand tapping urgently on his shoulder. Turning, he saw what Simna was pointing at.

Emboldened by the travelers' indecisiveness, a diverse collection of Skawpane's denizens began to emerge from their burrows, pits, sewers, and hiding places. Things with great glowing eyes and pincers in place of hands came crawling slowly toward the fountain. Tentacles writhed, and legs with joints in all the wrong places staggered stiffly out of dark recesses in the surrounding structures. They were not as well armed as the inhabitants of the slaughterhouse had been, but this time there were many more of them. It was as if the entire mephitic town had decided to creep forth to teach the interlopers a lesson.

Teeth clenched, Simna gripped his sword tightly. "Time for another fight, bruther. By Gowoar, there's a lot of them! I hope they don't realize how tired I am. Swinging a sword is heavy work."

"We are all tired," the herdsman observed. "Perhaps we will not have to fight."

"Not for this cursed 'water.' Useful for boiling a chicken or two, but we can't take it with us."

"Maybe we can." Ehomba was ignoring the swarming, slithering, advancing rabble to concentrate on the geyser. It hissed and sputtered angrily as it spewed from the earth. In his right hand he still held the sky-metal sword. Now he raised and aimed it—not at the salivating, noisome creatures that were humping their way toward him and his friends, but toward the geyser. This time the blue glow that emanated from the wondrous blade was so deep as to be almost purple.

"Hoy, long bruther," Simna exhorted him, "the enemy's over this way." Though fatigued, Hunkapa Aub and Ahlitah had lined up on either side of him.

Ehomba continued to point the radiant sword at the geyser. "Otjihanja told me that the sky metal can command more than the wind that rushes between worlds, and do more than send small ghosts of itself into battle. It also holds deep within its core the essence of the place where it was born."

Simna kept an uneasy eye on the advancing horrors. "So you're telling me it can spawn the heat of the fire in which it was forged? Somehow I don't think the ability to command heat is going to do us much good in Skawpane."

"Not where it was forged," the herdsman corrected his friend. "Where it was born."

Something leaped from the point of the sword to the geyser. A streak of impossibly dark blue, a flash of muted silver—Simna was looking the other way when it happened. There was a loud, violent cracking sound, like stone being shattered, only far more highly pitched.

One and all, the frightful denizens of Skawpane halted

their advance. They stared out of eyes that bulged and eyes that were slitted, out of compound eyes and simple eyes that could detect only movement. They halted—and then turned and began to flee.

Simna gaped in disbelief. Then he began to whirl his sword above his head as he charged after them, yelling imprecations and insults. Less inclined to resume the slaughter, his companions heaved a joint sigh of relief and remained where they were. The black litah was more tired than he would have liked to admit, and Hunkapa Aub's oversized hairy feet hurt.

Having satisfied his desire for verbal if not corporeal retaliation, Simna turned and trotted back to rejoin his friends. As he did so he caught sight of what had frightened off their potential attackers, and found himself shivering as he approached. Many remarkable spectacles had been sighted in old Skawpane, the great majority of them horrific in nature. But never before had its infernal residents witnessed anything like this.

Ice. Calling forth the temperature in which it had been birthed, the sky-metal sword had turned the geyser instantly to ice.

The gleaming crystalline pillar radiated a cold that, even at a distance, raised bumps on Ehomba's skin. Carefully, he sheathed the extraordinary blade, feeling the lingering cold of it against his back through both his shirt and the heavy leather scabbard. Simna and the black litah kept their distance, but Hunkapa Aub, so far from his beloved mountains, all but embraced it.

The herdsman was quick to intercept him. "Do not touch it, my friend. I know you welcome the cold, but you have never experienced a cold like this. You may stand close, but make no contact, or your skin will freeze tight to it." Listening, the shaggy face nodded understandingly, but even Ehomba's warning could not mitigate the man-beast's delight. He had been uncomfortably warm for a long, long time.

As cold continued to spill in vaporous waves from the sides of the frozen obelisk, it drove the hideous heat-loving inhabitants of Skawpane ever deeper into their holes and hiding places, leaving the travelers with the run of the central plaza and allowing them to relax a little. Already, the unrelenting torridity of the Blasted Lands was beginning to affect the newly forged frigid monolith. Beneath the baleful, remorseless glare of the sun, it started to melt. Immediately, water bags were unlimbered and their spouts carefully positioned to catch the rapidly increasing drip, drip. Ehomba allowed Ahlitah to lap from his bag.

"How is it?"

A thick, fleshy black tongue emerged to lick upper and lower jaws and snout. The big cat did not quite sigh with pleasure. "It is cold and wet and deliriously delicious, man." Fierce yellow eyes regarded the weeping shaft longingly. "Are you sure it's not safe to lick?"

"Not unless you want your tongue frozen to the column," Ehomba warned him. "Be patient. It looks as if the cold is keeping away the horrid inhabitants of this dreadful town." He glanced up. Cold, fresh, mineral-rich water was pouring from the pillar's summit as the sun began to reduce it with a vengeance. What ran off onto the ground formed small puddles that evaporated before they could grow very large.

"Soon we will have more water than we can carry. Then we must make haste to leave before these detestable creatures have either their hot spring or their courage restored to them." As the litah lowered its head, Ehomba impulsively reached out to tousle the thick black mane.

"I understand what you are feeling. I could use a bath myself." Turning together, man and feline gazed longingly at the streams of cool water that cascaded off the frozen geyser, only to vanish as steam or disappear into cracks in the ground. The waste was painful to observe.

When the last of the water bags had been replenished to overflowing, they took turns drinking their fill. The liquid that was streaming down the icy monolith was already starting to grow warm. Soon the relentless, abiding pressure from below would overwhelm the temporary cold the sword had drawn down from the sky, and the frozen column would once more become a boiling, frothing tower of scalding liquid.

But the abominable inhabitants of Skawpane did not know that. They continued to huddle in their cavities and hiding places, away from the visitors and the terrible cold that had taken possession of the very center of their community. Frustrated and helpless to interfere, they watched as the quartet of edible travelers took their time repacking their gear before heading out of town. Not east, as would have been expected, but westward into country so barren and bleak even the lowliest of the town's denizens shunned it. To the west lay country where not even a renegade beetle could survive. Truly, these mysterious visitors commanded vast powers.

Or else, the more cynical among Skawpane's citizens mused, they were controlled by idiocy on a cosmic scale.

*   *   *

Shouldering his pack, grateful for the weight of cool water against his spine, Simna glanced often back the way they had come as they left the last of Skawpane's twisted, warped buildings and equally skewed inhabitants behind.

"What do you think, bruther? When they get over their fear of your chilling little demonstration, will they come after us?"

Ehomba turned to have a look. Already the ominous outlines of the town were receding, swallowed up by intervening boulders and cliffs. Soon it would recede permanently into memory and nightmare.

"I doubt it, Simna. Many who sprang from the slaughterhouse to beset us died. Those who merely suffered a touch of cold are probably counting themselves fortunate. Behind all those oozing fangs and sharp-edged suckers there must lie intelligence of a sort."

"Hoy," the swordsman agreed, "and they can probably imagine what you'd do to them if they tried to give chase." He clapped his rangy friend on the back.

"I do not know that I would, or could, do anything." The herdsman protested mildly. "Really, if any of them came after us I think I would have to try and run away. I am very tired, my friend. You cannot imagine how these exertions drain me. To use the swords or the gifts in my backpack is difficult. I am not trained in the ways of the necromantic arts as are old Likulu or Maumuno Kaudom."

"I know, I know." Hearing only what he wanted to hear, the swordsman grinned broadly. "You're just a rank amateur, a babe in the brush, a hopeless simpleton when it comes to matters of magic. So you've told me all along. Well, fine. Let it be that way, since you continue to insist

283

it is so. I am satisfied with the consequences of your actions, if not the feeble explanations you offer for them."

Ehomba took umbrage as much at his companion's tone as his words. "I did not say that I was any of those things."

Despite the heat, Simna was enjoying himself. "But you still insist you are no sorcerer."

The herdsman drew himself up. "I am Naumkib. So I am neither a 'hopeless simpleton' nor a 'babe in the brush.'"

"Okay, okay." Simna chuckled softly. "Peace on you, bruther. You know, I wouldn't taunt you so much if you didn't take everything I said so literally."

The herdsman's gaze rose to fix on the high peaks of the Curridgian Range. They were markedly closer now. On the other side, he knew, lay Ehl-Larimar and the opportunity, at last, to fulfill his obligation. Those snowy crests held the promise of home.

Home, he thought. How much had Daki and Nelecha grown? Would they remember him as their father, or only as a distant, shimmering figure from their past? Many months had passed since he had made his farewells and set off northward up the coast. He fingered the cord from which had hung the carved figurine of old Fhastal, smiling to himself at the memory of her cackling laugh and coarse but encouraging comments.

He could turn for home even now, he mused. Forget this folly of abducted visionesses and possessed warlocks, of suspicious aristocrats and moribund noblemen. Put aside what, after all, were only words exchanged on a beach in a moment of compassion, and return to his beloved village and family.

Break a promise given to a dying man.

Lengthening his stride, Ehomba inhaled deeply. Other

men might do such a thing, but he could not conceive of it. To do so would be to deny himself, to abjure what made him Naumkib. Even if his companions decided today, or tomorrow, or before the gates of this Hymneth's house, to turn about and return to their own homes, he knew that he would go on. Because he had to. Because it was all bound up inside him with what he was. Because he had given his word.

Mirhanja had understood. She hadn't liked it, but she had understood. That was understandable. She was Naumkib. He wondered if the children did, or if they even missed their father.

Immediately behind lay hesitant horror. Immediately ahead lay—nothing. The ground was as flat as a bad argument, white with splotches of brown and pale red. Scorching heat caused distant objects to waver and ripple like the surface of a pond. Compared to the terrain that stretched out before them, the rocky gulches and boulder-strewn slopes they had crossed to reach Skawpane were a vision of rain-forest paradise.

Nothing broke the bleached, sterile surface in front of them: not a weed, not a bush, not a blade of errant grass. There was only flat, granular whiteness.

It was a dry lake, he was confident. A salt pan where nothing could live. There would be no game, no seeds or berries to gather, no moist and flavorful mushrooms crouched invitingly beneath shading logs. And most important of all, no water. At present they were well supplied, loaded down with the precious liquid. But the hulking Hunkapa Aub and the massive black litah needed far more water each day than any human. Despite their renewed supplies, he knew he would be able to relax only when they were safely across the blasted flats and in the foothills where springs or small streams might be found.

As for food, unless the mountains that towered skyward on the other side of the dry lake bed were closer than they appeared, both he and his companions could look forward in the coming days to dropping a considerable amount of weight. Hopefully, he reflected, that was all they would have to sacrifice.

XVIII

W hat an awful place!" His stride measurably reduced, Simna ibn Sind struggled to keep pace with his long-legged companion. Nearby, the black litah padded silently onward, head drooping low, long black tongue lolling over the left side of its lower jaw like a piece of overlooked meat.

"Hunkapa not like." Though the big hulk was suffering visibly beneath his thick coat of silver-gray hair, he plodded along determinedly, his head hung down and his arms almost dragging the ground.

Ehomba was in better shape than any of them, but took no credit for it. He was used to spending long days standing out in the merciless sun, watching over the village herds. Now he squinted at the sky. They had awakened early from the day-sleep and had been marching for more than two hours westward into the advancing evening.

"Take heart. The sun will be down soon." He nodded toward the mountains. They loomed massively before the weary travelers, but the foothills still lay more than a day's hike distant. Or rather, a night's. To avoid the worst of the heat, they had opted to sleep during the day and trek after dark. "It will grow cooler, and walking will become easier."

"Hoy, you mean it will become less hot." The swordsman wiped perspiration from his brow and neck. "Not in any way, shape, or form does the word 'cool' apply to this place."

In the course of their travels they had encountered many strange life-forms surviving in equally strange environments. From the blizzard-cocooned crests of mountains to the high dunes of the desert, from swamps shallow and deep to the vast open reaches of the Semordria itself, there had always been life, be it nothing more than a limpet or a leaf. Until now, until this tormented, perfectly flat plain of desiccated salts. There was not even, a panting Ahlitah pointed out, a warm worm to tickle a cat's taste buds.

With the onset of evening the heat fell, but not as fast as the sun. Even after dark, parching temperatures persisted. Mentally, walking was easier without the brilliant bright bloodshot eye of the sun staring you ruthlessly in the face. Physically, it was only a little less difficult.

Their meals, such as they were, had been necessarily skewed by their topsy-turvy schedule. Supper became breakfast, lunch a midnight snack, and breakfast, supper. Not that it mattered. Their stores were limited in quantity and consequently offered little in the way of variety. What one ate was often the same, meal after meal. Such victuals kept them alive, but their bellies were not entertained.

At least the moon was on their side, Ehomba reflected as they trudged along. Nearly full, bright as stibnite crystals and almost as hard of aspect, it allowed them to stride forth with some idea not only of where they were going, but also of what lay in their immediate path. By its providential brightness obviating the need for torches, it allowed them to advance with a modicum of comfort.

By midnight the air had cooled sufficiently to raise their spirits. Water was still in plentiful supply. In light of the other hardships they were enduring, Ehomba had not had the heart to propose rationing. When he finally did venture to broach the subject, he was shouted down by all three of his companions. They might not have much else, but at least they could drink their fill. Furthermore, the more they drank, the less weight they had to carry. And as Ahlitah pointed out, he was confident he would be able to smell water as soon as they reached the mountains. It might not seem like much, but even the herdsman had to admit that a long, cool drink compensated for much of what they did not have.

Resuming the march rejuvenated and refreshed but acutely conscious of the ominous presence of the sun lurking just over the eastern horizon, they entered an area of the salt pan that was not flat. Merged as it was with its identically tinted surroundings, it was not surprising they had missed seeing it from a distance. Though equally devoid of food or water, it at least gave them something new to look at and comment upon.

Towers of salt rose around them, not numerous enough to impede their progress but sufficient to alter it from time to time. Worn by the wind and the occasional infrequent storm, they had been weathered into a fantastic array of shapes. Amusing themselves by assigning names to the formations, the travelers competed to see who could identify the most outrageous or exceptional.

Pointing sharply to a column of whitened, translucent halite that had been undercut by the wind, Hunkapa Aub conveyed childlike excitement in his voice. "See that, see there! An ape bowing to us, acknowledging our passage."

Simna cast a critical eye on the structure. "Looks more like a pile of rubbish to me."

"No, no!" Moving close and nearly knocking the swordsman down in the process, Hunkapa jabbed a thick, hirsute finger in the column's direction. "It an ape. See— the eye is there, those are the hands, down at the bottom are the—"

"Ask it if it can show us a shortcut out of here," Simna grunted. Nodding to his left, he singled out a ridge of distorted, eroded salt crystals. "Now that looks like something. The jade wall of the Grand Norin's palace, complete with open gates and war turrets." He gestured with a hand. "If you squint a little you can even see the floating gardens that front the palace over by . . ."

But Hunkapa Aub was not listening. Elated by one discovery of the imagination after another, he was prancing from the nearest formation to the next, gleefully assigning a name to each and every one as proudly as if his fanciful appellations were destined to appear on some future gilded traveler's map of the territory. Ehomba looked on tolerantly. Of them all, their hulking companion was suffering the most from the heat. Simna obviously thought the brute was making a fool of himself, but Ehomba knew that no one is a fool who can find humor in desolation.

He found himself playing the naming game. It was irresistible, the first harmless diversion they had enjoyed in many days. Not only was it gently amusing, especially when made-up names for the same formation were compared side by side, but it helped greatly to pass an otherwise disagreeable time. He and Simna wordlessly agreed to compete to find the most suitable cognomen for certain structures. The game was left to them in any case, since the black litah found it repetitive and Hunkapa Aub was quite lost, happily adrift on a sea of a thousand multitudinous namings of his own.

"That column there," the swordsman was saying, "see how it sparkles and dances in the moonlight?" He singled out a formation spotted with many small crystals of gypsum. "I once knew a dancer like that. She would glue pearls and precious gems all over herself. Then when at the end of her dance she removed the last of her veils it was revealed that the jewels were glued not to the fabric of her costume but to her naked skin, and that all along they had only been glistening through the sheer material she had been wearing." He turned to his companion. "What does it look like to you?"

"I would not think of disputing such a deeply felt description." The herdsman stepped over a series of inch-high rills that ran across the surface in a straight line. Deposited eons ago by water action, they looked fragile, but were in fact hard as rock and sharp enough to slice open a man's flesh where it lay exposed between the protective straps of his sandals.

"Over there I see a fisherman's hut by the ocean," he declared. "Not the ocean below my village, but another ocean."

"How can you see a difference?" Simna squinted in the indicated direction.

"Because this sea is calm. It is rarely calm beneath my village. There are always waves, even on clear, windless days. And no Naumkib would build a fishing hut so close to the water. Too much effort for too little reward, as the first storm would wash it away."

"I see the sea," the swordsman admitted, "and the hut, but what makes it a fishing hut?"

Ehomba pointed. "Those long blades of crystal salt there near the bottom. Those are the fisherman's poles, set aside while he rests within."

"I could use a rest myself, and something to eat that isn't dried and preserved." The swordsman turned slightly in the direction of the formation and wandered away for a moment before rejoining the others on their chosen course. In response to the herdsman's slightly stern, questioning look, he shrugged diffidently. "Hoy, I know it's made of salt—but it doesn't hurt to dream for a few seconds."

"That's a sentiment I'll confess to sharing." Ahlitah had come up behind them. As usual, so silent was his approach that even the reactive Ehomba was unaware of his presence until he spoke. With his head, the big cat nodded leftward. "For example, over that way I can see a large herd of saiga standing one behind the other, fat and plump and slow of foot, just waiting to be run down and disemboweled."

Peering in the indicated direction, Ehomba had to admit that the resemblance of the broken ridge of salt to a column of plodding antelope was remarkable.

Evidently Simna was of like mind. "Sure looks real. Like they could take off in all directions if somebody made a loud noise."

"You're already making a loud noise." Crouching low and making himself nearly invisible even in the bright moonlight, the big cat had begun to stalk the wind-sculpted ridge. Realistic they might be, but the salt formations did not move. Ehomba was about to say something when the swordsman put a constraining hand on his arm.

"Leave him alone. All cats need to play. Don't you think he's earned a few moments of amusement?"

"Yes, of course. But he is being so serious about it." Uncertainly, Ehomba watched as Ahlitah continued to stalk the weathered parapet of halite crystals.

Simna shrugged it off. "I've never seen a cat that wasn't serious about its play. He'll catch up to us when he's through. Remember, he can cover a mile in the time it would take either one of us to run to that big ridge over there." He pointed. "See it? The one that looks like the entrance to a castle?"

Reluctantly, the herdsman allowed his attention to be diverted. Something did not feel right. Maybe, he thought, it was him. The heat was beginning to melt their thoughts. Behind them, the litah dropped even closer to the ground, maintaining its hunting posture as it stalked the salt. Try as he would, Ehomba could not see the harm in it.

Ahead and slightly to their right rose a massive hill of achromatic salts that had been eroded by the wind into a fantastic assortment of spires and steeples, turrets and minarets. The gleaming citadel boasted an arched entrance and dark recesses in the salt fortifications that during the day would not have commanded a second glance but which at night passed easily for windows. A breeze sprang up, advancing unimpeded across the dry lake bed. Whipping around the extravagant towers that had been precipitated ages ago out of a viscid solution of sodium chloride and other minerals, it imparted a carnival air to the formation, whistling and trilling through the hollows that had been worn in the salt. At a distance it almost sounded like people laughing and joking.

"Hoy, Etjole," the swordsman prompted him. "Come on now, don't let me win without a fight. I say it looks like a castle. What would you call it?" As they walked past, salt crystals crunching under their sandals, he studied the pale ramparts admiringly.

"I cannot argue with you this time, Simna. A castle or fortress of some kind. I could not imagine calling it anything else, because that is exactly what it looks like."

"Then we are agreed." Turning to his right, the swordsman started toward the silent formation. "Come on, bruther. Don't you want to see what it looks like up close?"

"I am certain it looks the same at close range, except that individual crystals of salt will begin to stand out."

Shaking his head, the swordsman continued toward the looming structure. "All this traveling in my company still hasn't made you a more jolly companion. Go on, pass up the chance to study up close a fascinating phenomenon you'll never see again."

As always, Ehomba's tone was unchanged, but his thoughts were churning fretfully. "Let me guess: You'll catch up to me in a few minutes."

"Depend on it, bruther." Turning away, Simna continued blithely toward the salt castle, moonlight reflecting off the hilt of the sword he wore against his back.

In front of Ehomba, nothing moved on the lake bed. No pennants of gleaming salt waved in the clear, stark light. No white-faced figures emerged from the weathered hill to greet him. Except for the barely perceptible breeze, all was silent, and still.

Frowning, he pivoted to look back the way they had

come. It was with considerable relief that he saw the reassuring oversized shape of Hunkapa Aub standing and waiting patiently not more than a few yards behind him.

"Come on, Hunkapa. If these two want to amuse themselves with silly nighttime fancies, they will have to hurry to catch up with us." The massive, hirsute figure did not stir. Ehomba raised his voice slightly. "Hunkapa Aub? Come with me. There is no reason for us to wait here until these two finish their games."

When the hulking shape still did not move, a puzzled Ehomba walked back toward him, retracing his steps across the lake bed. He knew he was retracing his steps because he could see where his feet had sunk a quarter inch or more into the bleached, caked surface. He was on the verge of reaching out to grab his ungainly companion's shaggy wrist when something made him pause.

Despite Ehomba's proximity, Hunkapa Aub had yet to acknowledge the herdsman's presence. No, the tall southerner decided: It was worse than that. Hunkapa Aub was ignoring him completely, treating him as if he wasn't there. Now Ehomba did reach out to take his massive companion's hand. He pulled, none too gently. He might as well have been tugging on a tree growing from the side of a mountain. Hunkapa Aub did not budge, nor did he react in any way. Instead, he continued to stare straight ahead.

Turning uneasily to seek the source of the brute's fascination, Ehomba found his gaze settling on a tall, heavily eroded pillar of salt.

A pillar of salt that looked exactly like Hunkapa Aub.

The resemblance was more than a fortuitous coincidence, went deeper than something that looked vaguely like a shaggy head attached to a cumbersome body and

295

limbs. The degree of detail was frightening, from the flattened nose to the wide, deep-set eyes. Edging closer, the herdsman found himself staring intently into hollow pits of fractured salt crystal. Should they shift, however slightly, to look back at him, he was afraid that he might cry out.

They did not. The image was composed wholly and unequivocally of salt; immobile, inanimate, and dead. Nothing more. But how then to explain the startling likeness? Not to mention Ahlitah's herd of sculpted prey and Simna's inviting castle. Reaching out, he took Hunkapa Aub's left wrist in both his hands and prepared to pull again, this time with all his strength. He did not. There was something odd about his hulking friend's hair. Usually it was soft and pliant, so much so that Simna often teased its wearer about its feminine feel. Now, suddenly, it felt granular and gritty. Releasing his grip, Ehomba put two fingers to his mouth and touched them cautiously with his tongue. The taste was all too familiar.

Salt.

Whirling, he raced back the way they had come. He found the black litah with his teeth sunk deeply into the side of a mound of slightly reddish salt. The big cat's burning yellow eyes were still open, still alert, but dimmed. As if slightly glazed over. With salt.

"Ahlitah, wake up, come out of it!" He pulled hard on one of the cat's front legs, then on its tail, all to no avail. Equally as heavy as Hunkapa Aub, the black litah was just as difficult to move. Stepping back, the herdsman saw to his horror that the sleek ebony flank was already beginning to show a crust of rapidly congealing halite crystals.

Uncertain what to do, he turned a slow circle. This part of the lake bed was a maze of mounds and pillars, knolls and motifs, configurations and oddly organic shapes. If he burrowed into some of the more recognizable forms, what might he find concealed in their brackish depths? How many of the formations were natural—and how many molded on unlucky travelers both human and otherwise who had preceded him and his companions to this occulted corner of reality? Did he dare dig within? High above, the blanched moon shone down and proffered no explanation.

His mouth set in a grim, determined line, he swung his backpack around in front of him and fumbled inside until he found the vial he was looking for. Little of the inordinately pungent liquid within remained. Hopefully, it would be enough. Since Ahlitah was the first and most seriously affected, Ehomba determined to try to emancipate the big cat first. But as he prepared to remove the stopper from the bottle, something off to his right caught his eye. He stared, then found himself staring harder, but it would not go away. Three pillars, streaked with brown and less so with red. One tall and two short, gazing back at him out of hollow, glistening eye sockets. Three pillars of accumulated, weathered, freshly precipitated mineral salts. Together, they formed a family of salt.

His family.

There was no mistaking the identify of the tallest figure. It was Mirhanja, complete to the smallest detail, her ashen arms extended pleadingly in his direction. He took an instinctive, automatic step toward her. Preparing to take another, he forced himself to halt. His right leg, his whole body trembled. A battle was taking place within, a war between himself as he was and himself as what he knew. It was a conflict that, if lost, would find him once more in the bosom of his family. Embraced by the ones he loved most in the entire world—and encased in patient, precipitating, all-embracing salt.

He would join his companions and their hapless predecessors not in crossing the surrounding sickly, bloodless terrain, but in becoming a part of it.

Always dispute what is happening around you, his father had told him. Never, ever, stop questioning everything and anything, even that which you perceive to be indisputably and undeniably real, for reality can play all manner of unpleasant tricks on the cocksure. Ehomba had grown up skeptical and politely suspicious of the world around him. As he was now.

Think! he screamed at himself. What has happened here? What *is* happening here? Ahlitah saw a herd of prey animals, and the salt became prey animals. Hunkapa Aub saw himself reflected in the salt, and the salt became his reflection. You see your family, the thing *you* most want to see.

But Simna ibn Sind had walked off toward a salt castle. Other travelers and animals could have wandered into this ghastly place and become embalmed by the salt, creating so many of the strange and now ominous formations surrounding him. But a castle couldn't just pick up and move. Therefore what they were seeing was being drawn, had to be drawn, from the hidden places of their own minds. Simna might dream a castle full of willing concubines, but he would want to take possession of the castle first. So the salt had, by inimical magicks unknown and unimaginable, risen up from the lake bed, precipitated out, and formed itself into a small castle for him to inspect. If he entered it fully, Ehomba sensed, his friend would never come out.

Reaching down to scratch an itch, his fingers came away with tiny white grains beneath the nails. Employing every ounce of energy and every iota of determination he could muster, he wrenched himself away from the heart-rendingly realistic figures of his family. As he did so, a cracking sounded beneath his sandals as he broke free of the encrusting salt that had already begun to crawl up his legs. He was free again, but for how long? And what of the fate of his friends?

No! he shouted silently. He had not brought them this far to lose them now, so near to their goal. Realizing that the nearly empty bottle of oris musk would not be enough to shatter the saline illusions the accursed landscape had precipitated around his friends, he fumbled anew with the contents of the backpack. But what could he possibly use? There was nothing, nothing he knew of that was stronger or had a more powerful effect on the living than oris musk.

No, he thought as he stopped digging through the jumble at the bottom of the pack. That wasn't true. There was something more powerful. Furthermore, he had plenty of it.

Slinging the pack around to where it rested comfortably against his shoulders once again, nestling against the twin scabbards, he unlimbered his water bag and tucked it firmly beneath his right arm. It was nearly full, brimming with the stuff of life hard-won in sinister Skawpane. Carefully he removed the stopper and let it dangle by its cord from the lip of the bag. The contents sloshed gently in response to his actions.

Turning his back on his imploring but inanimate family, he walked up to where the black litah stood frozen in the midst of suffocating halite. Taking careful aim with the mouth of the bag, he brought his right elbow and arm roughly against his side, squeezing the bag sharply. Water sprayed from the opening to drench the big cat. It struck his mane and shoulders, ribs and legs. It got in his eyes and nose.

For the first time in many long moments, Ahlitah blinked. Thanks to the water that had gone up his nostrils, this was followed by a sneeze of truly leonine proportions. Running down his flanks, the precious water dissolved away the salt. Even as the big cat was cleansed, fresh salt was trying to precipitate out around his feet, to make its way up his legs and trap him anew.

Shaking his head, the litah sent a shower of sparkling halite crystals flying in all directions. "What happened?" Wrinkling back his lips as only a big cat can do, he spat disgustedly to one side. "What have I been eating?"

Ehomba pointed out the places where the uncannily saiga-shaped lump of mineral salts showed claw and tooth marks. "Everyone likes a little salt with their meal, but there are limits. While you were trying to eat the salt, the salt was starting to eat you. It was not meat that was salted—it was your thoughts." Steeling himself, he turned and gestured in the direction of the three sculpted figures of his family. Now that he was fully conscious of the slow, terrible death they symbolized, he was able to look at them more clearly and see them for what they really were. This time they looked less like Mirhanja and his children than they did like three small pillars of accumulated whiteness.

Revelation proved sanguinary for Ahlitah as well. "I can't believe I was chewing so single-mindedly on that." His snarl of antipathy and contempt echoing across the lake bed, he brought one massive paw around in a great arc and decapitated the nearest formation. Lumps of shattered salt went skittering across the hard, crusty ground.

"Bring your water." Ehomba spun on one sandaled foot. "We have to free the others." He stamped down heavily as he walked. "And keep moving. Do not linger too long in one place. As swiftly as the salt distorts and affects your mind, it also clutches at your feet."

It took the contents of an entire water bag and part of another to free the hulking Hunkapa Aub from his saline entombment. When confronted with the reality of his mirrored self in salt, he could not be dissuaded from pushing it over. It smashed to bits, leaving a pile of salt rubble where moments before had stood a perfect likeness of the shag-covered man-beast.

Continuously brushing salt crystals from their arms and legs, they hurried on to the knoll of salts that had assumed the guise of a small castle. Breathing hard, Ehomba slowed before the sculpted entrance—but of his good friend and companion there was no sign.

Scratching ceaselessly as he fought off the persistent salt, Hunkapa Aub turned a slow circle. "Not see friend Simna."

"I don't smell him, either." Head back, the black litah was sniffing repeatedly at the air. "Between the new dampness and the old salt it's hard to scent anything else."

"Keep trying." Grateful for the moonlight, Ehomba strained to see through seams in the salt formations. They appeared to be taunting him, mocking his efforts to penetrate their encrusted secrets, laughing silently from origins he preferred not to contemplate.

His eyes widened slightly as he realized what must have happened. Whirling to face the blocky, crenellated formation once more, he aimed the water bag he was holding and directed Hunkapa Aub to do likewise with his. Bereft of hands, Ahlitah could only look on and watch.

Water gushed from the mouths of both bags to play over the flanks of the consolidated castle. Minarets dissolved into soggy lumps, and then the lumps themselves became components of thin briny rivers that flowed down the flanks of the formation. Turrets and spires sagged and crumbled, melding into the walls as they liquefied beneath the soaking assault.

It took more of their supply than the herdsman cared to think about, but halfway into the castle they finally caught a glimpse of Simna ibn Sind's backpack. Still riding high on the swordsman's shoulders, it gleamed dully in the moonlight. The surrounding, enclosing salt imparted a sickly blue cast to the exposed portions of his skin.

Moving closer and wielding the shrinking water bags like firearms, Ehomba and Hunkapa Aub dissolved the salt from around their friend's encrusted body. He had been completely entombed. Salt plugged his ears and formed a crust over his eyes. But his nostrils were still unblocked, though barely, the advancing salt having been held back by the moisture breathed out by his lungs.

Stiff and unbending, his body was dragged out into the open air and laid gently across Ahlitah's back. Lying him down on the ground was not contemplated, as it would just be returning him to the grip of the relentless, inimical salts. Water from still another bag was poured over him, drenching his body and clothing, soaking his face. When he finally revived, the herdsman did so sputtering violently and shaking his head.

Sitting up, he wiped animatedly at his face and took a

long, deep breath. "What happened? I feel as if I've come back from the land of the dead." Rising to his feet, he suddenly pointed and yelled, "That cursed castle tried to kill me! It grabbed me and tried to suffocate me!"

"Salt you down is more like it." Careful to keep moving his feet and arms, Ehomba proceeded to explain. "I think that if we had been five minutes longer in melting you out, the salt would have filled your nose and stopped your breathing. And your heart."

Wiping at himself as if he had just emerged from hiding in the depths of a cesspool, the swordsman found himself prone to a momentary case of the shakes. He was prepared to face death, had been ever since he had taken up the sword, but suffocating alive was among the least pleasant ways imaginable for a man to expire.

"Away from this place," he declared with a sweep of his arm. "Let's get away from here."

His companions needed no urging. The matter of their suddenly and severely depleted water supply, which they had worked so hard to obtain in Skawpane, was not mentioned. Commentary was unnecessary. Having utilized the greater portion of it to free themselves from the grasp of the alkaline prison, it would now have to be rationed severely, and quickly replenished. In the waning moonlight, the silhouette of the Curridgian escarpment loomed before them more meaningful than ever.

There would be water there, Ehomba knew as he moved forward at the run. The snowy peaks promised as much. The only question was, how high up and how far back would they have to go to find it?

Behind them, fantastic contours and extravagant shapes stood silent sentinel over the salt plain. They did not move, and none uttered so much as a whisper. Rising from pools of rapidly dispersing and evaporating water, crystals of halite and gypsum sparkled like diamonds as they precipitated out of the chloride-heavy solution. In most places such a wealth of crystals would have been zealously guarded and protected, for salt was necessary to the perpetuation of life.

Only here, in this forsaken and barren place between mountain and misery, had it turned deadly.

XIX

The Drounge

It did not know how old it was. It did not know where it came from; whether mother and father, egg, spore, seed, or spontaneous generation. It could not remember when it had begun or how long it had been wandering. It did not know if there were others of its kind, but it had never seen another like itself. It knew only that it was in pain.

For as long as it could remember, which might very well be for as long as Time was, it had been so. Without any specific destination in mind it had wandered the world, its only purpose, its only motivation, to keep moving. It sought nothing, desired nothing, expected nothing—and that was what it got. On its singular plight it did not speculate. What was the use? It was what it was, and no amount of contemplation or conjecture was going to change that. To say that the Drounge was resigned to its condition would be to understate the situation grossly. Alternatives did not and had never existed.

There wasn't an antagonistic particle in its being. By the same token, it was too compassionate to be friendly. Where possible, it kept its distance. When contact with other living things was unavoidable, as was too often the case, it rendered neither judgment nor insensibility. It simply was, and then it moved on.

Most creatures could not see the Drounge so much as sense a disturbance in their surroundings when it was present. This was to the benefit of both, since the Drounge did not especially want to be seen and because it was not pleasant to look upon. Occasionally, the sharp-eyed and perceptive were able to separate it from its surroundings. Whenever that occurred, usually in times of stress or moments of panic, screaming frequently ensued. Followed by death, though this was not inevitable. Murder was the farthest thing from the Drounge's mind. When life departed in its presence, apathy was the strongest emotion it could muster. How could it feel for the demise of others when its own condition was so pitiable?

For the Drounge was a swab. It roved the world picking up the pain and misery and wounds and hurt of whatever it came in contact with. A vague amorphous shape the size of a hippopotamus, it humped and oozed along in the absence of legs or cilia, making slow but inevitable progress toward a nondestination. It had no arms, but could with difficulty extrude lengths of its own substance and utilize these to exert pressure on its surroundings. Other creatures, unseeing, often ran into it, giving rise to consequences that were disastrous for them but of no import to the Drounge.

Open, running sores bedecked its body the way spots adorn a leopard. Scabs formed continually and sloughed off, to be replaced by new ones ranging in size from small spots to others big as dinner plates. They were in constant lugubrious motion, traveling slowly like small continental plates across the viscous ocean of the Drounge's body. Foul pustules erupted like diminutive volcanoes, only to subside and reappear elsewhere. Cuts and bruises ran together to comprise what in any other living being would have been an outer epidermis.

None of this unstable, motile horror caused the Drounge any discomfort. It did not experience pain as others did, perhaps because it had never been allowed to distinguish pain from any other state of being. For it, it was the way things were, the circumstance to which existence had condemned it. It did not weep, because it had no eyes. It did not wail, because it had no mouth. Though capable of meditation and reflection, it did not bemoan its fate. It simply kept moving on.

Unable to alter its condition, it had long since become indifferent to the aftermath of its passing. As well to try to change the effect of the sun on the green Earth, or of the wind on small flying creatures. Incapable of change, it felt no culpability in the destruction of those it came in contact with. It was not a matter of caring or not caring. A force of one of the more benighted components of Nature, it simply was.

It did not matter what it encountered. Large or small, the consequences were similar, differing only in degree depending on the extent and length of time that contact was made. The Drounge acted as a sponge, soaking up the world's injuries and pain. And like a sponge, when something made contact with it, it leaked. Not water, but hurt, damage, wounds, and death. The process was involuntary and something over which the Drounge had no control.

Why it kept moving it did not know. Perhaps an instinctive feeling that so much pain should not long remain in any one place. Possibly some atavistic urge to seek a peace it had never known. Survival, reproduction, feeding—the normal components of life did not drive or affect it. Staring relentlessly forward out of oculi that were not eyes in the normal sense, but which were misshapen and damaged and bleeding, it existed in a state of perpetual migration.

Gliding over a field of grass, it would leave behind a spreading swath of brown. Fire would have had a similar effect, would have been cleaner, purer, but the Drounge was a collage, a mélange, a medley of murder, and not an elemental. In its wake the formerly healthy green blades would quickly break out in brown spots. These would expand to swallow up the entire blade, and then spread to its neighbors. It was not a disease but an entire panoply of diseases, a veritable deluge of afflictions not even the healthiest, most productive field could withstand. After a few days the formerly serene grassland or meadow would stand as devastated and barren as if it had been washed by lava.

Sensing solidity, a herd of wild goats brushed past the patient, persistent Drounge as it made its way northward. Tainted blood and other impure drippings promptly stained their flanks. Some hours later, their thick hair began to fall out in ragged clumps. One by one they grew dizzy and disoriented, dropping to their knees or keeling over on their sides. Tongues turned black and open lesions appeared on freshly exposed skin. Pregnant ewes spontaneously aborted deformed, stillborn fetuses, and the testicles of rams shrank and dried up.

Eyes bulging, black tongues lolling, the toughest and most resilient of them expired within a day. Vultures and foxes came to feast on the dead, only to shun the plethora of tempting carcasses. Something in the wind kept them away despite the presence of so much easy meat. It was a smell worse than death, more off-putting than disease. The fennecs twitched their astonishing ears as they paced uneasily back and forth, keeping their distance yet reluctant to abandon such a tempting supply of food. Vultures landed near the bodies, fanning the air with their dark, brooding wings. Accustomed as they were to the worst sort of decay, a couple took tentative bites out of the belly of a stinking ram.

Within minutes they were hopping unsteadily about. Feathers began to fall away. The hooked, yellow beak of one bird developed a spreading canker that rotted the face of its owner. Within an hour both hardened scavengers lay twitching and dying alongside the expired goats.

Enormous wings spread wide as the survivors took to the air. For the first time in their relentlessly efficient existence, they had encountered something not even they could digest. The foxes and hyenas slunk away as if pursued by invisible carnivores armed with immense claws and fangs. Only the insects, who could sustain the losses necessary to make a meal of the deceased, found the ruminant desolation to their benefit.

Field or forest, taiga or town, it was all the same to the Drounge as it proceeded on its never-ending march. What happened when it passed through a city was unpleasant to the point of becoming the stuff of nightmare legend. Some called it the judgment of the gods, others simply the plague. All agreed that the consequences were horrific beyond imagining.

People perished, not in ones and twos or even in family groups, but in droves. Symptoms varied depending on what afflicted part of the Drounge each encountered.

Wounds refused to heal and bled unstoppably, until the unfortunate casualty shriveled like a grape left too long in the sun. Lesions blossomed like the flowers of death until they covered more of a sufferer's body than his skin. The daily clamor of the community; the give and take of commerce, the fluting arpeggios of gossip, the chatter of small children that was a constant, underlying giggling like a symphony of piccolos, was entirely subsumed in shrieks of pain and wails of despair.

So the city died, its inhabitants shunned by surrounding communities. Those who lived long enough to flee were denied sanctuary by their terrified neighbors. They wandered aimlessly, perishing in ditches that lined the sides of roads or beneath trees that could provide welcoming shade but were unable to mourn. Everyone who had come in contact with the Drounge died: the resigned elderly and the disbelieving young, the healthy laborers and the children who could not comprehend. They expired, and so did those who had been in contact with them. Those few who had seen the Drounge and remarked on its passage died differently, slaughtered by their panicked neighbors in a frenzy of ignorance and fear. Eventually, even the plague perished, exhausted by its own capacity for destruction.

And the Drounge moved on.

Nothing could stand in its way, and the perceptive got out of it. Those that were incapable of movement prepared themselves as best they were able, and expired as readily as those living things that could. The Drounge handed down no judgments, passed no resolutions, essayed no assessments.

Only solid rock barred its way or altered its course. Water it passed through as freely as it moved through air, sliding with damned grace into lake or pond and advancing by means of repeated humping motions. As on land, so it was beneath the surface of waves large and small.

Water plants withered and collapsed to the muddy bottom. The shells of unfortunate mollusks bled calcium until they deteriorated beyond usefulness. Abscesses appeared on the sensitive skin of amphibians, and the gills of passing fish swelled up until suffocation brought on a slow and painful death. Wading birds that ate the dead and dying fell from the sky as if shot, their eyes glazed, their intestines rotting. Emerging on the far shore, the Drounge left behind a body of water as devastated as any town or field. As always, in the aftermath of its passing, only the patient insects prospered.

The Drounge continued to move northward.

Eventually it reached a region it might have called home, had it possessed any thought of so removed a notion. For the first time in a long, long while it was able to advance without killing anything. Not because it had suddenly become any less lethal, the essence of itself any less virulent, but because there was so little life in its new surroundings to slaughter. It could not kill what did not live.

Dimly, through its persistent but restricted vision, it took note of rocks bare of bushes, of a soil so sterile it would not support the hardiest of weeds. An amazing place, as barren of life as the far side of the sky. But as if to ensure it could not relax, an occasional wandering or lost creature would materialize, only to make casual contact and die to remind the Drounge of the homicidal actuality that was itself.

Not many: just enough. A flowering grass that had somehow managed to establish itself in a shady crack in the blasted ground encountered the passing Drounge. Moments later its petals had dropped off, to skitter away in the detached grasp of a passing breeze. Then the stems bent, bowed by a sudden systemic affliction. The tiny stockade of glistening green blades yellowed and split. Within minutes the miniature oasis was no more, a flavescent smudge of decay against the sickly, pallid earth.

Where the snake had come from or how it had survived for as long as it had in that blasted land none could say. Heavy with eggs, it sought a place to lay. Searching for the shade of a boulder, it found instead the passing Drounge. Immediately, it began to cough, and to twist violently. The forked tongue flicked spasmodically. One long muscle, the snake writhed and coiled as if trying to choke itself. Eggs began to spew uncontrollably from the ventral orifice. Deposited exposed to the pitiless, blistering sunlight, they soon dried out, the desiccated life within never to see the light of day.

But for the most part the Drounge killed far less than usual, caused no havoc, induced no mass destruction. Apart from the few isolated encounters with weed and reptile, it lurched onward, enjoying an unusual period of grace and isolation. For a change, the only pain in its vicinity was its own.

It came eventually to a region of strange rock formations, peculiar spires and precipitates that contained the aspect but not the actuality of life. Composed entirely of inanimate minerals, they were immune and indifferent to the Drounge's presence. To its left rose a range of high mountains, their peaks ascending toward the clouds. Both would entail a detour, a delay in the march that knew no end, and to which the Drounge was wholly committed despite its lack of a purpose.

But between massif and hillocks lay an open plain, rising slightly as it approached the first foothills. It was almost perfectly flat, unadorned by plant life and devoid of rocky impediments. Offering an unobstructed route north, it was the path and direction the Drounge chose.

How long it had toiled forward over the arid plain before it once more encountered life it did not know. Time had no meaning for it, day being no different from night, summer accompanying the same suffering as winter. What life was doing in that place of desolation the Drounge could not imagine. It did not matter. It kept moving forward, always advancing, compelled to alter its chosen course to avoid solid stone but nothing else.

In some deep, buried, half-hidden part of itself it screamed at the creatures to change direction, to move out of the way, to do something to avoid contact. Having no lips, no palate, no tongue and no mouth, it could not shout a warning. It could only hope. But as had ever been the case with the Drounge, hope was a mostly forgotten component of its existence. What mattered, what was important, was that it keep moving, advancing, progressing. Why, it did not know. "Why" was a concept it could not afford.

At first it thought it would miss the creatures. They were highly active, agile, and traveling across the plain perpendicularly to the Drounge's course. If it had slowed down, if they had slowed down, contact could have been avoided. But they showed no inclination to accelerate or moderate their pace, and the Drounge could not. Catastrophe accompanied the Drounge the way remoras shadowed a shark.

Even so, a sliver of apathetic hope remained as it slid past first one, then another of the energetic vertebrates without making contact. They were an odd lot, the Drounge thought sluggishly. Paradoxical at best, mismatched at worst. A third member of the party trooped past without brushing against it or glancing in its lurching, pitching direction.

And then the fourth hesitated, reaching out as if feeling of the air in front of it, and grabbed a protruding wad of the Drounge's putrefying flesh just above one oculus.

Corruption spurted from the Drounge's fragile epidermis, surging forward to coagulate around the creature's fingers and wrist. Its eyes bugged and it gasped in agony as the relic residue of a thousand diseases and pestilences, of a million tumors and ulcerations, shot briefly through its flesh. Cinched by solidifying putridity to the left side of the Drounge, the luckless biped found itself dragged helplessly forward.

This was an unusual but not unprecedented occurrence. The Drounge knew exactly what would happen. Attached to its humping, gelatinous body, the trapped creature would find itself hauled along until the timeless poisons in the Drounge's system began to affect it the same way they affected every living thing. It would regain its freedom only when its pinioned limb rotted off at the wrist. Then the rest of the body would atrophy and die, most likely rotted away from within by the extreme contact it had made with the Drounge.

Instead of fleeing at the highest speed of which they were capable, the unfortunate's companions whirled and returned, rushing to catch up to him. Rushing to their own deaths, the Drounge reflected. No matter, no shame, no difference. It continued on its way, oblivious to their futile and soon-to-be-fatal efforts. Make contact with their friend or with it, and they too would die. Such had been the affliction of the Drounge's existence, and such would it always be.

Two of them stumbled and dodged about as if no longer in control of their own bodies. They were trying to react to something they could not see. Only the third now stared directly at the indefatigably advancing Drounge, peering into its seeping, pustulant optics, plainly sensible not only of its presence but of its bearing and appearance. Recognition, the Drounge knew, meant nothing. A minuscule part of it hoped the creature would keep its distance. The greater part of it was indifferent. After having induced tens of thousands of deaths, one or two more were of less significance to it than raindrops were to the sea.

At first it thought that the aware creature was digging into its own back, a pain the Drounge could have empathized with. Then it saw that the biped's own flesh remained inviolate. It was reaching into an artificial object that relied for motility on its organic host. Still avoiding contact with the advancing Drounge while making loud vocalizations to its companions, it withdrew from the sizable, lumpy object one that was smaller still.

Unlike the article that had given it birth, this small sac of treated and cured vacular material fit comfortably in its owner's palm. It had the shape of an onion, many thousands of which the Drounge had killed during its passage through formerly lush farmlands far, far to the south. Removing the tapered end of the sac, the vigorous biped proceeded to squeeze the bulb shape slightly. A small bit of thick, viscous paste oozed from the interior. Pale pink in color, it smelled sharply of rain-swept willow and other growing things.

Pacing the Drounge, the creature reached out and dabbed the bit of sticky mucilage on the spot where its companion's limb had become adhered. For a while nothing happened. The biped continued to trot alongside the lacerated flank of the Drounge, uttering comforting vocalizations to its entrapped friend, while the rest of its companions kept their distance.

Then something touched the Drounge.

This in itself was a most remarkable happenstance. Nothing touched the Drounge. It was the one that did all the touching; the imparting of death, the conveyance of misery, the transmission of suffering. So astonishing was the sensation that for the first time in living memory it reduced its habitual gait, slowing slightly the better to focus on what had occurred while simultaneously trying to analyze it.

It was not pain. Supreme among all living things on the subject of affliction, the Drounge was intimately familiar with agony in every conceivable, possible variance and permutation. This was something else. Something new and extraordinary. Unable to understand what had taken place, even in the abstract, it could only continue on its way, its direction and purpose temporarily muted but not swayed.

Instead of fading away, the phenomenon expanded its influence, until a portion of the Drounge the size of a pillow was fully involved. Within this segregated section of self, unprecedented processes were at work. Never having

in its entire existence encountered or experienced anything like it before, the Drounge was at a loss to give a
name to what was happening. It was not frightened. That
which bears the burden of annihilation does not fear. But
it was puzzled, if not a little confused.

Part of it, albeit a very small part, was changing. Meta-
morphosing in a most matchless and extreme fashion. It
took place so rapidly that the Drounge was unable to react,
nor did it quite know how to do so. Some sort of response
seemed called for, but it could not begin to know exactly
what.

The portion of itself that had engaged the creature foolish enough to initiate physical contact withdrew. Freed,
the unfortunate dropped away from the Drounge's flank,
falling to the ground while clutching its formerly impacted
upper member. By now that limb should have been diseased beyond recognition, should be little more than a
stick upon which a multitude of afflictions had worked
their foul dissipation. Moreover, the general infection that
was the Drounge ought to have spread to and throughout
the creature's entire slight, vulnerable body, reducing it to
a corrupted mass of dead and decaying tissue.

Nothing of the sort had happened. With the application
of the soft paste, all that the Drounge had inflicted had
been countered. The individual limb as well as the rest of
its owner had been miraculously restored to health. Climbing to its feet, the smaller biped held its formerly impacted
appendage and stared down its length as if examining an
unexpected apparition. It manifested no evidence of damage and its expression was absent of anguish.

To the Drounge this amounted to nothing more than an
incident. A striking incident, to be sure. One without

precedent. But in the long lexicon of its existence merely a footnote, a quip of fate, a momentary interruption in its everlasting painful passage through reality. The quartet of creatures whose path it had ephemerally encountered fell behind; their identities unknown, their insignificant purposes in life restored. The spot on its side where the second biped had daubed the bit of odd ointment tingled, but that was all. No harm had come to the Drounge. How could anything injure that which carried upon and within itself all the world's hurt?

A small flurry of movement caused it to look back, a gesture that required an effort no less painful than simply moving forward. It could not believe what it was seeing. Apparently indifferent to the damage that had almost been done to its friend, the taller of the two bipeds with which the Drounge had experienced contact was running. Not away from the northward path as would have been sensible, but directly toward the methodically advancing, only intermittently visible organism. The absurd, demented creature was chasing *after* the Drounge instead of racing at maximum speed in the opposite direction!

Self-evidently it was deranged. What could unsettle a sentient being so, the Drounge could not imagine. It did not increase its pace, nor did it slow down. Whatever mad, lunatic purpose motivated the biped was beyond the Drounge's ability to affect or understand. It did not matter. In the scheme of things, it made no difference whether the crazed creature lived or died.

It halted abruptly before reaching the stoically retreating Drounge. That, at least, was a rational decision. Perhaps the creature, momentarily maddened, had suddenly come back to its senses. One of its upper, absurdly spindly limbs was upraised. As the Drounge ignored it, the creature brought this member forward. Propelled through the air by this slight physical action, something flew from the end of the appendage. Idly, the Drounge identified it as the onion-shaped object the creature had been carrying earlier.

The bulb-shape struck the Drounge in the middle of its back. Humping implacably forward, it treated the barely perceptible impact with the same indifference it treated all such contacts. Whenever something touched it, it was invariably the other that suffered.

On impact, the bulb burst, spilling its contents. The thick, pale unguent spread slowly across the curving bulk of the Drounge. Still its presence was ignored.

Until it started to sink in.

The tingling sensation the Drounge had heretofore experienced only at one small place on its left side started to penetrate deeply. It was not unpleasant. On the contrary, the Drounge would have found it pleasurable had it possessed a means for describing such a sensation. In the absence of applicable referents it could only struggle with physical feelings that were entirely new. As a novelty, the effects of the expanding emollient were exhilarating. They could not last, of course. Within moments they would be subsumed within and overwhelmed by the raging internal dissipation and disease that constituted the Drounge's customary state of existence.

Proceeding with its advance, the Drounge waited for this to happen. It did not. Instead, the effects of the free-flowing, penetrating balm continued to spread. A strange feeling came over the Drounge, quite unlike anything it had ever felt before. It was as if its whole body had been caught up in something as wonderful as it was unexpected, though it possessed no more referents for wonderful than it did for pleasurable. It was changing.

For the first time in millennia, the Drounge stopped.

The singular tingling sensation now dominated every corner of its being, penetrating to the farthest reaches of self, replacing eternal agony and perpetual discomfort with—something else. This was not a small thing; *not* an incident, *not* an insignificant transient episode. Its very shape was changing, twisting and buckling with neoteric forces it did not understand. Could not understand, because it had no experience of them.

With a last convulsive, wrenching sensation of dislocation, the unforeseen metamorphosis achieved final resolution. The Drounge stood as before, inviolate and untouched. Only, something was different. It took even the Drounge a moment to realize what that was.

It was no longer in pain.

The absence of agony was so extraordinary a sensation that the Drounge was momentarily paralyzed. It was all gone, all of it—all the suffering, all the disease and decay, all the everlasting affliction that had combined to comprise its physical and mental existence. In its place was something the Drounge could not put a name to: a calmness and tranquillity that were shocking in their unfamiliarity. And something else. For not only had it changed internally, its appearance was radically altered as well. With a new inner individuality had come a new shell, a fresh and unspoiled outer self, courtesy of the tingling unguent that had affected a transformation far beyond what even its wielder could have envisioned.

Elation swept through the Drounge at its unexpected epiphany. Never having felt itself trapped, it hardly knew how to react to being free. Exhilaration was a sensation with which it had never before had to come to terms. Uncertain, tentative, it could only try.

As the tiny cluster of astonished, fragile creatures it had come close to killing looked on in wonder, the enormous butterfly that had materialized before their eyes spread six-foot wings of prismatic emerald and opalescent crimson and rose from the bleached desert floor, haltingly at first but with increasing confidence, into a cloudless and welcoming clear blue sky.

XX

Let me have another look at that hand."

Simna wordlessly raised the arm by which he had been attached to the lumbering horror. Rotting flesh had been miraculously renewed, nerves sutured, skin regrown, the bleeding stopped. With the impossible butterfly vanishing into the distance and his restored limb hanging healthy and normal from the end of his shoulder, his attention kept switching back and forth between wonders.

"By Gravulia, what—what was it?" he mumbled as his rangy companion critically inspected first palm and then individual fingers. "One minute I could see it clearly and the next, it wasn't there and something beautiful was."

Ehomba replied without looking up from his examination. "Disease is like that."

The swordsman blinked. The hallucinatory, spectacular butterfly was gone now, swallowed up by the sky and imagination, leaving him to contemplate his right hand. Moments ago it had been a putrefying, decaying ruin. Now it was restored. A small whitish scar, souvenir of a fight in a chieftain's hut on a distant steppe, had vanished from his index finger together with the more recent corruption.

"So it was a disease of some kind?"

"Not a disease. Disease itself, or some pitiful entity that it had become attached to. I am not really sure what it was, Simna. But there was no mistaking its effects. Even as I ran to help you I felt myself starting to grow weak and uneasy. If I had not been able to deal with it we might well all have died."

Feeling none too energetic himself after the mephitic encounter, the swordsman sat down on a rock. Nearby, Hunkapa Aub was studying the increasingly steep slopes that lay before them. The black litah was sunning itself on the brackish ground.

"The butterfly—" Simna looked up sharply. "Hoy, I remember you putting something on my hand! It set me free."

Ehomba nodded. "A salve prepared for me by Meruba. I was told that it was useful for dealing with cuts and scrapes, burns and punctures. When I saw what had caught ahold of you it was all I could think of to use." He gestured downward. "It cured your arm."

Holding his right hand in his left while gently rubbing it, Simna nodded gratefully. "My arm, yes, but that doesn't explain the butterfly." He shuddered once. "What I saw first, when it was visible to me, was no butterfly."

"No," the herdsman agreed solemnly. He smiled as he reminisced. "Meruba is known for her salves. It is said that, if applied in sufficient strength, they can cure anything. I used all that she gave me." Turning his head, his braids bouncing slightly against his neck, he gazed thoughtfully at the northern horizon. "Whatever it was that had hold of you, I think we healed it."

"Should've killed it," the swordsman grumbled. Releasing his hand, he started to shake it sharply.

"Hurt?" Ehomba looked suddenly concerned.

"Hoy, it throbs like my head the morning after a three-day binge! But it's nothing I can't handle, bruther." Rising from his seat, he straightened his pack on his back. Some of the straps had become loosened while he was being dragged along by the revolting apparition. "It's too damn hot here." He nodded briskly in the direction of the foothills and the rocky crags they fronted. "Let's find ourselves some cool shade and fresh water."

The ascent into the Curridgian Mountains proved arduous, but less so than their trek into the Hrugars. Deep gorges allowed them to avoid the need to scale the highest peaks, providing a natural approach to the towering escarpment. Where there was snow there was runoff, and the same canyons that guided them westward soon boasted of swiftly running streams and even small rivers. Ehomba was grateful they would not have to worry any longer about water. As they climbed higher the air grew cooler. The awful heat of the Tortured Lands receded until it was no more than a disagreeable memory.

Pines and redwoods, firs and kauris soon replaced weedy grasses and small-leaved brush, until they once again found themselves traipsing through forest. Ehomba and Simna were rejuvenated by the fresh air and increased humidity, while Ahlitah was largely indifferent. But Hunkapa Aub was positively exhilarated. Of them all, he, with his heavy, shaggy coat, had suffered the most by far from the unrelenting heat they had left behind and below.

He even welcomed the mist that settled in around them as they climbed a slope luxuriant with wildflowers, their petals splashed with extravagant shades of scarlet and teal and lemon yellow. As the moist haze thickened, the blossoms took on an air of unreality, their variegated faces staring brazenly at the shrouded sun, kaleidoscopic denizens of a languid dream.

Soon the mist had congealed to the point where even the black litah was hard pressed to espy a route upward, and they were reduced to following the stream that had cut the canyon. Though the humid air was still temperate and the climbing not difficult, Ehomba found himself glancing around apprehensively. Noting his friend's unease, Simna edged close.

"Hoy, long bruther, something's troubling you." The swordsman strove, without much success, to penetrate the haze. "You see something?"

"No, it is not that, Simna." As the herdsman licked his lips he tried not to suck in any of the prevailing moisture. "I was—I am—trying to remember something." Raising a hand, he gestured imprecisely. "It is this fog."

Simna took a look around, then shrugged indifferently. "It's fog. Accursedly thick fog, but just fog. So what?"

"I remember it."

The swordsman couldn't help himself: He laughed without thinking. "Hoy, Etjole, a man remembers the deaths he escapes and the lovers he's had. He remembers long, restful mornings and nights awash in celebration. He *doesn't* remember fog."

Ehomba ignored his friend's good-natured chiding. There was something not in the air, but about it. A quality that stirred a particular memory. He struggled to recall it.

Perhaps Simna was right. What was fog, after all, but droplets of moisture that hung in the air, too tired to rise as cloud, too lazy to fall as rain? How could anyone "remember" something so transient and ordinary?

Then he did. It was not just a fog, but *the* fog. The one that had tried to hold him back, the one that had attempted to enshroud and restrain him from ever beginning on this journey. It was the fog he had encountered not long after first leaving the village, so seemingly long ago. Failing to slow him then, it had come after him, abandoning its ocean home to confront him here, in these distant and foreign highlands.

Close by, the lumbering, mist-veiled mountain that was Hunkapa Aub called out uncertainly.

"Etjole, Hunkapa can't move. Hunkapa's legs not working."

A frustrated snarl sounded from just in front of the herdsman. Despite its great strength, the black litah too was finding progress suddenly difficult. Massive paws clawed at the sodden atmosphere in a futile attempt to advance.

The two humans were not immune to this sudden hindrance. Ignoring Simna's ensuing eruption of profanity, Ehomba concentrated on trying to take another step uphill. The sensation was akin to trying to walk through thin mud. It did not hold him back so much as slow him down to an unacceptable degree. At this rate they would be years getting through the mountains. Lifting his other leg, he struggled to take another stride. The result was the same. It was as if he had been wrapped in a waterlogged sheet not heavy enough to stop him, but sufficient to slow him dangerously.

Leaning forward, he put his weight into his next attempt. The gummy damp continued to cling to him, to drag him down and hold him back. Wanting to make certain that he had truly identified their adversary, he scanned every foot of the flower-laden meadow he could see, but with his range of vision reduced to a few feet, he was not able to make out any visible nemesis. For him to be able to see an enemy clearly in the fog, it would have to be right on top of him.

Which is when he was convinced once and for all that that was exactly the case.

"Go baaaackk...." It was an auricular specter, a verbal shadow, a ghost of a voice, as though wind had momentarily been manipulated and palpitated to form a word in the same ponderous manner as a baker kneads heavy dough.

The unexpected voice induced him to take one last look around, but there was nothing else to see; nothing but flowers and field and fog. Determined, he tried to push on, only to experience the same sensation of being slowed down and held back. He was covering ground, but trying to force his legs forward through the persistent impediment would soon exhaust him completely.

"Go...baaackk...." the sepulchral voice moaned. It seemed to come not from one particular place but from all around him. Which made sense, since that which was restraining him *was* all around him. But how to fight it? A man with a knife he would have known how to deal with immediately.

He searched in vain for a face, for eyes or a mouth, for something to focus on. There wasn't anything. There was only the fog, evanescent and everywhere present. "Why should I?" he asked guardedly, addressing his query to the damp, gently swirling mist.

The vaporous moan seemed to gather the slightest bit of additional strength from his reply. "Go back," it intoned in a dark whisper. "Go home." Airborne droplets of cool water eddied before his face. "It is all here, waiting for you. I have seen it. Disaster, complete and entire. You are doomed to unremitting misery, your quest to failure, the rest of your life to cold emptiness. Unless you end this now. Go home, back to your village and to your family. Before it is too late. Before you die."

This wouldn't do, he decided. Twice before, he had been compelled to listen to those exact same words—first from a seeress, then from a dog. Arms upraised in a gesture of defiance, he turned a slow circle and challenged the sky.

"A beauty gave me that augury, and then a witch. I did not heed *their* warnings, and I certainly will not heed this one!"

Nearby, his friend Simna ventured to comment hesitantly. "Etjole, you're arguing with the weather. That's a quarrel any man is bound to lose."

Ehomba begged to differ, but silently. Question he would, even the weather if need be, or he and his companions might never break free of the malicious atmosphere. They could not stay, and he would not turn back. Choosing, he reached back over his shoulder and drew the sky-metal sword Otjihanja had made for him. Crystallized iron caught the few isolated flashes of light that managed to penetrate the haze and broke them into sparks.

With his arm restrained by the cloying, clinging mist, he could not slash and cut with his usual ease, but he hacked away at the surrounding fog with as much strength and determination as he could muster. Results were immediate.

Bits and pieces of fog, cut off from the rest of the main body by the otherworldly blade, fell to the earth. Each squirmed glutinously across the ground as if seeking to rejoin the rest of the hovering gray mass, before finally falling motionless and evaporating. A louder moan surrounded him: a malign breeze off the mountain slopes wending its way among the rocks—or something else. He found himself wondering if fog could feel pain. It did not matter. There was work to be done, and he was the only one who could do it.

Patiently, wielding the sword with skill and care, he began to excavate a clear space for himself within the enveloping mist. As soon as it was large enough and his arms and legs were free, he cut his way over to Simna and liberated the swordsman. Hunkapa Aub and Ahlitah were next.

"Everyone all right?" he inquired. Looking at him, it was impossible to tell if the water pouring off his face and arms was perspiration or amputated mist. Assured that they had suffered nothing more than fatigue in their own efforts to free themselves, he turned and started work on chopping a path forward. Instead of wielding a machete against a wall of intervening jungle, or a shovel against a rampart of packed earth, he hacked away with something that was not of the Earth at that which was little more than nothing.

As he toiled, tendrils of fog strained to clutch at him afresh, reaching out with quivering slivers of damp gray for his arms and legs. He slashed away mercilessly, ignoring them as they fell among the flowers and grass, trampling the condensed moisture beneath his sandals. No more maybe-almost words teased his ears, but the moaning continued without pause. The fog did not bleed beneath his blade—it simply asserted its mastery of melancholy as it continued to do its utmost to detain him.

A man used to dealing daily with cattle and children was not about to have his progress denied by a recalcitrant mist. A tunnel appeared behind Ehomba and his friends as he pressed forward, a cylindrical tube in the fog into which the occasional grateful, sodden insect or arthropod found its way.

"Get off me!" he would shout from time to time. "Leave me be! I am near to my destination and will not be denied here. No mere weather, no matter how tenacious, is going to stop me!"

There was no reply. Only the continuous moaning, and the persistent, repetitious attempts to restrain his arms and legs. Occasionally he was forced to pause and hack clutching tentacles of moisture from the limbs of his friends. But for the most part, now that they once more had room in which to move, they were able to keep themselves relatively mist free.

He hewed his way forward for more than an hour. If the retentive, obstinate fog thought it could outwait him, or discourage him, it was more than wrong. It had never encountered anyone like Etjole Ehomba, whose arms rose and fell methodically, mechanically, as he cut his way forward, dead dew dripping like transparent blood from his blade of crystallized nickel-iron.

Then, realizing that all its efforts were doomed to failure, the fog began to dissipate. Vast quantities of it drew back, rising upward in the direction of the cold mountain peaks from which it drew sustenance, while isolated pockets fled downslope to evaporate. A few persistent tendrils continued to clutch at the arms and shoulders of the determined travelers, but these were soon cut away. As they ascended through the uppermost reaches of the fog bank, the sun returned, warming their damp bodies. The clinging fog had soaked Ehomba to the skin, but in the thin air the unobstructed sun made quick work of the lingering moisture.

A last gob of thick mist trailed him at a distance, darting and hiding behind one rocky outcropping after another. Used to watching for prowling predators while tending to the village herds, he kept track of it for a while, wondering at its intent. Perhaps it planned to drift down upon him when next he slept, covering his face, restraining not his arms and legs this time but his heart and lungs. He would not give it the chance.

Whirling, he rushed past a startled Simna to challenge the compacted cloud. Finding itself discovered, it immediately attempted to flee upward. The herdsman ran it down, catching up to it and dispatching it with his blade. Only the faintest hint of a moan rose from the wad of condensation as the meteoric sword-edge cut through its center, scattering droplets and inducing the rest of the gray blob to suicide beneath the unyielding rays of the morning sun.

Satisfied that he was no longer a source of interest to the vanished fog, or to any of its component parts, Ehomba sheathed the weapon and resumed his pace. Grass and soil in equal measure slid away beneath his sandals.

Free of the constraining, intemperate mist, they once again began to make good time. They had to. There was an obligation to fulfill, and a family and herd anxiously awaiting his return.

If anything else attempted to stop or slow them, Ehomba found himself musing, he hoped it would do so more openly and with some substance. He had not enjoyed fighting the fog. Instead of anger, or evil, there had been about it only an ineffable sadness, and he had found no satisfaction in slaying what was after all little more than a haunting melancholy.

After all, it had only, to its unfathomable, unknowable way of thinking, been trying to help him.

XXI

It was not long after they had left the inimical fog behind that they encountered the procession of humans and apes. Trudging along a trail that crossed the river gorge from north to south, the procession was heavily laden with baggage, from household goods dangling from stout poles supported by two or more individuals, to blanket-wrapped infants riding on the backs of females.

They shied in terror at the sight of Ahlitah and Hunkapa Aub, and Ehomba had to hasten to reassure them. Their accent was thick and heavy, but with repetition and gestures each side managed to make itself understood. These were poor folk, the herdsman decided, simple and unsophisticated. Judging from the expressions they wore, their burdens were more than physical.

"Ehl-Larimar?" he asked of several individuals. After a number of inquiries a long-faced macaque clad in heavy overcoat and cap finally responded. Raising its long arm, it pointed westward up the canyon and nodded.

"Good. Thank you." As Ehomba started past him, the ape reached out and grabbed his arm. Simna's hand went immediately to the hilt of his sword, while among the column there was an anxious stirring. Primate hands fumbled for axes and clubs. Ahlitah growled low in his throat, his claws seeking purchase on the hard ground.

Ehomba hastened to calm his companions. "It is all right. He is not hurting me." Glancing down, he saw that the macaque's face was fraught with concern, not animosity. "What is wrong, my long-tailed friend?"

It was uncertain if the ape comprehended the herdsman's words, but he certainly understood his tone. Releasing his grasp, he raised a spindly arm and jabbed a finger violently upcanyon. "Khorixas, Khorixas!"

"Hoy, what's a Khorixas?" Simna's hand had slid away from his sword, but his fingers remained loose and easy in its vicinity. "Maybe an outlying town this side of Ehl-Larimar itself?"

"Possibly." Smiling reassuringly, Ehomba stepped away from the visibly agitated macaque and retreated slowly, taking one careful step at a time. "It is all right. My friends and I can take care of ourselves." Even as he tried to explain he wondered if the ape understood any of what he was saying: These people spoke a language different from that of old Gomo and the People of the Trees.

Arm rigid and still pointing westward, the aged macaque rumbled "Khorixas!" one more time before lowering his hand. With a sad-eyed shrug, he turned and rejoined his comrades. When he paused briefly for a last look back at the travelers, it was to shake his head dolefully from side to side.

"Grizzled old fella must not care much for this Khorixas, whatever it is." Striding confidently forward, Simna kept a careful watch on the steep slopes that walled them in.

Nothing he saw or heard as they continued to hike upward led him to believe they might be walking into some kind of ambush, or a trap. Silhouetted against the scudding clouds, a few dragonets and condors soared on the updrafts. Marmosets and pacas scampered over the boulders and talus in search of nuts and berries. Thanks to the deep canyon, the travelers' line of march remained well below the tree line. The temperature dropped at night, but not precipitously so. When their blankets proved inadequate to the task of warding off the cold, Ehomba and Simna simply moved their bedding closer to the radiant bulks of Hunkapa Aub and the black litah.

They had just crossed the crest of the Curridgians, discernable by the fact that all streams now flowed westward instead of to the east, when they heard the first roll of thunder.

"Hunkapa no see clouds, no see storm." The hirsute hulk had his head tilted back while he squinted at the sky.

"It does not sound like that kind of thunder." Holding fast to his spear, Ehomba strode along in front, maintaining the same steady pace as always.

Simna ibn Sind cocked his head sideways as he regarded his tall companion. "There's more than one kind?"

The herdsman smiled down at him. "Many kinds. I myself have been trained to identify dozens of different varieties."

"Hoy then, if it's not a far-off storm clearing its throat that we're hearing, then what is it?"

"I do not know." A brilliant black-and-green spotted beetle landed on the herdsman's shirt, hitching a ride. Ehomba admired its glossy carapace and let it be.

"I thought you said you knew dozens of kinds of thunder?"

"I do." Ehomba's smile thinned. "But this one I do not recognize."

Whatever its source, it grew louder as they began to start downward. Its measured, treading rhythm was abnormal, suggesting an origin that was anything but natural. Yet the percussive volume was too loud to originate with anything man-made.

Only when they came around a cliff and entered a small alpine valley did they see that both of their assumptions were correct.

It had not been much of a village to begin with, and now it was in the process of being reduced to nothing at all. The stately thunder they had been hearing was caused by the concussion of hammer against stone. The stones ranged in size from small boulders to chinkers light enough for a child to move from place to place. The head of the hammer, on the very much larger other hand, was bigger than Ehomba.

It was being wielded by a giant—the first giant the herdsman had ever seen. The village elders knew many tales of giants, with which they often regaled their attentive, wide-eyed children. While growing up, Ehomba and his friends had listened to fanciful fables of one-eyed giants and hunchbacked giants, of giants with teeth like barracuda and giants lacking any teeth at all who sucked up their victims through straws made of hollow tree trunks. There were giants that swam in the deep green sea (but none that flew), and giants who lived in the densest jungles and never showed themselves (but some that were too big to hide).

There were ugly giants and uglier giants, giants who cooked their victims in a casserole of palm oil and sago pastry, and giants who simply swallowed them whole. Oura had once told of a vegetarian giant, and of another who was shunned by all others of his kind for washing his hair. Sometimes there seemed to be as many different kinds of giants as there were storytellers among the Naumkib, and that meant there were a great many varieties of giant indeed.

The one that stood before them using its great hammer to demolish the village was neither as horrific in appearance as he might have been nor as good-natured. Shoulder-length red hair tumbled in tangled tresses down his back and the sides of his head. Long hairs sprouted from pointed ears that stuck through the raggedy locks, and he had orange eyes. From his splotchety, crooked nose hung a booger the size of a boulder. His teeth were surprisingly white, glaring out from the rest of a baggy visage that as a face was mostly a failure. Dark and dirty treelike arms protruded from the sleeves of a vest comprised of many sewn-together skins, not all of them overtly animal. His furry lower garments were similarly fashioned, and his sandals with their knee-high laces bespoke the crudest attempts at cobblery.

He was three times the size of Hunkapa Aub, and when he swung the heavy hammer with its leather-clad head, the peal of disintegrating rock reverberated down every one of the surrounding canyons and gorges. Sweat poured from his coarse countenance in great rivulets, and even at a distance his stink was profound.

"Hoy, now we know what happened to the village of Khorixas." Simna's expression was grim. Another reverberant *boooom* echoed as the back wall of what had once been a fine two-story house came crashing down. "We also know why those hard-up folk we met a while back were migrating across the crest with their kids and all their possessions."

"We do not know anything." Ehomba was keeping one eye on the giant while assessing possible alternate routes with the other. The village lay directly athwart the most direct and easiest route westward and downslope. "We will go around," he announced resignedly. He started to turn away.

Hand on sword hilt, Simna all but jumped in front of him. "Hoy, long bruther, we have a chance to right a wrong here!" He nodded sharply in the direction of the crumbling village. "Whatever transpired between those poor wretches and this brute couldn't possibly justify the total ruination of their homes." He grinned knowingly. "Why, this great blundering ogre is *nothing* compared to the dangers you and I have dealt with these past months! Watch him work. See how slow he is, how ungainly his movements? We should teach him a lesson about picking on those smaller and weaker than himself and send him on his way. It will also earn us the undying gratitude of those simple mountain folk." His expression was eager. "What say you?"

Ehomba replied in his usual unshakable, even tone. "I do not need their gratitude, undying or otherwise." He nodded leftward, to where the giant was maintaining his steady rate of destruction. "Nor am I in the business of teaching lessons to rampaging giants or anyone else. My obligation draws me westward, to a destination that is, at long last, within reach if not sight." Supporting himself partially with his spear, he took a step to his right. "We will go around."

A disbelieving Simna's expression darkened. "I wouldn't have thought you a coward, Etjole."

The herdsman was not moved. "Or a fool either, I hope." Walking past the swordsman, Ehomba started up a narrow side canyon that led, if not due west, at only a modest inclination northward. Without a word between them, Hunkapa Aub and Ahlitah followed.

With his eyes Simna implored the others as they trooped past. When he found himself contemplating the last of the big cat's tail, he abruptly drew his sword. Waving it over his head and howling a defiant war cry, he spun and charged directly down toward the village and its ponderous, methodical enemy.

"Simna, no!" Ehomba's entreaties were ignored. Gritting his teeth, he started after his friend, hurdling grass and small rocks with long, lithe strides, holding his spear parallel to the ground beside him. Exchanging a glance, Hunkapa Aub and the black litah followed—at a sensible and leisurely pace.

Simna had already dashed in behind the giant to take a swipe at his ankles. The blow missed the main tendon but left a significant gash in the side of the left foot. Letting out a howl, the giant turned and brought his enormous hammer around in a sweeping, descending arc that would have smashed every bone in the swordsman's body—if he had remained standing where it was aimed. Quick as a jerboa, he'd darted out of its way. The wind of its passing ruffled his hair.

"Hoy, you great towheaded sack of pig piss! It's a little different when we fight back, isn't it? Come on, come on!"

He proceeded to taunt the giant with gestures as well as words. "Surely you can handle one tiny fella like me!"

Grimacing, the giant brought an enormous foot up and stamped down, only to find that once again Simna ibn Sind had skipped nimbly out of the way. Not by the margin the swordsman had intended, however. The giant was clumsy, it was true, but he was not as slow as Simna had first supposed. His defiant smirk began to develop a nervous twitch.

Ehomba arrived with sword in hand. He was furious, but not at the giant.

"What do you think you are doing?" he snapped at his imprudently energetic friend.

"Saving what's left of a village for the good of its innocent inhabitants." Panting, Simna stood close to the herdsman. "You pick your noble causes, I'll pick mine."

"There is nothing noble in a senseless death." Ehomba noted that the giant was watching them warily, trying to determine the orientation of its next blow.

"I don't plan on dying."

"No one does, but it happens just the same." Taking a deep breath, Ehomba addressed the giant. No matter who, or what, his adversary, he firmly believed in trying reason before the sword. "Greetings, imposing one! Why are you destroying the village Khorixas?"

Red eyebrows dense and tangled as berry thickets drew together. "What 'village' Khorixas? There is no village by that name." Callused and scored, a free hand indicated the ruins among which the oversized speaker was standing. "This miserable blot on the earth is Feo-Nottoa." The hand rose to smack sonorously against the broad chest. "*I* am the Berserker Khorixas!" The great hammer started to rise threateningly. "You should know the name of the one who is about to kill you."

"Why kill us?" Ehomba wondered aloud. "Why destroy this simple town?"

The head of the hammer lowered slightly, hovering. "I am a Berserker, and this is what Berserkers do. White teeth showed unpleasantly. "I am happy to be a Berserker. I like to destroy, and mangle, and exterminate. If I am fortunate, before I expire I will be able to eradicate every town and village in the southern part of the Curridgians." With his free hand he wiped his massive brow. "Annihilation, it is hard work."

"Hoy, it stops here!" Sneering, Simna gestured at his tall, laconic companion. "This is Etjole Ehomba of the Naumkib. Master of magic and all the necromantic arts, conjurer supreme, wizard of wizards, defender of the enfeebled and all who are preyed upon by bullies and ruffians!"

"I am not a bully," the Berserker Khorixas countered stiffly. "I am a professional." He squinted down at the two men. "And he doesn't look like much to me."

"Leave now." Simna took a challenging step forward. "Depart, flee, run away, before you are reduced to oblivion or slaughtered where you stand!"

"I'll take my chances," the Berserker Khorixas declared confidently, "but first I will make a paste of your bones to spread upon my bread for tomorrow morning's breakfast."

Simna stood his ground—making certain it was proximate to Ehomba's. As the stern-faced herdsman unsheathed the sky-metal sword and prepared to defend the two of them, the Berserker could be seen fumbling with the head of the majestic mallet. The coarse cord that se-

341

cured the protective leather cover was untied and the tough brown casing removed. Exposed to the clear mountain air, the silver-gray hammerhead gleamed metallically. Extensive crystalline striations caught the sunlight and held it. The swordsman's jaw dropped.

The colossal hammer of the Berserker Khorixas was forged of the same sky metal as Etjole Ehomba's ensorcelled sword. And there was a lot more of it.

Without preamble or warning from its owner, it was promptly brought around in a vast, sweeping arc, its passage through the clear mountain air generating a deep, reverberant humming. Simna leaped one way and Ehomba the other. The hammerhead struck the ground between them, ringing all the way to the center of the Earth and setting up subtle vibrations in the lush mudcress fields of Pridon on the opposite side. It was a blow that would have crushed lesser men to a damp pulp—or men less attuned to the behavior of creatures such as giants.

Despite the fact that his heart had sunk somewhere to the vicinity of his ankles at the sight of the unveiled hammer, Simna did not flee. Having precipitated the confrontation, against Ehomba's wishes, he was honor-bound to stay and fight. But not to stand and fight. That way lay rapid demise. Instead, he darted and dodged, making sure first of the location and direction of that deadly maul before dashing in close to strike at the giant's legs with his own sword. His exceptional agility and skill allowed him to deliver several stabs and cuts, but the wounds were shallow and only succeeded in further enraging the already incensed Berserker.

From a nearby slope, the black litah and Hunkapa Aub observed the battle. "Hunkapa not want Etjole to die," the shaggy hulk commented mournfully. "Hunkapa go and help!"

"You'll only get in the way." Ahlitah moved to intercept his ineloquent companion. "Leave it to the herdsman. Many's the time I've seen him extract himself from desperate situations." Fiery yellow eyes surveyed the arena of conflict. "He'll do the same here."

"And if he not?" Hunkapa Aub observed the flow of battle dubiously.

"Then he will die, and that prattling monkey with him. And I will try to find my way back to the veldt, and you to your mountains, and the sun will set tonight and rise tomorrow and the world take not the slightest notice of his strivings or ours. That is how it has always been and that is how it will always be." A muted snarl sent every small rodent within hearing scurrying for their burrows.

"Ehomba will find a way to win, or he will not. If he cannot defeat the giant, it's certain you can't."

"You could help too," Hunkapa Aub pointed out guilelessly.

"I have sworn to support him." The majestic ebony cat hesitated. "But I'd be in the way as well. There is a time to stalk, a time to pounce—and a time to wait. I think this is a time to wait. If you're sensible, you'll do the same."

So Ahlitah and Hunkapa held back and watched. Hammer blow after hammer blow descended, cleaving the air with monstrous streaks of its etched metal head. Each time, its intended targets jumped or twisted out of the way. But avoidance, too, demands effort, and both men were growing tired.

"Do something, Etjole!" Breathing harder and faster than was reassuring, Simna ibn Sind wielded his sword as he yelled to his companion. "Blow him into a mountain, bring down a piece of sky on his head!" Even as he shouted this advice, the increasingly desperate swordsman knew he was suggesting the impractical. With he and Ehomba forced to dodge as often as they were, any wind the herdsman called up was as likely to blow them off the mountain as it was the giant, while anything falling from the heavens would smash into the ruins of the village with an unearthly indifference to whoever happened to be standing there.

Astoundingly, instead of striking at the Berserker, instead of cutting at his legs and feet and trying to bring him down, Ehomba was doing his utmost to taunt him further.

"Bruther, what are you doing?" Simna was badly confused. "The one thing we don't need to do is make him any madder!"

But the herdsman seemed not to hear his friend as again and again he darted dangerously close to the giant before skipping spryly out of his way.

"*Ai,* you doddering dolt, you clumsy buffoon! Is this the best you can do? I am smaller, but too quick for you. No wonder you beat up on houses. Buildings cannot run away, or they too would make you look silly and laugh at you!"

Infuriated, the Berserker swung the great hammer in swifter and swifter arcs, until the air howled and shrieked in the grip of the artificial storm created by its wake. Unlike the tiny humans who were tormenting him, he did not tire, but appeared to grow stronger and more determined with each swing. The hammerhead hummed, whistling through the air like the piece of burning sky Ehomba's sword had called down to annihilate the imperious Chlengguu. Soon it was a terrible silver-gray streak, a blur that obscured everything behind it. Not even a swordsman as skilled as the redoubtable Simna ibn Sind could avoid it forever.

There was nowhere to hide. The stone structures of doomed Feo-Nottoa were as cardboard beneath that irresistible chunk of sky metal. Even a cave, had one been close at hand, would have been an insufficient refuge, for in the hands of the Berserker Khorixas even a mountain could be pounded to rubble.

An exhausted, tiring Simna, lungs heaving and legs aching, was bemoaning his likely fate even as he cursed his rash impetuousness, when Ehomba suddenly darted forward at what appeared to be the absolutely worst possible moment. The swordsman screamed a hoarse warning, but his tall friend did not hear. Or he heard, and chose to ignore it. Simna froze as the hammer descended, describing an arc that looked certain to impact the charging herdsman fully.

At the last instant, Ehomba dodged. Not back, away from the falling hammerhead, nor forward as a wrestler might have done in an attempt to slip beneath his adversary's guard, but sideways. As he did so he ducked just enough, brought around his own weapon, and with both hands swung it as hard as he could, forward and up. To Simna's experienced eyes it looked like a futile gesture. The sword was bound to shatter against the much larger, infinitely heavier hammerhead.

It did not. Too fast even for the swordsman to see, the edge of the herdsman's blade struck the backside of the swooping hammer. In so doing it imparted to that tremendous swing all the additional momentum of which its master was capable. Impelled forward and upward by the force

345

of its own rising on the backside of the swing and boosted by Ehomba's unexpected strike, instead of slowing down, the immense hammer continued to rise. Instinctively maintaining his grip, the startled Berserker Khorixas rose with it.

When he realized what was happening he contemplated letting go, even if it meant abandoning forever the incomparable tool. But by the time understanding penetrated that thick, unkempt skull, it was too late. The hammer had carried him too high. If he released his grip now he would fall long and far enough to break his neck, for even the spines of giants are made of flesh and bone.

So not only was he forced to maintain his grip, but he was compelled to strengthen it with the addition of his free hand. Berserker and hammer together, the one whistling and the other howling imprecations, rose into the cloud-free sky. Ehomba watched until giant and giant's weapon were a blot, then a dot, and finally a speck of indeterminate dust soaring over the southern horizon. Then he took a deep breath and started to shake.

"By Gowerben's footsteps, that's putting the arrogant assassin in his place!" A sweaty but elated Simna ibn Sind bounded down from the rock on which he had been standing and rushed to congratulate his companion. "Maybe it's as you say that you're no sorcerer, long bruther, but it's a master of unexpected gifts you are! I only wish that—"

The herdsman whirled on his friend with a fire in his eyes that for the barest, most intangible of instants exceeded that of the black litah. Rising and descending, his closed fist caught the swordsman flush on the side of the face. The report was loud enough to reach Hunkapa Aub and Ahlitah, who with the battle won were descending to rejoin their human companions.

Reflexively, Simna started to bring up his weapon even as he fell backward. Despite his shock, he caught himself halfway through the gesture. He landed hard on his thighs and backside. Not content with having delivered the blow, Ehomba strode forward until he was standing over the fallen swordsman. Glaring down, he shook a long finger in his friend's face. The hallucinatory blaze that had momentarily flared behind his eyes had vanished, but he was so furious that he trembled as he spoke.

"Never, ever, do anything like that again, Simna! Not in my presence or before my eyes, or I swear by all that the Naumkib respect and honor that I will abandon you to your infantile foolishness and let you perish!"

Stunned, Simna lay on the ground, gaping up at his enraged friend. From the first moment of their relationship there had been disagreements, debates, and disputations. But always words, words. Never blows. The only violence had been verbal. Clenching his teeth, he sprang to his feet, the bloodied sword dangling from his right hand. In an instant he was standing with head tilted slightly back, chest-to-chest with his companion, his unwavering gaze burning into that of the herdsman. Seeing this, Ahlitah growled and prepared to spring forward, but Hunkapa Aub reached down to put a massive hand on the big cat's rippling shoulder and restrain him.

The confrontation lasted only a moment, but to the tense pair of onlookers, one feline and the other only part human, it seemed the longest moment imaginable. Then Simna ibn Sind stepped back and, with slow deliberation, returned his reddened blade back to the scabbard on his back.

"You're a brave man, Etjole Ehomba. Brave and bold and maybe, just maybe, even wise. I've seen you do remarkable, astonishing things. But if you think that makes me afraid of you, you're wrong. Simna ibn Sind fears nothing living. Not soldiers, not giants, not even mystic and powerful sorcerers. And certainly not cattle farmers." Reaching up, he touched the place on his cheek where the herdsman's blow had landed. There would be a bruise there.

"I consider myself a fair and reasonable man, bruther. You don't want me to stand up for the evicted and downtrodden? Fine! I hereby relegate all my altruistic impulses to the bottom of my priorities for the duration of our partnership. In return, you'll keep your hands to yourself. I swear, I might allow one such blow to pass without redress, but I'll never let two."

Ehomba's voice had returned to normal. He looked away. "There is more at stake here, friend Simna, than your precious pride. Remember that I have a family I have not seen in far, far too long anxiously awaiting my return, and a home to go back to. You are burdened by no such responsibilities. You carry your home with you."

"Hoy, and after seeing these past many months how heavily such duties weigh on you, long bruther, I know for a certainty that it was I who made the right choice in deciding how best to contrive a journey through life. Homes!" His tone grew bitter and contemptuous. "They burn down or are pillaged, or storms and Earth-shakings destroy what a man takes years to build. Children die young, and wives grow bored and find excitement in unfaithfulness." He slapped himself on the chest. "I am a free man, Etjole! The whole world is my home, and everyone I choose to embrace is my family."

Ehomba's gaze was inclined westward, down the canyon that led to a no-longer-so-distant sea men called Aurreal. It stayed focused in that direction—as well as on other things. "The world may be your house, Simna. It is not your home. As for family, I wish you a real one someday." With a casual wave of one hand as he sheathed the apparently undamaged sky-metal sword with the other, he beckoned for his companions to follow. Hunkapa Aub fell into step on his right while the black litah ranged farther afield off to his left.

Simna dropped into his usual place close by the herdsman's side. He was smiling once again, his mercurial nature having returned to the fore, the disagreeable incident of moments ago seemingly completely forgotten.

"Tell me, bruther: What would you have done if the Berserker had let loose of his hammer as soon as it started to fly away with him?"

Ehomba smiled reflectively. It took a little longer than usual for the slight upward curve of his mouth to manifest itself, but he smiled. "Why then, my friend, we would have had to slay him before he could recover from his fall. Beyond that I did not have time to think. What the wise men and women of the Naumkib have given me does not allow me to perform more than one miracle at a time."

Simna scratched at the slightly sore spot on his face where Ehomba had struck him. "For a man who spends his days shooing along sheep and cows, you pack a virtuous punch."

"It is harder to knock down a steer than a man."

Ehomba declaimed this without so much as a smile. His attention remained concentrated on the path ahead.

The swordsman chuckled. "I only had a quick glimpse of his face before the Berserker sailed off into the sky. I wish I could be there when he finally comes down!"

Ehomba's tone was preoccupied, his gaze set. He strode rhythmically, easily, over the stony, pebble-strewn ground. *Not far now,* he told himself. It could not be much farther now. A part of him was aware that Simna had spoken, and was expecting a reply.

"Who said anything about him coming down?"

XXII

The view from the sun-swept ridge was breathtaking. Below, between the mountains and the sea, a lush plain dotted with small clumps of forest and the occasional gently rising hill ran from north to south as far as the eye could see. Homes and farms filled the land in between, forming neat patterns. Fronting a broad, sand-fringed bay was a denser concentration of streets and structures, of apartment blocks and businesses, warehouses and amphitheaters, schools and parks. Like the mandibles of a beetle, coral-stone breakwaters enclosed the outer bay, creating shelter and a safe harbor for dozens of incoming and outgoing ships. Their sails spotted the water like the gulls that shadowed them.

Etjole Ehomba stood with one foot resting on a rock, leaning forward, his right arm resting on his thigh. From the semitropical plain and sea below, a warm, slightly moistened breeze rose upward into his face, making him blink and ruffling his braids. There were times these past many months, more times than he cared to remember, when he doubted whether he would ever stand in such a spot, inhaling such a view. Yet there it was, spread out below him, benignly welcoming his arrival.

Ehl-Larimar.

A voice, high-spirited and characteristically confident beyond reason, sounded next to him. "Hoy, long bruther—there it is." As the swordsman contemplated the breathtaking panorama, a flock of opalescent macaws flew past below them, cawing a raucous welcome, their wings glistening in the subdued sunlight as if coated with powdered gems. "Goyvank knows until now I was never really sure it existed."

"Hunkapa like." The largest member of their party grunted approvingly. "Pretty place."

"Too many people." When Ehomba glanced warningly at the big cat, Ahlitah growled irritably. "I know, I know: I can't eat anyone. At least not until after we've recovered this waylaid female."

"We are conspicuous," the herdsman reminded them unnecessarily, thinking out loud, "but this is another large and cosmopolitan city. A seaport as well. With luck our presence will go unremarked upon by the authorities until we have accomplished what we came for. Time is therefore most important."

"Hoy, since when wasn't it?" Simna commented dryly. "Myself, I'd like to take the time to linger and sample the delights a grand city like this surely has on offer, but after we've taken the treasure—and the lady, of course—I know how vital it'll be for us to depart posthaste." He winked at his lanky companion. "It was clever of you, bruther, to engage two such big and strong associates as the carpet and the cat. Either of them can haul more gold and jewels than the two of us put together."

"I am certain they have that capability." Ehomba's reply was devoid of sarcasm.

"And after we've made our escape, we'll head back through these same mountains." The swordsman was well satisfied with his imagined plan of action. "Outraged as they'll be, the authorities might pursue us for a while, if they manage to pick up our trail, but I've yet to meet the soldier who'd challenge all the country we've recently traversed, even on pain of lashing." He grinned at the herdsman. "Besides, they'll have no sorcerer along to help them deal with hypnotic, swallowing salts and the eager denizens of places like Skawpane."

Ehomba started down the mountain. The last mountain, he knew. "First there are questions we must ask of the natives. We need to find out where this Hymneth makes his home, what sort of defenses he keeps close around him. We need to see if anyone knows of the Visioness and where she is being held."

"And the treasure," Simna reminded him enthusiastically. "Don't forget to ask about the treasure."

Ehl-Larimar was as attractive within as it had been from a distance, with luxuriant, carefully tended parks, clean streets, and a healthy and attractive populace. Yet beneath the overt prosperity and occasional opulence there was an eerie sense of ill-being, as if everyone, rich and poor alike, were suffering from some nonfatal but persistent malady.

As Ehomba had hoped, while their presence was remarked upon, it caused no unusual stir among the locals. Once they succeeded in wending their way down to the harborfront, the travelers found themselves swept up in the usual swirl of commerce and industry, just another clutch of exotics in a sea of hardworking foreigners and industrious visitors. Other than the occasional curious glance, no one paid them the least heed.

Not only did the harborfront provide the anonymity Ehomba sought, it was also among the best places in any large city to obtain information. But whenever they mentioned Hymneth the Possessed, initially cordial locals shied away in quiet terror, and even wayfarers from distant lands found hasty excuses to take themselves elsewhere.

Eventually and by means of persistence (and the quiet, unspoken threat posed by Hunkapa Aub and Ahlitah's presence), they learned the location of their quarry's fortress home, as well as the knowledge that it was rumored he kept within its walls a woman of surpassing beauty who hailed from a far land. They now knew where they had to go. It was, as Ehomba put it in his pragmatically understated fashion, now simply a matter of going there.

They found temporary lodging in a waterfront hostel that catered to visitors from the far reaches of the Aurreal, and there they slept and rested all that night and through the following day, until their second night in Ehl-Larimar brought them the darkness they sought.

High, thin clouds obscured much of the light reflected by a quarter moon. The temperate climate of the coast allowed them to move quickly and effortlessly through the city. Once away from the harbor, urban activity began to decline. Those citizens who happened to chance upon the resolute travelers needed only to catch a glimpse of the mass of Hunkapa Aub, or the glowing yellow eyes of the black litah, to hurry on their way without pausing to ask questions.

Toward the high, somber castle they climbed: not by the winding, stone-paved road that provided access to conventional visitors, but up a hunters' trail that ascended from the city toward a broken peak lying between fortress and sea. This time Ehomba let the big cat lead the way, its sharper-than-human senses alert for signs of patrolling soldiers or armed citizens. Once, Ahlitah left the path between the brush and trees to pounce. His attention had been momentary diverted by an unlucky rabbit. Having never encountered at any time in its short life on the city's outskirts a predator of the size and aspect of the litah, it was too paralyzed with fear to scream. Swallowing his snack in two bites, the unapologetic big cat resumed the ascent.

Changing direction before the modest summit was reached, they turned slightly south and east to follow the ridgeline until they found themselves standing in the brush that grew thickly above and behind the castle. Looking down, it was easy to see that its master was the ruler of a rich and prosperous land. Turrets and battlements had been designed with an eye toward appearance as well as efficacy. Only the finest building stone had been used in the construction of the fortress. From within the keep as well as along the walls, flickering lights testified to the presence of oil lamps and torches.

They waited there, crouched down among the concealing chaparral, grateful for the pleasant, balmy night. Owls hooted from within the dark shadows of tall trees, to be answered by nocturnal dragonets whose occasional flights provided a diversion for the tarrying travelers. Moonlight shining through their wings, they preyed on the bats that darted and dove above the treetops in search of moths and other insects, homing in on their victims with shrill, high-pitched squeaks. Between their oversized eyes and ears and long snouts lined with hundreds of thin, sharply pointed teeth, there was not much room left for the rest of their efficient but homely reptilian faces.

The moon had passed its zenith and was waning toward morning when Ehomba shifted from the one-legged herdsman's stance in which he had been resting. "It is time," he declared simply. Taking the point from the black litah, he led the little company toward the castle.

Their initial impressions of its superior design and solid fortifications were confirmed by close inspection as they sidled in single file along its back wall. Nowhere could they find a loose stone to dig out, or a hole through which to squeeze. High above, serene sentries paced their posts, never thinking to look straight down. Why should they? Who would dare to try to sneak uninvited into the fortress of Hymneth the Possessed, and, more to the point, who would want to?

It was Simna ibn Sind, more familiar with castles and imposing stone structures than his tall friend, who suggested they try the storm drain. Large enough to allow all of them passage, even Hunkapa, it penetrated the foot of the castle wall near its western edge. An iron grating blocked ultimate ingress, but though well blacksmithed, it had not been designed with an intruder the size of Hunkapa Aub in mind.

Lying sideways in the opening and bracing his feet against the interior wall, their shaggy companion gripped one of the bars of the grate in both huge hands and pulled, intending to remove the bars one at a time. Instead, there was a muted grinding noise as the entire grate came away in his fingers. Hasty inspection revealed that, as might be expected of iron that had spent much time standing in water, the footings of the bottom bars were rusty. Not rusted through, but no longer possessed of their original strength, either. That was important, because it had allowed Hunkapa Aub to remove the grate quietly as well as quickly.

With Ehomba still leading, they took turns crawling through. The drain opened into a grooved, stone-faced flood-control channel that ran the length of a spacious courtyard. Thus concealed below ground level, they were able to approach close to the back of the keep itself without being seen.

Approaching whistling forced them to halt, trapped with little more than the shadow of the building for cover. If they were discovered here, inside the main wall but outside the keep, they would have no choice but to retreat back the way they had come, knowing that the castle's defenders would subsequently be alert to any further encroachment and thereby making a renewed intrusion far more difficult. The whistling intensified and grew nearer. Simna silently removed his knife from his belt, only to have Ehomba put one hand on the swordsman's wrist and a long finger to his lips.

Around the corner sauntered a member of the household staff. Enjoying the windless, invigorating night air and oblivious to his immediate surroundings, he was on his way to work in the castle scullery when he blundered into the travelers. Stepping forward in a single stride, Ehomba put his right forearm around the man's neck and pulled, lifting and squeezing at the same time. In utter silence, the startled kitchen aide reached up with both hands to claw at his assailant's forearm. His eyes bulged and his lips worked, but, devoid of air from his lungs, no sound emerged.

Slowly, as if he were falling into a deep and gentle sleep, his eyes closed and his flailing hands and twitching body went limp. Without ever removing his forearm from the man's neck, Ehomba gently lowered him to the ground. Simna stepped forward to whisper admiringly.

"That's a fine move for a peaceful herdsman to know."

"Sometimes it is necessary to restrain a frolicsome calf from hurting itself." Almost invisible in the shadows, Ehomba moved forward, his sandals barely whispering across the courtyard flagstones. "There was no reason to kill him. He will sleep until morning and wake with nothing worse than a sore throat."

A grinning Simna silently sheathed his knife. "It's a kindly invader you are, long bruther. If all my adversaries were as considerate as you, I'd have fewer scars in embarrassing places."

"So you would if you had led a more restrained life." Finding a wooden door, the herdsman tried the iron latch. It opened at a touch, with an agreeable absence of noise.

They were in.

It was a storeroom of some kind, piled high with crates and containers of household goods. Though virtually pitch-black inside, there was among their company one for whom poor light and even the near absence thereof posed no obstacle. Following close behind Ahlitah, they made their way through the storeroom and into a hall beyond.

"Unless the interior layout of this pile is utterly differ-ent from every palace I've ever been in, there should be some kind of central chamber or meeting place." Simna gestured forward. Beyond the storeroom, feeble but ade-quate light filtered in through distant windows and ports, allowing them to advance with greater confidence. Once again Ehomba took the lead.

Sounds drifted down to them from the upper reaches of the fortress, but they were isolated and few. This late at night and this early in the morning, few denizens of the castle were stirring. Guards patrolled the main gates and outer wall, not the interior living quarters. Ehomba was concerned about the possibility of encountering free-roaming dogs but, oddly, none were about. Despite his in-terminable curiosity it was, however, a problem to which he could at the moment devote but little thought.

"Here, this way." Advancing, the herdsman gestured for the others to follow him to the left. Proceeding silently through a travertine-trimmed archway, they found them-selves in the high-ceilinged, central chamber whose exis-tence Simna had earlier propounded.

It was utterly silent. Moonlight entered through stained-glass windows of unsettling motif high above the floor. The swordsman was excited to discover that the floor was paved not with slabs of granite or even marble, but with semiprecious stone such as rhodochrosite and lapis, agate and onyx. There *was* treasure here; ample treasure. He could smell it.

"Now all we have to do is find the room where the Vi-sioness is held," Ehomba whispered. "We will take a ser-vant prisoner and seek the information from him." His voice was low and tight with expectancy. "Simna and I have dealt with guards before. With luck, we will be able to spirit her out of the castle and back along the route we used to enter. By daybreak we will be away from the city and safely in among the mountains."

"Hoy, that sounds grand, bruther. But what about the treasure?" Deeply concerned with other matters, Simna hovered close to his lanky companion.

"The Visioness first," Ehomba reminded him tautly. "When we have her, then we will discuss the matter of treasure. Better to worry now about guards, and whether this Hymneth the Possessed sleeps near at hand to the one called Themaryl."

"Tonight, he does not sleep!" The booming voice was shockingly loud and immediate.

Illumination flooded the audience chamber as the fifty fine lamps that lined the enclosing walls and hung from the high ceiling came simultaneously to life, filling the imposing room with light. Whirling as one, the four travelers found themselves staring at the far end of the chamber. There was a throne there, raised up on a high but modest dais. Seated on the throne was a towering, striking figure clad from head to foot in burnished armor of florid design and elegant execution. Bejeweled floor lamps of solid malachite blazed on either side of the chiseled seat of state, their light glimmering off the gold and azure armor.

From beneath a helmet of alloyed red and green gold, eyes blazed with no less intensity than the plethora of dazzling lamps. One mailed arm was upraised. As it lowered slightly, so did the light of the fifty lamps, reducing the blinding brilliance that flushed the chamber to a more tolerable level. Straight-backed and steely-eyed, white of hair and lean of muscle, a venerable soldier-sage stood to the left of the throne and slightly to its rear. Near the foot of the splendid dais fluttered two ominous, independently hovering puffs of malevolent black vapor.

The intruders scanned entrances and alcoves, but the rest of the chamber was deserted. There were no concealed guards, no approaching platoons of heavily armored soldiers, no murderous dogs snarling and snapping madly at the ends of handlers' chains. Only the imposing figure seated on the dais, and the single venerable attendant.

Simna's hand drifted away from his sword. The black litah rose slowly from his crouch. Around them, saturated wicks flickered and sputtered softly, fed by finely sieved and blended oils. Ehomba searched the helmet-shrouded eyes of the towering figure seated on the throne, and those same deep-set, intelligent eyes gazed unblinkingly back.

"'A master of the necromantic arts,' the Worm said. 'A questioner of all that is unanswered.'" Leaning forward slightly on the dais, Hymneth the Possessed, Lord of Ehl-Larimar and Supreme Ruler of the central Aurreal coast all the way from the Wall of Motops to the frozen northlands, leaned his chin on his fist as he considered the taller of the two humans standing before him. "Have you really come from all the way across the Semordria, the eastern ocean?"

It took Simna a moment to find his voice. Swallowing hard but uncowed, he boldly took a step forward. "Not only from across the Semordria, but from far to the south as well."

The armored specter ignored the swordsman. For Hymneth, Simna ibn Sind did not exist. Nor, except as transitory curiosities, did Hunkapa Aub or the black litah. He had words only for the tall, slim, spear-wielding figure clad in simple shirt and kilt who met his gaze without flinching.

"I must say that you don't look the part." After holding the stare for another long, thoughtful moment, the Possessed sighed and sat back on his throne, dropping his arms to the sculpted dragon-headed rests. "After all this waiting, it's something of a disappointment. However, when it comes to reading tomorrows, even the Worm is not omnipotent."

"By Gosthenhark, we're due some respect here for what we've done!" Insults Simna could deal with, but he could not and would not be ignored. "This is my friend the Naumkib Etjole Ehomba, who comes from a land so far to the east and south you cannot conceive of the distance."

"Can't I?" Already, Hymneth was sounding bored.

"He is a wizard of inestimable wisdom and power, controlling forces you cannot hope to defeat." Straightening proudly, the swordsman touched a thumb to his chest. "*I* am Simna ibn Sind, virtuoso of blades and sixth-degree adept in the warrior arts of my homeland. We have not come all this way, defeating dangers and overcoming obstacles beyond your imagining, to be treated with contempt. We mean to have from you the Visioness Themaryl of Laconda, unwillingly abducted from her family and home, and return her to her people." He took a step back and then added hastily, "And whatever treasure of yours we can carry off with us as well."

Hymneth the Possessed nodded slowly, his posture and attitude indicative of a weary patience. The senior soldier at his side remained standing at attention, having moved not a muscle or, insofar as Ehomba could tell, an eye, during the entire confrontation. As for the amorphous blobs of black effluvium, Ehomba knew what they were.

"Well spoken," the Lord of Ehl-Larimar deigned to comment. "While I generally dislike volubility in my soldiers, you exhibit the kind of blind and dumb courage that can sometimes prove valuable. I might have use for you." Before a defiant Simna could reply, Hymneth returned his attention to the silently watching Ehomba.

"When first I was warned of your coming, I was concerned. Not afraid, mind, or worried, but concerned. It is a foolish man who is not concerned with the unknown. This consideration troubled my thoughts, and became so persistent as to unsettle my sleep. Then, things changed. Or rather, something of great importance changed. So much so that it no longer became a matter of interest to me whether you reached Ehl-Larimar or not." Behind the helmet there surfaced the suggestion of a smile.

"This came about because I became immune to anything you could do. Believe me, when the change took place it was a revelation as welcome as it was surprising." He leaned his head slightly to one side. "I look forward with complete indifference to whatever you may choose to do next."

Simna whispered tersely to his laconic friend. "He's bluffing. No matter how powerful he is, he knows nothing of our strengths or powers. Therefore he can't be as disinterested as he says." When Ehomba did not comment, the swordsman decided to go on the offensive. Raising his voice, he challenged the armored figure slumping on the throne.

"If you think you can intimidate us with words, then you've no idea of what we've gone through in the getting here." His fingers slid meaningfully to the hilt of his sword. "It doesn't matter if you're alone except for that old menial and a couple of black puffballs, or if your whole army is waiting just outside this room. We demand that the Visioness Themaryl be brought before us—and that's just for a start."

The helmeted skull nodded slowly. "As you will see, I can be quite an agreeable fellow." Turning slightly to his right, he gestured toward the shadows. "There is no need to send for her. She's right here."

From out of the darkness strode the abducted enchantress of far-distant Laconda. Trailing pale blue chiffon and silk, her flowing tresses bound up in a snood of gold wire set with sapphires and tourmalines, she seemed to glide across the floor toward the dais. Having been smitten with her aspect in a vision, Simna was no less overwhelmed by her loveliness in person. Though he had known many comely women, they were as thistles compared to the radiant rose that now stood before him.

Commanded to appear, he expected her to halt well short of the throne. She did not. As he searched for hidden chains or restraints, she mounted the dais until she was standing directly alongside the throne itself. Reaching out, she placed one hand on the metal-clad shoulder of Hymneth the Possessed. The swordsman hunted in vain for evidence of handcuffs or leg shackles.

And then she smiled.

Simna's lower jaw dropped. Beside him, Ehomba said nothing. Hunkapa Aub and Ahlitah waited behind the two men, confused and uncertain, not knowing how to react or what to do next.

To say that Hymneth was enjoying the effect the Visioness's actions had on his visitors was to understate the delight he hardly showed. "As I told you, something of a transformation has taken place here in Ehl-Larimar." Without taking his eyes from the stunned intruders, he murmured encouragingly to the woman standing by his side. "Tell them—my dear."

As it had been in the vision, her voice was molten gold, each syllable a chord in an infinite celestial cantata. "I am sorry if you have gone to much trouble. It is true that when I was abducted by Hymneth I was overflowing with hatred for him and all that he might stand for. Brave men and women died on my behalf, trying to liberate me. For that I am now and forever will be sorry. At the time and for many months thereafter I grieved for them even as I hoped another might come who would deliver me.

"Imprisoned here, a 'guest' who was not permitted to leave, I was well treated. I kept my own counsel, and nursed my anger and loathing, until eventually it became a thing separate and apart from me. Once that happened, I was able to stand back from it and consider more dispassionately my surroundings. Only then was I able to bring myself even to speak civilly with my captor. Only then did I come to appreciate his profound qualities."

"Profound qual—" Simna whirled on Ehomba. "Bruther, why don't you say something? Are you hearing this?"

Glancing down, the herdsman nodded. "I am hearing it, friend Simna."

Drawing herself up to her full height, the Visioness declaimed clearly. "I have chosen to remain here of my own free will. As his amenable consort, Hymneth has offered me the co-regency of Ehl-Larimar. I have accepted. I regret any personal inconvenience this may have caused you, but you may console yourselves with the knowledge that you are free to remain or depart, as you see fit. You will not be harmed."

Simna could not believe what he was hearing. "He's drugged her! Or she's been ensorcelled! She's not free to voice her own mind. Break the hex, Etjole! Free her from this corrupting stupor so that she can speak the truth!"

The herdsman leaned slightly on his spear. "No, Simna. I do not think she is suffering under a spell. I have been watching her posture, her lips, her eyes. She is herself and none other. The words she speaks are hers, and come from the heart as well as the mind. She truly means to remain here."

"Then—everything we've gone through; the battles we've fought, the dangers we've overcome, the lands and towns and armies and seas we've struggled to pass at the repeated risk of our very lives, it's all been for nothing? For nothing?" When again his friend did not reply, the swordsman sat down heavily on the exquisite, highly polished gemstone floor. And then he began to laugh.

His laughter grew louder, and wilder, echoing through the length and breadth of the great hall. He began to rock back and forth, both arms wrapped around his stomach as the laughter spilled out of him in long, rolling waves. Only when he had come close to laughing himself insensate did the calmly foreboding voice from the throne speak again.

"Unlike the beauteous Themaryl, I hardly ever feel sorry for anyone. People make the lives they live. I regret to admit that in certain quarters of my kingdom I am not considered a compassionate ruler. But tonight, though I would like to laugh with you, mercenary, I find that I cannot. I can only—feel sorry for you." He turned back to the silently staring Ehomba. "So you see, necromancer from across the Semordria, if such it is that you are, you are defeated before you can begin. That which you came to fight for no longer exists. Your reason and rationale have evaporated, like smoke." Steel-clad fingers reached out to cover the back of the Visioness Themaryl's perfect hand.

"Ordinarily, I would not be so generous to those who slink uninvited into my home, but my consort has spoken. You are free to leave, or stay, or do whatever you want. It is of no import to me. Enjoy the city if you like. Ehl-Larimar has much to offer the tired traveler." He nodded in the direction of the silent old soldier. "If you wish, Peregriff will find lodging for you tonight within the castle. Since I have no reason to deal with you as enemies, I suppose I might as well treat you as guests. Tomorrow you may dine with me. And with my incomparable, compliant consort." Turning his hand, he lifted hers up in his, bent forward, and kissed it. Seeing this was enough to set Simna ibn Sind to laughing uncontrollably all over again.

"No."

The seated swordsman's hysteria halted in mid-laugh. To the left of the throne, the impressive white eyebrows of General Peregriff narrowed ever so slightly. At the foot of the dais, tiny red eyes began to emerge and take shape within the cryptic depths of the cancerous black vapors.

Having started to rise from his throne, Hymneth the Possessed paused and peered across the reflective, lamplit floor. His voice was composed, even—but just the slightest bit perplexed.

"What did you say?"

"I said, no." For the first time since the lamps had burst

to life in the regal audience chamber, it was Etjole Ehomba who stepped forward. "We cannot avail ourselves of your hospitality, or that of your kingdom." Lowering the tip of his spear, he pointed slightly to his left. "The Visioness Themaryl is coming with us."

Hymneth's voice grew quietly, dangerously frosty. "I am afraid I do not understand. She does not wish to go with you. She does not wish to return to Laconda or the life she knew there. She wishes to stay here with me. Of her own free will. You yourself acknowledged as much only moments ago."

The herdsman nodded. He had come a long way and was very tired, as if he had spent days chasing runaway animals through the hills and gullies back of the village. "When I first set out on this journey, not knowing how or when it would end or where it would take me, I did so because I had made a vow. A promise to a dying man who called himself Tarin Beckwith, of Laconda North. He made me swear not to rest until I returned the Visioness Themaryl to her home and family. This oath I reluctantly made. I have traveled far and at great expense of effort to fulfill that obligation. I intend to do so."

The wide, helmeted head was shaking slowly from side to side. "There is reason, and then there is insanity, but the likes of this I have never had to deal with before. Do you mean to tell me that in spite of her declared wishes to remain here you intend to take her back, by force if necessary?"

Ehomba nodded stoically. His voice never changed. "By force if necessary."

With the abruptness of a rogue wave shattering upon an unsuspecting shore, Hymneth the Possessed stood bolt upright before his throne and bellowed thunderously at the impious intruder.

"By Besune, this is worse than madness!" He was trembling with rage. "In spite of all the sleeplessness you have caused me, I offer you your life, and you demand death!" Reaching out toward the intolerable interloper, he made a cup of his extended fingers. "Since you so devoutly seek your doom, here it is, master of a doubtful magic. Here in this hand. Come and get it!"

Without a word, a grim-faced Ehomba let go of his spear. It had not yet struck the floor before he was running forward, reaching back over a shoulder to draw the sky-metal sword. A stunned Simna frantically began to scramble to his feet. Hunkapa Aub tensed, and the black litah let loose with a snarl that rattled the hanging banners high overhead. Rising to his full, dominating height before the throne, Hymneth the Possessed spread both arms wide to restrain the alerted Peregriff and shield the startled Themaryl. Then he let loose with an inarticulate howl of his own as he flung one arm forward at the tall, rangy herdsman racing toward him.

The dart that had been concealed within the sleeve of his armor struck the onrushing herdsman in his right shoulder. Without pausing, Ehomba reached up and pulled it free. Tossing it to one side, he showed no ill effects from the virulent poison it contained. Nor would he, thanks to the immunizing contents of his water bag, thoughtfully treated months ago by, as Simna was fond of saying, a long brother.

His gaze narrowing slightly, the ruler of Ehl-Larimar brought his other arm forward and uttered a word so loathsome and vile that the Visioness was compelled to clasp both hands to her ears to shut out the echo of it that lingered in the air. In response to his gesture, eyes now fully formed and ablaze, the two clouds of sooty vapor that had been hovering impatiently by his steel-booted feet ballooned to the size of black buffalo as they sped gleefully away from the dais to intercept the impudent, foolhardy human.

XXIII

Ehomba met the onrushing eromakadi head-on, without trying to dodge or step clear of their charge. In an instant he was enveloped in black cloud and completely obscured from view. Simna held his breath. Even so, he was less agitated than his companions, who unlike him had not had the benefit of seeing the herdsman deal with eromakadi. But as the minutes passed and nothing happened and Ehomba did not reappear, the swordsman found himself growing more and more uneasy.

Then a soft whistling became audible. It grew louder, until it dominated the room. The vaporous substance of the eromakadi began to twitch, then to jerk violently, and finally to shrink. Moments later everyone could see Ehomba, standing with sword in hand, inhaling and inhaling without seemingly pausing to breathe. Into his open mouth the eromakadi disappeared, sucked down like steam from a kettle traveling in reverse, until the last frantic, faintly mewling black tendril had been swallowed.

Without word or comment of any kind, an Ehomba none

the apparent worse for the experience resumed his assault on the dais.

"An eromakasi!" Balling one hand into a fist, a surprised Hymneth raged at the onrushing herdsman. "What have you done with my pets, eromakasi?" Flinging his closed, armored hand forward, the Possessed opened his fingers the instant his arm was fully extended.

Ball lightning flew at Ehomba. It was olive green in hue and crackled with energy. Raising his blade, the herdsman parried the verdant globe. Deafening thunder rattled the reception hall. Simna and the others were momentarily blinded by the shower of green sparks that flew from the sky-metal sword.

Even as Ehomba was opposing this latest assault, the lofty figure seething before the throne of Ehl-Larimar was readying another. Hymneth continued to fling spheres of sickly green energy at his attacker as the herdsman persistently warded them off. In this manner Ehomba, though his approach was slowed by the need to fight off the tall sorcerer's successive attacks, sustained his advance on the throne. As he drew nearer, the ball lightning flew more often. Employing reflexes honed from years of fighting off predators intent on stealing from the Naumkib flocks, he struck down one blazing assault after another. The frenzy of emerald sparks that struck from his untiring blade outshone the far more subdued glow of the chamber's lamps.

Swinging the sword in short, deliberate arcs, he gained the first step, and then the second. If Hymneth the Possessed was growing anxious or uneasy, the evidence of such a condition remained his and his alone. His face remained hidden behind the magnificent helmet. His defense was as unremitting and incessant as Ehomba's advance, and he showed no sign of weakening or abandoning his position before the throne.

Surmounting the last step, Ehomba batted aside a lethal, crackling globe half his size and was swallowed up by the consequent deluge of rabid green sparks and shattered shafts of lightning. Emerging from this cataract of emerald energy, he brought his blade around in a low feint, then swung it up over his head and brought it straight down, edge on, with both hands. Hymneth the Possessed, Lord of Ehl-Larimar, was in the process of throwing another orb of lightning when he saw or sensed what his attacker intended. Quickly raising both mailed arms over his head, he crossed his wrists and caught the descending sword in the V they formed.

Green and white sparks erupted from the point of contact and the concussive wave thus generated knocked Peregriff, the Visioness Themaryl, and Simna ibn Sind off their feet. Only the larger and more powerful Ahlitah and Hunkapa Aub were able to remain standing, and even they were staggered by the force of the detonation.

When Simna's vision cleared and he could once again discern the drama being played out in front of the throne, a loss of feeling and belief gripped him the likes of which he had never experienced before, not even when as a child he had been cruelly assaulted by his peers. As receding thunderclaps rolled through the chamber and off into the distance, he saw the remnants of the shattered sky-metal sword lying scattered everywhere: on the steps leading up to the dais, on the floor, on the throne itself. Stare at them as he might, they did not slowly revive, did not become dozens or hundreds of new, smaller blades as they had in far Skawpane. They had been smashed into ragged shards and strips of twisted steel, like the vulnerable metal of any common sword.

At the foot of the steps lay a crumpled, motionless figure.

"Etjole!" Heedless of whatever the domineering, armored figure commanding the dais might do, the swordsman rushed forward. Hunkapa Aub and the black litah were right behind him.

Throwing himself on the prone torso, Simna used both hands to wrench the valiant herdsman over onto his back. Ehomba's eyes were closed and his body limp. There hung about him a sharp, acrid smell, as if he had been singed by something as lethal as it was invisible. The swordsman shook the smooth, lean shoulders; gently at first, then more forcefully.

"Etjole! Bruther!" To his frantic entreaties there was no response. Pressing an ear to the herdsman's chest, Simna's eyes grew wide as he detected no sound from within. Hastily moistening a palm, he held it in front of the herdsman's unmoving lips. Nothing cooled his skin.

"It can't be." He drew back from the motionless body. *"It can't be."*

Dipping his maned head low over the prostrate form, Ahlitah listened and sniffed once, twice. Then yellow eyes rose, flicking first in the direction of Hymneth the Possessed, then meeting those of the stricken swordsman.

"It's over, Simna. He's dead. The herder of cattle is dead."

And he was.

Ehomba felt no pain. In fact, he did not "feel" at all. He knew instinctively, unarguably, that he was dead. Dead at the hands of another. Hymneth the Possessed had killed him. This knowledge caused him neither regret nor discomfort. Those were concerns that belonged to the world of the living, and he was no longer a part of that. He did not think of his condition as a failure, or lament for his lost family, or sorrow for anything left behind. After death, everything changed.

He was conscious that some time had passed, though whether seconds or years he could not have said. At first he had been aware of being above his body, utterly divorced from it and from everything of the living flesh. Very quickly thereafter and without any sense of transition or traveling he found himself in a void, an immeasurably vast space that would have been completely dark except for the presence of distant, unblinking stars. They were not the stars one saw in life. Somehow they seemed much closer, yet infinitely distant. There was no sense of ground, of up or down or direction, or of the presence of the Earth. Only the void, stars—and souls.

He thought of them as souls for lack of a better term. Present around him in the starry vastness was everyone who had ever lived. Though they were packed together in a single immense, amorphous mass, there was a feeling of adequate space between individuals. It was crowded, yet with no sense of crowding.

There was no movement of bodies. Everyone hung limp, drifting, eyes open and unblinking as they contemplated the star-washed heavens with a silent fusion of curiosity and wonderment. Ehomba was surprised to discover that he retained a sense of body, of the physical self. Gazing about, he was unable to identify or categorize individuals either as to sex or age. There was only the powerful, detached feeling of being surrounded by uncounted people.

He was able to sense more than this from only one nearby individual, whom he felt to be a foot soldier of young to middle age who hailed from an earlier eon. Only his eyes conveyed any familiar impressions at all. No one breathed, or smelled. It was possible that they, and he, could hear, but there was no noise, no sound in the accepted sense.

He was conscious of understanding words without actually hearing them as modulated waves pressing against his inner ear. The words were simply "there." Otherwise it was infinitely peaceful and quiet despite the drifting, floating mass of humanity. There was an inescapable feeling of equilibrium, of everything and everyone being held in silent, sensationless suspension. This despite a steady, unending flow of new arrivals who added wordlessly to the ever-increasing volume of individuals.

The only words he could comprehend seemed to be whispering "What time is it?" and "Does anyone here know the time?" Though conscious of, aware of, others around them, this was all that anyone could think of to say. Ehomba found it interesting that no one asked, or thought to ask, what day it was, or what month, or what year. Only, "What time?"

That, and endless self-reflective queries of "Didn't I just get here?" This gently querulous mantra was repeated over and over, yet without any feeling of repetition or tedium. There was never any sense of more than one minute passing before the question was heard again from another source, and then another, and another. "Didn't I just get here?" This even though an immense amount of time had obviously passed. How many millions, or billions of times the question had been ethereally posed Ehomba could not have said. It was the same for him as for everyone around him. The feeling, the certainty, that regardless of real time, no more than a minute had ever passed.

There was one other sensation. An inescapable, powerful, overriding sense of purpose to It All. What that might be, he never got a feel for. Catechist that he was, he was pleased to believe that there was a reason, a purpose behind It All, just as he was disappointed not to learn what that might be. It was frustrating, though he never felt frustrated in the familiar sense of the term.

There was no heat or cold, no feeling of weight. No pain or pleasure. Physicality without sensation. Just a sense of being—and the Purpose. No sense of a deity, either, or of anyone or anything watching or manipulating. Just souls, people, accumulating, wondering about the Purpose . . .

Standing tall and assured before the throne, Hymneth the Possessed straightened his helmet, which had in the course of the preceding clash been jolted slightly askew, and regarded the tableau of intruders below him.

"See to them, Peregriff."

"Yes, Lord," came the always prepared voice off to his left.

"As soon as they have recovered from their bathetic grieving, find out what they want to do. Offer the mercenary a position with the army—not my household staff. I'm not in the habit of recruiting the potentially vengeful. The cat is clearly intelligent beyond the level of his more modestly proportioned cousins. I suspect it will want to leave. Let it. As for the bloated rug-creature—I'm not sure what to do about it. Hopefully, it will depart in the company of the cat, and without soiling the floor on its way out." Turning to his right, he extended an arm.

"Come, my dear. I think this has been enough entertainment for one night."

Crouched alongside the motionless body of his tall friend, a disbelieving Simna cried unabashedly, the tears spilling copiously down his cheeks. "You crazy, single-minded fool! You gaunt, self-righteous bastard! Hoy, you weren't supposed to die! What am I going to tell your family?"

"Excuse me," murmured Hunkapa Aub as his huge frame inclined over the corpse, "would you please step back, Simna?"

"What difference will it make?" The swordsman sobbed angrily, consumed by passion and self-pity. "Why should I—" He broke off, sniffed long and hard, and gaped uncertainly at his oversized companion. "Wait a minute here. What did you say?"

Eyes of arctic blue gazed back at him. "I asked you to please step aside. I need room."

"You need . . . ?" The swordsman's expression narrowed. "All of a sudden it's not 'Hunkapa need' or 'Hunkapa want Simna move.' It's 'Would you please step back, Simna'— glib and polite as a thrice-bedamned court orator." He straightened and took a couple of steps backward, staring hard, hard, at the massive, looming figure. "By every god-damned god I've ever sworn by—what's going on here?"

"I need room in which to work." Having concluded his hasty but thorough examination of the herdsman's corpse, Hunkapa Aub rose to his full height, tilted his shaggy head back until he was gazing at the ceiling, closed his eyes, and stretched both arms up and out.

Opposite, Ahlitah was in stealthy retreat, muscles tensed, head held low. "I knew there was something about him. I knew it."

"What's that?" Simna shouted across Ehomba's prostrate body at the big cat. "What did you know?"

The black litah growled softly, its rending claws fully extended as they scraped backward across the floor. "He never *smelled* stupid."

"*Simbala!*" cried Hunkapa Aub, imploring forces that lay deeper than his words. "*Acenka sar vranutho!*"

A brilliant white glow appeared above his head, a fierce effulgence that pulsed with scarcely restrained energy. Descending on the far side of the dais, Hymneth the Possessed and his new consort paused and turned. Behind the helmet, the ruler of all Ehl-Larimar—blinked.

Eyes closed tight, chanting to himself, Hunkapa Aub lowered his arms until both hands were pointing at the floor—and at the prone figure of Etjole Ehomba. "*Haranath!*" he rumbled, and the pulsating, glittering orb responded. Drifting down from its location above the shaggy head, it impacted the body of the herdsman, and sank into it like milk into a sponge. A pale brilliance suffused the slender cadaver, overflowing it with radiance from head to toe. Eyes still shut, Hunkapa sustained the incantation as an obviously agitated Hymneth released the Visioness Themaryl and started hurriedly back around the base of the dais.

"'A master of all the necromantic arts' is coming, the Worm said—but it never described what he would look like!" Raising one hand, the sovereign warlock threw a crackling, virulent green sphere at the hulking hirsute figure. Lethal lightning darted straight for Hunkapa Aub's eyes.

Standing bolt upright, engulfed in a torrent of unadulterated white energy that was the shadow of the lingering breath of a billion unfinished, unfulfilled souls, Etjole Ehomba caught the sickly emerald globe square in the chest. It exploded on impact, shriveled green spikes flying off and spilling away in all directions like startled snakes. As Ehomba started toward him, Hymneth once more began throwing sphere after destructively lambent sphere. Those directed at himself the herdsman shattered with a simple wave of his hand, each finger armored with the massed white energy of a million souls. Any orbs aimed at Hunkapa Aub he merely deflected, sending them crashing destructively into the far corners of the quaking hall.

Crouched off to one side, Simna ibn Sind watched the clash of forces whose scope he could not judge and whose strength he could not imagine, and found himself struck most by something that was less than overwhelming but just as distinctive. Throughout all that had happened, his friend Ehomba had never lost his poise. His expression had been the same when first he had attacked Hymneth, when he had lain before the swordsman in death, and now when he was—what was he? Simna did not know. He was a man of the blade and not of the mind. As always, struggling with the latter caused him far more pain than any edge, no matter how sharp.

Ehomba's advance was deliberate and relentless. No matter what Hymneth threw at him, no matter how awesome the energy or irresistible the might, the herdsman continued to approach. Green and white lightning flooded the great chamber and obscured much of what was happening at its far end.

Until a burst of verdant ball lightning taller and wider than Hunkapa Aub smashed the shell of protective white energy that surrounded Ehomba. Exhausted but triumphant, perspiring heavily within his armor, Hymneth the Possessed prepared to raise his tired, trembling right hand one last time.

"Now, whatever you are become, we'll make an end to this, *and* to the secret master who has manipulated you all along!"

Like his expression, the herdsman's voice never changed. "I am Etjole Ehomba, of the Naumkib, and no one manipulates me." Parting his jaws and before Hymneth could bring his arm up and forward, he spat forcefully at the supreme sovereign of the central coast. Two dark, wet, black blobs flew from his lips, to strike the looming, armored figure right in the eye slit that creased the upper part of his helmet.

Hymneth's arm continued to rise—only to halt, quivering, halfway from the ground. The imposing figure stumbled once, shook itself, then staggered sideways. There came a metallic cracking sound as deep fissures appeared in his armor, running from magnificent helmet to mailed foot. The Visioness Themaryl screamed as the ruler of Ehl-Larimar collapsed sideways onto the floor. Struck by the half-digested essence of not one but two eromakadi, he lay in his useless armor, unmoving where he had fallen.

Reaching for his sword, Peregriff started forward, only to be intercepted by a still uncertain but increasingly confident Simna. Holding his blade out in front of him, the swordsman ventured a strained smile.

"No, my venerable friend! By Gequed, we'll see this thing done with by those who matter. You and I are insignificant components of any final rendering."

An awkward pause ensued while Hymneth's general glared down at the itinerant swordsman. Then he nodded, once, and dropped his hand from the hilt of his weapon. Together, both men turned to look.

Rushing forward, Themaryl had knelt beside the supine figure of her monarch. Concern wracked her countenance, but there were no tears. Fearful, she looked up at the rangy, solemn-visaged herdsman.

"Is—is he dead?"

"No." Ehomba studied the motionless figure somberly. Bits and pieces of fractured armor were starting to slough away from the body. "Only paralyzed, and that I think just from the shoulders down. Eventually, he should recover all movement."

She started to smile gratefully, then thought better of it, and instead turned her attention back to the recumbent torso.

Breathing hard, Simna ibn Sind joined his tall friend in gazing down at the motionless form. "Hoy, only paralyzed? Why leave the job half finished?" He aimed the point of his blade.

"No, my friend." Reaching out, Ehomba forestalled the swordsman's fatal intent. "That is not what I came for."

Simna eyed him imploringly. "By Gulvent, bruther, he tried to kill you! He *did* kill you! Speaking of which . . ." The swordsman turned to look at the indefatigable hulk that was Hunkapa Aub. Through his fur, the biggest member of their little party was smiling.

"I get it!" Simna blurted in sudden realization. "You weren't really dead! You were faking it all along."

Ehomba shook his head slowly. "No, my friend. I was dead. Well and truly dead. I know, because I spent time in the place where the dead go."

"Tell me," asked Hunkapa Aub seriously, "what is it like, the place where the dead go?"

"Slow," the herdsman told him. Reaching out, he put a firm hand on the swordsman's shoulder and smiled reassuringly. "I knew that I was going to die, Simna. It had been foretold. Not once, but three times. Once by a seductive seeress the memory of whose beauty and wisdom I will always treasure, once by a dog witch whose insight and affection I will always remember, and once even by a fog whose persistence I will never forget. 'Continue on and die,' they said—and so it had to be before we could triumph." Turning, he gazed gravely at the still unmoving body of Hymneth the Possessed: warlock, sorcerer, eminent ruler of illustrious Ehl-Larimar.

"But that was as far as their predictions went. Nothing was said about what might happen *after* I died." Raising his eyes, he smiled gratefully at the imposing, attentive, fraternal figure of Hunkapa Aub. "Nothing was said that would preclude my being resurrected."

Simna gaped at him, struggling to digest the import of his friend's serene words. Then—he grinned. The grin widened until it seemed to encompass the majority of his sweat-streaked face. And then he began to chuckle softly to himself. It never grew loud or boisterous like before, but it did not go away, either.

"Two sorcerers. All this time I've been traveling in the company of *two* sorcerers." Turning, he confronted Hunkapa

Aub, whose eyes had become suddenly wise as well as blue. "As many days and nights as I have spent in your company, as many evils and dangers as we fought side by side, and I never suspected. I never *would* have suspected."

Hunkapa Aub's smile widened slightly. "Not all wizards look alike, good swordsman. Not everything in life appears as one imagines it to be. And it is not required that one be human to be a master of the thaumaturgic arts."

Simna could only stare and shake his head in lingering disbelief. "Why? Why the sham and the continuing charade? Why did you let the people of Netherbrae keep you in a cage and throw food at you and torment you with insults and curses?"

Clasping both immoderately hairy hands behind his back, the hulking wizard considered Simna's flurry of questions. "You would not understand, good swordsman. Even a sorcerer needs to learn by experience. I was traveling through that part of the world when I was accosted by the simple, shallow folk of that otherwise charming mountain town. I could easily have avoided capture, or freed myself at any time. But I was, and am always, curious as to what would motivate otherwise apparently intelligent and compassionate people to act in such a shameful fashion toward another of their fellow beings who had done them no harm. One can learn much about one's peers by spending time in a cage.

"Then you appeared in Netherbrae, and freed me. Finding you more interesting than anything else that tempted to engage me at that time, I chose to accompany you on your journey. It promised much of interest and elucidation. Suffice to say, I have not been disappointed."

"But why the pantomime?" An unsatisfied Simna persisted. "Why didn't you just tell us who and what you were from the beginning?"

Hunkapa Aub's smile was as sage as the look in his eyes. "Wizards have this 'effect' on people, good swordsman. In the presence of one they become muted things and no longer act themselves. I wanted to study you as you are, not as you would have become had you known my true identity."

Simna stammered angrily. "Study us? And what have you learned, maestro of a mumbling disguise, from the specimens you chose to keep so long in ignorance?"

"The best thing there is to learn about another. That you are good, all of you. Yea, even you, Simna ibn Sind, though you would argue long and hard to deny it. I know you well. You, and the great and noble cat." Raising his gaze, he considered the lanky figure of Etjole Ehomba. "Your friend and guide I am still not entirely sure about." Hirsute shoulders rose and fell in a prodigious shrug. "I think I will stay with you a while longer. I sense there is still more to learn from your company."

"Well, it's a good thing you turned out to be more than the untutored, shambling simpleton you seemed to be," Simna declared, adding hastily, "I mean nothing untoward by that, master. Who would have thought you the more powerful sorcerer than Hymneth the Possessed?"

"Who said I was more powerful?" Hunkapa Aub's smile faded. "I caught him unawares, after he had been tired and worn down by your friend Etjole. I did not defeat him. Ultimately, it demanded the combined efforts of both of us."

"Hoy, however it was done, the important thing is that you were able to overcome him." The swordsman glowered down at the recumbent, motionless figure from which ruined metal was sloughing like a second skin. As he did so, his eyes widened.

Exposed to the flicker of lamplight without his omnipresent armor, Hymneth the Possessed, lord of the central coast and absolute ruler of Ehl-Larimar the sublime, was after all had been said and done not all that he had appeared to be.

Curly black hair almost as thick as Hunkapa's covered the barrel chest as well as the long, massive forearms. But beneath the bulky upper body were tapered hips and shockingly short, stunted legs. These too were intermittently overlaid with still more of the thick body curls.

Formerly strapped to and now detached from the undersized lower limbs and feet were a pair of whitened, dying legs that had been taken from a much taller man. Amputated from an unknown owner, these fleshy prostheses were dying before the onlookers' eyes, the magic that had kept them attached to the warlock's feet having been shattered along with the rest of his protective spells. Nothing less than stilts made of meat, they had covertly provided a good portion of the lord of Ehl-Larimar's imposing height.

Atop a bull neck sat a massive head that seemed too large for the rest of the body. Thick, almost blubbery lips fronted a prognathic jawline. The ears were overlarge and set toward the rear of the skull. Most striking of all was the forehead, sloping well back from the thick, bony ridges that shaded the eyes. The raven hair atop the head had been trimmed short to eliminate the profusion of greasy curls to be found elsewhere on the squat body. It was a surpassingly ugly face, a visage that fluctuated uneasily between homely and repulsive. A face that was not quite human, though Ehomba knew what it was. Simna recalled a recent statement of Hunkapa Aub's.

"It is not necessary for one to be human to be a master of the thaumaturgic arts."

Hymneth the Possessed was a neander.

The partially paralyzed wizard was impotent to smash in the faces that were staring down at him or strike the pitying expressions from their countenances. Defeated, frustrated, revealed, naked, and exposed, he could only moan and howl helplessly.

"Go on; look, stare, gawk at me. My people wonder why I never appear among them unhelmeted or without armor. It's because if they saw me like this, as I *am*, they would repudiate me despite all my power and no matter what threats I rained down upon them. My forebears are from the far north, from the frozen wastes that cap the roof of the world. There they huddle, miserable and cold, dying young and struggling to eke out an existence I would not bequeath to a bird. Driven there by the 'healthy' ones. By people like yourselves." Unable to move more than his head, he glared defiantly up at a silently watching Ehomba.

"Only *I* was different. Only I devoured everything the wise ones muttered and mumbled, storing their knowledge within my heart as well as my head. I studied, and learned, and vowed to make a life different from theirs. A life of power and dominion over those who shunned and jeered the neanders.

"When I had learned enough, I found my way here, to Ehl-Larimar. The journey almost killed me, but I took the throne from the weakling who sat upon it and remade it in my own image. I extended my control to encompass all of the central coast. I could have done more, could have conquered farther to the north and south, but I did not. Power I'd wanted, and power I'd gained.

"Having attained so much, still I was not satisfied. Having acquired power over the real world, I sought the same over the supernatural. I immersed myself in whatever necromantic lore I could find. But nowhere did I encounter a spell that would render me human. That would make me 'normal.' On learning that there was nothing I could do to alter my ugliness in the sight of people, I resolved angrily to surround myself with beauty." Lifting his head, he nodded as well as he was able.

"The consequences of that obsession you see all around you. This castle, its furnishings, even the attendants and retainers who serve me within its walls; everything has been chosen as much for its attractiveness as for skill. It, and I, lacked only one thing: a consort. Someone to sit by my side, to be my queen. Feeling this great emptiness inside myself, I determined to seek out the most beautiful woman in the world. I found her, and took her from her lackeys and lickspittle suitors, and brought her here. A vain hope, perhaps, but I thought that given time and consideration and honor, she might come to at least tolerate, if not to love, me."

Kneeling beside him, the Visioness Themaryl took up the refrain. "He stole me away from my home and my family. My anger was boundless as the sea and the land I was carried across. I would neither converse, nor dine, nor sit with him.

"Then in the very late of one evening, when I thought the castle asleep, I stole downstairs in my endless search for a means or route of escape, and caught him slumped over his table, drunk—and unhelmeted. At first I was repulsed. But my constitution is not frail. I approached, and looked into his face that was half unconscious, and I saw the pain there." She sighed deeply, remembering.

"After that, it was different. I was cautious, and I believe that he was afraid to chance too much, but in time we came to know one another. All my life I have been courted, and promised, and drawn back from a chorus of suitors and swains that sometimes seemed to stretch from my home to the moon itself. I found them all much alike: vain, unambitious, conceited, too much in love with themselves to love another." She rested a hand on the exposed, thickly bearded chest. "Here I found something—different. If your journey homeward should take you back through Laconda, please assure my family that I am well, and content with my lot."

Simna finally stopped laughing. Shaking his head at the irony of it all, he gave his tall companion a friendly slap on the back. "Well, that's that, I suppose. All this way to rescue a princess who doesn't want to be rescued. Let's have a look around for the treasure and then I suppose we'll be off. There's nothing to hold us here any longer." He started past the herdsman, heading for the main entrance to the audience chamber.

For the second time that remarkable night, Etjole Ehomba said, quietly but firmly, "No."

"No?" A querulous Simna turned. "No what?" He gestured toward the toppled Hymneth and his angelic attendant. "You heard what she said. She wants to stay here."

"Nothing has changed, Simna. You heard what I told *him*. It does not matter." Walking over to where he had earlier dropped his spear, Ehomba recovered the weapon. Returning to the prone form of the Possessed, he brooded aloud over his lack of options.

"I vowed to Tarin Beckwith, a man of noble mien and honorable intention, on the occasion of his last breath, that I would return the Visioness Themaryl to her family. Though I have come a great distance and been too long away from home and friends, I intend to do this thing."

Her exquisite face upturned to him, Themaryl gaped in disbelief. "But I want to stay! It is as your friend says. I have cast my lot with this person. I will not go with you. Do not ask it of me."

"I will not," Ehomba replied. So saying, he bent down and slipped a slender but muscular arm around her waist. Lifting her up, he slung her over his shoulder, a position that found her stunned and outraged.

"Let me go! Put me down this instant! I, Themaryl, command you!"

"Only one woman commands me, and she is not here." Holding the kicking, flailing form firmly against his shoulder, he turned to the stupefied Simna. "Tie her hands before she thinks to try and draw my remaining sword, or to go fumbling in my pack. Quick now, Simna!"

"What? Yes, bruther. Hold her."

The swordsman was a master of blades, not knots, but he bound the wrists and legs of the Visioness securely enough with cord drawn from the richly brocaded curtains that framed one entryway. Unable to raise himself up or move more than his head and neck, Hymneth the Possessed raved and ranted at the meddling interlopers, vowing all manner of punishment and torture if they did not release her at once.

Seeing his master's distress, Peregriff was about to call out to the castle guard for assistance, only to find himself instantaneously confronted by a sleek black feline shape.

"I'd hold my tongue if I were you," Ahlitah warned the senior soldier. "Or I will." Prudent as always, Peregriff held his peace.

They left the general hovering over his master and calling not for armed soldiers but for medical assistance. No crawling along damp, filthy storm drains for them this time; they strode boldly out the main entrance to the fortress. The startled twilight guards scrambled to react, only to shy away from the presence of the long-striding Hunkapa Aub and the triumphantly snarling black litah.

Thus did the four visitors and one unwilling other depart the temperate and accommodating land of fabled Ehl-Larimar. As they did so it was hard to tell who was making the most noise: the enraged and disbelieving Visioness Themaryl, or the master of blades Simna ibn Sind, with his ceaseless grumbling about their failure to even look for, much less obtain, any treasure. Only Ehomba's promises of riches to come kept the seriously aggravated swordsman from remaining behind. The herdsman mollified his sorely disgruntled companion somewhat by placing him in charge of the Visioness and her security.

For the first time in recent memory, a determined Ehomba found himself heading deliberately and purposefully east.

XXIV

As if to confirm that their luck had changed, by dint of a hard march and fortuitous timing, they reached distant Doroune just as the *Grömsketter* was concluding the return leg of its tour of the trading towns and cities to the south. A joyous reunion there was, with Stanager Rose and all her crew astounded yet pleased to encounter their former passengers once again.

No one was disappointed that their eastward crossing of the Semordria was less eventful than before. Following Captain Rose's instructions, they allowed themselves to be put ashore well to the southwest of Hamacassar and its twitchy time guardians. By traveling south and then east from the point of disembarkation, they also avoided Laconda North, where because of the difficulties arising from their previous visit they would have been less than courteously received, and reentered Laconda itself from the west.

Simna was concerned that they might have difficulty approaching the capital quietly if the citizens of that prosperous province recognized their long-absent Visioness, but he needn't have concerned himself. After the long and tiring journey, her aspect was less than regal, and they arrived in the city without incident.

Disclosure of the Visioness's presence among them occasioned scenes of riotous joy among the populace, and the travelers were conveyed without delay into the presence of the Duke and his family.

All Themaryl's relations had gathered to salute her return: father and mother, doddering grandparents, gabby aunts and uncles and innumerable cousins. Haggard and drawn, she was forced to endure embrace upon embrace.

"Oh my delight," one uncle declared upon looking at her, "you do look like you've had a time of it!"

"I am not the same person I was when I was taken from here, Bennrik," she replied stiffly. "Things changed, and I changed with them."

"But you are home, back in the bosom of your family and your people, and that is all that matters." Duke Lewyth rose from his modest seat of power to gesture grandly at the outlandish quartet of foreigners who stood together and formed an exotic island in the midst of the rejoicing throng of aristocrats and courtiers. "And for that we have these stalwart, brave strangers to thank!" Smiling graciously, he nodded at Ehomba.

"Have you anything to say to the people of Laconda on this joyous occasion, sir? Any words you might care to speak will be received with gratitude and appreciation."

It was Simna who spoke up, raising his voice above the general clamor. "You have to understand, noble sir, that my friend here is no orator. It is more in his nature to . . ." He halted as, to his considerable surprise, Ehomba not only stepped forward but mounted the royal dais to stand opposite the Duke and next to the Visioness Themaryl. He did not bother to raise his hand to quiet the crowd, but instead simply began speaking in his usual calm, measured tone.

"I vowed to the dying Tarin Beckwith of Laconda North to return this woman to her home and family. This I have done." As he spoke, he ignored the Visioness's sullen, unyielding scowl. "My obligation to him is at last fulfilled." Turning to her he asked simply, directly, and utterly unexpectedly, "Now that I am free of any responsibility in this matter, I would like to know what it is that *you* want."

She gaped at him. For an instant she thought that the tall, singular southerner was taunting her, making fun of her condition. But in spite of herself she had come in the course of the long journey back to Laconda to know him at least as well as any of his odd clutch of companions. In all that time, she had never seen him taunt, or ridicule, or mock anyone. Was it possible that the query was an honest one?

She did not have to meditate on a reply. Nor did she hesitate. "I want to go back to Ehl-Larimar."

Ehomba nodded. Below, surrounded by celebrating, unwitting Lacondans, a dreadful realization was dawning on a profoundly confounded Simna ibn Sind. Hand on sword hilt, he began backing toward the nearest door.

To say that Themaryl's family was not pleased by her pronouncement was to understate the matter rather severely. Their vociferous objections to her announced departure manifested themselves in the form of clutching hands and the subsequent arrival of alarmed troops. Bearing in mind that these were her own people, Ehomba and his friends perpetrated as little violence as possible in the course of fleeing from her homeland. Despite the destruction of the sky-metal sword, the herdsman still had its oceanic counterpart and his walking spear to scatter the hostile. Where those uncommon weapons proved inappropriate to the task, he commanded the contents of his seemingly bottomless backpack.

The *Grömsketter* was unavailable to take them back, having embarked on an expedition up the Eynharrowk from Hamacassar, but they eventually managed to make contact with the crew of the legendary oceangoing three-master *Warebeth*. News and stories travel fast on a river, and her captain had heard of the exploits of Ehomba and his companions. For a few of the remaining pebbles in the herdsman's possession, he agreed to carry them westward back across the Semordria, a body of water with which Simna, at least, was becoming all too familiar.

The pall that had hung over the fortress of Ehl-Larimar's supreme ruler vanished at the announcement of her return. A downcast, disbelieving Hymneth greeted them in his private quarters. Unarmored, trembling so violently he could hardly rise, he embraced the woman he had never expected to see again. Smiling reassuringly, she rested her head against his and gently stroked the side of his misshapen, elongated face.

In the course of his difficult and less than exemplary life there had been much that had intrigued Hymneth the Possessed, and even more that had infuriated him, but he had rarely, if ever, been as bewildered as he was now.

"You brought her back. You crossed half a world to take her away from me, and then you brought her back." From beneath inhuman, bony ridges he stared at Ehomba, his confusion palpable. *"Why?"*

"I fulfilled my obligation to a dying man. Once I had done that, I was free." The herdsman nodded at Themaryl. "She has a good heart, and became less overbearing during the course of our return to her homeland. Though under no formal obligation, I felt obliged by circumstance to grant her one request. That request was to return here."

Hymneth pulled slightly away from his restored consort. "This will not change me, you know. I am still Hymneth the Possessed, lord of the central coast and of all Ehl-Larimar. Supreme ruler of this part of the world."

"I know." Ehomba smiled enigmatically. "I can only hope that you will now do a better job of it."

With that, Etjole Ehomba and his friends departed that naturally blessed but ill-governed province and once more made the difficult trek back to Doroune and the eastern coast. There they waited until they made contact with an especially bold captain and crew who agreed to attempt a crossing of the Semordria to the southeast, in hopes of landing their well-paying passengers not in the delta of the Eynharrowk, but somewhere nearer a certain small southern coastal village.

When Hunkapa Aub announced that he was remaining behind, regretful farewells were exchanged. While Simna delivered himself of effusive praise and a few obligatory coarse jokes, and the black litah growled diffidently and offered up a sociable paw, no words were exchanged between the shaggy sorcerer and his dark, lean counterpart. Simna knew that much passed between them, even if only by glance and gesture, that he was not a party to. Nor, frankly, did he want to be. As for himself, he chose to remain with Ehomba, reminding him yet again of his promise to reward a certain itinerant herdsman with wealth and fortune.

And so it was that after adventures too many and tortuous to mention, the three remaining travelers found themselves put ashore at the trading town of Askaskos, from which it was but a moderate and easy journey north to the last, small village on the southern coast. To Ehomba, the look on the face of his wife as he appeared outside their house was worth more than all the knowledge he had accumulated in the course of his travels, and all the riches he might have claimed. His children, grown since last he'd seen them, clustered close, Nelecha gripping his waist so tightly that it impacted his breathing.

Mirhanja and the other villagers extended a ready and grateful country welcome to the comrades of their wandering son. There followed several days of celebration and feasting, during which Simna ibn Sind in particular proved highly voluble on the subject of their many extraordinary exploits.

It was during one such evening feast, while Simna grandiosely held forth on the difficulties of crossing the wide and perilous Semordria, that Ehomba confronted the black litah. Belly full, half asleep, the big cat ignored the attentions of the young children who giggled into his mane and toyed with his tufted tail.

"What will you do now?" Ehomba asked him. "Compared to the distances we have covered together, it is not so very far to the veldt where first we met."

"Not so very far, no," Ahlitah responded. "But far enough. Haven't thought much about it. I have trouble thinking when my stomach is full."

Nodding, the herdsman sat down beside the noble head.

"The domesticated herds of the Naumkib are extensive and require constant vigilance. This is because the hills where they graze are full of predators. One such as yourself would be a welcome ally to those who must spend long hours watching over them."

The litah considered. "You saved my life, but I no longer owe you. The debt is repaid in full."

"More than in full," Ehomba admitted readily. They sat in silence for a while, listening to the sounds of happy feasting and tolerating the children's antics, until the litah spoke again.

"Among these predators that trouble you, are there cats? Cats like me?"

Ehomba's expression was grave. "Too many to count. Lionesses and she-cheetahs, leopards sleek of flank and smilodons long of tooth."

"It is a long way to the veldt." Ahlitah growled uncertainly. "You would trust me to guard your flocks and not devour them?"

His chin resting on folded hands as he watched the nearby celebration, the herdsman shrugged. "I have trusted you with more than a cow these past many months. Besides, those who stand watch over the herds also share in their bounty."

"And I would still be free to leave at any time, to run when the need overcame me?"

Ehomba glanced over at his massive, clawed companion. They had been through much together. "I would not ask of another that which I could never ask of myself."

The litah snorted. It was his way of saying little while saying much.

* * *

There came a morning when Simna ibn Sind confronted the other companion of his journeys well to the north of the last house. While admiring the supple play of cloth against the bodies of the young women who came to draw water for the day's activities, the swordsman hesitated at first to speak his mind.

"Come, my friend," Ehomba told him. "Something is troubling you."

"Hoy, I don't want to insult you, bruther, or the hospitality of your friends, which has been all that a man could ask for."

"And yet you are not content," Ehomba observed sagely.

"It's not that the food isn't good, or the accommodations unsuitable." The swordsman struggled to find the right words, then finally decided to plunge ahead. "It's just that I've spent my life trying to avoid places like this, Etjole." He made a sweeping gesture. "Maybe this is enough to satisfy a cat, but I don't belong here." He took a deep breath. "Also, there's the little matter of some treasure you've kept promising me. I knew when I first met you that you had access to some. I thought you were searching for it yourself. Then I believed you when you told me that it could be found in Ehl-Larimar. The only reason I'm here now is because I've kept on believing you." His tone and expression hardened.

"I've put myself in death's way for you more times than I care to count, bruther. Now I expect some reward."

Ehomba gestured at the sharp-edged mountains, the quiet village, the pristine air and peaceful surroundings. "Is this not reward enough for you? Were not the adventures we had treasure enough?"

The swordsman did not reply directly, but instead

grinned while briskly rubbing the thumb and forefinger of his right hand against one another. Ehomba sighed. "There is no treasure here, Simna." He squinted up at the cloudless, impossibly blue sky. "Would you not like to go for a walk on the beach instead?"

"Listen to me, Etjole! You promised me that—" The shorter man halted his nascent tirade. A wide, sly grin spread across his weatherbeaten, sun-scoured face. "A walk on the beach? By Goulouris, long bruther, I'd be happy to take a walk on the beach. I'd nearly forgotten about the beauty of the beaches above your village."

There were children playing at the water's edge when they arrived. Ehomba's daughter was among them, and he tried his best to explain to her the reason behind the comical antics of the funny man from the far north who threw himself on the shore and rolled about wildly, laughing at the top of his lungs while throwing fistfuls of pebbles up in the air and letting them land on his face and body. Eventually, the teary-eyed swordsman rose and began to gather some of those pebbles. Laughing Naumkib children helped him, delighting in his joy and praise when they handed him a particularly large or bright pebble.

Simna ibn Sind spent a pleasant and gratifying morning at the seashore, collecting pebbles until his backpack was half full.

"I'm not a greedy man," he told Ehomba when he was sated. He hefted his pack higher on his shoulders, and the weight of diamonds within clinked as they shifted and settled. "This little is enough for me. I'm going to go home and buy myself a small kingdom."

Ehomba regarded his friend gravely. "Are you sure that is what you really want, Simna? To own a small kingdom?"

The swordsman hesitated, his smile fading. For a long moment he stood there, listening to the waves roll in to rustle the beach of diamonds, to the music of children playing, the chatter of merapes on the rocks offshore and the cries of seabirds and dragonets. Then he looked up at his tall friend and grinned anew.

"No, long bruther, I'm not sure that's what I want—but I am going to give it a try."

Ehomba nodded sadly. "Come into the village with me and we will arrange for the supplies you will need. I can give you some directions, and an introduction to a certain helpful monkey you may meet."

Simna left the following morning, the herdsman escorting him as far as the fifth beach north of the village, where the fog began.

"If you're ever in the far northeast," the swordsman told his friend, "seek out the khanate of Mizar-lohne. That's my homeland, and I'll settle myself somewhere nearby." He grinned one more time. "There are always kingdoms for sale thereabouts." He sighed ruefully. "Who knows? Perhaps I might make another journey to find Damura-sese."

"You have been a good friend, Simna ibn Sind, and a boon companion." One last time, Ehomba put a hand on his friend's shoulder. "Travel well, keep alert, and watch where you put your feet. Keep looking, keep searching, and perhaps one day, with luck, fortune might smile upon you and you might find Damura-sese."

The swordsman nodded, started to turn to go, and then paused. The sun was not yet high and it fell in his eyes, making him squint. "One last thing, Etjole. One thing I must ask." He moved closer so he would not have to squint as hard. "Are you, or are you not, a sorcerer?"

Turning away, the herdsman gazed off into the distance and smiled: that same familiar, enigmatic smile Simna had come to know so infuriatingly and so well in the course of their long journeying together.

"I have told you and told you, Simna. I am only a student, an asker of questions, who knows barely enough to make use of what the wise ones of the Naumkib provide me."

"By Gunkad, long bruther, answer the question!" Not to be denied or put off any longer by clever evasions, the swordsman fumed silently and stood his ground, both physical and forensic.

Ehomba looked down at him. "Simna, my friend, I swear to you by the blue of the sky and the green of the sea that I am no more a 'sorcerer' than any man or woman of my village, be they herder of cattle, hewer of wood, thresher of grain, or scraper of hides."

The swordsman met his gaze evenly and looked long and hard into the eyes of his friend. Then he nodded. "What will you do now?"

"Watch over the cattle and the sheep. Be with my wife and children. In the time I was gone, my son reached the age when all Naumkib are initiated into the lore of adults. That is a task I must begin tomorrow."

"Hoy, I wish I could stay, and I don't want to offend you, but I'm really not interested in sitting through some quaint ceremony where a boy learns how to castrate cattle or dock sheep or paint his face with vegetable dyes." With a last regretful grin, he spun on his sandals and headed north, pausing once at the top of a ridge to turn and wave. Then he vanished, welcomed and swallowed up by the sea fog that hung perpetually over the coast north of the village, and Ehomba saw him no more.

On the morning of the following day the herdsman took his son Daki out of the village, heading inland. Mirhanja packed them a lunch and bade them good-bye, but not after extracting from her husband a promise to be back well before nightfall.

The trail father and son trod was narrow and overgrown in many places with weeds and vines, so that it was difficult to see. It wound its obscure way into the grassy hills behind the village until it terminated next to a plain rock face at the end of a shallow canyon that looked exactly like a hundred other similar heavily eroded canyons. Clearing away some brush and dead twigs, Ehomba exposed a narrow, dark opening in the weathered granite. Preparing torches from the ample supply of dead wood that lay scattered about, the two men entered.

The downward-sloping floor of the tunnel had been worn smooth by centuries of running water and sandaled feet. They walked for an indeterminate time before their torches were no longer necessary. Daylight filtered in through cracks in a ceiling that was now high overhead. A little farther on, the tunnel widened and became a chamber. Very soon thereafter it widened a great deal more, and became something else entirely.

The slim but well-built Daki, wearing a solemn expression others would have immediately recognized as being derived from his sire, contemplated the sight before him with respectful reverence but without awe.

"What is this place, Father?"

"This is where the Naumkib come from, Daki." Raising an arm, Ehomba swept it before him in an expansive gesture to take in all that there was to be seen. "Too long ago to remember, our people settled here and built this place. They accumulated boundless knowledge and untold riches."

The youth looked up at him. "What happened to them?"

Ehomba patted his son on the shoulder. "When one feels one has no more to accomplish, the next thing one attains is boredom. The Naumkib abandoned this place. In ones and twos, in groups and in families, they scattered to the far corners of the world. Gradually they mingled with other peoples, and became one with them, and were content. Only a few remained behind."

"Us," the boy realized. "The people of the village."

"Yes. To not forget is a great responsibility. A legacy must be looked after, Daki. Not necessarily expanded upon, or exploited, but looked after." He started forward. "Now come, and I will show you more of yours."

They spent the remainder of the day exploring the deserted towers, and the great library, and the majestic arenas of knowledge. Daki marveled at the walls of solid gold, and the gemstone utensils the vanished inhabitants had left behind in their silent kitchens. Together, father and son turned the pages of ancient tomes bound in sheets of solid ruby, chosen not for its beauty but for its strength and ability to protect the far more valuable paper pages that lay between those crimson covers. They visited the observatory, with its telescopes still pointed at an especially large crack in the roof of the enormous cavern, and its congruent cupola with the ceiling that showed innumerable constellations fashioned from all manner of precious stones.

A captivated Daki did not want to leave, but Ehomba had to insist. "Your mother will be angry at us both if we are late," he reminded his son as they began the long hike back to the tunnel.

"Is this where you found the answers to all the questions you keep asking, Father?" the boy asked as they ascended wide stairs of marble and agate and sparkling goldenstone.

"No, Daki. This is where I find only more questions. I promise you: Someday, when you are a little older, we will come back here, as all men and women of Naumkib must, and you will find, whether you want to or not, many questions of your own."

The youth considered this reply as they ascended. Then he nodded slowly, hoping that he understood. "Does it have a name, this place? Or is it just called Naumkib?"

"We call ourselves the Naumkib," his father replied. "The ancient city and place of learning is, and always has been, known as Damura-sese." He smiled as they neared the entrance to the tunnel. Mirhanja would have supper ready, and he was hungry. "The rest of the world knows it as a story, a rumor, hearsay. We keep it that way."

Daki picked up one of the torches they had left behind. "Part of our legacy?"

"Yes, son. Part of our legacy. A little secret of the Naumkib."

"But not the only one," the boy observed, displaying the wisdom for which his family was noted.

"No, Daki. Not the only one."

Etjole Ehomba, who was an honorable man, made his

way with his son back out of the celebrated lost city, whose riches lay not in its fabulous trappings but in the learning it held, and back to the modest house by the sea, where as he had sworn to his friend Simna ibn Sind he was no more a renowned sorcerer than any man or woman of his village, be they herder of cattle, hewer of wood, thresher of grain or scraper of hides.

Printed in the United States
21524LVS00001B/242

9 780446 522182